The Sol Majestic

Also by Ferrett Steinmetz

Flex
The Flux
Fix
The Uploaded

The Sol Majestic

FERRETT STEINMETZ

TOR

A TOM DOHERTY ASSOCIATES BOOK
New York

THE SOL MAJESTIC

A Tor Book
Published by Tom Doherty Associates
175 Fifth Avenue
New York, NY 10010

www.tor-forge.com

Tor® is a registered trademark of Macmillan Publishing Group, LLC.

The Library of Congress Cataloging-in-Publication Data is available
upon request.

ISBN 978-1-250-16819-1 (trade paperback)
ISBN 978-1-250-16818-4 (ebook)

Our books may be purchased in bulk for promotional, educational, or business use.
Please contact your local bookseller or the Macmillan Corporate and Premium
Sales Department at 1-800-221-7945, extension 5442, or by email
at MacmillanSpecialMarkets@macmillan.com.

First Edition: June 2019

Printed in the United States of America

0 9 8 7 6 5 4 3 2 1

To Gini:
Who else would I dine with?

The Sol Majestic

1

Three Days, Fifteen Hours, Thirty Minutes to Savor Station

You can starve for the next three days, Kenna tells himself, eyeing the bigger kids down in the station lounge. *Or you can take a beating.*

His gut rumbles as he wills himself to walk down the corrugated steel corridor. There are four of them, well-fed workers' sons hulking with gene-enhanced muscles. They laugh as they push lightballs back and forth at each other on their smartphones, playing some networked game. Their duffel bags rest by their feet.

One of those bags holds Kenna's nutricracker allotment.

There is no more food within a million miles, not until the transport ship docks at Savor Station. Maybe not even then, depending on what ambassadors Mother and Father find to curry favor with.

He tenses his shoulders. This is the worst part: getting their attention.

"I crave your pardon," Kenna says, wincing, hating the way he's defaulted to feeble politeness. Mother's influence.

The four kids turn. The adult passengers also roll over to watch, swaying in Kevlar hammocks above, exhaling puffs of marijuana smoke as they lean in to watch the festivities. The cramped spaces and long boredoms of interstellar transport transform any personal friction into public performance—a constant pressure that's eradicated Kenna's ability to cry.

The biggest kid—of course it's the biggest kid—curtsies mockingly. "M'lord," he says. Everyone laughs.

"You absconded with my food," Kenna insists. "I mandate its safe return."

"Have your valet buy you some new food."

"I have no valet." Kenna has never had a valet. His parents had had one, as children, and they sing him to sleep at night with the tales of his great-grandparents and their hundreds of servants—but Kenna counts himself lucky if he finds a maintenance closet to sleep in. "And I will not pay when the nutriments are rightfully mine."

All four stand up. Kenna finds himself grateful he has nothing left to steal—Father has spent years trading away family heirlooms to survive, and so Kenna has no smartphone, no smartpaper, no duffel bags full of food. Just his bony black body and his reputation as a Philosopher.

Or, rather, his reputation as someone who might *become* a Philosopher. He's supposed to be guiding galactic leaders to peace, not whining at bullies in a transport ship. Mother derived her Inevitable Philosophy before she was thirteen, Father unlocked his at twelve—and though Kenna meditates daily, hoping to find a belief so Inevitable it guides his every action, he's sixteen and long overdue for inspiration.

He's almost too old for a Wisdom Ceremony. He's let his starving body taint his mind. Though he should leave these low boys to their food and seek out his Inevitable Philosophy, here he is wasting time trying to fill his belly instead of his mind.

"*We* don't have your food," Big Kid lies, sniggering. His buddies nod in time, like marionettes. "And even if we did, isn't your mother Queen of Saving the Starving Millions? I thought she crooned in advisors' ears to convince *real* emperors to unlock their granaries. Shouldn't you starve yourself first?"

I do, Kenna almost says, but he knows how that conversation will go. The crowd will excoriate Mother and Father, tell Kenna the Philosophies should have died after they failed.

Father, whose chest is tattooed with his Philosophy—*I will lead my people out of darkness*—has lectured Kenna on how Philosophies fall into disrepute, then rise like phoenixes. Until Father can bring the wayward leaders back to the fold, regaining the generosity that wise leaders once aspired to through grand Philosophies, the rank and file will mock them for their struggle. *There's nothing an empty soul enjoys more than watching enlightened men fail,* Father says.

Yet Kenna had *so* wanted to give these boys the benefit of the doubt. He'd trailed them for a day to ensure he wouldn't accuse the wrong person. He'd watched them wolf down vending machine jerky to satisfy casual hungers, while Kenna had only stayed alive by rationing his duffel bag of bulk-purchased nutricrackers across months of lean journeys.

If Kenna had an Inevitable Philosophy, neither the bullies nor the belly cramps would bother him. If Kenna had an Inevitable Philosophy, he could walk away serene, his actions guided by higher concerns than mere survival. If Kenna had an Inevitable Philosophy, he could persuade these boys of the righteousness of sharing resources in scarce quarters, guiding this grubby ship to the compassionately Inevitable enlightenments that benefited empires.

But he has no Philosophy. And since there's only one way to get his food back, he kicks the kid in the crotch.

Big Kid's eyes crossing is wondrously satisfying—a stunned glare that seems to say, *I thought you'd lecture me on how no lie could balk an Inevitable Prince.* Terror flows as the other kids realize that no, Kenna is not that kind of prince.

He grabs two duffel bags as the adults above yell down scorn, jeering that a Prince of the Inevitable Philosophies should be *concerned* about the poor, and Kenna hauls ass down the corridor, hoping the other passengers won't interfere.

Alas, the thieves' terror ebbs as they realize Kenna was not *that* kind of prince, but neither was he an assassin-prince who could kick their ass with years of martial training. Kenna's a street urchin with credentials, and starved for two days to boot. And so they run him down, and kick him in the ribs, and take their bags back.

"There!" The biggest kid upends his duffel bag to rain down empty wrappers over Kenna's head. "We ate them already, you freak! And you know what? They tasted like *shit!*"

They did, Kenna thinks, imagining the sumptuous meals Mother told him of, detailing seven-course meals with a fixated lust that could have passed for pornography. His finest dining has been a cup of ramen noodles.

He crawls into a bathroom stall.

Kenna curls up on the toilet seat, holding his bloodied nose to stanch it because of course there's no toilet paper. He watches the stall's timer count down to kick him out in ten minutes. On the graffiti-smeared bathroom screen overhead display, a little graphical spaceship-dot creeps toward Savor Station, with a clock to mark the remaining time: 3:15:23.

There had been a third choice, Kenna realizes, blood trickling down the back of his throat. He could starve for three days, *and* take a beating.

But he doesn't cry. You can't drink tears.

2

After Sixty Minutes on Savor Station

Kenna sucks on a plastic bead as he follows the eight-year-old girl around Savor Station, trying to work up the nerve to mug her.

She's pudgy, dressed in a little blue uniform, a kid wandering through the crowded hallways like she's in no danger at all. The tracker tag on her wrist makes Kenna think maybe she isn't. She cruises to a stop to watch some cartoon advertisement on the overhead monitors, reaches into an oil-stained bag of meat jerky to chew on it absently. Kenna hates her for the way she can eat without paying attention; put jerky in his mouth, and it would fill his whole world.

He sucks harder on the bead. More saliva. Fools the stomach into thinking something's on the way, which of course it isn't unless he mugs this little girl.

He pushes past tourists consulting overhead maps, edging close enough to grab the bag. He should. He *has* to.

Kenna hesitates again.

The girl moves on, wandering into the glassine cubicles of merchants' stalls, darting between shoppers' legs. She passes a shop heaped with tubs of fresh fish, flopping as they're released from expensive time-stasis cubes; the salt-ocean smell makes Kenna wipe drool from dry lips even though he's straying dangerously close to the tawdry commerce areas. He steps toward the fish, like a man in a dream—and as he stumbles forward, the security cameras whirr to focus on him. The merchant senses Kenna's stray-cat approach, quietly shifts his body to deny him access.

Could he beg the merchant for scraps? Kenna takes another dazed step forward, reaching out plaintively. The merchant's lips tense as he readies well-worn excuses: *if I give scraps to one boy then I will be swarmed by beggars, a purveyor of quality goods cannot be seen surrounded by hobos, I'm sure you understand.*

Kenna turns away, knowing exactly what the merchant will say before he utters a word. He's dodged many embarrassments by intuiting potent visions extracted from body language, and Kenna has paid dearly the few times he's ignored his instincts.

Yet he's glad the stalls don't have jobs posted. He'd sell his labor for a fish. Mother and Father would never talk to him again, of course—*you don't* learn *a trade, your Philosophy is your trade.* They have left Kenna behind in the common areas while they negotiate meetings with Savor Station's visiting politicians, hunting for an opportunity to lend their wisdom to powerful legislators. But though Kenna tries to remember his parents' lectures on providing insights so profound that leaders will pay to hear them, his growling belly drowns out their voices.

They've been Inevitable for so long they've forgotten how to fear death. They hesitate whenever they lecture him, squinting with the effort of attempting to translate their enlightened experience into Kenna's debased state; the only time he's seen them falter is when they try to explain how they unlocked their Inevitable Philosophy. *You find strength in the suffering of others,* Mother intones, or Father tells him, *Once you realize what's truly at stake, you come to realize how little you matter.*

But Kenna's felt his heart stuttering from malnutrition, and once again his nascent Philosophies fall away when survival calls.

The girl ambles on, waving cheerful hellos as she strolls between the stalls; Kenna scans the market for better targets. The other shoppers, maybe? No. They're big. Healthy. His hands shiver from malnutrition. They'd yell for security right away, he'd get jailed, shaming Mother and Father.

He imagines justifying this crime to them. *They had food already; I didn't. She didn't need that food; I do.* Yet he's already heard them whispering consultations with each other, fretting how all the Princes of old had *their* Wisdom Ceremony before they were fifteen. Kenna's sixteenth birthday was a month ago, and now Mother and Father's muttered discussions have taken on the panicked hiss of monarchs debating whether Kenna can continue to be the Inevitable Prince if he does not shape his Inevitable Philosophy.

Being arrested might be his final fall from grace.

Kenna should hate them. Instead, he envies their Inevitability. Mother and Father's bottomless compassion gets them up in the morning; their love keeps them moving when Kenna wants to curl up and die. They're waiting in some old politician's lobby, chasing flickering embers of power. Once Father's Inevitable Philosophy convinces the right potentates, he'll lead his people out of darkness.

When Father chants *I will lead my people out of darkness!*, Kenna can feel the limitless strength bound in those words—yet though Kenna spends hours meditating upon the revolutionary changes that should be made for the benefit of all, the best philosophies Kenna can muster are pleasant platitudes that crumple into guilt whenever Kenna's stomach growls.

Kenna has no people. He has no compassion. He has no Philosophy. All he has is a girl with a bag of meat jerky—a girl skipping into Savor Station's main arteries.

Kenna follows her, chest hitching with self-loathing.

It's more crowded here, his every footstep blocked by bag-toting porters and gawking tourists and miniature forklifts ferrying crates. Though this curved ring is wide enough to hold hundreds of passengers, the space is all elbows and bulkheads, which makes sense; each square inch cost thousands of dinari to build, a sliver of safety constructed in pure vacuum by brute labor.

Kenna creeps closer. The girl babbles at a porter, discussing some show; he sidles up, sliding his fingertips across the bag's tantalizing oiliness.

All he has to do is clench his fingers, and yank, and run.

He imagines the girl's shocked face as he tugs the jerky from her hands, that little-girl shock of discovering that anyone can take anything from you if they're big enough, and he realizes this is what it would take to survive:

He would have to become a bully.

Kenna howls. Startled, the girl drops her jerky, but Kenna does not notice; he's pushing people aside, fleeing. He cannot stop crying, but he can move so fast that no one has time to notice his tears. He wants *so badly* to throw all this honor aside to stuff his mouth with meat and be happy and shivering . . .

. . . but he is not a thief.

Oh, how he envies thieves.

Do you have to be so dramatic, *Kenna?* he can hear Mother chiding him. But she's carved away everything that doesn't advance her Philosophies—she's whittled herself down to perfect postures, to primly smoothed robes, to unceasingly polite rules of etiquette.

If he had an Inevitable Philosophy, he would never lose control. But he does not, so he runs.

His legs spasm. Kenna collapses by a long line of people—Savor Station is criss-crossed with lines, lines of people getting passports, lines to get on ships, lines to fill out job applications, lines to—

DO YOU LOVE FOOD? a sign flashes.

The sign itself is written in a flowing, sugary goodness, a message in frosting. It writhes like a dancer pulling veils across herself, highlighting a carved wood booth crammed into a corner.

Wood, Kenna thinks. *What madman hauls wood across solar systems to put it in a lobby?* He knows vandals; on the transit-ship, this would have been carved to pieces.

Yet even in the elbow-to-ass room of Savor Station, people make space for this little alcove, as if the dark wood booth is an ambassador from some great kingdom. It has a confessional's solemn pall—but the people lined up before it have the expectant looks of lottery contestants, chatting eagerly about their chances and wringing their hands as they fantasize about winning. A stiff pressed linen curtain gives privacy as each new person steps into the booth, muttering well-practiced speeches. The line's end is nowhere in sight.

The sign contorts, bowing, then unfolds into a new set of letters: THE SOL MAJESTIC.

Kenna has no idea what that means, but he longs to be a part of it already.

The sign is whisked away as though by a breeze; smaller words float across the empty space like lotus blossoms drifting across a lake. THE MOST EXCLUSIVE RESTAURANT IN ALL THE GALAXY. ONLY EIGHTEEN TABLES. RESERVATIONS MUST BE MADE TWO YEARS IN ADVANCE.

BUT ONE TABLE IS RESERVED EACH NIGHT, FREE OF CHARGE, FOR THOSE WITH THE LOVE TO SEE IT.

Kenna clambers to his feet.

TELL US WHY YOU LOVE FOOD.

This is insane, this is stupid, this is foolhardy. He should comb the marketplaces again, see if anyone has dropped food on the floor. But Mother and Father will not return from their political sojourn for hours, and this . . .

. . . this . . .

Kenna staggers down the line. His legs ache before he reaches its end. He settles behind a rumpled family of middle-aged tourists, who welcome him with a bright-eyed wave and a "Why not?" gleam in their eyes. A group of fashionable Gineer hipsters, their smooth skin taut from gene-treatments, fusses about the delay as they settle behind him.

He settles into his own silence, lets others do the talking. They speak breathlessly about cuisine.

It takes a while before Kenna realizes *cuisine* means *food*.

They speak of tenacious ice-eating mosses, planted on asteroids, sent on trips around the sun, retrieved to harvest the bounty for a once-in-a-lifetime salad. They speak of deep-sea creatures evolved at the bottoms of vinegar oceans, so delicate they have to be kept in pressurized containers, released via special mechanisms to explode in your mouth. They speak of artificial meat-fibers spun across rotating tines in cotton-candy strands, a protein that melts on your tongue to saturate your whole mouth with thick umami.

What is umami?

He's never eaten well, but he thought he at least understood the *language* of food. Mother spoke of noodle soups and roasted ducklings. These meals sound like exhibits.

They discuss meat. Kenna relaxes; he understands meat, even though all he's ever eaten has been vending machine jerky. But these people discuss blubber, siopao, Silulian black-udder, p'tcha, vacuum flanks, sashimi. They trade the names like chips on bingo cards, brightening when it turns out two people have consumed the same oddity, exchanging indecipherable dialogues on bizarre concepts like flavor profiles and top notes.

Kenna should not be here. But leaving would mark him as a fraud. He has had enough humiliation for the day.

There's enough humiliation for everyone, he's glad to see. As they draw closer to the confessional, people are rejected with an astounding rapidity. You are asked, Kenna is told, to discuss why you love food, though most don't make it past their first sentence. A beautiful actress stumbles out, hands on her broad hips in irritation, to inform the crowd she'd had *auditions* that lasted longer.

The nice family people standing before him—so educated, so smart—explain that some days, Paulius does not find anyone at all to let into his restaurant. Paulius has exacting tastes. It is said on days like that, Paulius sinks into a deep depression, though Paulius is more known for his fits of rage.

And the nice family goes in, one at a time.

And the nice family is ejected from the booth, one at a time.

The Gineer hipsters flutter their hands at Kenna, as if loath to touch his ragged clothing. "Get in," they hiss. "Get it over with."

Kenna slumps in. White linen curtains close behind him.

Before him is an elegant table, draped in a white tablecloth, standing before a blank white screen. A wooden chair, curved like a cello, rests on the floor, inviting Kenna to take a seat.

Kenna sits down, crossing his hands to prevent himself from fidgeting. He half expects a buzzer to go off before he speaks.

Instead, he stares down at the tablecloth. It has indents where would-be vandals have left outlines of dicks, but the tablecloth is made of some special ink-resistant fabric.

The screen pulses gently, a reminder.

Kenna clears his throat.

"I . . . I don't think I love food."

Nothing happens. Is there some secret signal that nobody's told him about? *Has* he failed already, and is too much of a yokel to know?

"I can't be certain. Mother and Father—*they* had grand meals. They warm their hands by those memories, savoring banquets they had with Grandfather, reliving those courses one by one . . .

"I don't have those recollections. I've had canned meat, dried noodles, pickled eggs. If I . . . if we . . . ever came back into favor, would I . . . appreciate anything else? I can't tell. All this surviving is killing me.

"Mother and Father, they're—they dream decades in the future. I can barely imagine tomorrow. And I think if I got one meal, one good meal, to show me what life I could dream about, then maybe I could . . ."

He drifts off, uncertain what he could do. His life is defined by absences. He can't envision what he *could* do, because he doesn't love food, he doesn't love people, he doesn't love anything, and how can you become something when all you've known is nothing?

"Maybe I could have a Philosophy," he whispers.

A soft whirr. Kenna jerks his head up at the noise; he's still in the confessional. He'd started talking and had forgotten about The Sol Majestic, forgotten about Paulius, he'd poured his heart onto the table and why is that screen rising into the ceiling?

The door concealed on the confessional's far side swings open, revealing a sunlit orchard.

There are no orchards in space, Kenna thinks. He freezes, so he does not hurt himself in his madness.

But through the door are blue skies, knotted tangles of grass, twisted boughs of trees heavy with fruit. *Rows* of trees, retreating far into the distance. A zephyr of sun-warmed chlorophyll ripples his hair.

The trees' branches are wrapped around stainless steel water pipes that snake across the landscape. A geodesic dome's triangular struts slash across the sky. Surely, he would not have imagined *that*.

He creeps his way toward the exit, expecting some security guard to block the entrance. But no; he steps over the threshold, and his battered shoes sink into soft loam. His fingers close over a tree branch's knurled hardness, and the sensation of something growing beneath his fingers is like touching miracles. Kenna inhales, and it's not the stale scent of recycled body odor and plastic offgassing; it's the clean smell of rain and leaves.

He plucks a hard oval of purplish-green off a branch: a grape? He rolls the fruit's waxy surface between his fingertips, puzzled at its hard flesh. Weren't grapes supposed to be squishy, like the jam in the vending machine sandwiches? This smells like the light crude oil coating your skin after you bunk in a cargo ship's engine room. Is it safe to eat?

He's never eaten anything that hasn't come wrapped in plastic.

Kenna drops the fruit and stumbles forward, seeking something simpler. He pushes his way into a curved valley with long rows of curlicued vines lashed to wooden poles.

A tall, potbellied man strides across the vineyard toward Kenna, jabbing a silver cane into the soft soil for balance.

Kenna's breath catches in his throat. The man is coming for him. The man who owns the vineyard.

The man—Paulius?—ducks under the vines without lifting his blue-eyed gaze away from Kenna, as though he has memorized every limb in his garden. The man's own limbs are slender—long graceful arms, a dancer's legs, all connected to one bowling-ball belly. Whenever he ducks, his long, white ponytail swings madly, knotted in silver cords. He steps over the hillocks quickly, as if an emergency calls for his attention but he refuses to give up the dignity of walking.

The man is dressed in thigh-high black boots and a white ruffled vest, but somehow the rain-slickened vines leave no marks upon him. He is wrinkled and tan—not the fake orange tan of tanning booths, but the light leathery patina one acquires from hard work in fine sunlight.

He holds a brass bowl in his free hand, thrusting it forward. Steam wafts upward.

He deposits the bowl into Kenna's hands gravely. Kenna looks down; the bowl thrums warm against his palms, rimmed with circuitry, the soup cradled within perfectly still. The bowl has its own artificial gravity generator at the bottom, pulling the soup down so it can never spill.

Kenna trembles. This bowl is worth more than everything his family owns, and yet Paulius—for it *is* Paulius—has handed it to him as though it were nothing at all.

Paulius bows.

"The first rule of appreciation," Paulius says, his voice mellifluous, "is that it is impossible to savor a thing you have been starved of. This applies to food, lovers, and company. So I must feed you before I can teach you. Drink deep."

Except Kenna *can* savor it. Though his stomach punches the inside of his ribs, desperate for nutrients, Kenna peers into the coppery broth before him. Little globules of fat wobble upon its surface, glimmering like holograms. Glistening dark meat chunks bob at the bottom. He inhales, and the rich chicken scent fills his nostrils, fills his brain, fills his world.

Then he thumbs the gravity release button and sips it. Or tries to. His hands betray him, pouring it into his mouth. Kenna fights his body to sip genteelly instead of gulping. He's sobbing and coughing, making dumb animal noises in front of Paulius . . .

Paulius grabs his shoulder, his fingers so strong they root Kenna to the earth. "Your breath stinks of ketone. I know how long a man can starve, and you are at your limits. Please. *Eat*."

Freed from restraint, Kenna dumps it down his throat. His belly heats up, radiating warmth like a tiny sun. His muscles twitch as his blood feasts on the broth, ferries it out to his limbs, suffusing him with a rapture greater than any orgasm.

His ass hits the ground. He sprawls in the soft earth, feeling his emaciated body rebuilding itself, feeling the sunlight's warmth on his brown skin.

Paulius kneels down beside him, nodding as Kenna's chest hitches. This isn't just the broth; it's life, it's a connection to this land Paulius has created, and—

He loves food.

He loves *something*.

As Kenna realizes how close he was to dying, dying in all the ways that really counted, he curls up and cries.

3

After Ninety Minutes at Savor Station

"So why didn't you eat the olives?"

Paulius has draped a robe over Kenna's shoulders as he leads Kenna across the orchard, headed for a small frosted-glass door set into a polished aluminum wall. Kenna clutches at the white linen lapels, reveling in the feeling of clean cloth; he's worn his filthy Inevitable Robe for so long he can no longer distinguish between the stained cloth and his squalid skin.

"I thought they were grapes," Kenna replies, looking back at the gravity bowl. It's worth more than some spaceships. Paulius simply left it where Kenna had dropped it.

"Why didn't you eat the grapes?"

"I—knew not how to eat them."

"You don't know how to eat *grapes*?" Paulius leans in, his thin-lipped mouth pursed with grave concern. Kenna feels the sickness roiling within him, a rotting cancer uncovered by Paulius's examinations. Kenna's stomach is a landfill of rubbery microwaved mockmeats and sugared pastries that crumble like plaster dust to the tooth.

"For lack of opportunity only," Kenna explains. "We've fallen from fashion. My parents, they travel the stars in an attempt to bring the Inevitable Philosophies back to the people who once followed them, but . . . until they succeed, we lack a planet to call our own. And the foods on starships are built to last."

"So what did your mother make you when you had a bad day?"

"She microwaved a tub of macaroni."

"And when you could buy any sweet, you bought—"

"Frosted Chocobombs."

"Why?"

"They had the most calories."

"Oh, Kenna." Paulius's silver-braided hair twitches as he shakes his head, like a cat's tail as it stalks prey. "You can pack yourself into ships to sail the vacuum, work for men who speak no language you understand, sleep beneath a sky that glows in colors you never realized air could be. Yet when you find that ramshackle stand nestled in all that exotic lustre, the one that sells the dumplings you ate when you were a child, then—then no matter how far away you are, your mouth will bring memories flooding back. Food is what anchors us. Food's how we find our way home.

"And you . . ." He tenses; his silver cane lifts an inch from the ground. "Your home is a collection of *vending machines*."

Paulius's cold fury is reassuring. Kenna's body itches with sickness. The broth burbles in his belly, the most organic thing about him; his bones and muscles have been formed from the extruded fats and olfactory compounds sold in plastic packages.

But Kenna is no longer worried. Paulius will protect him. And a man who can tend to an orchard in space's hard vacuum can work miracles.

Paulius's gaze lifts away from Kenna, up toward the hexagonal polarized windows looking out into space. He bares china-white teeth at the blank panels above, which glow with dispersed sunlight.

He begins to tap his teeth, slowly, like a metronome.

Paulius squints, searching for something high above him. *There's nothing up there,* Kenna thinks. But as Paulius sweeps his cane-tip out across the lambent radiance, outlining imaginary figures across that blank artificial sky, Kenna sees what hangs above them:

A blank canvas.

Paulius giggles, an infectious titter. He frowns, tapping his teeth harder. Then another chuckle, and he mutters "yes."

Each giggle is a new idea, Kenna realizes. He strains his eyes to look up at the sky, hungry to see what Paulius sees. Paulius is assembling concepts, trying to piece something together—

Paulius raps his cane across Kenna's shins. "How long has it been since your mother and father have been properly served?"

"They were children. Younger than I."

Paulius jitters like he's filled with electricity, making tentative gestures in every direction as though the world is filled with too many possibilities to commit to one movement. "I can't give you what we serve. Don't you see? That's *my* food. What you need is, is—it's *your* food. We don't make that here."

That mad spark leaps to Kenna. "But you will."

"We *will*! Banquets in the classic style, fit for the finest leaders! Scented osmanthus blossoms! Hami melons, dripping dew! Cold fish cakes! The entire kitchen will have to be refitted! We'll train our staff to serve each course in purest Inevitable Philosophy etiquette! By the time we're done, you will know what home *is*!"

Paulius thrusts his cane into the air, as if leading a parade—then looks back, realizing no one but Kenna is here to see him.

Yet Kenna's chest heaves. For the first time, he's excited to see what happens.

Is that what an Inevitable Philosophy feels like?

Paulius drags Kenna toward the glass door. "Come on."

Kenna passes through the door, and a flashbulb panic sears his nerves as he realizes there are *laborers* in this kitchen—flush-faced men and women chopping roots. Mother and Father always covered his eyes whenever Kenna tried to watch the transport-ship repair squadrons—as if manual labor was a disease he could pick up through casual contact.

Yet the smells of The Sol Majestic's kitchen are so intense that Kenna forgets he has eyes.

The yeasty scent of bread dough fills his nose, so pungently alive that Kenna realizes all those crackers he ate were like fossils preserved in plastic packets. Then a moist salty oiliness squirms into his nostrils, a scent Kenna cannot identify until he sees a burly woman sliding a knife into the belly of a great golden fish and realizes *this is what the sea must smell like.* Everywhere some new delicious scent plucks at his nose, these mysterious aromas opening up channels to his stomach . . .

Paulius tugs on Kenna's shoulder: "*Come on!*" Kenna stumbles into the narrow corridor between an oven's furnace and three men chopping a great purple branch into perfectly round slices. He's terrified he'll bowl someone over, making brute contact—but everyone in The Sol Majestic's kitchen is aware of their neighbors. They step out of Kenna's way with military precision.

Kenna's staggering through the least of The Sol Majestic's dangers: there's the scrawny young boy hauling a cauldron of bubbling sun-plasma, the tall androgynous technician speeding time back up on a stasis cage crammed with sharp-pincered crabs, the two men swinging a six-horned animal carcass up onto the butcher block.

Kenna has lived side-by-side with soldiers, hitchhiking back home on the cargo ships with him; these cooks are tougher. Their hands are criss-crossed with half-healed knife cuts and puffy burn scars. They reach fearlessly into flames. When Paulius slides in between two women dicing braided liquorice cords into perfect cubes, their knife-blades unconsciously turn toward him, like solar panels rotating toward the sun, trying to lure Paulius into judging their work.

Who knew creating something corporeal required such courage?

Paulius pushes by, batting people out of the way with his cane. The chefs notice Kenna trailing behind. They squint, wondering what chef is in trouble—and then, when they note Kenna's cheap robe and see Paulius's hand clutching Kenna's wrist, they make a pained noise.

"Scrimshaw! SCRIMSHAW!" Paulius yells, headed for a bright red door at the kitchen's far end. The plain door makes Kenna realize how beautiful this kitchen is. The chefs wear stylish snapped-collar outfits bridging a rainbow of colors, from a commander's red to a dishwater blue. Their silver knives draw showers of sparks when they pull them from the auto-sharpening stations. They work on brushed-copper ovens, scrubbed spotless, bathed in light from the stacks of stasis cages that freeze time and dispense a cold blue glow of Cherenkov radiation—

But that battered red door is painted aluminum. It's the one thing in The Sol Majestic's kitchen that doesn't need to impress, which means it contains the most impressive thing of all.

"Scrimshaw!" Paulius yells, a doctor calling across a crowded emergency room.

The door bangs open.

A tall, dour woman plants one steel-toed boot onto the kitchen floor, as if she is an explorer claiming this planet for the first time—

Everything stops.

Kenna wonders, for a moment, if the stasis cages have malfunctioned. Knives hover in mid-air. Women hauling boiling stockpots wrestle sloshing fluid to a halt. Gineer chefs with their hands beneath a broiler pause, looking anxiously over their shoulders.

This is the woman who signs the paychecks, Kenna thinks.

She lowers her thick-rimmed black glasses, peering down at Kenna through crystal lenses. Kenna should have popped a scrubba-freshener before he got here, burnished the oil residue off his dark skin. But how could he have known?

The queen of the kitchen is as cold as a coat hanger, a plain woolen black coat draped over a form even more emaciated than Kenna's. She's tall as a parapet, peering down at everyone through old-style glasses, crouched like the legends of old dragons; a terrible intelligence radiates from her. She's a black hole of information, drinking in every detail, revealing nothing.

Yet her bristling irritation broadcasts her desires to Kenna. She demands one thing: perfection, at the lowest possible price. And no one has yet given it to her. Her hair is an unflattering bowl cut, dyed a deep and artificial jet-black for a woman her age. Kenna is certain that the unstylish hair is a trap, designed to lure out those unwise enough to comment upon it.

"*Scrimshaw!*" Paulius all but hurls Kenna at her feet. The kitchen, seeing Scrimshaw's attention flicker down to someone else, resumes operations.

"Yes?" Her voice is a bemused whisper, yet it cuts through the clatter of plates.

"New plan."

"New plans incur new expenses. I'm against."

"The old menu? Deleted." Paulius flicks his hand across the air like a man erasing a chalkboard. "Our *new* cuisine will be a fresh take on the Inevitable Philosophies!"

He thrusts his hands down at Kenna, a boy demonstrating this new puppy's lovableness to a skeptical parent. Under Scrimshaw's chill black eyes, the half-headed bruises on Kenna's cheekbones throb back to life, fresh breezes blow through his shabby Inevitable robe, his unwashed armpit-stink wrinkling his nose.

Scrimshaw clears her throat, a hiss like a dying air scrubber, preparing to dismiss him—

Kenna clambers back to his feet, never breaking eye contact with her.

You are a prince, his mother had reassured him as she dabbed sealing fluid on his cuts after the bullies had beaten him. *Find your Philosophy, and the universe will pour your cups full of pride.*

Scrimshaw believes him to be a vagrant. Half an hour ago, Kenna would have agreed. But with Paulius, they will use this kitchen to reforge a lost empire for one meal, the corroded glory of the Inevitable Philosophies restored through lacquered duck and boiled cowpeas—and Kenna is the Prince of the Inevitable Philosophies.

His spine snaps straight. He realizes how many years he's kept it bent.

Five fingers close into one fist. The Philosophies speak. He brandishes his fist at Scrimshaw.

"Inevitable." Kenna's whisper is inexorable, a planet swinging around the sun like a haymaker.

Scrimshaw's upper lip twitches. It takes Kenna a moment to recognize the gesture as a smile. Then the smile is tucked away as neatly as a handkerchief shoved into a pocket as she sighs, her nostrils flaring.

"*Must* we pretend each of your new love affairs is as earthshaking as the one before, Paulius?"

Kenna's veins frost, that Inevitability vanished—which means it wasn't Inevitable.

Did Paulius sense that Kenna longed for the company of men?

The idea of making love to such a grandfatherly man makes Kenna's skin itch like it was flaking off, but . . . Kenna's seen predators lurking on the transport ships. They're threadbare, wheedling, obvious men who'll offer to show new boys the ropes, yet in the end there's only one rope they ever show. Clammy sweat prickles Kenna beneath his clotted robe as he prepares his usual brush-off speech—he's an Inevitable Prince, his heirs are carefully chosen, Mother and Father would never allow a coupling with no chance of progeny—

"*Love* affair?" Paulius's outraged squawk, loud enough to cut across the kitchen, floods Kenna with reassurance. "When have I *ever* bedded a customer? Especially not one a third my age—"

"Not the boy." Scrimshaw's words are a guillotine, beheading useless arguments. "The *menu*. You're a living avalanche, Paulius, eternally perched to rumble headfirst into love affairs with some new idea. The boy's not a boy. He's an excuse for adventure."

"You see?" Paulius turns, wide-eyed, to Kenna, then flutters his hands in Scrimshaw's direction as though presenting criminal evidence in a trial. "Only this calculating clockwork concoction would confuse 'excuse' with 'inspiration'. This callous creature's heart doesn't beat—it *accrues*."

Scrimshaw stands impassively, motionless except for a single rotation of her wrist: *get on with it.* Her tedium at Paulius's impassioned production crushes Kenna's lungs in one liver-spotted fist, leaving him breathless.

Paulius is flamboyant, confident, a born performer. Kenna is certain that Paulius believes what he is saying; the man triggers none of his fine-tuned senses that shield him from con artists. But the problem with performers is sometimes they perform so well they fool themselves. Does Paulius believe in Kenna, or the thrill of the performance?

How many other sad castoffs has Paulius helped? And, perhaps, abandoned when they turned out not to fit into Paulius's glorious narrative?

"And don't you *dare* speak of my past inspirations as though they ceased to matter simply because they no longer affect our menu!" Paulius splutters, playing the outraged prosecutor, pacing in tight circles before her as he draws the kitchen's attention. "Great cuisine changes *lives,* you fetid fetter. What good is it filling bellies if we never touch a heart? Even you, *you,* must see the necessity of helping a wayward Philosopher to dream . . ."

"The Inevitable Philosophies are clichéd," she ripostes. "Their food was franchised, commercialized, homogenized. People were tired of it long before you were born."

"That's why it's perfect," Paulius retorts. "We will revive the unexpected."

"Our patrons expect the best meal of their lifetime." She angles her hand, a gesture like a fencer parrying. "It would take years to elevate a hoary cuisine to our standards. Merely sourcing the exotic ingredients would take—"

"A day."

Scrimshaw reels. "A day?"

"I'll burn connections."

"For *this*?"

Paulius kisses the top of Kenna's head, dry and chaste. "The Prince's future is at stake. I can do no less."

"Even if you do burn connections—a life-threatening resource I would urge you not to drain for this paltry exercise—I will not shut down the kitchen *again* to go chasing some wild dream. We have reservations, some from people who took the relativistics years ago. By the time they return home, their families will have aged to dust, a sacrifice made so they can dine at the finest restaurant in all the stars. I will *not* see them disappointed."

"That's fine," Paulius says. "We'll work double-shifts until we learn the Inevitable Philosophies. Our old menu in the afternoon, our new menu in the morning."

"The chefs have already threatened to strike over their current workload, Paulius. They won't stand for—"

But Paulius has twirled away to pound his cane upon an aluminum chopping block. "*Oh, my slaves to food!*" he cries. "*We have another cuisine to unearth! It lies in a moribund coma, drowned in a bog of bottled sauces! The Inevitable Philosophies are ripe for our plunder, needing the sweat of your brow and the tip of your tongue to pry its cuisine back from the grave! Who will help me descend into the Underworld to haul back this sweet, sweet Eurydice?*"

"*Yes, chef!*" The chefs thrust ladles into the air, stab the air above them, roar their approval.

"You see?" Paulius blows his staff a kiss. "What you have never understood, you old black manacle, is this kitchen is not a business. The Sol Majestic is a temple of *transformation*. And we *will* worship our heathen gods."

Paulius curls his arm around Kenna's shoulders, drawing against him protectively, and Kenna feels safer and warmer than he ever has in his whole life. Kenna is certain that this is a personal love, that Paulius would bankrupt himself before he abandons Kenna to languish without this grand, antiquity-exhuming meal—

Yet Scrimshaw's gaze is as dead as a blank monitor. "We will not be able to afford paying them overtime for more than two weeks."

"I'll use my cut of the profits to pay them for three months."

"You've spent your profits. You have enough left to pay them one month."

"You're a boat anchor," Paulius hisses. "You're a bureaucratic cancer. You're peripatetic poison, poured into the porch of my ear . . ."

"So a month is acceptable, then?"

Paulius holds up eight fingers, four on each hand, wriggling them inches from Scrimshaw's glasses. "Not a month, you dried bean. *Two* months. I pay a month of overtime, the restaurant pays for four weeks—eight weeks total."

"Four weeks, Paulius. You'll run overbudget. *That,* I'm afraid, is . . ." She clucks her thin tongue against porcelain-white teeth. "Inevitable."

"I'll leave."

Kenna's stomach tightens around the broth in his gut; he hadn't meant to cost Paulius the restaurant. Scrimshaw inhales through her nose, drawing her head back, more draconic than ever. Kenna half believes she might breathe fire. "You won't."

"Don't test me, you corroded shackle. I've made sacrifices for this place. I keep these hoary old standards on the menu at your bequest."

"I allow you to change ninety percent of the dishes every season!"

"What remains is the most tedious stuff! Transglutinated beef-strands and spherified chicken alginate!"

"I mandate only that two courses out of twenty-three are *guaranteed* to please. The rest can be sacrificed on the altar of your experimentation. If you find that too tedious, perhaps you *should* leave."

"Perhaps I shall." Paulius flicks dirt from underneath well-manicured fingernails. "What would you tell the customers who have arrived after two years in hibernation, I wonder? How would you explain the automatic loss of a Firewar Star rating when the head chef leaves?"

"How would you explain fleeing yet *another* job?"

Kenna feels the tension vibrating between the two of them. The rest of The Sol Majestic's kitchen has returned to chopping, emulsifying, foaming—confident in tonight's service.

"Eight weeks," Paulius says. "Or pack my bags."

"Six weeks," Scrimshaw hisses. "Or pack your own."

He whirls on one heel, grabbing Kenna's hand. "So be it."

"But at six weeks," Scrimshaw relents, her fingers rippling like sea anemones, "I'll authorize the expenditure to put Master Kenna and his parents up as long as this takes."

Kenna hadn't realized she'd known his name.

Paulius reaches back to pull his braid out across his chest, begins rebraiding it into fussy little knots. "Put the boy up? In a hotel? Why?"

"I doubt his parents planned to stay for six weeks. Or would you leave them living in the ducts?"

Paulius's knife-scarred fingers skitter through his braid, running up and down the cord like agitated spiders.

"Done," Paulius says.

Kenna waits for them to shake hands. Instead, they breathe in and out three times, their gazes locked like swordsmen in a battle, each refusing to be the one who slinks away from this confrontation. Come the third breath, they both turn away.

Scrimshaw shuts the red door. Paulius collars a passing chef.

"Pack the Escargone with basic supplies. Two—no, three weeks' worth. I'll burn connections as soon as I determine what other supplies we have to get in, oh, and tell Rèpondelle to round up the boy's parents." He makes a tiny hop, stamping both his feet on the floor, half a jig. "Oh, I have *so much* research to do!"

Then he crouches down, ducking below the kitchen's sightline, leaning heavily on his cane. He slides his fingers around the back of Kenna's head; his grip is so weak, the pressure on Kenna's neck is a mere request to come closer.

Kenna acquiesces. Paulius presses his sweat-fevered forehead to Kenna's.

"Thank you," he whispers. In The Sol Majestic's maelstrom, touching heads creates a tiny chapel for Paulius to reveal his secret exhaustion. "Thank you for gifting me something new."

As Paulius's skull trembles against his, Kenna senses the sickness ravaging Paulius's body. Paulius feels like a bird, frail bones and thin muscle; something devours him from the inside.

It is an intimacy Kenna has never felt before: an acknowledgment of weakness, shared through touch.

This restaurant, Kenna realizes, is no hobby. It is a survival mechanism. Paulius must endlessly stoke himself with grand visions, or his failing body will collapse and never rise again.

As if to confirm this, Paulius inhales one ragged breath, then leverages himself back to his feet with his cane. When he stands, he is once again Paulius: indomitable. Unstoppable.

"I'm afraid we must part for now, my friend. But never fear— you and I will smuggle a meal worthy of igniting your passions past Scrimshaw's starvation budget. Stay close: I shall return."

You and I. Kenna adores the way Paulius effortlessly credits him. And though it may be foolish, risking affection on a man who may only see him as an opportunity to perform, Kenna chooses to drink deep of this newfound camaraderie.

The danger, of course, is that instead of friendship, Paulius will give Kenna a meal and a sales pitch before ejecting him back into the void, where Kenna will spend his life wincing as he recalls the time someone purloined his lineage to fashion a show. A smarter man would tuck in his napkin and wait for nothing more than a free meal.

Yet he remembers how he felt in the confessional booth: a blank husk wheezing dead words. He'd starved on a diet of pure cynicism. Believing in Paulius, in this meal, nourishes him in a way he can't explain. He must risk his heart. He must.

Paulius taps chefs on the shoulder, commanding them to come with him. Kenna follows, but does not know the kitchen's rhythms. The chefs move to their own time, and Kenna realizes Paulius had fed him the beat. Within moments, Paulius has disappeared out a side door.

Kenna cruises to a stop next to a freshly peeled pile of fluted potatoes. The remaining chefs pay him no attention; they have to decompress airsquid from their pressurized containers, sew pieces of meat through a canopy of crisped turnips, sizzle pans of nuts. A chef scoops the golden nuts high in the air, like a comet soaring, then whisks the pan underneath to catch every last one as it falls, as beautiful as any dance.

Kenna hears the wooden *thok-thok-thok* as a chef juliennes an iridescent root into precise ivory matchsticks. He cranes in, pushing dangerously close, marking the way her fingers curl protectively to hold the vegetable, her knife chopping so fast that Kenna wonders if she is gene-enhanced.

Kenna's right hand slips around an imaginary knife, rocking it back and forth. The fingers of his left hand curl over an imaginary root. His admiration is a sad weakness—Mother would twist his arm until his tendons strained, haul him to Father for a lecture on the necessity of intellectual purity.

The chef slows her pace, angling her blade toward him, stepping aside to display the way she pinches the blade with her forefinger and thumb, the way she juts her knuckles forward to protect the fingers of her guiding hand. She exaggerates her body motion, rolling her shoulders, bobbing her head as she rocks the blade through the root. Kenna bobs along with her, an uncertain grin creeping across his face as he catalogues her technique . . .

Then she hip-checks Kenna to one side, her chopping speeding up to a blurred machine-gun *rat-a-tat*. She fixates on the roots with the urgency of a pilot making a rough docking.

Did she realize I'm debasing myself by watching? Kenna doesn't know the kitchen etiquette; perhaps he has embarrassed her. He opens his mouth to fumble out an apology—

Scrimshaw's black shadow falls over him.

"There you are." Scrimshaw's voice is like steam, hot and ephemeral, making sweat prickle across the chefs' cheeks. "I've arranged for comfortable lodgings for you and your parents. The hotel has just upgraded their virtual reality hoods at the hotel, so you can play any game you please. If you'll come with me, Master Kenna..."

Scrimshaw reaches down to guide him to his new home.

Kenna hugs his hand against his chest, as though it might fly away to meet her grasp. He knows Mother and Father would disapprove, but—

He needs to learn the kitchen's secrets. Even though labor is the exact *opposite* of Inevitable Philosophies.

"I cry your pardon, Madame Scrimshaw. But . . . if it were okay by you . . . I fear I would be far more comfortable ensconced in the bustle of your kitchen than pent in any kind cage of a hotel. *If* that were to be okay. By you."

Scrimshaw's face is old, and unreadable. Kenna freezes, a rabbit trembling under a hawk's shadow.

Then a smile uncurls like a flag across Scrimshaw's face.

She nods—no.

She *bows*. The chefs around her mirror the motion.

"Welcome to the kitchen, Master Kenna," she says, then adds: "For now."

4

The First Night at Savor Station

Kenna is used to the sleepy travelers' rhythms on spaceships: the yawn-and-roll of people in the bunks, the shuffle of duffel bags, the erratic ploddings around the corrugated steel walkways to kill time. Nobody hurries on spaceships, except perhaps in that mad rush before touchdown; the space between stars is large.

Whereas every chop of Sol Majestic's knives propels them toward the evening's service. They bang open oven doors, pour hissing clouds of liquid nitrogen into steel bowls, stuff cuts of meat into the long ceramic gravitizer tubes before flipping the switch to cook the protein beneath the heat of planetary pressures.

The guests are coming.

The dishes must be assembled.

Kenna's main goal is to get out of the way. The chefs tolerate nothing that obstructs the upcoming service, and should Kenna accidentally bump a line cook he would be ejected as an enemy of the kitchen. The air thickens with shouted orders, leaving no room for Kenna's questions.

Yet if Kenna perches near an assembly station, anticipating the chefs' motions so he darts aside before they mutter protests, the chefs offer him rewards for good behavior. They tilt the saucepans and run spoons down the middle, so Kenna can see the demiglaces' consistency. They slip him scraps, pausing to register Kenna's blissful reactions with such pleasure they might as well be watching a theater show. They make flourishing gestures as they wave sensors across the dishes, demonstrating the rows of complex readouts that ensure the scent-profiles contain no unwanted surprises. They even allow Kenna to push a finalized dish underneath the scanners that verify the portions are the correct size and shape.

Most important, when Mother and Father burst into the kitchen, desperate to see their son, the staff closes ranks around Kenna, obscuring him until a woman in a sharp red tuxedo can be summoned. The woman greets them with a smooth politeness, mirroring their concern for their son's whereabouts before deflecting the conversation into the necessity for an interview to fathom the mysteries of Inevitable cuisines.

Kenna cannot hear the conversation over the kitchen's clatter; his view is blocked by pot-washers ferrying stacks of plates. But the flashes of the red-tuxedoed woman's body language are like watching a conductor sweeping her baton across an orchestra. She is her own stage, first moving in syncopation with Mother and Father to reflect and catch their movements, then shifting to take the lead so her gestures inspire emotion from Mother and Father.

Kenna knows how Mother and Father long to be listened to. They have spent their lives in poverty, crouching on the doorsteps of powerful men who have discarded them like last year's fashion. Yet the woman in the red tuxedo leans in close to hear them; Kenna feels if she missed a single syllable from Mother or Father, she would scoop down and pluck it off the ground to present it to them as though it were a gold coin dropped from a wealthy man's purse.

By the time she suggests perhaps a private interview to consult them about their Inevitability might not be amiss—a proposal Kenna catches via a dove-like flutter of white-gloved hands—her veneration has captured them wholly. They follow, straightening their robes.

"And that's why we pay Rèpondelle the big bucks," a chef mutters—then, as if embarrassed to acknowledge she has broken the silence they have wrapped Kenna in, darts off to poke her finger into a tub of jellied larks' tongues.

And Paulius is woven through the night's service, tasting, measuring, interrogating. The guests have sat down for their first drinks, and now is the critical time where The Sol Majestic's perfection must be hammered into place. Paulius is everywhere, consulting on the look of this dish, searing a caul of cheese beneath the broiling flametongue of the salamander, debugging the bioprinter as it catches on a spool of carpaccio. Occasionally he stops to ruffle Kenna's hair.

But Kenna catches the signs of Paulius's fatigue. The way he leans on his cane when no one's looking. The delirious way he closes his eyes between tasks.

He looks tireless, but Kenna sees the cost.

The service draws closer. Kenna scurries through the bustle of hips and knife-tips to watch as the ingredients are combined into dishes. They are not food as he understands it. These are tiny blobs of taste positioned on a plate's canvas, so beautiful Kenna would cringe to eat them; he imagines clumsy fingers sinking into the clean geometrical lines of a cut of fish that floats atop a shimmering river of degravitized salt water, smudging the clean ribbon of dark sauce artfully curved across the platter, and Kenna shivers in revulsion. Eating this art would be like peeing his name across a mural.

Yet his stomach, his traitorous stomach, rumbles as the chefs spritz the trout with atomized air scented with the leafy scent of riverbanks, preserved from the planet the fish was caught in, tiny clouds caught and shaped by microgravity controllers to keep the fish moist as the moment it was caught—and to give diners the illusion that they are perched high in a tree, staring down through a dusky mist.

The rhythm reaches a crescendo as Kenna counts each course brought out to the diners, savory dishes sweetening as they approach the dessert course. Twenty-three dishes. Twenty-four. He jerks awake, sitting on top of the humming ultrasound dishwasher. Is that twenty-five? Did he miss one? Despite the broth in his belly and the chunks of meat the chefs have passed him, Kenna feels his body extracting the last of the nutrients from everything he has eaten today, then trying to weave all that natural healthiness into bones made from expiration-date pastries. The effort sucks the sugar from his brain, his body falling into deep slumber as it closes down for repairs. Twenty-six dishes. He thinks. Twenty-seven.

Darkness.

A cheer hauls him out of paper-thin sleep. The night's service is over. Kenna clambers down, furious he missed the excitement; the fumellier offers him a hit from the Majestic's prodigious marijuana supplies. And why shouldn't he? All the other chefs are taking tokes, popping open bottles of beer, celebrating another successful night. Kenna sucks the smoke in deep, chokes; everyone claps him on the back, offers him a glass of wine.

Who knew the camaraderie that work brought? Mother and Father gestated their Inevitable Philosophies through scrupulous self-reflection, abandoning earthly bonds to generate certainty, but . . .

The staff here is so joyous at having survived another night's service that their celebratory good will overflows to anyone nearby.

They joke that if they give him the best wine, Kenna will choose them. A boastful mock-scuffle breaks out, each chef claiming the dish they will make for the Inevitable Prince tomorrow. They interrogate Kenna as to his preferences; their sentences waft into the air like the marijuana smoke, skirling into nothingness, and Kenna stares at the fans overhead.

Soon he is leaning against the ultrasound dishwasher, but the chefs push him aside; they clean pots, sing songs, discuss what repasts a transport ship hobo would find appetizing. Kenna tries to speak, but his tongue flops in his mouth like a fish the chefs have released from stasis. His words bubble in his skull like the bubbles

in this champagne flute, fizzing out the top of his head and popping into nothingness . . .

Someone carries him. Paulius. His gait is uncertain. Kenna tries
to tell him to get his cane. But Paulius crouches over, tucks Kenna
into a cot. There are a few other chefs in cots around him already,
some snoring deeply, some reading, some blowing plumes of
marijuana smoke into the vents.

He's not tired. There are still things to watch in Mono No Aware.
Kenna is no child. He is

He is

He is asleep. And for once, his dreams are not Inevitable, but
fiercely, gloriously mundane.

5

The First Morning at Savor Station

The one thing Kenna knows about beds is that you must fight for every minute you stay in them. Beds are a prized luxury on the transport ships. He has slept in one only seven times in his life. Four of those times have been in medi-clinics.

A bed is a tiny vacation. Nobody's feet are jabbing into your back, no stranger is stepping on your face. Your body heat suffuses the blankets, enfolding you in a warm hug from yourself.

Yet the moment you exit the bed, the vacation is over. Beds are rented by the hour.

So Kenna sleeps in the cot the same way he has slept in every bed: his fists knotted in the blankets, eyes squeezed shut, pretending to be asleep until an attendant ejects him from this soft kingdom.

Except the chefs are getting up around him. They awake with a jolt, craning their necks around to see what got them up. Then they get up furtively, snatching their shoes from the floor, tapping a dozing friend on the way out and jerking their chins toward the door. Their friends mouth silent thanks before pulling on their shirts.

It was like this on the ships, Kenna thinks. Ride long enough on any transport ship and you come to know the hum of the engines. There were merchants who lurked along the shipping lanes, offering to cut the transport captains in on their profits. If you heard the ship's thrum shift from the steady pulse of long-distance haulage into the pitch of sublight speeds, you could position yourself by the docking bay to get first pick of the salesmen's merchandise.

Mother and Father had lectured Kenna over the way he'd sleep through anything: *Once you have hauled your Inevitable Philosophy up to your conscious mind,* Father had said, *it will be as though words are written on every wall. You will not sleep; your dreams will prod you to action.*

Your childish dreams are anesthesia, Mother had said, disappointment inscribed on her face. *They muffle your actions. How do you expect to acquire an Inevitable Philosophy, Kenna, staring at the insides of your eyelids?*

Except the insides of every transport ship held the same corroded walls, the same bullies waiting to mock the fallen Prince, the same reminders he couldn't afford the upper decks' sumptuous entertainments.

Yet in The Sol Majestic, Kenna's waking hours are better than dreams.

Is this what an Inevitable Philosophy feels like?

His head is light as a balloon; he lets the covers slip to the floor without a single regret. But there's an orchard outside. And an Escargone, whatever that is. And a procession of half-naked chefs, sipping black coffee as they pad through the Majestic's back corridors to the loading dock.

The dock, lit by overhead fluorescents, is just large enough for pallets to be delivered from the inbound spaceships—a battered steel space, functional but not elegant, with shuttered delivery doors on every side. Thirty chefs have crowded in, whispering, their heads tilted like radar dishes toward some obscured cargo in the room's center.

Except as Kenna walks in, they each bob their head in respect and move backwards, their sleepy faces blossoming into cryptic smiles that they offer to him like gifts.

Kenna would normally recoil from such welcome; boys are only friendly to him as cruel jokes, luring Kenna into revealing his hopes to them so they can fashion more cutting insults. Only scowls are honest.

But this is already dreamlike. They were so kind last night.

He thinks of Father, discussing his Inevitable Philosophy: *each step will feel preordained, Kenna. Once you know what your life's purpose is, you will walk fearlessly into black depths.*

Loading docks are treacherous places, for a Philosopher. No Inevitable thoughts can be birthed in a place where men are reduced to cart animals—and if the poison of laborious sweat doesn't befuddle your brain, the temptation of commercialized physical delights will.

Yet the steel pallet doesn't feel as though it could destroy Kenna's future. It's a waist-high pallet, wrapped in taut black plastic so no light-fingered dockworker is tempted by its contents.

Yet it has no RFID tags dotting the plastic. Without scannable tags slapped across its surface, the station's automated forklifts couldn't have delivered this pallet here—knowledge Kenna feels soiled for knowing.

"Paulius must have burned connections," one whispers. The others bob their heads in agreement a tick too quickly; Kenna feels that soap-bubble consensus of convulsive affirmation, concurring before they're forced to acknowledge they don't actually know what that means.

The chefs pace in slow circles around the pallet, keeping a cautious distance as though it might be radioactive—which it might be, for all Kenna knows. How could this even be here? Paulius welcomed him to the orchard less than eighteen hours ago. Kenna has spent his entire life traveling on ships, has catalogued their speeds: even if he assumes Paulius can afford the fastest of automated courier-ships, the ones that stick their cargo in stasis cubes so they don't have to worry about crushing their human passengers to jelly, it would still take at least a week to get a shipment from the nearest systems out to Savor Station. Only military-grade ships can split dimensions, and that tech's zealously restricted.

As with most things, the rich are faster than the poor. But even the rich remain tethered to the laws of physics.

Paulius could not possibly have summoned a dockful of Inevitable Philosophy supplies in less than a day.

But how can Kenna be sure, unless he opens it?

The pallet feels like a present to Kenna, or at least what he imagines a present would be if Mother and Father gave gifts. The chefs cloak the pallet in an eager silence, shushing each other's theories as they jostle as close as they can get without actually claiming it, looking to Kenna as though he will preside over some unrehearsed ceremony.

And Paulius is a showman, isn't he? Wouldn't it be like Paulius to leave a special supply cache for Kenna the Inevitable Prince to open?

One gift couldn't destroy his Philosophy, could it?

Kenna presses his palm against the pallet's smooth plastic.

The chefs exhale, the orgasmic noise of a crowd watching fireworks explode.

Emboldened, Kenna presses down. He wants to rip off the wrap in one convulsive gesture, but then he would know what's inside. Kenna's had so few pleasures, the joy of having something to anticipate is almost better than the pleasure itself.

What's underneath is soft. Kenna had expected to find a can's hard ridges, or the firm crunch of some unknown vegetables, but the pallet's soft as a pillow.

What will it taste like? How will he eat it?

He wedges his fingernail underneath the wrap . . .

"Back, you savages!"

A young woman as thin as a mantis pushes her way through the crowd, her cheekbones sharp enough to cut flesh. She wears a striped red-and-gold chef's outfit—one of the highest ranks in

Paulius's kitchen, which Kenna finds comforting—but her sweat-stained collar is unsnapped, revealing light bronze skin flecked with blue mold. She wears great brass goggles with smoked lenses, so big Kenna would swear their weight should snap her scrawny neck; her short, straight black hair sticks out in every direction.

She grips a wooden cask in her hands, brandishing it like a grenade.

"You know what old Montgomery needs to live, you backstabbers!" she cries. "The sensation! The novelty! You'd bury me in a bland grave!"

Kenna squints. The cask is not a weapon—it's made of stained wood, the size of a bucket, blotched with wet mold-growth. Montgomery thrusts it forward, elbows locked, keeping it far away from her center mass as though she intends to drop it.

Yet the chefs stiffen in a paralyzed rictus, their fingers curling themselves to catch this cask, cringing as if not catching it might spell the end of their career. They form a protective circle around Montgomery, who swings the cask around in wild arcs to keep it faced toward them, as though she was brandishing a crucifix at a crowd of vampires. The chefs hunch low, ready to dive underneath to catch it should Montgomery wobble.

Their eyes flicker toward Scrimshaw's red door, hoping for their boss to save them.

"You were sleeping, Montgomery!" a lowly black-striper pleads, bowed low to dive underneath the cask.

"Prevaricators! You're all prevaricators of the highest order! I never sleep! I have bitches to tend! And speaking of bitches—" She rattles the cask; something doughy flops against wooden staves. "She wants to die, you know! I have carried this bitch on my back across star systems, cajoling her with nostrums to prod her back to existence, using all my skills to keep her vivified! A good shake"— she rattles it again, and lesser chefs faint—"and this sad bitch would deliquesce into mold! And *then* where would you be, ay?"

"Let them alone!"

No one is more shocked than Kenna to hear himself speak. The chefs turn to face Kenna; their disbelief lends him strength. He won't let them suffer when this is his fault.

"The chefs here had no plans to broach the integrity of your possessions," Kenna tells her. "*I*, however, did. So if you plan to punish anyone—punish me."

Montgomery snorts, then bends down to scrutinize him, her lenses whirring as those brass goggles focus in on him.

"The boy," she murmurs. Her head bobs with metronome regularity. "I suppose you *do* have claim."

She reaches back, her limbs unsettlingly spiderlike, to nestle the cask into a webbing of mold-furred leather straps on her back. The chefs breathe a sigh of relief as Montgomery strokes the cask, then clasps her hands in apology, bowing to the room.

"An overreaction," she purrs. "I thought you gents failed to understand my condition."

"And I failed to understand this pallet was your purvey."

"My *purvey*?" Her laugh is like a can of bolts rattling down stairs. "No, that pallet belongs to Paulius. I swiped his shopping list before he . . . burned connections." Her sly grin is a dancer sliding a veil aside to give an indistinct glimpse of her body beneath. Kenna knows Montgomery is the only one in this room who understands how "burning connections" works, and she keeps that knowledge locked up.

"So he did order in supplies."

"Not just any supplies, my sweet project." Montgomery licks imagined flavors off her fingertip. "Ingredients old Montgomery here has never tasted lie beneath that tarp—racks of funky mushrooms and salted seagull eggs and some crazy herb called rehmannia. And while old Montgomery owes you a debt for—"

"You're all of thirty, ma'am," Kenna says. "I refuse to recognize you as old."

She thumps her chest, releasing a skirl of mold that sets Kenna coughing. "Age isn't tallied in years, boy. It's the sum of your experiences. There are newborn octogenarians and teens as old as pharaohs. Interview doddering nursing home victims; see if they've done half the things I have. I'm antiquated. I'm dying as you look at me."

"From the mold?"

She raises her eyebrows—which Kenna can only tell via the lifting of her goggles. She reaches down to her belt, which is bandoliered with an assortment of eyedroppers, patting each before settling upon the one she needs. She shakes it like a thermometer before squeezing its contents into a hole in the cask.

Something in the cask sighs, a yeasty breath. She pats it like a baby's bottom.

"No, no, boy," she says. "My sweet moldy bitch helps keep me alive. She's never the same twice. That's what a woman with my condition needs."

"I'm sorry—your condition?"

She stiffens, bracing for revelation. "I'm a Sensate."

Kenna's irritation is upended, tumbling into sincere pity. Kenna's more used to the transport ship chemists, sore-pocked men who specialize in siphoning whatever synthetics they can tap from the ship's engine supply-lines, then refashioning them into haphazard drugs. But he knows addicts too well. And Sensates, addicted to novelty, are among the worst passengers on transport ships— needing to travel to new planets to satisfy their quivering need to see new skies, but trapped like cats in a cage during the trip.

Some clawed themselves bloody, unable to tolerate staring at the same walls for a week. Some bolstered themselves against the monotony of starship travel by hurling themselves into unwise relationships with incompatible companions, recognizing the impending heartbreak but taking solace in a new flavor of drama.

They'd seemed so miserable to Kenna. The Sensates would babble endlessly, relentlessly, about the joys of what it would be like to frolic in the red-frothed waves in the ruby seas of the next port— but a day after running naked on the beach, the experience lost its luster. Once the newness was gone, sameness rubbed against them like sandpaper. And they'd scrape funds together for their next trip, anguishing at the routine of menial work, forever itching to be anywhere else . . .

Montgomery snaps her fingers close enough to Kenna's eyes that he flinches. Then he recognizes the insult he's given her; to an addict fighting their compulsions, pity is poison.

"I see you're familiar with my condition," she says.

"I am, but . . . you're restricted here. Working in the same place, manufacturing the same meals? That would destroy the Sensates I've met . . ."

"I don't *work* here," she sniffs, offended. "Paulius knows of my condition, and convinced me to stay for a time. He knows I'm a culinary Sensate, restricted to new tastes. I spent years enduring the traveling prisons of transport ships until he convinced me if I stayed at the best restaurant in the stars for a time . . ." She looks longingly at the pallet. "People would bring the new foods to me."

"Of course I'll share. But . . ." Kenna looks at the pallet; there's enough food under that wrap that the chefs could all eat until their bellies burst. "There's no need to go waving your cask about. Even were I greedy, I'm sure Paulius would ensure you got a taste . . ."

"This is your food, O Prince," Montgomery admits. "Paulius ordered it in for you, and I can't say you don't deserve it. But if I watch you eat balut—whatever that is—then by the time *I* have a piece, I'll know what it looks like, I'll know what it smells like, I'll know whether it tastes fair or foul . . . I won't have the encounter's *fullness,* in all its glittering anticipation. And if you know us Sensates, Master Kenna, you know—well, the anticipation is all that sustains us."

But I had anticipated the taste as well, Kenna thinks.

Kenna has never been given a gift, so he's never had anything to give. Now that he has a wealth of options, he finds that wealth makes him sullen. *That was mine,* he thinks. *Paulius left it for me.* Even Montgomery acknowledges he has the right to take it.

He should rip it open. He won't get this opportunity again; in six weeks, his meal will have passed and he'll be poor again, while Montgomery will be feasting on whatever new foods Paulius orders in . . .

. . . and he will know forever that when he was rich, he was no better than the people who shat upon him when he was poor.

"You may slake your fill on this pallet," Kenna says quickly, before he regrets it. "On one scant condition."

"Which is?"

"You inform me what's in the cask."

Watching her smile is like watching ice crack. "Dinner rolls."

Kenna would ask for further explanation—but in a way, the cask's mystery is sweeter than knowing.

Montgomery leans her full weight on the flexing plastic wrap, head hung low, palms spread open as if the pallet is all that holds her up.

She presses her cheek to the taut wrap, slithering along it, sniffing—and then, driven wild, she reaches over with the trembling need of a woman pulling the sheets off her lover to grasp a fistful of . . .

. . . bright orange silken robes.

She tugs a long robe out from underneath the wrap, crumples it, presses it against her face as though somehow this might be food. "No," she whispers, tossing the fluttering robe back into the crowd as if they might explain it to her, then shreds the wrap to push deeper into the pallet. She digs frantically, scooping plumes of bright fire-colored robes into the air above her, each so light and fragile they open like parachutes before drifting down onto the scuffed loading bay floor.

He should feel sorrow for Montgomery. Instead, he marvels as he plucks one from the air.

"Those are Inevitable Philosophy robes." Kenna's robes are puckered knots of black stitches, more thread than fabric; he would have purchased new clothes long ago if Father hadn't forbidden it. *This is our last link to our people, Kenna,* Father had said. *If we don't wear the sacred robes, how will people know us?*

It had always seemed like foolish pride. But as the silk flows over his knuckles like textured water, spilling down around his wrists, Kenna realizes he has never seen his Father's robes as Father does. Father sees the tattered silk-scraps, sewn clumsily into place like butterfly wings tangled in a spider's web, and uses memory to knit them into a recreation.

"These are what I should be clad in." Kenna's hushed words send the gossamer-light robes billowing away like jellyfish.

"I know that! You think I don't know that?!" Montgomery shakes two fistfuls of robes like rainbow pom-poms. "What in the frozen void will I do with *robes*?"

"You will do nothing with them," Paulius says, appearing in the far doorway. "The front of house, however, will need to be garbed appropriately for the service. Now put those back, you've already torn some. Don't you realize how delicate those are?"

It is as though Paulius has broken a spell. Montgomery pushes her goggles back across her forehead, surveying the shredded robes with gold eyes that look like pools of olive oil, pinched at the edges with an epicanthic fold. Like any addict, Kenna realizes, she only recognizes the damage she's done after she's jarred out of her need.

Muttering frantic apologies, she begins creasing the robes back into their original shapes.

Scrimshaw stomps into the dock, her steel-toed boots sending echoing booms through the chamber. "*What is this?*"

Paulius is the only one who does not flinch. "Robes."

She pinches one earpiece of her thick plastic glasses, as though she can somehow focus them to find a better explanation. "I can see it's robes. Why do we have a pallet of robes?"

Paulius's disdainful head-shake causes his braid to twitch. "For the front-of-house. This is a dinner for the Kings of an Inevitable Philosophy, Scrimshaw. Rèpondelle will tell you: we cannot scrimp on proper outfits for such a gala."

"Fine. But we employ twenty servicemen who'll need regalia."

"And Kenna! And his parents."

"So: twenty-three outfits. Whereas laying there, taking up precious space in my dock, are at least five *hundred* silken robes."

"I didn't have time to *bargain,* Scrimshaw. What, do you think I'd bring the tailor out here to suit up everyone *personally* in your absurd six-week deadline? No, I had no choice! I had to buy every outfit she had!"

She snaps her fingers before holding out her palm expectantly. "The bill of lading, please."

Paulius plucks a receipt from his suit pocket and drops it from an inch above her palm, so as not to make contact with Scrimshaw's flesh.

Scrimshaw glares at the bill with malice enough to burn a hole through it. "This is a massive expenditure for an excess of useless material. What do you expect me to do with it?"

Paulius flicks his fingers toward her as though trying to get snot off his nails. "Make it into money, my dear manacle. It *is* what you do, after all."

She scowls. Then her plucked eyebrows rise. She cruises to a stop before the pallet, gazing off into space, rubbing fabric between her fingers contemplatively.

"And *you* lot." The chefs mouth silent explanations as Paulius turns to face them, practicing apologies. Paulius uses his cane to push them aside as he makes his way to the loading dock's far door. "Did you think I would smuggle in appallingly rare foods and then leave them in a corner for you to stumble across like yesterday's laundry? Is *that* the second-rate entertainment I gift to the finest chefs in the known stars?"

Each chef clasps their palms against each other in an isometric pressure, not quite daring to applaud, not yet. Montgomery hugs her cask to her chest, whispering reassurances into the barrel. Yet as Paulius leans down to unlatch the loading dock door, he pauses, lapping up their suspense. He grants them a single bemused smile as he hears them groan in anticipation.

"Honestly." Paulius rolls his eyes. "You'd think you worked at Belle du Balle, not The Sol Majestic."

Paulius flings the door upward.

The front-of-house staff charges into the loading dock like a parade, golden robes flowing around their bodies.

Effervescent delight pops out of Kenna, an unprincely laugh that Kenna's mother would silence. The other chefs whoop in approval, a thunderous adulation as the waiters step through the door in choreographed precision—the first wave snapping open tables with rich red tablecloths and arranging them on the ground, just as the second wave, carrying covered copper bowls perched atop tented fingers, swoop in to drop the sample bowls into place.

Kenna's eardrums flex as taiko drums boom into the room— speakers, it must be speakers, there's no room for the barrel-sized drums to be played, but the speakers Paulius has placed are so fine that Kenna can practically taste the sweat of half-naked men pounding drums.

The servers whirl to face the chefs—the same waiters from last night's service, transformed. Last night, they carried dishes stiffly, immersed in service. These robed waiters march around the tables wreathed in wildness, like bright-scaled fish gliding through water—or perhaps red dragons swooping through the air. They roll their hips to send the diaphanous fabric soaring. They smile with bold fierceness, so positive they have brought Kenna joy.

This is what it was like for them, Kenna thinks. *This is the glory of the Inevitable Philosophies.*

For the first time in his life, Kenna can understand why Mother and Father might tow a bedraggled son on rusted starships, sacrificing everything to limp from hopeless situation to even more hopeless situation. If they could bring this majesty back to life . . .

Mother and Father had shown him videos. Yet those videos were tiny, caged in smartphones scarcely bigger than Mother's palm. To be surrounded by such glory . . .

The waiters thrust a hand backwards, fingers seizing the grip on the cloches that hide the dishes' contents. The chefs lean forward, with Montgomery pushing her way to the front.

A waiter—Kenna thinks it may be the red-tuxedoed woman from last night, but he cannot be sure, her face vanishes from memory like a dream whenever he's not gazing directly upon her—looks to Paulius.

Paulius leans back like an emperor, waves a lazy approval.

The waiters lift the cloches off the plates in a smooth ripple, revealing tiny piles of ingredients, each identified by a stiff parchment placard: *Rehmannia. Haw jam. Artocarpus. Fermented seahorse milk. Balut. Sailwhale flank.* And more . . .

The ingredients glisten enticingly under the lights, piles of raw meat-red and lambent purple jelly and lumpy milk-white: Kenna glances upward, noting Paulius has attached lights to the loading bay's ceiling.

Montgomery charges in toward the ingredients, head down, clutching her cask between bicep and chest like a football. She stammers to a halt, transfixed, tracing tiny circles around the edge of the plate. She falls to her knees, subsumed by the tiny gray eggs, sniffing and smelling. The chefs stand back, respecting her ritual.

She slides an egg into her mouth, feeling its bumps with her tongue, blissed out as she sucks upon it, purring as she strains the egg white through the pebbled shell . . .

"All right," Paulius says. "Give her some alone time. That's why she stays here."

"When do we get our taste?" asks a green-striper.

"You know we don't do sweets before savory in this kitchen, my poppet. You are aware the Escargone needs preparation, yes? That the rest of you must sous chef your own supplies for the contest?

So haul, my lovelies, haul, to stock the Escargone high with all these new ingredients. After our time-ship is prepared? *Then* you may nibble. Now work quickly, before these samples die under the lights . . . or before Montgomery loses control."

Montgomery now chews a shell experimentally, the hard flecks leaving gashes in her gums. The chefs gaze at her longingly—Kenna knows that for all the shortcomings of the Sensate lifestyle, he will never taste anything as intensely as Montgomery relishes these eggs—and then trot off to help load the Escargone.

Kenna follows, curious to what the Escargone is. The chefs shoulder the heavy crates scattered through The Sol Majestic's kitchen—again, no RFID tags—and, with audible grunts, haul them to the back of the kitchen where through a heavy airlock lies . . .

. . . another, smaller kitchen.

Whereas The Sol Majestic's kitchen is spacious enough to allow Kenna to move, the smaller kitchen's packed as tight as a military ship. The chefs crowd around the entryway, having to enter one at a time, shouldering past each other as two men crouch inside to strap supplies to the walls. Their hips bump against a tiny dishwasher as they drop the perishables into old-style bucket freezers. The stoves fold up, boards fold down to create chopping boards, and in the back there are two hammocks tied to the wall and a cramped toilet seated directly underneath a showerhead.

Kenna's shoulders creep together, anticipating the cramped workflow lurking in the Escargone. There, The Sol Majestic's airy aesthetics have withered into brute functionality. Once that door latches shut, Kenna knows, the stoves will broil both chefs and food. By the time the chefs finish packing the supplies away, only two narrow corridors remain. Kenna has taken cheap flights like this before. Their cooking will become a jigsaw puzzle; removing a pot from storage will require something else to be stowed.

He's lived on transport ships his whole life.

This kitchen was made for him.

Except his brains would boil in there—locked in a cramped space with workers, all he'd focus on would be tawdry techniques, and his grand thoughts would evaporate.

He's meant to lead nations. He's already wasted too many years daydreaming. He can't give up his Inevitable Philosophy; Mother and Father have told him the universe is counting on him to speak truth to power . . .

"This is Stage One," Paulius tells him.

Paulius's thigh-high black boots and ruffled vest have vanished, replaced by blue Kevlar janitorial footie-scrubs. It's the outfit only desperate travelers buy; they're durable and completely inabsorbent. Sweat dews on the inside of those outfits, dribbles down to collect into stink-puddles that must be shaken out at the day's end.

Seeing Paulius stripped of his grand outfits is horrifying. Kenna finds The Sol Majestic's kitchen-stripes comforting—knowing which chefs have achieved mastery to guide the other chefs. Yet in this cornflower-blue peasant's outfit, Paulius could be any transport ship traveler.

Doesn't Paulius fear losing his authority? Wasn't that the reason for his gaudy outfits—to broadcast his imagination's superiority? Does Kenna understand Paulius at all?

"That cramped scullery is meant for long transport," Kenna observes, changing the subject. "I'm failing to see why we would use such a cramped space when we could rise early to use this kitchen . . ."

Kenna threads that "we" in subtly, fearful Paulius has used his magic to create a place Kenna would feel comfortable cooking—

Paulius takes the "we" with a skill of an athlete catching a ball. "This is how we cheat Scrimshaw."

It's never occurred to Kenna that Paulius cooked. He thought a man like Paulius had people cook *for* him. Yet Paulius does not seem diminished by his labor; he's excited to teach.

Kenna is excited. He could learn to cook, couldn't he? Everyone had to cook, once upon a time. Boiling noodles, surely the greats had to do that . . .

"How can we . . ." Kenna glances at the Escargone's watch-piece mechanics, notes the thick circuitry-bands looping around the outside, a tangle of chips and glowing wires that reminds Kenna of ancient sigils.

". . . I remain uncertain how we'd cheat Scrimshaw with a tiny pantry," he admits, braced for Paulius's disappointment, yet proud he has kept himself pure enough to be unknowing of logistics.

Paulius grabs Kenna's wrist, pulls him over to the Escargone with the excitement of a boy showing off his greatest toy, presses Kenna's palm against the circuitry. Though Kenna's hand goes numb, he loves the way Paulius reacts to his ignorance; Paulius isn't disappointed, as Mother and Father always are. He is honored by the opportunity to show Kenna something.

"You feel that?" Paulius asks.

Kenna feels secure enough with Paulius to say no.

Paulius rubs his cheek against the Escargone. "It's what you *don't* feel. You don't feel the thrum of the ship rotating. You don't feel the force fields' vibration. You don't feel anything, because these circuits sever the inside of this pod from time itself."

"So your capsule is akin to . . . a stasis field?"

"Brilliant, Kenna! But the opposite. Stasis fields create pocket dimensions that slow the time within to a crawl. This"—he pats the ship once, twice, three times, as though he can't believe his luck in getting it—"speeds time *up* behind that door. Much trickier. When you slow things down, so what if a few extra seconds pass during months of stasis? But speeding up—ah, one misplaced decimal and you'd open that Escargone an hour from now to find my dusty skeleton entombed like a Pharoah. It's terribly dangerous, locking yourself inside hyperaccelerated time fields. But all the fun stuff is."

"So how long will you . . ."

"Once that door slams shut, great engines will speed time up inside. Scrimshaw won't see me for hours—but I won't see that desiccated warden for weeks."

"I'm afraid I still don't fathom how that assists you . . ."

Paulius steps inside the Escargone, tapping the ingredients strapped to the walls like a game show host displaying fabulous prizes. "That old oubliette gave me just six weeks to prepare your meal. Six weeks! That's not long enough to learn how to cook the Inevitable Philosophies properly, let alone transform them."

"I've never seen such a transformation." Kenna cannot believe his luck. He's dreaded talking to Mother and Father, weathering their disappointment at his occupying his time with such trivial things such as food—and now Paulius has created a magical portal for him to shed his Philosophies in, emerging as a common cook . . .

Why does that idea keep bobbing to the surface?

"Yet you *will* witness the transformation! That's the point, Kenna. I'll show you how this works. But Stage One is reviving the simple dishes so we can make them with the skill of old." Paulius twirls a knife on his finger. "There's no sense in trying to improve a dish if we can't experience it at the summit of its glory. So we make the same dishes over and over, trusting our palates to lead the way."

Kenna does not know how to cook, or to eat. This will be a master class in cuisine: the easiest dishes, starting from square one. He tells himself this is not a trade; it is an education.

"I pray . . ." Kenna swallows back drool. "I pray you shan't find such repeated efforts tedious."

"It is *terribly* tedious! Yet it's not. Cooking isn't one skill, Kenna—it's a hundred different skills we mash into one word. It's knowing how to crush an herb to impart the perfect flavor-perfume. It's knowing how flavor interacts with the goose's skin. It's knowing how the roast's heat will change its scent. You may cook the same goose a hundred times, but that's a hundred skills you improve with each dedicated dish, until one day you fire on a hundred cylinders and eat the face of God."

Yesterday, Kenna couldn't imagine the pleasure of a full belly. Now, his dreams have swollen to encompass the potential thrill of a meal he has made himself, of having internalized The Sol Majestic's rhythms, of basking in Paulius's approval as he lifts one perfect spoonful of his own creation to Paulius's mouth . . .

Yet as he imagines that spoon's weight in his fingers, he can feel his brain shutting down. Empty spaces once reserved for nothing but pure Philosophy now cluttered like supply closets with mundane tradecraft.

And for what? A full belly and a warm cot?

He must become greater than his desires. Mother and Father want him to become a Philosopher. *Paulius* wants him to become a Philosopher. Great monarchs await his guidance. He cannot give in to this simplicity when the complexity of ideas calls to him . . .

"And once we learn how to make the perfect lacquered goose, Kenna, determining its simplest possible form, then comes Stage Two—adding complexity. Chefs are all show-offs, Kenna. They add flourishes they don't need, scrawl 'signature' styles across the suffering faces of once-great meals—but some of that complexity adds depth and flavor. Yet we don't know which of these elaborate preparations are pretentious frippery and which are the beams of the station, as it were. So we scour the ancient recipes . . ."

". . . and make all the complex dishes, to see what sticks."

"Precisely." Paulius taps Kenna on the nose, sending a thrum of pride down Kenna's spine.

"And Stage Three?"

Paulius clasps his hands against his Kevlar jacket-bib in prayer. "Once we've determined what the best version is . . . we extract its essence."

"It's . . ." Kenna thinks of the dabs of food painted across last night's dishes. *Each bite must be like a firework of flavor bursting across the back of your tongue.* The highlights of a thousand recipes, compressed into a single bite, one morsel enough to send your eyes rolling . . .

He *wants* to learn.

But at what cost?

"You understand. You *do.*" Paulius turns from him, rummages through one of the boxes lashed to the Escargone's wall. "But you have a greater role to play in this culinary theater than mere sous chef."

When Paulius turns his back upon Kenna, it's as though he has slammed a door shut on Kenna's dreams. Kenna does not know what a sous chef is, yet finding out he will not be one is like a fist closing around his heart.

"I cannot imagine a greater role, sir."

If Paulius understands how thoroughly he has eviscerated Kenna, the thought does not stop him from rooting through a box. "Your vision is occluded, O Prince. Mine sees the entirety of the stage. Alas, I shall be locked in the Escargone with my three best chefs, slaving until tonight's service needs me—and the one thing you must understand above all, Kenna, is that The Sol Majestic is a temple, and we are faithful acolytes to the service. I'll have little time to teach you."

Betrayal pulses through his body, but also relief—perhaps it's better if he remains an inspiration, rather than sullying his hands with work. "Then what am I to do?"

Paulius shakes out a ceremonial robe so vividly orange and red it reflects shimmers of fiery light across the Escargone's interior.

Paulius drapes the robe around Kenna's shoulders. Kenna flinches—his body is filthy—but Paulius casually places a robe worth more than Kenna's entire family upon him.

Paulius takes a step back to admire him. Kenna wants to slip away, but in the Escargone there is nowhere to hide.

"As a poor boy, you have mastered the art of slipping by unseen,"

Paulius says. "Now you must learn to be comfortable with being viewed. For as the Prince, all eyes will be on you come your meal."

"Yet I fear I am not—"

"No. You *were* not. Allow me to give you this gift, Kenna. Let me show you who you were meant to be."

Kenna wants to flatten himself against the Escargone's walls, trying to blend in, but then he would dirty the robe. Paulius's generosity is like sonar, echoing through him, mapping out how little Kenna has to offer. Kenna is a sodden rat, creeping along transport ship walls, he would shrivel in the spotlight—but Paulius needs him to be a performer. Is he being used for his publicity, his royal lineage wrung dry for spectacle? There's the possibility that he'll be tossed aside like table scraps when all this is done.

But there's also the hope of becoming the leader Paulius claims he is.

Paulius steps forward, pushing Kenna out into The Sol Majestic's kitchen. Kenna does not want to be seen like this, he's a gilded-lily fraud, but Paulius is inevitable, forcing Kenna to either shove Paulius back into the toilet-shower or to step into the Majestic's sunny light.

At least most of the chefs will be in the Escargone, tasting the shipment, Kenna thinks—but no. The ingredients have been brought into the kitchen, and the chefs are at their stations.

Yet The Sol Majestic's rhythm has shifted. Before, the chefs intermingled, consulting each other, tasting each other's dishes. Now, each chef is tense-shouldered, chopping ingredients furtively, glancing over into their neighbor's pot then looking down at their own dish as if to ask, *Why didn't I think of that?*

Amazing. Yesterday, he was unaware cooks took pride in their work, and today he finds them *competing.*

"*My sweet slaves to food!*" Paulius cries, making sweeping gestures with his palms like leaves falling toward Kenna's feet. "*May I introduce to you . . . the Prince of the Inevitable Philosophies!*"

"*Hail Prince Kenna!*" Kenna is grateful that they suppress their smirks. They respect him because Paulius has exalted him—as, presumably, he has exalted others—yet there is still that merriment of everyone settling upon the same absurd thought simultaneously, that Kenna is the most magnificent specimen to ever grace their kitchen.

But the glory of The Sol Majestic, Kenna thinks, is that they treat the absurd with deadly seriousness. When the chefs return their attention to their dishes, they whisk harder, determined to win Kenna's love.

"I'll be gone for three hours, your time." Paulius snaps his fingers; two chefs clad in blue footie-scrubs salute before marching into the Escargone. "When I return, you will have selected the chef who will be your servant."

"*Servant?*" To Kenna, the chefs here are like the glorious birds in the atrium outside—he'd admired them, but never thought he'd *own* one.

"Yes, Kenna. All you've had is soup and leavings. I can't give you a meal fit for a prince unless you can appreciate it like a prince. I have authorized one of my chefs—just one—to be excused from service, her whole job to cook you five meals a day. She will walk you through what food can do."

"Which one?"

Kenna hopes if he feigns ignorance, Paulius will select someone for him. But Paulius, naturally, is ahead of his game. "I told you, Kenna—you'll choose."

Choosing makes Kenna sick. His life has been a series of rejections—by Mother for his poor meditation skills, by Father for being sixteen and still not having grasped his Inevitable Philosophy, by the rich for having fallen into poverty, by the poor for having failed them. Inflicting failure upon someone else will turn him into the people he loathes.

Paulius squeezes Kenna's shoulders like a coach preparing to send an athlete off the bench. "Impoverished children make tough choices out of scarcity. A prince makes tough choices out of abundance. You are a prince. Any of my staff would serve beautifully as your personal chef—but let's see what instincts you have, hmm?"

"Yet I know naught about any of these fine workhands—"

"That's why you have three hours to talk to them, dear lad. This is the interview."

"And if I choose wrong?"

The question sets Paulius's nostrils flaring. "There's only one wrong choice in life, Kenna—to bump along like a twig in a stream. You will choose a chef by the time I return, or I shall be cross. *Quite* cross."

Paulius storms into the Escargone. "Slow the Universe!" he cries, and two waiters, having discarded their silken robes for workman's wear, heave their shoulders against the door until it latches into place with a *bang* that Kenna is sure they feel on the other side of the station.

There is a small hatch, a circular window that Paulius glares through. He snaps his fingers, the sound lost behind the thick smoked glass, and the waiters throw a massive switch. Purple flares coruscate around the circuitry—not with the flash-and-burst speed of lightning, but with electron particles slowed to the speed of fat, buzzing flies.

The window brightens, flaring like a supernova—which makes sense, Kenna thinks. The kitchen fluorescents are pumping out billions of photons, hours of light compressed into a second's output. But if he squints, he sees Paulius has disappeared from the window, and a thick cardboard sign has been taped over it:

CHOOSE.

6

Three Hours to Find a Chef

Kenna is onstage now, an audience of chefs laying out ingredients to draw his attention. A blue-haired girl, her dark skin laced with tattoos, deftly chops apples into rose shapes to lure him closer.

A lanky Intraconnected has spun spiderwebs of thin meat-strands between antlers, plucks the wet fibers like harp strings, a protein tapestry to draw him in. A pudgy Colpuran scoops up great handfuls of tiny nanobots from steaming stewpots, smears them along the smooth edges of a head-sized cube of translucent agar. He gestures enticingly as the bots march through it, automated ants threading the neutral growth culture with preprogrammed mazes of appetizing tastes.

A pair of twin brothers has filled the gravitizer's narrow tube with turtle eggs; the instant Kenna glances in their direction they crank the G-forces, crush the eggs into an omelet cooked by the force of its own compression.

How do you eat the meat-strands? Kenna looks for a nearby fork, sees none, wonders if they would gasp in horror if he peeled filaments off the bone with his grubby fingers. Is there a proper place to start eating the cube?

He is uneducated, but the chefs' flashy efforts make him feel dumb. All the things he needs to learn—he cannot learn this in six weeks. It would be a betrayal to learn the laborers' ways, but Paulius is correct: Kenna must learn to appreciate what they make.

He had their respect, back in the loading dock. He wanted them to think of him as a prince. But now he must choose one of them, and he will choose for such monstrously stupid reasons that he may as well be a child thumbing buttons at random.

He overhears a whispered conversation: "Have we *held* auditions for one of Paulius's pet projects before?"

"Well, they're all different, you know that." Kenna turns to flee, and—

CHOOSE, the sign says.

They saw you turn to run.

Then they'll see you stride back, won't they?

He paces among the countertops, fixating on the dishes, keeping one shoulder interposed between himself and the chefs. With luck, he can turn this roiling anxiety into a regal diffidence. It's partially successful; the chefs do not speak without being spoken to. Yet they hover, mouths parted to offer advice, a brittle kindness tapping on Kenna's door.

These silk robes are too light to carry authority. It's like wearing toilet paper. He needs battle armor for this kitchen. And the dishes are puzzles, presented with no instruction manuals. Seafaring bivalves that open up like birds' mouths when they scent his breath, revealing blobs of blue meat nestled in pearlescent shells; pools of hissing green soups like boiling emerald lava.

A prince would know how to eat these.

Perhaps what he seeks from Paulius is not an education in labor, but an end to ignorance.

Kenna stands before the antler-tree, the filaments fine as spun sugar. There is no spoon. Should he reach up and yank it into his mouth?

He could ask. But if he will be a barbarian, then let him be a bold one. Kenna will grab fistfuls, pull this inverted animal mockery tumbling to The Sol Majestic's floor, and when the chefs see him for the ignorant savage that he is he will shout what did they expect, he *told* them who he was . . .

The smell of broth.

That rich chicken scent whisks aside his other concerns, like a man pulling the curtain shut on a window. Kenna never knew he could be embraced by an odor, but that soup is a warm hug that tells him everything will be all right. And why not? The last time he had it began the most perfect day of his life.

Food is what tells you when you're home, Paulius had said.

Kenna finds himself drifting toward the broth's origin. The broth swirls in a great silver pot, steaming, being stirred by . . .

The most beautiful man Kenna has ever seen.

Kenna is grateful the man is tending to his broth so fiercely that he does not look up, because Kenna is certain that he is grinning a great goofy smile—yet his numb fingers find nothing but slackness in his cheeks, a gobsmacked expression that Kenna attempts to reshape into something normal.

Kenna has not kissed anyone. His parents have always tracked his relationships closely, worried he might soil the royal bloodline. And Kenna has always been a mock-prince, with nothing to offer his beloved, and so he has mashed years of lust beneath hard necessity.

But the necessity melts away, leaving only hardness.

Yet the man pays such tender attention to his broth, bending down to smell it with flared nostrils, closing his eyes in rhapsody as he breathes in and then grabs a sprig of rosemary. The broth-stirrer's face is pale as cream, frowning at the soup in perplexity, a combination of determination and befuddlement that Kenna wants to kiss away.

The broth-stirrer is not particularly clean, Kenna notes. His station is a confused jumble of herbs and smeared spoons. His blond curls peek out insouciantly from underneath a knit cap placed imperfectly on his head; Kenna resists the urge to adjust it, slick back those curls for him. He wears a lowly black-striper's uniform, cut across his lean-muscled arms—arms bulging with the unsightly experience of arduous exertion, not the studied porcelain smoothness that yoga has shaped Father into. Yet Kenna longs to trace his fingers along those firm curves.

This is a student, Kenna realizes, only a year or two older than himself. *I shouldn't be so close to someone so beneath my stature,* Kenna thinks, but the thought vanishes as quickly as a shooting star.

Kenna positions himself behind the broth-stirrer, eager to command attention—but the broth-stirrer sighs and rolls a pinch of salt between his fingers. He pokes at the broth disconsolately with a wooden spoon.

"May I taste your broth?" Kenna says, then winces; that sounds so *sexual,* why did he say that, why, why?

Surprised, the broth-stirrer drops his spoon into the pot, then almost plunges his hands into the boiling liquid after it, then scatters herbs across his work station as he hunts for a ladle to fish the spoon out. Which is good; he's not *that* skilled with his hands. Perhaps he's not so soiled by his work that he and Kenna will have something to converse about.

Then he notices Kenna. The ladle clatters to the floor as the broth-stirrer stands to attention, his hand twitching in an aborted salute. The other chefs politely muffle laughter, turning away before they embarrass him.

Sighing, the broth-stirrer—his embroidered name marks him as BENZO—slumps away to fetch a clean ladle, then fishes the spoon out of the pot. "Oh, you don't want to taste my, uh, broth, sir. It's not done."

A boy that beautiful, that dedicated, shouldn't sound so hangdog.

"Don't call me sir." Another wince; Kenna shouldn't order anyone around anyway, and he doesn't want to accentuate the social fractures that already stand between them. "When will it be done?"

Benzo sucks air between his teeth, a reluctant mechanic about to inform the ship's captain how much this repair will cost. "It's taken three years so far."

"You've been making the same broth for three *years*?"

"Not the same broth, silly." Benzo's "silly" is spoken like a flirtatious punch to the arm; Kenna clings to that friendliness like a life preserver. "I make a fresh batch every morning."

"And you've done that . . ."

Benzo chuckles, a preemptive gesture to ensure Kenna doesn't mock him first. "For three years. Yeah. I get up, fetch a fresh chicken from stasis, butcher it, start a broth, distill yesterday's broth, dice the aromatics, make a raft to clear it, and simmer it until my face is parboiled from steam. And in the end . . . well, here."

He flings his hands out in a chaotic *what-the-hell* gesture, then plucks a silver tasting spoon from a bowl. He skims off a serving, guides the spoon onto Kenna's tongue . . .

Which doesn't feel awkward until Benzo makes eye contact and sees how hungry Kenna is.

Benzo swallows thickly, as if realizing how intimate this is, feeding his food to another man. The tip of Benzo's spoon slows on its way to Kenna's lips, Benzo's pale eyebrows furrowing as he silently asks, *Hey, is this okay?*

By way of reply, Kenna clasps Benzo's hand in his, guiding the broth to his mouth. He can feel Benzo's muscles stiffening at the skin contact.

Benzo's skin is the summary of everything Kenna loves about Mono No Aware. Kenna closes his eyes, pressing his fingertips against the ridged knife-scars on the back of Benzo's hands, savoring the way Benzo's skin is still flush from oven-heat, inhaling the clean scent of freshly cut celery clinging to Benzo's fingers.

Then the golden broth coats his tongue, and Benzo has to step in to catch him as Kenna's knees melt.

Benzo's arms are as strong as they look.

"Aww, no, you don't—you don't want that," Benzo says, propping Kenna against a chopping table before dabbing sweat off his forehead. His fine cheekbones, already reddened from the broth, have deepened two full shades of red.

"That's *exquisite*," Kenna says, springing off the table to wave the spoon in Benzo's face.

". . . the broth."

"The broth, yes."

Benzo smiles, then shakes his head as though waking from a dream. ". . . no! That's awful, don't you see? It's . . ." He ladles a cupful of broth into a wineglass, swirls it before Kenna's eyes with the vigor of a man attempting to summon a genie. "It's fatty."

The surface of the broth is stippled with microscopic glimmering dots of fat.

"It's cloudy."

If Kenna squints, he can make out a thin vortex of a haze.

"And—here, try it again. You'll see."

Benzo thrusts the fine-stemmed glass into Kenna's hands; some slops on Kenna's fine robe. That would have panicked Kenna in a past life, having the most expensive thing he had ever worn stained— once stained, an Inevitable Robe cannot be cleaned, to demonstrate the permanency of error—but with Benzo, Kenna has a prince's grace.

Except he will never be a prince if he continues to consort with Benzo. Inevitable Philosophies are not born in kitchens, or factories, or junkyards.

Kenna turns to one side so Benzo cannot notice the dark splotch seeping across the breast of his once-in-a-lifetime robe, and sips at the broth contemplatively, feeling rich heat shimmer straight down to his stomach.

"Tastes fine to me," Kenna says.

Benzo's panic brings apologies bubbling to Kenna's lips. He wishes he could find honest fault in this broth, for his lack of criticism is driving Benzo mad.

"No, no, no!" Benzo grabs the snifter from Kenna's grasp, slugs the broth back, swishes it around his mouth as he squeezes his eyes shut.

He's seen the other chefs sampling dishes; when they taste, it is

a fluid motion, closing their eyes blissfully as though they are taking in the overture at an opera, marking the rise and swell of the
flavors on their tongues.

Benzo, however, sweats as he samples. He sloshes the broth like
mouthwash, exuding the desperation of a man trying to pass a test.
His expressions shift as he proceeds through the stages of exami-
nation, each as distinct as a forklift shifting gears—ratcheting into
the next segment as he tests for spice quotients, tests for mouthfeel, compares it against past flavor profiles, breaks down the oiliness. Kenna cannot help but feel this process is too mechanical,
but he has no idea how to guide Benzo to better appraisals.

Benzo spits the remains into the sink.

"No." Benzo's whispered negation is the sadness of a spouse
caught cheating. "That's—there's too much salt. The celery is overwhelming. This is supposed to be a neutral stock we can use in
any dish, and it's . . . it's imbalanced."

Benzo is deranged, Kenna thinks. The Sol Majestic cannot be
that exacting. But the other chefs busy themselves in an orchestrated compassion, not letting Benzo see how they've noticed he
has fallen short once again.

"I diced onions for nine months before Paulius used one. Then
I cooked chickens for a year. One boy made stock for five years and
wasn't good enough."

"But he made it, right?"

"He was just short of six years when Paulius took him aside. Said
his palate wasn't good enough. And then . . ." Benzo blows into
his fist, spreads his fingers, mimics a leaf floating away on the wind.

"Well, *I* think your broth is top-notch. Do you know it saved
me?"

". . . no."

"I assure you it did. I was emaciated when I arrived. I hadn't eaten
a bite in four days. Yet when Paulius carried your broth to me . . ."

"He did?"

Paulius probably just grabbed whatever was close at hand, but there's no harm in letting Benzo believe he's special. "When he brought me *your broth,* it was like . . . A fire that limned me from top to bottom. An incandescence that showed me what food *was*."

"Really?"

Benzo's excitement is a teetering domino that could be knocked over by the slightest criticism. Yet Kenna cannot muster a scrap of complaint. Perhaps these antler-meats and gravitized omelets and carved apple-gardens are delightful, but the broth is plain as Kenna. He understands it.

"Will you make me something?"

"What?"

"I don't know. What is it you chefs consume? You can't eat grand meals 'round the clock, can you?"

"That's my job, actually." Those delicate cheeks darken again. "I cook the line meals. For the kitchen. It's . . . simple fare, to keep their bellies full."

"Then make me something simple."

Benzo runs to the pantry, so eager to be asked to demonstrate his skills that he never questions what's right for Kenna. He returns with a crusty loaf of bread, a hunk of cheese, and three tomatoes in a wire basket. He carves out a hunk of butter, tosses it into a sizzling pan, the air humming as the stovetop's induction coils burn red.

He cuts out four ragged slices—the chewy crust flakes open as he sinks the knife tip in, the inside so fluffy that cutting a straight edge would be impossible—and slathers them in more butter, then slices the tomatoes into perfect circles and spreads them across the bread, then crumbles cheese onto the tomatoes.

"You don't want to slice the cheese," he tells Kenna. "You want it nice and gooey. So it'll spread across." He hands Kenna a lump, which is so different from the plastic yellow stuff he's eaten out of vending machines; this is a creamy white, translucent, squeaking between his fingertips. It feels alive.

He pops it into his mouth and his toes flex happily.

"There's other kinds of cheeses, you know," Benzo says. Kenna did not know. But now he is happy to contemplate what colors cheese might come in.

A sliver of doubt slides into his contentment: he should be asking about The Sol Majestic's guests, studying the wisdom of the rich and potent, readying his Inevitable Philosophy.

Yet Kenna crowds in as Benzo slides a spatula underneath the sandwich to flip it over, needing to see what shade of golden brown the crust is, what Benzo will do when the cheese oozes out the sides and sputters in the pan. He's so close that he is hip-to-hip with Benzo. Benzo doesn't step aside to let Kenna gawk; he stays right where he is, a little cryptic smile floating across that angel's face, letting Kenna push up against him.

And when he flicks the sandwich onto a plate and bisects it with his knife, Kenna's swallowing back saliva.

Benzo holds up the half-a-sandwich playfully by Kenna's mouth. "You ready?" he asks. "I'm not gonna feed this one to you, though."

Kenna takes the sandwich from Benzo as though it were a benediction. It feels like life, so hot his fingers puff up. He crams the grilled cheese into his mouth, the crust crunching beneath his teeth, the gooey cheese oozing between his teeth, the tomato bursting into . . .

. . . when Paulius arrives three hours later, he stinks of duck and sports a ragged gray beard.

Benzo and Kenna have made what they call "Cheese mountain," a heap of cheeses brought in by the fromager. The fromager has blindfolded them both, placing samples before them, seeing whether either Kenna or Benzo can identify the cheeses they've had today by taste alone.

Kenna and Benzo are laughing. Benzo isn't doing much better than Kenna is.

". . . have you chosen?" Paulius asks.

Kenna whips off the blindfold. Paulius's blue Kevlar is runneled with burn marks, stained dark with grease; the other chefs stumble out of the Escargone woozily, like sailors on a bender.

Benzo shivers under Paulius's shadow.

"Oh! Yes!" Kenna wraps his arm around Benzo's brawny shoulders, pulls him close. "Him."

Paulius has the grizzled stare of a man readjusting to a larger world. He peers blearily over the antlered meat-strands, the threaded agar-cube, the now-stasised omelette, the rows of elaborate dishes waiting forlornly for Kenna's attention.

He scratches his beard, disgruntled. "You had . . . all those fine meals laid out for you." Then: ". . . O Prince." He sniffs at Benzo; not disdainfully, but as though there's something about the lad he's not understanding. "You had twenty dishes within arm's reach, each a repast that would garner a Culinary Star from a Firewar reviewer, certainly the best meal you'd have had in your life, and . . ." He exhales through his nostrils, rustling his mustache.

Paulius turns to look at his chefs, as though somehow one might offer a theory. ". . . and you don't even *try* what they offered?"

Kenna takes the remainder of the grilled cheese sandwich off the plate, now cold and greasy and still so very delicious, and takes a bite. "Ah yes. That. I incorporated your wisdom."

"Elucidate?"

"All that glory your chefs laid out for my repast? That's Stage Three cuisine." Kenna offers the sandwich to Paulius, who turns it over in his hands, flexing it enough to watch the oil drip out onto the tile. "This? This is Stage One. The simple dishes. I must walk before I can run."

Paulius takes a big bold bite that stuffs half the sandwich into his mouth. He bobs his head as he chews it messily, Benzo chewing his fingernails as he waits for judgment.

After Paulius swallows, he grins.

"Brilliant," he says, pulling up a stool to cut himself a slice of cheese.

7

The Third Day at Savor Station

Every sixth day, The Sol Majestic rests. Benzo does not.

Kenna hears Benzo rise well before the station's dimmer-lights switch to daycycle, even though there is no service today. He pads after Benzo into the kitchen, where Benzo starts the broth routine again: cycling down a stasis cube to fetch a chicken, the feathers still on. Meandering through the orchard's garden to pull some fresh carrots from the ground, brushing off the dirt, smelling them before tossing the unworthy ones into the composter. Getting out the pots and setting up his station.

He's not alone. At least half the chefs are up, yawning as they thrust their knives into the electron-sharpeners' crackling slots.

"Do you ever take a day off?" Kenna asks.

Benzo lowers the feathered chicken into the scalding water, swirls it around the pot. He frowns down at the chicken, parsing the question.

"Paulius said I was close."

Actually, what Paulius said after sipping yesterday's broth was *You used too much salt, too much rosemary, too few onions. It's cloudy because you overcooked the carrots. And I can tell you skimmed off the fat. If you get the balance right, you shouldn't have to skim.*

For all Benzo knows, Paulius won't even taste his broth today. The glass porthole to the Escargone gleams with compacted photons, a paper sign reading LACQUERED DUCK OR BUST taped across the inside. Kenna's heard Paulius will try to pack four months into today, though his chefs may hamper that effort; they stagger hunch-shouldered out of the Escargone to run weeping through the station's rings, hugging surprised strangers and exclaiming at Savor Station roominess.

But Benzo isn't doing this to best Paulius. He's making broth to best himself. Benzo is hell-bent on making not just one perfect broth, but a sequence.

That seems oddly ambitious for a line chef. Yet the kitchen bustles with grand experiments.

This must be Paulius's influence. Ordinary people could not aspire to such greatness. Kenna has seen the layabouts on the transport ships inhaling weed and exhaling shattered dreams; none could have mustered such ambition without a superior intellect to goad them.

Though as Benzo hoists out the sopping chicken to pluck feathers off the still-steaming wings, Kenna wonders whether Benzo can achieve his goal. *The kid was just short of six years before Paulius took him aside,* Benzo had said. *Said his palate wasn't good enough.* Kenna remembers tasting blue-veined cheese crumbles and doing almost as well as Benzo in the fromager's guessing game . . .

"*She* wants to speak with you," a rumpled yellow-striper says.

Kenna feels proud, as though he has passed a test. There is only one *She* in The Sol Majestic worth discussing, and the yellow-striper assumed correctly that Kenna understood. He nods, heading toward Scrimshaw's red door at the kitchen's rear . . .

The yellow-striper yanks him back hard enough Kenna has to steady himself on a wooden chopping block. "You *never* go to the red door!" Her nostrils flare. "Nobody emerges from the red door as an employee. I wouldn't even send one of Paulius's favorites in there without a warning . . ."

"Then where is she?"

The yellow-striper waves two fingers next to her eyes, lunging at Kenna repeatedly in a strangely ostrich-like movement before flipping her palm open to him in a *capisce?* movement.

Kenna does not capisce.

"Oh right," she says, embarrassed. "You're not keyed into our social network. She's in the loading dock."

Kenna shouldn't be surprised that everyone here has biomatrixes installed, but then again surgery is a small price to pay for working at The Sol Majestic. Though it is a large price for Scrimshaw to pay, as biomatrix implants are top of the line even by Intraconnected standards.

He squeezes Benzo's shoulders to apologize for leaving, but Benzo has gotten out pliers to pluck the pinfeathers. Benzo's existence has shrunk to a chicken, and Kenna finds something comforting in that.

Scrimshaw sits in a perfect siddhasana position in the center of the loading dock, a clipboard in her lap. Towers of folded robes surround her, as though she were a goddess holding court in a fabric temple. Judging from the angles of the stacks, all faced inward toward her, Scrimshaw has personally sorted every robe on the pallet.

"Master Kenna." She sweeps her hand across the robe-free space she has left for him to sit. "I must discuss The Sol Majestic's future with you."

He pulls his heels underneath him. Mother has taught him to meditate for years, grabbing his neck to correct his slouching. Yet when even Mother gets into siddhasana position, she is tight as a cord; Scrimshaw's relaxed, yet her lean thighs are pressed flat against the floor.

Kenna wants to ask Scrimshaw if she has studied yoga. From her bowl haircut and her unflattering thick plastic glasses, he's pretty sure Scrimshaw views her body only as a carrying case for her head.

"What level of honesty do you require?" Scrimshaw asks. "Choose carefully. Most people melt under levels of total truth."

Kenna suppresses a shiver. *You're not behind the red door,* he thinks. *You're not being cast out. Yet.* But from the way Scrimshaw's fingers impatiently tap the clipboard, something dreadful lurks within these stacks of robes.

"I'm poor," Kenna says. Admitting that to her is like scourging himself with whips: a necessary pain to prove worthiness. "I cannot afford the luxury of lies."

Scrimshaw's approving smile is as quick as a single frame in an animation, vanishing before Kenna can prove it wasn't an illusion. She purses dry lips, weighing her approach.

"These robes will bankrupt us before your meal arrives."

She's as calm as a coroner taking a dead man's pulse. Her gray eyes smother Kenna's initial laughter: this is no joke.

"Paulius isn't entirely awful at negotiating, when he cares to be." She rubs Kenna's hem between thumb and forefinger, drawing his attention to the quality. "He got quite a good price for them. The problem is, each robe is worth three months' salary to the average man. Bargaining the tailor down to the equivalent of a month's salary per robe is useless when he has purchased . . ." She runs a finger down her clipboard, tapping her fingernail upon the total. "One thousand, two hundred and three robes."

Sitting down, Kenna feels dwarfed by the stacks of robes, as though they might topple over and bury him. Though he has been here two days, The Sol Majestic feels as eternal as a culinary church—a place where bills never came due. Except as Scrimshaw flips over the clipboard to present it to Kenna for his verification, he sees the Majestic as she does. The beauty disappears, replaced by business—a mass of expenses sagging into a deep bankrupt void, a ponderous weight threatening to snap and drag the owners into poverty.

How does anyone ever develop a Philosophy when they're weighted by such petty concerns?

Yet Kenna himself is a weight. In his attempt to help, Paulius has dropped such a load onto that strained web that it will now snap.

"What can I do?" Kenna is glad he hasn't eaten. Every bite shrinks the Majestic's profit margin. Gods, Benzo spilled chicken broth on this expensive robe and Kenna didn't even try to blot it off . . .

"This invoice will come due in thirty days. Another sign of Paulius's sad inexperience; net 30 would be excellent terms for perishables, which frequently go bad before the week is up. But for intersolar apparel sales, net 120 is more standard—assuming that we have one hundred and twenty days to transport the robes to our store, sell them, and have the cash from the customers to pay the bill. Purchased in bulk, like this? He would have done better to have doubled the price per robe, but given us a hundred and eighty days to sell them before the bill came due."

"It's easy enough to follow." Though Kenna squirms, wishing these tawdry financial concerns weren't so simple; he's halfway toward learning a trade. "Plus, we're not a clothing emporium."

Scrimshaw adjusts her glasses as though they pain her. "As you say. And even were we renowned for our suits instead of our soups, it's not like a discredited religious sect's formal wear is in high demand. This is doubtlessly why the tailor was so eager to sell them."

"Can't we . . . refuse to pay?"

"No matter how far humanity travels, all merchants remain a whisper apart. Fail to pay this invoice on time, and word will get out. Other merchants will sense our blood laced in the water and tighten their terms—or worse, demand cash up front. The Sol Majestic rests on a foundation of top-flight ingredients sourced from across the universe. If the merchants believe they might not get paid for their investment, they'll offer us different selections. Customers would notice the degradation. Firewar reviewers would swarm in to recalculate our rating. It would be a slower death—cancer instead of the guillotine—but just as certain."

"Then try for a—what do you call it?—a refund."

"A worthy proposition, but just as poisonous. Paulius is seen as a genius. This gives him great bargaining power; merchants use the fact they sell to Paulius to drive up their other prices. Should we skulk around cleaning up his messes, presenting him as the kook that he is, we would splinter The Sol Majestic's reputation. And that presumes the tailor, who doubtlessly took a rare opportunity to sell her backstock, has any incentive to take them back."

"But . . . you think I can help."

She scrutinizes the clipboard. Shyness is not something Kenna ever expected from Scrimshaw. "I do. Do you track your Q-rating?"

"Not since some ruffians absconded with my smartphone back on a Taurean transit-jump."

"Then here." She brushes her fingertips across the clipboard before tossing it into his lap; its surface glows like a sunset, its screen blossoming into red Worldwork tracker-charts. Kenna tries to look as though he gets handed smartpaper nanocomputers every day.

He flips through his Worldwork graphs, which are mostly barren. On the Intraconnected worlds, where wall-mounted cameras record your every waking moment from a hundred different angles, the immense Worldwork servers analyze your performance—and, for a fee, rank your talent in every skill you've demonstrated that day. Though no Intraconnected he's met has ever failed to pay the Worldwork fees; not only is it a point of pride for the Intraconnected to boast they are the 38,212nd best kite-fighter in the known worlds, but no Intraconnected employer will hire you unless you can document a Worldwork ranking above the fiftieth percentile in your chosen profession.

For the non-Intraconnected, who sport gaps in their lifetime camera footage, they offer different services: mostly, tracking your Q-rating. The Q-rating is a sum total of your social network mentions, blog posts, overheard conversations where you're brought up, writings inspired by concepts you've devised or helped amplify: complex calculations of millions of vectors measure how often people think of you. Politicians and celebrities have high Q-ratings; duels to the death between the first-and second-ranked Q-raters are surprisingly common, as are carefully negotiated love affairs.

Kenna can watch his family's influence crumble by watching the degenerate downward curve of his Q-rating. He doesn't have celebrity numbers, but he *is* a prince of a sort—and though he's never asked to generate clouds of gossip whenever he steps on a transport ship, he's never found a way to suppress that communal interest.

But Kenna's Q-rating has declined each week since he was born. Sometimes, after Mother gave him another lecture on how disappointing it was that Kenna had yet to find his Inevitable Philosophy, Kenna would pull up his grandparents' charts and compare them to his. His grandparents' charts were towering mountains, their numbers thrusting into the rarified air of the thirty-seventh rank—widely discussed even on worlds that didn't follow the Inevitable Philosophies.

He pulls Grandmother's chart up to verify what he knows: that jittering line wavers steadily downward from the moment of her birth. The Inevitable Philosophies were birthed in a revolution, a marvelous fusion of old traditions with new insights. Anyone could become an Inevitable Philosopher, no matter how humble their origins—though of course, the new Philosophers always had to be endorsed by the old guard. It had been sold to leaders as a movement that cleansed heartache.

But the Inevitable Philosophers did not trouble themselves with political realities. Nor did they seek office, considering it to be a distraction from their goal of inciting Inevitable Philosophies in the worthy.

Kings came to us asking how to feed their people, Father had said as he bound Kenna's wounds. *We chastised them for having insufficient belief.* And so Father and Mother flew from minister to minister, assuring their hidden acolytes that abject poverty had tempered the Inevitable Philosophies into something more pragmatic—but even the most fervent believers now felt it better to practice their Philosophy in secrecy.

Kenna pulls up his Q-rating again. He rides the ragged edge of the eighty-eighth rank, which seems low, but that's ridiculously high for a boy too poor to blog. And—

"Yes?" Scrimshaw asks, her amusement dry as parchment.

"I've jumped six points. In two days." The Q-ratings are logarithmic—a six-point jump indicates he's vaulted over billions of people.

"Indeed."

"Is that—"

She leans over to tap a vertice on Kenna's chart. The charts fold themselves away to reveal a sweating Paulius on a fish-eye lens, his white beard-stubble speckled with fig seeds. He holds up a sauce-covered duck to the camera with the restrained grief of a man carrying his dead son.

"Seventeen different recipes." He presses the duck to his nose, smearing the crackling fat across his face. "And it's *shit*!"

He hurls the duck against the shower-toilet in the Escargone's rear. But his arm catches against a box strapped tight to the walls, and the duck entangles in the rubber shower curtain instead, flopping hoisin sauce in a hideous dead duck marionette. Paulius howls, a raw-throated shriek—then vaults over a chopping block, his ass sending brown sugar crashing to the floor, before ripping down the curtain and curb-stomping the duck.

The other chefs move in. For a moment, Kenna thinks they are pulling Paulius away. But no. They too are curb-stomping the duck.

"This should be a meal fit for a *prince*!" Paulius shouts down at the tangle of bones and meat, lurching drunkenly away to retain what's left of his dignity. Cramped, he sidles between two chefs and scoots past the dishwasher before bumping up against the camera.

"This duck." He clutches a stove with the intensity of a man who might heave it out a window. "This duck is an insult. An insult to a boy who needs just one meal to reignite the passions of his Inevitable ancestors. That boy—a *good* boy, a supremely *wise* boy— deserves a duck that will lend him its wings. Let the Prince soar."

Paulius whirls upon the three chefs, thrusting his hands into the air in triumph, an effect only slightly spoiled by his accidentally punching an overhead compartment. "*Will we give Kenna his duck, boys?*"

The chefs chuck the mangled duck contemptuously into the incinerator. "*Yes, chef!*"

"*Will we let the Prince soar?*"

"*Yes, chef!*"

"*Then let's reset this kitchen and try again!*" The feed irises out.

Kenna clutches the clipboard against his chest, as though he can somehow transmit a hug to Paulius. "Is he . . . all right?"

"Yes, yes. That video took him three takes. But as he predicted, it's gone viral." Scrimshaw rolls her eyes. "Gods forbid the Inevitable Philosophies become popular again and Paulius doesn't get the credit . . ."

"Wait—how has that gone viral if he filmed it yesterday? Isn't the video still propagating across the communication-points?"

"We lease an ansible for the station. We can't afford transmission-lag, not with our guests."

The smartpaper nanocomputer pulses beneath his fingertips. By itself, the smartpaper is worth more than all the trips Mother and Father have booked. But smartpaper with an instant-communication stream to planetary datafeeds? That's a ridiculous luxury rappers boast about, right up there with immortality genes and cloned sexbots. Kenna feels the ridiculous urge to pull up a few real-time newstreams, just to watch the headlines from other planets on the far side of the mapped 'verse.

Instead, he thrusts the clipboard back into Scrimshaw's lap, feeling small underneath the shadows of Inevitable robes. All this wealth, necessary to keep this insane restaurant spinning in a remote station. If they don't sell the robes, then the lease will fail, the chefs will be unemployed, the meals will stop coming.

It's business. But business is survival. His eyes have been opened.

Kenna cannot stay here. He knows he cannot stay here. But he needs the *idea* of The Sol Majestic. These two days at the Majestic have been a refutation of the idea that the world is all rust-pocked transport ships and exalted beggary. Once his meal is done, he will return to dreary transit, yes—but *somewhere,* people are working bringing beauty to the universe, and that's good enough for Kenna.

If The Sol Majestic dies, so will Kenna.

"How may I help?"

Scrimshaw's fingertips dance across the paper's surface; blooms of cash flow out from financial forecasts, social network analyses ripple across the smartpaper's luminescent surface, cast neon reflections in her glasses. Scrimshaw's gaunt face slackens as she drinks in the data, her pupils jittering as she inhales it into her brain . . .

She closes her eyes, setting the clipboard aside. Kenna recognizes the gesture as a unilateral disarmament; she will ask Kenna to do something deeply uncomfortable, and for that she will abandon her charts.

"The good news," she says, "is we do not need to sell all the robes before the invoice comes due. Selling enough to cover our costs will do. And they are cheap, allowing us a roomy profit margin; we'd have to sell perhaps a third of them in the next four weeks to break even."

Kenna remains patient as Scrimshaw pushes past her instinct to think in numbers. Her perfect siddhasana position has distorted as she leans forward—a slight incline, but from Scrimshaw that might as well be prostrating herself upon the floor.

She cares for him, in her own way, Kenna realizes. Yet what

could she possibly ask of him that he would fear? His own death would be trivial; he's barely existed.

He reaches out to take her hands. They're all bone, no warmth. Scrimshaw's black eyes widen in shock at the unexpected contact.

"Scrimshaw, I give you full permission to tout me in any way you see fit," Kenna says. "Mother and Father will be glad to have the Inevitable Philosophies discussed again—though I warn you, they may protest your interpretation of the faith. Yet if you must make my meal a public celebration to invite celebrities to, then . . . well, I submit my body to your marketing needs."

Scrimshaw kisses Kenna's fingertips. "My dear boy," she says, nuzzling her wrinkled cheeks against his knuckles. "My dear, dear boy."

Kenna sits still as a mannequin, confused, embarrassed.

She tugs him closer so they are almost nose-to-nose. "What we have planned thus far is a generic celebration, Master Kenna. Paulius has gone too far this time: the celebrities we must court will not come to just any fête. No, Master Kenna, I have looked over the ceremonies the Inevitable Philosophies have to offer, and there's only one ritual worth discussing."

Kenna feels the station lurch underneath him as he understands what she is asking. He would faint, but Scrimshaw's tight grip keeps him rooted to consciousness.

". . . No."

"It's your right to say no, Master Kenna. You only get one Wisdom Ceremony. You only get it because you have found your Inevitable Philosophy. And if you lie in order to force this celebration to happen, you will have to live the consequences of that lie to your deathbed."

His Inevitable Philosophy.

She's asking him to abandon his Philosophy, and instead peddle some tawdry commercial to save The Sol Majestic.

He imagines lying to Mother, to Father. He imagines reporters interviewing him, his Q-rating skyrocketing, as the Inevitable Philosophies are reborn in The Sol Majestic's white-hot publicity. He imagines all those secret practitioners finally able to admit *Yes, I have my own Inevitable Philosophy, just like the Prince, it guides my every motion.*

He imagines emperors coming to ask Kenna for his advice, for at his Wisdom Ceremony Kenna announced that he at last had found the Thought That Cuts Through Obstacles, a belief so potent no man can be said to have a soul without finding it.

He imagines upholding that lie's monstrous weight all his life, realizing if he wavers in this fabricated belief then faith in the Inevitable Philosophies will gutter and die.

He won't just fail. He'll take his religion with him.

"*Do* you have an Inevitable Philosophy, Master Kenna?"

Scrimshaw asks the question with a feather-light hope, as though Kenna hasn't been avoiding Mother and Father all his life, as though Kenna would have come stumbling into The Sol Majestic's confessional booth had he anything to live for.

Kenna staggers to his feet, grabbing the robes for support; they tumble downward, catching air, knocking other stacks over, turning the loading dock's battered titanium floor into a turbulent silk sea.

Kenna flees. And does not look back.

8

Timeless, Until the Decision

Crying, Kenna has learned, calls enemies to you. There is nothing for the poor to do in transport ships but gossip, and a weeping man is a good day's entertainment for them.

Walking makes you invisible.

He strides past the incoming cargo bundles, ducks underneath the tree-like unpacking robots who peel tarpaulins off the pallets with multi-jointed limbs and then sort the supplies to ready them for their new destinations. He does not waver as the dented steel forklifts roar toward him, feeling a vague disappointment as the safety-sensors buzz on before they swerve around him.

Yet even though he's fled to Savor Station's darkest reaches, Kenna cannot escape The Sol Majestic's radiance.

The sorter-bots separate out plastic containers of rust-colored spices. The crates dribble juice from accidentally crushed fruit down upon him as he walks beneath. His hairs stand on end as he passes the ceiling-high banks of hot electric stasis lockers, an expense well beyond most cargo bays' means. He walks around the usual stacks of recycler filters and gear shafts, but Savor Station's stock-in-trade focuses upon perishables.

"*Hey!*" A dockworker shouts, threading her way through the machinery.

Human contact gives Kenna a hot flush of shame. The other transport-children snuck down to the cargo bays, played chicken with the hulking forklifts to prove their bravery, but Kenna was a prince. The one time he'd played dodge-bot, Mother had refused to speak to him for days, routing her requests through Father, disappointed that a boy who *should* be seeking his Inevitable Philosophy had instead fraternized with dockworkers' kids.

Do you have an Inevitable Philosophy, Master Kenna?

Mother can recite hers proudly: *I will save the starving millions.* Father wears his tattooed over his left breast: *I will lead my people out of darkness.* Together, they have sacrificed their lives to travel in humble poverty, pleading at diplomats' doors, trying to change the fate of planets—while Kenna's grandest dreams have been inspired by a servant's soup.

The dockworker storms over—and pauses, taking in Kenna's robe. She plucks at her overalls, determining whether the fancy outfit means Kenna outranks her. Then she squints at the chicken-soup stain darkening Kenna's robe and scratches her eyebrow, uncertain . . .

"I am afraid I have lost my way," Kenna says, feeling too lost already. "Direct me to the exit, and I shall abdicate your premises."

"Gonna have to scan you," the dockworker says.

Normally, Kenna would bristle at the implication that he had stolen something. But he remembers Father's words: *Possessing a Philosophy is what differentiates us from an animal, my son. I love you now as I would a pet. I hope one day to love you as a man.*

Bad enough not to have a Philosophy. What would Father say if he knew Kenna was thinking of faking a Philosophy? To save a *restaurant*?

The guard must smell the stink of deception on him.

Kenna is hustled out into the food mall, the door slamming shut behind him. The air dances with food-scents—the light orchid smell of tea vendors, the sweet foam of vegetable mousses, the buttery sizzle of fresh crepes poured across a grill. Tourists mill between the stalls, jerking their heads around as they spot a kimchi vendor—"The Original Sauerkraut Station!" a sputtering neon sign advertises—and make excited cooing noises as they elbow Kenna aside to get a dishful.

Kenna's gaze drops to the tile floor. If he denies himself a look at the foods, he won't feel so bad when he can't afford them. His stomach cramps are a convulsive reminder—he ate well last night, but in six weeks he'll be back to counting nutricrackers.

Maybe sooner, if he doesn't lie to save The Sol Majestic.

And what if he refuses to lie? The chefs' conversation floats back to him, freshly infused with a mocking tone Kenna is positive wasn't there originally: *Have we held auditions for one of Paulius's pet projects before? Well, they're all different, you know that.*

Kenna knows all too well the difference between a performance and a relationship. Mother has told him endless times: *Philosophers bond, politicians perform.* Too many Inevitable Philosophers lost themselves courting magistrates who mimicked popular Philosophies only to gain votes. Those Philosophers thought themselves brothers to kings, only to find themselves tumbling from grace once their chosen allies found more expedient collaborators.

There's no shame in using people who would use you, Mother says. *The trick is to know when their performance is coming to an end.*

And Kenna wants to believe The Sol Majestic is not all that holds him and Paulius together. He wants to believe that he is deeply beloved by Paulius for some quality he himself cannot see.

And before, he always wondered how those lost Philosophers of old could be so foolish. But now he understands. He might lie just to keep that glimmer of hope alive—to believe that someone would love him for who he is and not for what he can provide.

He clenches his fists, infuriated at himself. Kenna can fathom everyone's motivations except for the man he needs to understand most . . .

A soft hand closes around his biceps. Kenna spins around, mouthing denials—he stole nothing, he's not that kind of boy, he's just a traitor to his religion—yet instead he finds a stout Colpuran man with brightly braided hair backing away.

"My sorrows for startling you, dear sir," he asks, his voice like syrup poured over pancakes. "May I—may I offer you a bowl of bhelpuri?"

Kenna's stomach contracts again, driven mad by food's proximity. "I fear I have no currency to spare."

The man pats Kenna's chest, smoothing Kenna's robe down, keeping his fingers straight as if to demonstrate to Kenna there's no thievery at work—an oddly submissive, yet tender, gesture. Kenna stiffens, suspecting sales techniques—Mother and Father have warned him how shameless traders mold themselves to your desires.

"No coinage necessary, my friend," says the Colpuran. "I merely have sympathy."

He reaches into a worn-out pushcart brightly decorated with Day-Glo knotted ropes to match the braids in his hair, and brings out a wax paper boat filled with a vinegary salad. It's a work of art, a tiny medallion of puffed rice heaped with finely cut carrot curls and chutney blobs. The hot smell of spices and fresh onion fills Kenna's mouth with thick drool. Kenna gulps the saliva back, cringing—no normal boy would have such a full-body reaction to a small bowl of food.

Instead, the merchant beams, proud to inspire such a reaction. He pats his cart, as if telling his best friend, *Can you believe this?*

The merchant looks down at the bhelpuri cupped in Kenna's hands as if he has presented Kenna with a fine sculpture. This salad is the merchant's dream, Kenna realizes. Like Benzo, the merchant has sacrificed everything in the pursuit of one perfect dish—nestled by Savor Station, where he labors for pennies in the hopes of finding the stray Sol Majestic client who truly appreciates the genius he assembles in small wax paper cups.

The hairs on Kenna's neck prickle. Mother has always tugged him past the sales carts, jerking his robe so he couldn't peer into the stalls, informing him he shouldn't watch merchants debase themselves for dinari.

Yet Kenna feels honored to hold this dish. This merchant has been nurtured by The Sol Majestic's radiance, drawn here by Paulius's mad dream. The Sol Majestic is aptly named, as Savor Station sits in a planetless solar system that's composed entirely of rubble belts and gas clouds—all that's here is the warmth of a single sun, and a supply post conveniently stationed to serve as a stopping point between impossibly empty stellar journeys.

Without the Majestic to draw tourists, Savor Station would be nothing more than another grubby trading spot where ships docked to refuel and let weary travelers stretch their legs.

Kenna has avoided knowing traders' lives too well, but he's seen enough on transport ships to understand the life this merchant has condemned himself to by coming here—dozing off after a long day with his cart chained to an overpriced sleeping tube, paying too much for fresh ingredients shipped here across solar systems, endlessly refining the same tiny salad to perfection.

Mother and Father travel across the galaxy to sell their Philosophy—and so, in its own bizarre way, has this man.

The bhelpuri's scent is sharp, rising up from the soaked rice, plunging a pleasant knife into Kenna's tastebuds. Kenna's palms tremble as he realizes the merchant wants to spread the joy of salad. The dinari is what he charges to survive.

Dumbfounded, Kenna asks, ". . . you said you had sympathy?"

"You are the Prince, are you not?"

The trembling stops.

The merchant pulls his pushcart closer, as though he wishes to bring it in on the conversation. "Forgive me, but I saw you on Paulius's broadcasts." He senses Kenna's discomfort, directs Kenna's gaze to the other food merchants. "We all watch his videos, you see. And I thought . . . well, perhaps *I* should know about these Inevitable Philosophies. Not that I'm proffering food for trade—I just wished to express support in your journey, perhaps learn what kept you going through such hardship . . ."

If the merchant wasn't so kind, this wouldn't be so cruel.

All I must do is tell him how the Inevitable Philosophy is the light that wakes you from troubled dreams, the shining beacon that removes worry, Kenna thinks. *And if he still frets after he has come into the faith, I can tell him his Philosophy is not strong enough, that he must meditate more, and he will feed me for giving him such wise advice . . .*

He shoves the bhelpuri back into the merchant's hands; the merchant looks so wounded that Kenna's heart aches.

He wants Kenna to tell him that finding an Inevitable Philosophy would somehow make all this sacrifice not hurt.

Tell him he hurts because he's unworthy, Kenna thinks. *Lie to him and a thousand others, and you'll spend your days with your belly full.*

Kenna pushes his way past the merchant, lurching past the endless restaurants embedded in the curve of Savor Station's walls—a Gineer brasserie where inhumanly handsome attendants take blood samples before printing out protein-rolls tailored to your genetic preferences, an Intraconnected cafeteria where hunched women in shawls slop out buttered noodles into cracked dishes. This is a culinary paradise; most space stations have just a row of vending machines spritzing artificial food-odors at passerby.

These multitudinous chefs were drawn to The Sol Majestic's tidal pull, like coral huddling around a hydrothermal vent at the bottom of a cold ocean. They subsist off of Paulius's leftovers, the tourists who've come searching Paulius's dream and will eat well while they wait for him. If The Sol Majestic goes bankrupt, all this dries up.

Kenna must become either a tawdry salesman pushing a false Philosophy or an executioner.

And he is stumbling blind, pushing through the slow-moving procession of those waiting to get their shot at The Sol Majestic's confessional booth. The station fuzzes out as he retreats, headed back to where he feels comfortable . . .

"Hey," Benzo says. "You okay?"

It's as if Benzo's cautious voice allows him to think again.

Kenna finds himself curled up against the pitted metal walls of a transport-ship crawl space, neck aching from being jammed at an angle; these were the places Mother suborned as their meditation chambers, slanted leftover space crammed in beneath the engine blocks. Benzo does not yet clamber into the tiny space with Kenna, awaiting permission—but he takes in the drifts of rust-flakes showering down as servicemen tromp up the stairs above them.

Benzo's presence feels like a spotlight, thrusting Kenna onto Paulius's stage again.

Still, Benzo must have spent some time tracking him down. He's been through so much effort that Kenna cannot bear to send him away. But he can't quite welcome him, either.

"My status is acceptable." Kenna tries to sound like he normally lounges in a starship's piss-stained hollows.

"Okay." Benzo's brow furrows as he tries to find something in this isolated prison cell to make pleasant conversation with, fails, then sunnily reaches for something in a satchel.

He brings out a grilled cheese sandwich in a plastic ziplock baggie. The baggie is fogged from the heat, gooey with melted cheese. He extends it toward Kenna, luring him.

"I thought you might be hungry. And, you know, I know you like this, at least."

Kenna's unsure whether to feel unworthy or relieved that he has such a good friend. ". . . would you, perhaps, do me the honor of your company?"

"Sure." Benzo gets down on his hands and knees to crawl in through the triangular opening, and for an instant Kenna thinks Benzo might cross the tiny space to embrace Kenna, cuddling him in his moment of need. He imagines Benzo's firm stomach pressed against his, Benzo's muscular thigh pushing his legs apart—no kissing, just holding Kenna tight and feeling that desire vibrating like a plucked guitar string . . .

But Benzo respectfully sits as far across the crawlspace as he can, hugging his knees to conserve space, though his sneaker-tips brush coyly against Kenna's feet. Kenna recoils. Kenna is stained, leprous, doomed to be a charlatan or the man who slaughters the dreams of Savor Station. Nobody should touch him.

Benzo offers the sandwich. Kenna's belly groans.

"I could use some repast," he admits, blushing. "Thank you."

The baggie is filled with gloppy cheese and mushy bread, having steamed itself into one delicious goo Kenna will have to scoop out with his fingers.

"Hold a moment," Kenna says. "Weren't you brewing broth?"

Benzo laughs, smooths out his shaggy hair. "I mean—yeah. Sure."

"But you were going to fashion a flawless broth."

He shrugs, pulling his feet back. "It's cool. It's my day off. I'll try again tomorrow."

It *is* a big deal, Kenna realizes. Kenna feels certain nothing had gone wrong with Benzo's broth yet; Benzo had abandoned an as-yet-unblemished shot at perfection to help his friend.

Benzo's sacrifice sucks the air from the room. Kenna can't make a big deal about it; this friendship feels so comfortable because they don't have to talk about how it works, it just does.

He tugs open the bag, slides his fingers inside. The rich scent of Gruyère smothers the crawl space's industrial metal tang. He thinks of Benzo leaving a chicken congealing in the pot to grill this up for him. The thought is warmer than any sandwich.

You'll cost Benzo his job.

That shouldn't matter. Jobs don't matter. Nothing should matter except for the search for truth.

Still, Kenna sucks the cheese off his fingertips.

Benzo studies a crease in his pockets, trying to give Kenna a semblance of privacy, despite the fact that he has to hug his knees so as not to touch Kenna's legs. His feet tap in erratic patterns, as if his whole body is allergic to this silence.

"I get sick, too," Benzo declares. "Thinking of the day I go."

"You shan't leave." Kenna hates to lie to his friend. "You'll devise the perfect broth, and then Paulius shall make you one of his line cooks."

"Ooof." Benzo blows a half-whistle through pursed lips. "No." He rubs his neck, forehead almost touching his knees. "No, no, no."

"No?"

Benzo's lip twitches. "I thought everyone in the kitchen knew."

"I fear I'm new here."

"I guess—well, yeah." He exhales through his nostrils, the energy leaking from his body. "That's right."

Kenna almost laughs, thinking Benzo had a brainfart—but the way Benzo now focuses on the exit, mapping out escape routes, tells Kenna that Benzo remembers exactly when Kenna arrived. He's swollen with such hidden shame that he imagines this buried secret is the first order of business whenever his name comes up, even though no one in The Sol Majestic has said a word to Kenna.

Perhaps they haven't spoken because they are ashamed for Benzo. Kenna doesn't know. But he does know he loves Benzo, so he leans over to ruffle Benzo's blond curls.

"Will you be . . . all right?" Kenna braces himself for terminal news, wondering if Benzo also has some degenerative disease.

"I'm gonna make broth." Benzo spits the words as if he expects Kenna to contradict him. "*Perfect* broth. Way better than any slave could make."

. . . *slave?* Kenna wonders.

As Benzo flinches, Kenna realizes he accidentally spoke the word out loud.

"Indentured servant," Benzo corrects Kenna, uncurling in this cramped space, forcing Kenna to retreat into the corner. "Slaves are illegal. Technically. But . . . *She* buys the endebted by the boatload off of credit-ships."

Benzo lowers his voice to whisper "She," unused to speaking his Mistress's name out loud.

"And *She* said the reason I had been born into debt was because my kind did not know how to strive for perfection. So I made Her a bet. I bet Her an endebted boy could make one flawless dish. And if I do . . ."

Kenna nods, knowingly. "You'll be free."

Benzo's easygoing face contorts into a scowl so bitter that Kenna winces. "No. If I pull this off, She'll have the best chef in all Her houses. I'll never be free, even if I win the bet." His eyes go flinty. "My children will be, though."

You're too young to think about having children, Kenna thinks. *You're only a year older than I am.* But to a slave, Kenna realizes, children are a sign of hope.

Benzo's quivering now, a frustration so deep that he forgets Kenna's existence. Kenna should move to help, but despair slows his reaction—Benzo wants children. What if Kenna's misreading the affectionate way Benzo grasps his shoulders? There's no romance on the transport ships—merely crude offers and flat innuendo, bolstered by a crowd of bored passengers who cheer on their favorite couplings with the zealousness of an audience watching a live-action soap opera. People catcalled whenever anyone made a move upon the Desolate Prince, sending suitors scurrying for cover, leaving Kenna to know every flavor of rejection, yet not one flavor of adoration. And there's no good way to ask if Benzo is bisexual, not now. It wouldn't matter anyway. They're friends. Even if they never kiss, they're friends.

"You must have mustered quite the reputation for bravery," Kenna whispers. "Making a wager like that."

Benzo's anger melts when he sees Kenna is serious. "Most people—they get sad. At least they do at The Sol Majestic. They think I sold my family for generations now—I took out a loan to bet myself here. Scrimshaw says I should have at least tested my palate before I confronted Her. They don't . . ." He swallows, lost in concern.

"Hey." Kenna squeezes Benzo's kneecap to distract him. "You

forged a path to The Sol Majestic. You already possess prodigious skills."

"I don't, actually." Benzo's rueful grin is the most kissable thing Kenna has ever seen. "She brought me to the one place where I couldn't charm other people into cheating Her. Paulius would never serve my dishes to customers unless they were impeccable."

Kenna's disconcerted to think Paulius wouldn't compromise The Sol Majestic's quality to save a man's life, and even more disconcerted to find he agrees with Paulius. The service is the service. The dishes must not be bent to human foibles. The meals are set to inhuman standards, so that mere men must shatter and regrow themselves to reach its perfection.

He ignores what that revelation says about what Paulius should do to him if he cannot provide Paulius with a ceremony worthy of his skills. Paulius is kind, and loving, and righteously brutal.

"Well, you *shall* show Her." Kenna shakes Benzo's kneecap harder. "You shall perfect the broth. And every night, you shall place a dish of that broth next to every meal you serve Her, to demonstrate how wrong She is about the endebted."

"*That's my dream!*" Benzo leans over to hug Kenna, bangs his forehead on a corner, pats Kenna on the thigh instead. "You get me, buddy. You get me."

Except Kenna is certain that if The Sol Majestic closes prematurely, She will not consider the bet a draw. Closing The Sol Majestic will condemn generations of little Benzos to slavery.

"That's a good sandwich." Benzo nudges the bag toward Kenna. "You should totally eat it."

Kenna chews, the cheese so delicious he cannot help but lose himself in the rich taste of friendship. He may be a monster. But Paulius has been his friend far more than his parents, Benzo has been kinder to him than the fallen diplomats who once followed the Inevitable Philosophies. His mother fights for the starving millions, yet never the starving son.

He will lie, he realizes. He will lie for The Sol Majestic.

* * *

Now Kenna waits before the Escargone's metal hatchway, waiting to give Paulius his gift. The Sol Majestic will continue to exist, if Scrimshaw can leverage this publicity into sales.

He supposes he should tell Scrimshaw first—but though he is fond of Scrimshaw he does not love her. He loves Paulius. And the first time he speaks these words of betrayal, agreeing to dismantle the principles his family holds dear, he wants it to be to someone who will understand how much that means to him.

The oval window flickers and blurs as Paulius and his chefs move at hummingbird speeds. Kenna sits on a stool; is he a dog, waiting for his master?

The high-pitched whir dims, the movements in the Escargone slowing to human speeds. The door cracks, hissing greasy steam laden with body odor out into the kitchen's fresh air; overhead recyclers click on, sucking up the fumes before they can taint the food.

The chefs tumble out, thrusting fine crystal champagne flutes into the air, the fizzing drinks slopping over before they whirl upon each other, toast again, and guzzle the champagne in exultant gulps.

"Make way!" Paulius bellows. "Make way for the meal!"

Paulius strides behind them, carrying a glistening, golden-brown duck on a tray. He holds it with the reverence of a man carrying the king's crown.

Then he sees Kenna, seated patiently, and sobs.

"Of course." He sets the duck down and grabs Kenna's cheeks to kiss Kenna's head, fingertips smearing honey across Kenna's lips. "You knew, my dear boy. You knew we'd succeed for you. And you wanted to *see* it!"

He whirls upon the other chefs, who are pouring themselves a fresh round of triumph. "You see? This is why we work! Because"— he sucks in a ragged breath, almost choking on his sentiment—"the boy appreciates what we do!

"Oh, Kenna." Paulius slices a piece off the duck, a firm pink meat encrusted with sauce, guides it to Kenna's mouth. "You deserve this. You deserve the best duck we can give you."

Kenna pushes the duck away with his fingertips. "Paulius." He swallows, his rehearsed speeches falling away under Paulius's rapt gaze. The other chefs storm into the kitchen, wanting to watch Kenna's reaction.

Thank God Paulius is so close. He can whisper. "I—I've agreed, Paulius. I'll do the task. For you."

Paulius blinks owlishly. ". . . do what?"

And Kenna realizes: *Paulius doesn't know.*

Then: *Of course Paulius doesn't know.*

Paulius styles himself as a savior of foods and people alike, at least until they prove themselves unworthy. Once Paulius understood the distress he was placing Kenna in, he would be obliged to leave the meal behind. Paulius is a man of wild passions—yes, he would condemn Benzo to slavery if the broth was imperfect, but he also allowed a novice boy to fumble around his kitchen because he thought an endebted child deserved a chance to be free.

Should he recognize his meal had become Kenna's dilemma, Paulius would have to sacrifice the Majestic just as he had casually dropped that gravity-bowl back in the orchard once Kenna had drunk his fill. And Paulius never considers the consequences, no more than he did when he bought a pallet of silken robes—he acts, aftermaths be damned.

He'd thought lying about his Philosophy would reveal Paulius's heart. Now he realizes it would merely shift the performance to a different stage. Either Paulius is so kind that he would shutter everything to protect Kenna's future, or is so committed to believing himself a benevolent tutor that he would destroy The Sol Majestic rather than see himself for what he is.

Now Kenna realizes why Scrimshaw hates Paulius so. Paulius has lurched from dream to dream, leaving Scrimshaw to piece together the practicalities. Scrimshaw conceals the jagged edges so

Paulius's genius can work, because either Paulius's heart or his ego is impossibly fragile when nicked.

Paulius works miracles only because he does not realize their cost.

The duck is beneath Kenna's nose, drops of sauce oozing off a dark meat slice. Paulius's eyes brim with tears, grateful to bring this perfection to Kenna.

". . . do what, Kenna?"

"I've . . ." Kenna's throat is dry as rust. "I've unlocked my Inevitable Philosophy."

"That's wonderful," Paulius says. "Try the duck."

Kenna tastes nothing. He tells Paulius the duck is perfect. The kitchen erupts into applause.

This is the first lie, Kenna thinks. He vows to count every one.

9

Five Weeks, Three Days Until the Wisdom Ceremony

Savor Station's most luxurious hotel consists of one gleaming brass hallway, locked off from the rest of the station by engraved titanium bars. Kenna types Scrimshaw's passcode into a cool blue keypad; the gateway chimes, opening inward.

Kenna creeps along the brushed-brass walls, making his way toward his parents.

Kenna's a newly minted liar who hopes to convince Mother and Father of an imaginary Inevitable Philosophy—but the wealth of empty space here magnifies his fraudulence. The hotel's hallway is ostentatiously wide, big enough for two people to waltz in. Mother and Father have always complained of being stuffed into ships. Whenever they arrived in a place with room to maneuver, Mother and Father ran around like little kids, flinging their arms out wide.

But Mother and Father had grown up planetside. Kenna had grown up in cramped ships, where every square foot carried crippling maintenance costs. Crowded spaces bring comfort. For Kenna, big spaces are where disdainful receptionists glare at him from across a chilly air-conditioned room, where Mother discreetly elbows him to sit up straight, where Father hisses that if Kenna demonstrates dishonor then the ambassador might cancel their appointment.

Who has more dishonor than a boy who lies about his Inevitable Philosophy?

The door swings open. Kenna braces himself; of *course* entering his passcode would have alerted Mother and Father. He had hoped to at least get through the doorway before they lectured him on the bad habits he would pick up sleeping with low-class cooks. He won't even escape the hallway before Mother and Father pummel him with words.

Father steps out. Kenna ducks his head, palms together, bowing deep enough to ward off Father's wrath . . .

"Son." That booming voice has swayed emperors. "Gaze upon me."

It takes Kenna a moment to process the word "son." Father has referred to Kenna *as* his son before, but has never called him anything but Kenna.

Father never speaks a word he does not intend.

Surprised, Kenna glances up—and Father bounces on his toes like a boxer entering the ring, arms crooked out to hug Kenna. He looks strong enough to wrestle warships.

Father has retained a battered dignity over the years, but his spine has been contorted by a lifetime of bowing. His brown eyes have turned rheumy from blinking back tears. Clad in a pristine robe, however, Father no longer looks like the tattered remnant of an old religion, but the vanguard of a new and exciting order—a man reforged in the fires of poverty to usher in a new era of Inevitable Philosophies. His graying braids have been dyed jet black and freshly woven with polished glass beads.

"Son." Father smacks his lips as he accustoms himself to the sound of this kinship. He moves to sweep Kenna up in a hug—

That's not me, Kenna thinks, retreating, *your son would have an Inevitable Philosophy—*

And as Father embraces him, Kenna realizes the difference between *being tended to* and *being loved.* Father has always given him polite shoulder-squeezes. But this? This is the sun-warmed hug a man gives to his loved ones.

Kenna melts into Father's arms, clutching Father's broad

shoulders as Father clasps Kenna around the waist and hoists him high, rubbing his cheek against Kenna's.

He could stay here forever, drunk on the warmth of his father's skin.

If I could find an Inevitable Philosophy before the Wisdom Ceremony, Kenna thinks, *I could feel this way forever.* But he never will. An Inevitable Philosophy cuts like an axe; Kenna is a bungie cord, bending floppily to necessity.

If there are Gods, Father always says, *the only prayers they listen to are hard work and good planning. So leave your prayers on the ground.*

Nevertheless, Kenna prays for an Inevitable Philosophy.

Father sets Kenna down and *inspects* Kenna. He snorts, as he plucks at Kenna's robe.

Kenna freezes. Father has seen right through him, of course— Kenna's false Inevitable Philosophy is like watching a dead vidstream, all emptiness and static. Father will do what he always does when Kenna fails. He will stand statue-straight, disappointment choking his throat shut. Then he will give the slightest shake of his head and walk away, except this time he will never return . . .

Father pinches the chicken-broth stain on the robe between two fingers.

"Is that Kenna?" Mother asks, emerging from the hotel room. Kenna's been so dizzied by Father's affection that he only now realizes they've never left the hallway.

Yet Father is tugging on Kenna's robe, high enough the hem threatens to expose Kenna. Mother's happy face creases into a frown as she crouches over, examining him.

Kenna steels himself. Their parental chastising has always been a two-person show: Father glares balefully, regretful to be in a room with him, whereas Mother frets and fluffs, hauling him off for lectures. Except this time Father will walk away forever; what lectures could rehabilitate the whorish merchant his son has become?

Mother, too, is resplendent in her new robe, her dreadlocks

freshly topknotted, her face scrubbed clean to show her beautiful oil-brown skin. She keeps her robe sashed tight around her waist to keep it from tangling around her ankles. She moves in precise bursts, each step transitioning to some new and perfect stance.

"Is that a stain?" Mother kneels to examine the robe pinched between Father's beefy fingers.

It takes Kenna a moment to recognize the tone in her voice: *worry*. She's always been concerned for him, but never worried.

"Look at it," Father says. "He doesn't know."

"Of *course* he doesn't know."

"He has not endured the fourth estate's abject distortions."

"Oh, Kenna." Mother sweeps him up in a tight hug; for once, it does not feel like she is teaching him a grappling technique. "You cannot be seen sporting blemishes. Not anymore. The gatherers of lies circle you like starfighters, knowing you have come into your power; they seek to dismantle your truth. For them, the debasement of wisdom provides *entertainment*."

She waves him into the room, head hunched down as if she expects bloggers to pour into the hotel at any moment.

Entering the hotel room first feels like being jettisoned into space. Mother and Father have never let him enter a room ahead of them before; his life consists of peering around their elbows to get glimpses. Yet he is propelled into a vast beige room, one so big there is nothing within reach—just a wooden table, four comfort-couches with Virtual Reality Hoods, and a discreet fold-up screen in case privacy is needed. He could run in circles and never bump into furniture.

He wants to be in the kitchen, where everything serves a purpose. He wants to smell hot peppers frying, feel the chill of liquid nitrogen–cooled dishes cascading down to tickle his ankles, feel sweat prickling between chefs as they engraved meats with the plasma cauterizing units.

This hotel room creates nothing. It's a mausoleum. Yet it's the isolation Mother and Father always wanted for him; a bare place to delve into his thoughts and emerge with the treasure of a Philosophy.

Father's chest puffs up as he enters, though, taking strength from these gaudy surroundings. He snatches a smartpaper computer off the table, displays a mailbox overflowing with emails. Kenna reads glimpses—*all seems meaningless* and *the suffering* and *seek your wisdom*—as Father flicks through pages' worth of messages until they blur into a misery-laden stream.

Father grins.

"They're hearing our voice again, Kenna. Having wandered lost, they've come to realize they need someone to guide them to truer paths—and finally we have a way to turn our voices to thunder."

Kenna reaches out to read the mails individually. Mother whips the tablet away.

"Now, only the poverty-stricken contact us," she says, placing it back on the table. "But soon our message will reach the people who can help them. The diplomats. The advisors." Her fingers clench as though she longs to grab royalty's collar. "The *emperors*."

Father preens. "I'd always insisted on finding a new patron to revitalize us, hadn't I? I hadn't thought of a restaurant owner, but . . . this Paulius has reach."

"And surprising insight, for an entrepreneur. Sending Kenna to a training camp where he does nothing but taste Grandmother's foods? I would not have required so earthly a bond to our glorious past, yet it seems to have ameliorated Kenna's limitations."

Mother extends one slender arm, wiggling her fingers; Father reaches out to intertwine fingers with hers, a polished gesture, as though they are about to do a pas de deux. "It was right to come here."

As always, Kenna feels a powerful need to be anywhere but here. The love Mother and Father feel for each other is so intense that their holding hands is like a force shield glimmering into existence around a warship.

Except this time Mother and Father extend their free arms, urging him into their embrace.

He shuffles forward, feet numb, as their arms drop over his shoulders.

Much like the lacquered duck, Kenna discovers that grand glories brought by falsehoods bring no pleasure.

Mother whips the robe off Kenna.

"*Hey!*" Kenna dances behind her, grabbing at the robe, but Mother moves toward the incinerator.

"This is blemished. We should have trained you better for this day, Kenna—but ah, even our faith wavered."

"For *what* day?"

"With our resurgence in popularity come the reporters. They brought down our great-grandparents. They mocked the faith. They twisted our words until we appeared to be nothing more than ticks. And even such a tiny thing as a stain"—she bares her incisors at the robe's faint discoloration—"will mark you as a *hick*. They'll turn you into some backwoods dispenser of maladies."

"But that's my robe!"

"Tch." She sucks air between her teeth. "Scrimshaw can get us new ones."

Scrimshaw is going broke, Kenna wants to say. He doesn't dare. No true Philosopher concerns himself with low money.

"The Sol Majestic has a dry-cleaning wing," Kenna lies. "Their guests, they . . . stain their garb all the time. With unearthly ingredients. Paulius, he . . . offers to cleanse their apparel. At no charge!"

Mother hefts the robe, dubiously weighing the miracles Paulius might produce. "Kenna, the very point of these robes is that they cannot be cleaned. Like the Inevitable Philosophies themselves, once stained, no amount of effort can restore them. We wore shabby robes back when we had no choice—better a stained pride than none—but now? We can afford to be profligate."

Kenna debates grabbing the robe and running, but Mother has always shrugged off his grapples.

"It's . . ."

His belly aches. This lie might be the one that eviscerates him. *Get used to lying,* he thinks, digging his fingernails deep into his diaphragm. *You have a lifetime of fraud to perpetrate.*

". . . it's the robe I wore when I discovered my Philosophy!"

Mother's grip on the robe slackens as she presses it against her breasts, a serenity creeping across her gaunt face, as if absorbing Kenna's enlightenment from it. His nonexistent enlightenment.

Her dreamy expression seeks permission from Father, who nods gruffly. "I guess we can allow for a new tradition." Father frames the robes between his fingers, as if taking a test-shot for a vidblog. "'A stain is a small price to pay for Inevitability.' Yes?"

"Yes!" Mother lifts the robe up high, then allows it to slide off her fingers as though she is raining grace down upon Kenna. Her lips compress, slyly, with feigned nonchalance; she's never been as good a liar as she believes. "So tell me, Kenna, what is your Inevitable Philosophy?"

This, at least, is the part of the lie Kenna has mapped out. "I will speak only at my Wisdom Ceremony."

"You see?" Father says. "His Inevitable Philosophy ignites, and for the first time our son—our *son*!—forges tactics for a bold future! That's right, Kenna; reveal your Philosophy to no one. Germinate it in isolation. Let no one drop a speck of doubt in your rich soil."

"The speech you give at your Wisdom Ceremony will reshape not only the galaxy, but you," Mother says. "Spend these next weeks in meditation sharpening the truth so you will cleave all doubt when you speak."

This will be my final respite, Kenna thinks. *Five weeks at The Sol Majestic. Five weeks with Paulius, and Benzo, and Scrimshaw. Five weeks helping devoted men turn effort into beauty . . . and then a lifetime of lies.*

"This will be a good place to study," Father says. "Free of distractions."

. . . what?

"Free of reporters," Mother says. "Free to find your truth."

No, no, Kenna thinks. *No, no, no . . .*

"I can't—" Kenna turns in circles, half-naked in his smallclothes. The hotel room a mausoleum, friendless, a tomb to seal his dreams. "This isn't—"

"Now, Kenna," Father says. "You're a prince. Your Philosophy can't be improved by hanging around workmen, even fine ones like Paulius owns. But *we'll* be with you. Every step of the way."

Mother extends her hand to interlace her fingers with his. "You are our son."

Kenna finds the words he has always craved to hear are heavy enough to crush his heart.

Father shuts the door, walling him away from The Sol Majestic.

10

Five Weeks, Two Days Until the Wisdom Ceremony

Once you have hauled your Inevitable Philosophy up to your conscious mind, Father had said, *you will not sleep; your dreams will prod you to action.*

The umbral lights above him dim to dusk, then darken to the black night, calculated to adjust his circadian rhythms; Kenna cannot sleep. Liquid nanoengines in the bed lovingly massage his shoulders, biosensors triangulating his tensest muscles to squeeze the stress away; still Kenna cannot sleep. The bed whispers hypnotic, brain-numbing lullabyes; still Kenna cannot sleep.

Kenna has no Inevitable Philosophy.

He will not sleep until he finds one.

He needs to talk to Paulius. Only Paulius can properly witness his suffering. Kenna imagines crouching in the transport ship's puke-stained hammocks, talking to the mothers combing lice from their daughters' hair: *They locked me in a comfortable room where all I could do was play VR games.*

They would stave his ribs in for such audacity.

But the VR games are the nutricrackers of the mind, dazzling holoworks that provide triumphant fever-dreams, yet you wake to realize you've done nothing. The Sol Majestic's kitchen will lace your body with scars: knives gash your fingers into bloody flaps, red-hot pans will sear blistered trails into your flesh, liquid nitrogen spills will freeze your skin into nerveless gray permafrost.

Yet when you are done, all you see is that green asparagus threaded with black licorice, three stalks placed equidistant on a perfect, bone-white plate.

He can endure being taken away from that crucible of creation. But he can't pretend the sacrifice means nothing. Mother and Father would know he was lying if they knew how he loved The Sol Majestic.

He has to talk to Paulius. Only Paulius would understand this horror of a blank page left unwritten. Yet Mother has snored for two hours. Guarding her baggage on the transport ships has made her sleeping form taut as a mousetrap, ready to snap shut on any intruder.

It takes Kenna a full twenty minutes to creep his toes out from under the covers and down to the floor.

Yet the comfort-crèches assist him. When he dares to sit up, noise-cancelling algorithms muffle the sound. Mother twitches, ever-vigilant, and Kenna's breath goes ragged; if they caught him sneaking out, they would see the lies written on his face. He would no longer be their son.

He is in the hallway. Freedom.

He thumbs his way past the hotel gate, sneaks across Savor Station's scurrying nighttime. A spaceport can't afford to sleep. The overhead lights are dimmed, but the maintenance crew rolls the benches away, shines UV lights on the walls, scanning the station for metal fatigue. Others sweep detritus off the floor, dumping plastic into recycling bins; every ounce of plastic they can recycle is an ounce that doesn't have to be shipped across solar systems to replenish their supplies.

Kenna's not even certain he can get into The Sol Majestic; he avoids getting too close to the entryway's chipped obsidian surface, threatened by its monolithic nature. Paulius created a temple for food, and so the entrance for customers is hewn out of glistening volcanic rock, shelved with thorny plants in sandy crevices. Placed against Savor Station's smooth titanium walls, it looks like a gateway to some alien dimension.

Instead, Kenna pads around to the service entrance, stares into the retinal scanner, hoping Scrimshaw has added his biometrics to the authorization list.

The door glides open.

Tears blur his vision. He's never seen The Sol Majestic's dining room. But for him, this long kitchen, cut into a maze by flat chopping surfaces and ovens, *is* The Sol Majestic.

He is gratified to see signs of life as he creeps past the pantry of humming stasis cubes. Two chefs spin a great sticky candy floss ball off a pan of caramelized sugar, delicately coordinating an antigravity device so as to not shoot burning sucrose in each other's face. A gaggle of waiters, sleeves rolled up, slam shots of lion's milk and place drunken bets on a combat hologame. Montgomery, spidery in her brass goggles and mold-eaten chef's outfit, crouches over velvet-black curtains and squeezes a glimmering blue fluid out of an eyedropper into something Kenna cannot see.

And as always, the Escargone's flickering light, that celluloid shadowplay of Paulius working at hummingbird speeds.

The motley crew stop their games as Kenna stumbles forward, drunk with relief, headed for the stool in front of the Escargone. The shot glasses are lowered to the table, agreeing Kenna is a problem to be solved but unsure who is fit to handle him.

A smarter man would sidle up to these chefs, get to know their names, start casual conversations that he would ultimately steer onto the topic of old kitchen gossip. But he can't think of a way of asking them about Paulius's past protégés that wouldn't degenerate into him begging for knowledge.

Instead, Kenna strides ahead, stiff-legged, focusing on the Escargone's porthole-light, refusing to blink until water fills his eyes.

He can identify Paulius's movements, even speeded up. There are no other cooks left to assist Paulius; they refuse to cram themselves into that gastronomic oubliette for weeks of their time, so he works in isolation, perfecting Kenna's next dish.

Kenna needs Paulius. It is shameful to need a man so badly, to be in such need of benediction that you will be his dog, waiting outside his doorway until he deigns to acknowledge you, but that is who Kenna is. If he must reveal his tender belly to The Sol Majestic's workers, then he will, because even if Paulius's benevolence is an illusion then Kenna needs this illusion . . .

"Hey!" a stern voice says. "Clear out."

The shock of being spoken to makes Kenna blink. Montgomery has pushed her goggles back across her forehead; her light bronze skin is flecked with violet mold, her hair dotted with spores, and so the area around her eyes where her goggles had been is the only place that shows unblemished skin. Somehow, that clarity makes her honey-colored eyes dangerous.

She flicks knifelike fingernails in Kenna's direction, once, twice, a peremptory shooing motion.

Kenna grabs the stool, fingers tightening—she will have to carry him out. But he'll fight her . . .

Chairs scrape across the floor behind him. Muttered apologies: "Sorry, Montgomery." They file out of the kitchen, keeping their distance from Kenna; an apology for pointing unwanted attention in his direction.

Montgomery drapes a heavy dishcloth around his shoulders, the towel's weight a terry cloth hug. "You cold?"

Kenna is cold. He hadn't noticed.

"Paulius might be a while." Montgomery worms long fingers through a hole in her red-and-gold striped chef's outfit to scratch her armpit. "You want a treat to pass the time? I have one of the oddest repasts in the universe, should it suffice."

Kenna's stomach is a stone. But Montgomery's gruff kindness is more filling than any banquet, so he clambers down from the stool.

Standing up feels like he's broken a spell. This solemn vigil would have been ridiculous. Solitude is supposed to help gestate Inevitable Philosophies, but Kenna is broken; isolation makes him orbit around the same discomfiting thoughts over and over again until they swell to occlude his vision, destroy his memories of anything good in life, reduce him to an embarrassingly adolescent eternity.

If the Majestic has taught him nothing else, it's that he needs a friend to take him aside before he loses all perspective.

"Come," Montgomery says. "The Bitch is generous today. I can spare a mouthful."

She lopes off, leading him to a recessed corner. Velvet-black curtains surround a stainless-steel sink, flecked with white flour. Mounted behind the curtains is a planetarium projector, beaming a hemispherical black hologram projection of outer space so it floats above the sink, cold stars shining down.

As she approaches the shadowy stage, she whirls upon Kenna, crouching. She makes fluttering calming motions with both hands, shushing him as though he might wake a sleeping infant.

"There." Her drum-tight face loosens in ecstasy as she peers into the sink, the blissful relief of a junkie pushing heroin into the vein. "There's my sweet Bitch."

Something within burbles, a soft slow exhalation.

"Go on." Montgomery nudges him. "Look."

Kenna jerks forward a step, stops. For the first time, he understands Montgomery's Sensate nature; in a way, this delicious tension is better than any revelation. He's honored she has entrusted him with her secret, so he pulls aside the curtain with the painstaking deliberation of a poor boy opening up his only Christmas present.

Resting in the sink is a small oaken cask; the one she brandished at all the chefs when she was making her way through to the robes.

Resting in the cask is a pulsing, baby-sized wad of dough.

The brown dough undulates, it bubbles, having swollen out the cask's rim to extend slim tendrils. It grasps for the curtains at clumsy plant speeds, yet something's mesmerizing in its motions. The dough's color ripples through spectrums of delectable browns, from the rich dark brown of a freshly baked pretzel to the wheat-colored swell of dinner rolls, puckering into the crackled texture of a biscuit-top.

Kenna feels an ache in his chest, which swells to a distracting annoyance.

He realizes he has forgotten to breathe.

Tiny bubbles stipple the dough's surface, blossoming like flowers across a field. They burst in elaborate geometric patterns—an encoded communication?—releasing puffs of electric blue fungus that drift down to coat the sink. The dough ripples again, an unconscious shrug, flopping yet another questing tendril out, its skin swelling into—

Montgomery whisks the curtain shut with a showman's grace, scattering yeast granules across Kenna's robe. "She's got a hypnotic quality to her, I think. Comes with the way she interfaces with your brain."

"What . . ." Kenna leans back on the chopping block behind him, gripping the hard wood, using it as an anchor to remind himself of the existence of something other than that beautiful Bitch. "What *is* that?"

"Oh, that's not the question." She draws her goggles back down over her eyes, then peers into the sink, cocking her head to and fro like a pecking bird. Then she eases her hand in, twisting her arm back and forth with the careful air of a man attempting to crack a safe. "Question is, what can she do?"

She emerges with an ice-cube-sized palpitating chunk of unearthly dough.

"What is that?" Kenna repeats.

"Do you trust me?"

"No."

A rolling eye-twitch. "Trust me."

She grabs his head, her long nails catching on his braids; as he opens his mouth to protest, the dough-globule sticking to her fingertips reacts to his breath's carbon-dioxide warmth, shivers in orgasmic rhapsody before sending sticky shoots spasming down the back of his mouth.

Kenna swallows, stringy tentacles hauled halfway down to his stomach by unthinking peristaltic motion. They swell at the moisture, turning spongy, trapping the retching boiling up from his belly. He bites down; the dough flows through the gaps in his teeth, taking root in his throat.

He claws at his mouth. Montgomery grips his wrists, digging her fingernails in until Kenna's hands pop open, then flattens his palms against her collarbones. Kenna yanks away, but Montgomery is immovable as a titanium beam. The smoked lenses of her brass goggles whirl and click as she focuses upon him, and there is something comforting in her insectile confidence.

Montgomery has a flinty love; he feels it in the way she holds him against her.

"Breathe through your nose."

Gagging, Kenna surrenders to her orders. Octopoid strings hammocked across his throat vibrate at the rush of incoming air, peel away as they reposition themselves to allow Kenna wavering breaths. Montgomery thumps his hands against her chest once, twice, as if in approval. Kenna coughs as doughy strands peel away from his uvula to creep down his tongue . . .

"Almost there," Montgomery reassures him.

The dough seeps into his tongue's papilliar bumps, digging deep—

Warm bread dough fills his world.

Not just any bread dough; the crackling bread fresh from Benzo's pan, but amplified. The crust crispier, the yeast richer, the browned bits perfectly toasted, and that heady scent of Benzo curled up close to him—

All intertwined with the silky taste of chicken broth, the two melded together like somehow you could make a crispy sandwich out of wet soup, and those overlaid with the crumbly salt of the fromager's goat cheese, woven with how good that first sugar-shock of Frosted Chocobombs felt on an empty stomach on those rare occasions Mother let him choose from the vending machine, melded with . . .

It's love. Food is love. All the memories of food, plucked from his brain and mixed into one heart-stilling emotion-swell, the thin threads of Kenna's happinesses melded into one great moment . . .

When Kenna swallows, the dough slips bonelessly off his tongue and into his stomach.

"No worries, you poop it out," Montgomery says. "I think if you had a different biology, you'd have just taken part in some alien reproductive cycle. But if the Bitch has a home planet, I've yet to find it."

He's panting, and it's not just the lack of air. Montgomery's presence makes him coltish, embarrassed; he's never had sex, but he's pretty sure it's that intense.

"What *is* that?" he asks for the third time.

The dough in the sink makes a thin keening noise, like helium squeaking out of a balloon.

Montgomery kneels down to slide a black leather valise out from under the sink. "The lady who asked me to tend to it called it 'Sirusian Sourdough.'" She roots through a clatter of glass bottles, holding them up to her goggles, tossing them aside. "In truth, she made up the name, and was most likely hoping to ditch a shipment of forbidden contraband before she was arrested. She needn't have bothered; the Bitch would have liquefied in a few hours, without assistance."

She settles upon a curlicued bottle with ash-pale grains within, dumps out a palmful, weighs it experimentally. She sprinkles it in a dash at a time; the keening noise dwindles.

"I have carried this fine Bitch on my back across star systems, asking endlessly what she is or where she is from; no one knows the answer. Alas, the Bitch is old, and wants to die. She must be constantly cajoled with nostrums to prod her back to a viable existence. I've determined through trial and error what she likes, mostly, but it's hard going. I wish I had a better sense of what makes her happy, but . . ."

She leans down into the sink, poking the bulbous surface fondly. It makes a squeaking noise.

". . . Maybe one day I'll bring her home."

Kenna massages his throat, that warm chicken-and-bread flavor still resonating like a tuning fork. "I see why Paulius retains your services."

Montgomery rolls her shoulders, deflecting the compliment with an irritated shrug. "I'd do it gratis, but I'm not stupid enough to turn down free money. Besides, the Bitch is filled with endless challenges. Perfect companion for a Sensate, really."

"I admit I'm unfamiliar with labor, but . . . is tending to a blob of alien genetics a full-time job?"

She shoves the valise back under the sink hard enough that bottles rattle. "I don't *work* here, kid. This is one stop in a grand journey. Once the tarnish dulls the hull, I'll move on."

"Okay, but . . . how much time do you spend tending her?"

She palpates the Bitch as though expecting to find some new malady. "My moldy darling needs maintenance every—well, call it thirty-seven minutes and fifteen seconds."

"You feed her every half an hour? Without fail? When do you—"

"I've *had* dreams." Montgomery's pupils are constricted pinholes. "I refuse to succumb to temporary comas when I've seen so damned little of the universe."

She *is* an addict, Kenna reminds himself. Needing something new every day. Then he remembers that spider-scrabbling twitch of the Bitch in his gullet—and instead of revulsion, the thought fills his mouth with drool. One taste, and already he's primed to associate that crawling sensation with purest love.

The urge to beg for another sample is humbling. And he only has the memory of three good meals.

"This must be . . . intense . . . for someone with a history of fine dining," Kenna says.

"Another reason I don't sleep." Montgomery slides down the sink, elbows hooked across the ridge, letting her legs sprawl loose-limbed across the floor. "The customers have a hard enough time of it. I know of three old men who've taken up permanent residence at the Station, working as janitors, putting together their meager savings for a single, annual, shared taste. I don't dare let anyone who works here try her; they'd beat me to death and tug her corpse to shreds."

The good feelings seep out of Kenna, leaving chill wariness behind. "Yet you bequeathed me a sample."

She cracks her neck lackadaisically, then locks gazes with Kenna.

"Well, I figured if Scrimshaw thought you could take one hundred percent honesty, you could handle a ride with the Bitch."

Kenna's surprised exhalation turns into a reluctant grin. This entire feeding session has been an elaborate setup for a talk; he admires the subtlety with which she cleared out the kitchen, then ushered him into her trust.

"So . . ." His stained robe feels like lies skeined across his body. "So you are aware. Of my, uh . . ."

It's amazing, how the incline of her head can convey such compassion. "Your fake Philosophy, yeah." She whistles, low and long. "Don't envy you that."

"But how did you . . ."

"So many secrets." She makes a plucking, pincer-like gesture with stiff fingers, which Kenna eventually recognizes is a mockery of knitting. "Everyone lies, here. What'll happen to them once I leave? I swear, I'm the only one who sews everything together."

Kenna's relieved sigh feels so bottomless he deflates, sliding onto the tiled floor facing Montgomery. He wanted someone else to know of his sacrifice; here she is.

". . . have you got a Philosophy?" she asks. "I mean, not a real one. One that'll satisfy the punters."

"Don't call them punters." Kenna remembers the bhelpuri merchant, all those sad emails tossed onto Father's desk, everyday people straining under such desire they creaked under their weight.

"They deserve something. They deserve a *real* Prince. A nobleman who—who can light the way for them again."

"You realize your religion's only six generations old, right?"

Kenna's cheek feels as numb as if she'd slapped him in the face.

"You Philosophers only got thirty years of *real* power." Montgomery scratches the back of her neck, a doctor reluctantly diagnosing an embarrassing disease. "Your great-grandparents got lucky enough to catch some potent people's ears, sold a lotta self-help vids in their day, but . . . you were a fad, not a religion."

Kenna turns to Paulius, as though Paulius would emerge from the Escargone to argue of *course* the Inevitable Philosophies are meaningful, Paulius has his own Inevitable Philosophy, it's why he's spending months locked in a tiny jail cell even though his body burns with disease.

The porthole flashes brighter, as if sensing Kenna's distress.

"You don't even have your own ceremonies!" Montgomery cries. "Your cuisine's ripped off from ancient cultures, your robes are modified dashikis with splashes of old pop art. The people who made the Inevitable Philosophies ransacked whatever looked cool from old civilizations other people ignored! And the Philosophies your parents have, they're not philosophies—there are no insights behind them. Their Philosophies are more like a glorified to-do list . . ."

"Even allowing for your high-handed notion that what we do is a fad," Kenna says, pressing his back against the chopping block, "you still need me to comport myself improperly to sell your robes." His throat convulses as he pronounces the word "sell"; that's the first time he's admitted what he's doing out loud. "Sell enough robes to—"

"To keep the Majestic solvent, yes, yes." She lights a cigarillo, stabs the air with it. "Paulius will help. He's good at bringing fads back to life. But . . . have you considered letting the Inevitable Philosophies die when this is done?"

Kenna gets up to leave.

She leans over to press him back against the cutting block, a gentle pressure that brooks no interruption.

Montgomery takes a long fearful drag on the cigarillo, sucking in bravery with the carcinogens, then pitches it aside.

"The universe," she tells him, her eyes a bright burning gold, "is a big place. So big we don't even know where *she* comes from." She glances over her shoulder toward the burbling mass in the sink. "I'm not saying to stop the Wisdom Ceremony. But your position isn't hereditary, despite how much of a show your parents put on. Back in the glory days, all a Philosopher needed was an incandescent willpower and a willingness to toe the party line. If Paulius works his culinary spell, then acolytes of every shade and state will come forward to plant their lips 'pon your parents' parts. Which means *you* don't have to spend your life shackled to this lie. You could disappear afterwards. I'd give you some money."

"Money?" Kenna says, horrified.

"You don't know how to care a little. You go all the way. Like the way you abandoned that shipment to let me have my way with it. Like you did with—" She jerks her head to the Escargone, that tiny window now flashing erratically. "With *him*. Kid, if you stay and watch everyone live their lives according to something you made up, it will eat your heart. And *no* one deserves to go down with *that* ship."

"No." The word pops out, reflexive as a hiccup. "No, we—we are the muscle that moves the universe. We lead our people out of darkness. We save the starving millions . . ."

"Your mother couldn't save a starving son."

"That's not her goal!"

Montgomery slams him back against the cutting block, teeth bared. "Then her goal's *irrelevant*! What good is a religion if it can't feed your fucking child?"

He grabs her arm, pushing *his* fingers deep into her wrist—and yanks her to one side so she loses balance, sending her plowing face-first into the floor.

Ice water floods his veins. It felt so *satisfying* to hurt someone who'd demeaned the Philosophies. All those years of mockery—he shouldn't have hurt her, but he wants to do it again.

"It's not *about* that!" He scrambles to his feet, retreating, afraid of what else he might do to her. "We suffer! Because we *have* to make it better for everyone else! We *have* to!"

Montgomery snurbles a great mouthful of blood back out of her nose. She looks fearful but unbowed, a cornered rat, someone who clearly didn't expect to be losing this argument. She snaps her words off like gunshots:

"What a fucking ego trip."

She hauls herself up the cutting block, dribbling blood down its side; Kenna snaps to his centerline, steps back into trap pose. Except his trap pose has never helped him in a real fight; Mother's fighting tactics never work against actual bullies.

She sees him lapsing into fighting position, lowers her head like a bull about to charge. "Your parents' savior complex," she sneers. "That *blinds* them. How can they help anybody when—"

The porthole's luminescence darkens from a soft lightbulb-yellow to an eye-watering violet.

Montgomery stops in mid-sentence, crouching to face this new threat.

The violet intensifies, solidifying, a blue-shift violet that Kenna finds both naggingly familiar and filled with inchoate danger.

"Shit," Montgomery mutters, deer-frozen in terror. "Jesus, you dumb cocksucker, you forgot to take your meds—"

The soft light sharpens into diamond-sharp refractions, filling the porthole so full of that dead blacklight that the glass cannot contain it. The light expands convulsively; a ragged oval luminescence that swells to occupy the door, a light so strong it shines through steel.

A dimensional portal.

Montgomery leaps for the door. "*No!*" she yells. "*You can control it! Stay inside! Stay* inside *the ship, Paulius*—"

But that imploding light bursts open in a splatter, disgorging a jittering figure in the shape of a man.

The man shoots out of the gateway like a freight train, smashing into an oven hard enough to buckle the metal. His whole body vibrates, skin turning a mottled blue as his lungs chug like a motor engine running at top throttle, sucking in air and extracting every ounce of oxygen . . .

He's moving at inside-Escargone speeds, Kenna realizes. *He got jettisoned out of the time field without the ship slowing down, so he's moving at sixty times our speed—*

Kenna hammers the Escargone's emergency off switch as Montgomery shrieks, takes the juddering body in her arms, wrestles Paulius to the floor like a flopping eel. A siren goes off, red lights whirling across the kitchen floor.

The hollow sound of massive engines powering down takes forever. Paulius's impossible machine-gun motions slacken into rapid-fire feats of athletic prowess, then into a dying man's weak flailings. Montgomery holds him tight against her chest, eyes closed, face up toward the ceiling as if in serene prayer.

Not prayer, Kenna thinks. *She's using her biomatrix implants to call for assistance.*

He bolts over, kneeling, ready to offer Paulius comfort.

Paulius's eyes are wide with the astonishment of someone who didn't expect to find himself alive, and isn't sure he's made it out of the gates yet. His mouth hangs open in lopsided horror, lips crayon-blue; he whoops in ragged breaths which make a tiny crunch with each lung-expanding inhalation.

Kenna does not want to know what's making that tiny crunch. But his eyes are drawn to the noise's source:

Paulius's waist is smashed.

His blue overalls are tented with jagged outcroppings where shattered bones poke up. Kenna looks up, seeing the dent where Paulius careened into the oven.

He can't look, but the floor is an equal horror: the grooves in the tiles well up with Paulius's blood. How fast had Paulius been moving? If a week passed at Paulius's time for every two hours here, and it took Kenna half a minute to shake off the shock and shut down the Escargone, then how long was Paulius lying unattended?

An hour. Maybe half a day.

Paulius might die before the paramedics arrived. And what medical assistance did Savor Station have, anyway? The smaller stations only had traveling medics, men who arrived for periodic checkups, and if you had an inflamed appendix it might burst before a physic flew out to see you . . .

No. No. Montgomery had summoned someone. Savor Station was large, well-equipped. They'd have at least a docbot.

"Kenna." Paulius's voice is a phlegmy cough wrapped around slurred consonants.

"Don't talk." He wants to hug Paulius, but Montgomery has her arms curled protectively around his ribs, shielding his broken body.

"No. You—" Paulius sobs, a terrible and bottomless sound. "You can't tell *anyone*. What you saw."

Paulius sees Kenna's confusion. He turns a wince into a parody of a titter, baring his teeth in his best imitation of a smile.

"No one," he repeats, then sinks back into Montgomery's embrace.

What just happened? Did Paulius somehow . . . teleport out? Men can't *do* that. Yet in The Sol Majestic, anything is possible, even dreadful things . . .

Chefs come charging in. How could they have waited so long? And then Kenna realizes: this has taken maybe two minutes, tops. They charge in, then recoil back, faces turning white as leeks.

"The Escargone," Montgomery hisses as the other chefs run to get towels, run to alert Scrimshaw, run away from the terror. "It *malfunctioned*."

Kenna gives his uncertainty as a gift to Paulius, going numb as the sirens draw closer.

11

Five Weeks, One Day Until the Wisdom Ceremony

Kenna has slept alone in closets while his parents took shuttles to curry favor from some politician. He has cried himself dry inside toilet stalls. He has wandered through spaceports, too poor to purchase a single entertainment, waiting for Mother and Father to return.

He thought he understood loneliness.

Yet the docbot's waiting room is blackest purgatory.

Not that the holding area is dark: it is floodlight-bright, every surface gleaming. Six plastic bucket seats sit in a semicircle around the door to Paulius's operating room, each with ugly humped curves to dissuade people from falling asleep. Once an hour, a warning bell chimes and sprinklers blast down a chill alcohol mist to sterilize the chamber. Boxes of nitrile gloves are recessed in the wall.

He can hear Scrimshaw and Montgomery muttering through the door, the docbot's monotone voice offering cold probabilities. Captain Lizzie, Savor Station's owner, has arrived, and Kenna is curious to meet her; she was a surgeon of some repute in a past war, and she has kindly offered to interpret the docbot's sometimes-cryptic diagnoses.

In another room, Kenna can hear buffing knives whirring as a bone-printer re-creates Paulius's shattered hip from old X-rays.

No one else from The Sol Majestic is allowed to attend, or else they'd all be here. Even though it is the dead of the night. Which makes sense—after scrubbing the kitchen sterile and calling in a repairman to fix the broken oven, Scrimshaw had commanded the traumatized kitchen staff to get some sleep while they could.

Yet no one questioned Kenna's presence here.

He can't determine whether that is a quiet benediction, or proof of his irrelevance.

Kenna puts on gloves, plays with the masks, ignores the cut-up clothing in the corner—Paulius's suit, cut away by the docbot's insectile scalpels so it could slide IVs into Paulius's veins, the even cloth-strips deposited into a recycling container.

That shredded suit is like seeing Paulius's flayed skin.

Paulius *can't* die. He is Inevitable. Kenna pulls up games on Scrimshaw's smartpaper, loads his corneas full of dancing dots designed to distract him—but within a few seconds he thinks of Paulius shivering on The Sol Majestic's floor, and then his brain rebounds off the concept of Paulius's mortality.

The ceiling drips down prickling mist.

Knives carve replacement bone.

The docbot drones out muffled survival prognostications.

The door hisses open. Lizzie, the station captain, strides out in her trim gold-and-gray uniform. She's pale, gaunt, vacuum-scarred, far shorter than Kenna thought a station captain would be. But her gray eyes are as clear as radar, sweeping across the room to size everything up.

"It's not good," she says.

She addresses him as though they're old friends. Kenna relaxes under her competence; her words carry the weight of a dossier she's compiled on Kenna.

"But there's room for hope," she continues. "Soon as the fabber finishes that hip, that door will lock shut and the docbot will perform the surgery. I've got to delegate some tasks to clear my schedule—and then I'll be standing in the room, in case something goes wrong."

"Is that likely?"

"My faith is in the docbot. But my hand is always on the override switch." Kenna remembers the legends he'd heard about Captain Lizzie—once the Angel of Sauerkraut Station, a teenaged girl so talented with the surgeon's knife that warring soldiers had declared a truce at her station lest they lose her skills.

Captain Lizzie glances toward the ceiling, the twitch of someone with biomatrix implants receiving a message.

"Anyway," she says. "Scrimshaw and Montgomery will fill you in. Pack in for a long day, O Prince."

It's been *a long day,* Kenna thinks, then realizes the station has yet to click over to dawn-shift.

Scrimshaw slides open the door to Paulius's room enough for her to squeeze out, then urges Montgomery to squeeze out too. Montgomery holds the Bitch-cask up as she comes out, blocking Kenna's view. He cranes his neck to see how Paulius is doing; Scrimshaw clucks her tongue.

"Better not to look," she says sadly.

Montgomery shivers as she exits Paulius's chamber, turning away from Kenna and Scrimshaw to drop the cask and face the wall, eking out privacy. Her fingers creep over her shoulders, giving herself a tiny shoulder massage that expands into a self-hug.

Scrimshaw sits down next to Kenna, clasping her knees with an old woman's daintiness. "The surgery will begin within the hour. But we can't stay with Paulius. We have to go back."

Kenna realizes he's been only able to bear this waiting room nullhell because he was counting down the time until he had company again. "Back to where?"

"The kitchen, of course," Montgomery says bitterly, dribbling a blue substance into the cask. "The Bitch never takes a break, and neither does the service."

"People have traveled for months to get to this dinner," Scrimshaw explains. "Spent their life's savings. Paulius is irrelevant; what matters is the meal. Would you like to come back with us? To do small jobs in the kitchen?"

"No!" Kenna slides away across the chair until he bumps against the knobbed armrest, putting as much distance between himself and Scrimshaw as possible. How could she make the kitchen work when a great man lies dying? Even Scrimshaw hangs her vulture's head low, as if acknowledging what a callous, money-seeking monster she is.

"He needs me." How egotistic, assuming Paulius cares for him. "To look after him."

Montgomery yanks up the cask, lean biceps bulging as though she wants to crack the wood. "He's surrounded by monitors. We're all on biomatrix alert. If something happens we'll come running, and if that happens none of us can help anyway. Face it, kid, Paulius is either gonna die or he's not, we're useless, and wasting away in this stupid waiting room won't help—"

"Montgomery."

Scrimshaw's single word hits Montgomery's "mute" button. Montgomery's grip tightens on the cask, as though considering staving Scrimshaw's head in—

—but the docbot mutters a status update, and Montgomery whips around to check on Paulius's condition.

Scrimshaw coughs politely, point made.

"Fine," Montgomery snaps. She taps her goggles, focusing on Kenna. "You and I, Little Prince, we'll have words. Just . . . remember." She jerks her head back toward Paulius's room. "Remember."

She storms out of the room, hauling her cask.

Scrimshaw reaches out to pat his knee—but her hand hesitates in midair before she places it primly back on her lap.

Kenna feels a vague embarrassment sublimating away. Scrimshaw shielded him from one of Montgomery's rants, and maybe she's right that Paulius wouldn't want the service stopped—merchants don't stop, but neither do Philosophers like Paulius, and The Sol Majestic muddles his conceptions of both—but he's still mad at her anyway.

"Well," she says. "*I'm* glad you're staying here."

It would be egotistical to agree, so Kenna studies a packet of face masks mounted on the wall.

"Don't worry," Scrimshaw continues. "Anticipating your desires, I convinced Lizzie to put a station camerawatch on your parents. If they take a route that intersects with you, we'll send the best interference to ensure you retain your privacy."

". . . interference?"

"Rèpondelle." Scrimshaw's head bobs in satisfaction at the mere mention of this person's name—which, given how prudent Scrimshaw is with praise, fills Kenna with confidence. "Our front-of-house supervisor. Trained to manipulate the truculent back to satisfaction. She's gifted you with breathing space once before, though I doubt you remember it."

When Mother and Father burst into the kitchen, worried to see their son, they close ranks around Kenna, obscuring him, until a woman in a sharp red tuxedo can be summoned . . .

"The woman in red," Kenna says.

"Yes. Her. Though I doubt she'd be pleased you remember."

"Why not?"

"She wears many faces. Keeping her confined to one makes her nervous. In any case, the kitchen has your back, Master Kenna. Guard Paulius for us." She taps the smartpaper in Kenna's hands. "Keep us alerted should he require assistance."

She rises, the meeting concluded—yet before she moves to tap the door's exit button, she slumps against the wall. Her sinewed strength drains away to reveal a geriatric woman in an old coat.

Before he can rush to her side, she clamps her teeth together, a predatory throat-ripping gesture that saps his water. Those tensed teeth are sizing up something she isn't certain she cares for, ready to devour something too weak to survive.

"Tell me, Master Kenna." Old as she is, Kenna fears her. "Was I—wrong to gift you with one hundred percent honesty? Should I have obfuscated the Majestic's peril?"

That something she does not care for, Kenna realizes, is herself.

"I'm worthy of truth." It is hard to stare straight into those chill gray eyes. "But I still resent you."

Her lips curl as she swallows her sorrow, turning self-loathing into bitter smiles.

"So long as I'm hated for the right reasons."

She exits. Kenna takes a chilly solace from her departure; if the Queen of the Kitchen says that Kenna deserves a place by Paulius's side, then he must mean *something* to Paulius.

Kenna waits.

The noises behind Paulius's door must be ordinary surgery, Kenna tells himself. But even muffled, the whir of sterilized sawblades slicing through Paulius's bone resonates through Kenna's body until he clasps his hands over his ears. Moist sucking noises, like an old man toothlessly slurping Jell-O, ooze through the door's cracks to lick Kenna's eardrums.

Paulius is being rebuilt. The repair is messy.

Lizzie stands behind that door, which gives Kenna strength. He has not heard her smack the emergency override switch, and the slicing noises have an assembly line's square-edged precision. Yet it comforts him to know someone human stands by Paulius in this needy hour.

A bleep from the smartpaper: *Parents inbound. Interference dispatched.*

A videocamera feed blooms across the crumpled-tissue smartpaper on his lap, a high overhead shot showing Mother and Father marching across a repair bay, headed straight for the docbot clusters. They walk with one arm flung dramatically out in the other's direction, interlacing fingers in a lover's hand-hold—but walking at a pace that threatens to clothesline the noontime shift's maintenance workers.

When threatened, Mother and Father take up space in cramped

places to emphasize their royal nature. They are Inevitable, prepared to inconvenience anyone to get their wayward son back to his studies.

A light touch, at the base of the shoulder. Mother and Father whirl angrily, their faces melting into sheepish confusion when they see the woman in the red tuxedo not *quite* bowing before them— but she flexes her knees like a ballerina, spreading her arms in a circle to make room to encompass their immense presence.

A furrow of confusion. They remember her, but not her name. No matter; the red-tuxedoed woman remembers *their* names extravagantly, all but begging their autographs. Her bland face reflects their concerns, wondering what great concern brought them out to this place of low labor.

The flat-carbon smartpaper speakers are not good at transmitting audio over the waiting room's hiss and whirr, yet Kenna hears snippets of objections—*he was to stay in our room* and *he must feel compassion for kings, not cooks*—

The woman in the red tuxedo agrees with everything they say. Her body trembles like a tuning fork, resonating with their wisdom. Yet somehow, with careful interjections, Mother and Father's great-winged circle closes around this unassuming woman, stepping closer as if she is the only audience worth speaking to. They come to realize the compassion that calls Kenna to Paulius's bedside proves their grand instincts have fallen on fertile soil, that meditating upon death is the insight Kenna needs, that they *are* peckish, that perhaps a selection of fine teas would help quell the rumble in their bellies.

The red-tuxedoed woman leads them off-camera, their heads bobbing to her tune.

A knock at the waiting room door; Benzo pokes his head in. He keeps his distance from the cold metal walls festooned with nozzles to refill the docbot's medical supplies. Then, seeing Kenna, his broad face opens into a brief but sunny grin, before remembering what a solemn space this is.

He ambles in with a studied casualness. His black-striper's outfit is rolled up at the sleeves, revealing sturdy forearms; Kenna ponders trailing his fingertips down the veins on the underside of
Benzo's arms and feeling those heathen muscles tense.

Benzo says nothing. Kenna realizes he's *staring* at Benzo, which
is stupid, so stupid, why is he so awkward?

But Benzo stares back at Kenna, swinging a wood-woven picnic basket back and forth. He squeezes the handle at the apex of
each swing, knuckles tightening around it, trying to work up the
strength to say something.

Kenna doesn't want to know what he might say. Maybe Benzo's
thinking the same thing Kenna is, in which case what would they
do with that physical intensity, sitting ten feet away from a flayed-
open Paulius? And maybe it's something else, in which case Kenna
wants to hold on to this flirtatious dream for a little longer.

"Did you manufacture your broth today?"

Kenna hates himself the moment he says it—why didn't he let
Benzo talk first? Why didn't he relish this silence, like a Philosopher should?

Benzo lets out a hissing laugh, like a ship emergency-venting
pressurized air, then mops his blond curls back on his forehead.

"You know, I was gonna make broth," he says. "But then I
thought, hey, what if I make the perfect broth today, on the day
Paulius can't taste it?"

It takes Kenna a moment to realize Benzo's made a joke. Kenna's pure laughter makes Benzo puff out his chest. "Seriously?"

Benzo's grin wilts as he sets the picnic basket down on the floor.
"Nah, I made it," he confesses, the moment vanished as he plops
into the seat next to Kenna. "It wasn't very good."

Kenna's heart breaks a little.

Benzo reaches down to fumble with the basket, lifting the lid
up enough to give Kenna a peek inside. There are four bread loaves,
swaddled like children in checkered blue fabric.

"I gotta remember to thank Montgomery," he murmurs, tracing

a memo on the biomatrix implants in his skin. "She took over my station so I could bake four kinds of bread for you. She *never* works prep duty. Don't know what got into her. In any case, I'm sorry it's only four breads, normally I'd pop into the Escargone and make you ten different kinds, but nobody in the kitchen will touch that thing now, they actually walk around it in a big circle like it might bite them . . ."

"*Hey.*" If Kenna doesn't interrupt Benzo's breathless monologue, it might go on forever. "I fear I feel no hunger."

"I got a job, Kenna. I'm educating your palate. And I gotta tell you, there's such a difference between peasant bread and pumpernickel, it'd be a shame if you never knew it . . ."

"I'm holding *vigil*. You can't—you can't eat when someone languishes in surgery . . ."

Benzo takes his hand.

Kenna's breath, his heartbeat, every neuron in his brain converges on the warm sensation of Benzo's fingers closing around his.

Benzo took his hand once before, to feed him soup, yet this tenderness holds no such excuse. Benzo's fingers move lovingly across Kenna's skin, like ice skaters moving across a frozen pond, leaving tingling trails behind.

Benzo's saying something, but Benzo's firm touch pushes the language out of Kenna's head. At best, he notices Benzo's bristly stubble, realizes Benzo had no time to shave today, wonders what it would feel like to lean over and press his lips to Benzo's.

Then slowly, like an animal resyncing with time after being in a stasis cube, his brain catches up to make sense of Benzo's words:

"You can't do that, Kenna. Trust me, I—you don't get a lot of good moments, working for Her. You don't get to choose your happy times, they just show up whenever She's not paying attention. So you learn that when you get a good moment, no matter when it arrives, you've gotta grab it *hard,* because . . . well, who knows when you'll get another chance?"

Is Benzo asking him to kiss him?

Benzo is totally asking Kenna to kiss him.

But if Kenna's wrong, then things will be awkward. So awkward.

Except Benzo's stopped talking, and he's still holding Kenna's hand. These seats sit so close to each other, hip-to-hip.

Benzo's eyes are planet-blue and earnest, reflecting Kenna's terror. Benzo, too, has so much to lose: Kenna is technically his employer for the time being; if he's wrong about this then he might not get to stay with Kenna anymore, and how would the kitchen gossip about his foolishness then?

Benzo's lips open, just a bit, as if begging to be kissed.

Kenna realizes he has to kiss him. Benzo's risked enough. Kenna must risk it back.

But what if Kenna's wrong? This is a docbot ward. What if Benzo's awkward because of all the sorrow? What if . . .

No. Enough overthinking.

Just do this.

Kenna moves forward, close enough to scent the butter on Benzo's breath. Benzo trembles, closing his eyes . . .

. . . and the hourly sterilization spritzes them with alcohol.

They splutter, the kiss ruined, spitting disinfectant—and as Benzo scrubs his tongue with his palm, he chokes out a laugh.

Kenna giggles.

All that latent tension converts into an acknowledgment of how *ridiculous* this is—this elaborate dance they're doing, this gravid seriousness—and when Benzo makes eye contact, it's like wildfire sparking off Kenna. They snort back sniggers, trying not to give in to this giggling amusement, but every time Benzo makes eye contact it's this clean honesty of *God, aren't we idiots?* and they *are*, it's so ludicrous to circle each other like boxers when they clearly love each other, and whenever they exchange glances it opens a door past all this silly posturing to show how much affection is there for the taking.

They laugh until they're best friends.

The door to the operating room cracks open. "Everything all

right?" Lizzie asks, drawling it as though she's talking to lunatics. Kenna realizes how crazy this must have sounded from inside the operating room, especially with Paulius still teetering on death's door.

Benzo chokes out a "We're glorious."

Lizzie gives them a quick nod, as if to say *I've seen stranger things in war,* and closes the door. Even though they're in the waiting room and she's supervising an operation, Kenna feels like she's giving *them* privacy.

That sensual moment's been cleansed from the room. There were no kisses, and won't be today. Yet in some weird way, this newfound comfort is better.

It feels like something to build a relationship on.

"Come on," Benzo says, wiping off the picnic basket. "Let's try the bread before we get doused again."

The bread's pretty good.

The friendship is better.

12

One Afternoon Closer to the Wisdom Ceremony

"Do *not* order me around like I'm one of your re-homed wageslaves!"

Montgomery's words haul Kenna out of a gummy dream, his back aching from the waiting room chair contortion.

"If you won't help the boy," Paulius says, "I'll crawl to the Escargone myself."

"You wouldn't."

Kenna grasps for consciousness, face beaded with disinfectant, slipping out of the chair onto the floor. He's slept fitfully in the hours that Paulius has been in surgery, a dusky exhaustion-hell.

Paulius's anguished groan shoves the fog away.

Montgomery's arm snakes out, hauls Kenna in.

The recovery room is cramped, the ceiling an orthodontic nightmare of needles, the monitors on the walls blaring a threatening bloodred as Paulius attempts to heave himself off the bed. Scrimshaw holds him down, pushing her weight onto his chest as though attempting CPR; she is backed by a slender armada of antennae-like docbot extension arms, which advance nervously as they dart back and forth in attempts to inject Paulius with a sedative.

Paulius thrashes, sending vibrations through the medical tethers connecting him to the docbot—the blood pressure cuffs, the pulse oximeters, the heart monitors, even his long white braid, all jiggling like an obscene puppet show.

"Bring me to the Escargone!" Paulius huffs. He clenches his

teeth as the stitches across his naked body flex. "It is *inspiration* that feeds a man! I will *not* leave that boy to wander! I will—"

And then he notices Kenna, and relaxes quickly enough that Kenna wonders if a sedative-arm got to him. But no. He lifts his arms in greeting, allowing Scrimshaw to shove him back against the pillow. Yet Paulius's mouth creeps into a hesitant grin, as though he can't quite believe that this angel, that Kenna, has come to see him.

"Kenna," he whispers, a tear trickling from one eye. "I should have known you'd never leave."

Gravity shuts down. Kenna is wafted aloft on the happiness of realizing he was right, Paulius needed him here.

They need each *other*.

"I was by your side, sir," he gasps, his lungs a vacuum. "All along."

Paulius's exhausted smile is as radiant as any sun.

This is a betrayal, Kenna thinks without a scrap of regret, this beautiful oxytocin acceptance flooding his veins. *This is what I should have felt when Mother and Father hugged me.*

Scrimshaw bats away an inbound sedation needle.

"No," Montgomery rumbles, pushing Paulius and Kenna apart like a referee separating two boxers. "No, no, *no.* I brought you in here to talk him *out* of this damn-fool plan, not talk him *into* it."

". . . what damn-fool plan?"

"He wants to hole up in the Escargone to heal."

Paulius's mouth crooks in a disdainful sneer, as if to ask, *And what's wrong with that?*

Kenna can't see why that'd be a bad idea himself, with the impending Wisdom Ceremony; why shouldn't Paulius bring a nurse with him into the Escargone, compress the painful weeks of recovery into a single afternoon's time to emerge hale and hearty?

Yet Montgomery snorts like an angry dog, prepared to brain Paulius with her cask rather than let him near the Escargone. Scrimshaw looms over him with a teacher's grave disappointment. Even the rows of sharp-toothed docbot instruments ripple as though they might surge forward to grab his tongue.

"Okay." Kenna waves his hands in peaceable circles. "What, precisely, makes you believe Paulius's course of action is suboptimal?"

Montgomery thrusts her fingers deep into her hair, pulls hard. "He's got *Niffeneger* syndrome, for the Gods' sake!"

Kenna's skin goes clammy with embarrassment. He'll have to admit ignorance twice in short order.

Paulius touches his fingertips to his forehead, squeezing his eyes shut. "You speak as though it's a fatal disease."

"It *is* a fatal disease," Scrimshaw snaps.

"*Life* is a fatal disease. We all have our own terminal velocity. I merely have a more colorful endpoint than most."

Scrimshaw rolls her eyes, a magnificent rolling, like stars wheeling overhead. "*Most* people's terminal velocity doesn't involve actual freefall through an atmosphere, you gossamer-dreamed lout."

"I'd *kill* to die so close to civilization, you rickety old birdcage. My days will end in a black void, feeling my eyeballs frost over, and *you know it.*"

"You act as though I'm eager to see the end of your financial contributions, when you know damned well I've taken every risk to ensure your dimensional stability . . ."

Kenna makes a time-out "T" with his hands. "Fine people— before we continue this most studied sniping, may I request an explanation of this Niffeneger syndrome?"

Both Scrimshaw and Paulius cross their arms and study the walls, pointedly ignoring each other. Scrimshaw taps one rubber-soled boot against the plastic floor; in response, Paulius taps his fingers against his bicep in a counter-rhythm, both using tiny noises to war peevishly.

Montgomery blinks, twice, as if to ask *Are you shitting me?* and then kneels next to Kenna. "Okay. So. You're familiar with dimensional splitters?"

"The most expensive warships in existence? Yes, I believe I'm familiar."

"Yeah. Well, a couple hundred years ago some bright boys got the idea to try to breed humans with the capacity to fold dimensions."

He stifles a disbelieving cough. "That's ludicrous. You couldn't possibly breed a dimensional splitter into a human body. They have to siphon mass from stars to get it to work."

"Didn't say it was easy, kid. Or that they were entirely successful. Only way they could do it was to splice nanobots into the people's genes, and those nanobots drew power from . . . somewhere. High-powered techno-juju. But the 'bots had a loading time that made bureaucracies look nimble. Couple of times a year, these folks would build up enough of a charge to crack open a rift, and . . ." She clasps her hands together as if in prayer, then makes a diving motion as if plunging through dimensions. "Poof."

Kenna frowned. "I'm guessing this fine tale does not end with an army of super-engineered warriors."

"No, it does not. Because for one thing, even though they tried to breed in some navigation senses, space is *large*. Far too large for meat-brains to calculate with efficiency. For every planet, there's ten trillion planet-sized gaps. Most walked straight into vacuum. If two somehow charged up at the same time *and* landed on the same planet, they might land continents apart. Or plummet through the upper atmosphere."

"So they discontinued the program."

"We assume. All we know is when you breed a race who can teleport anywhere, well, it's hard to keep 'em down on the farm. One escaped to planetfall, made a little love, and we have reconstructed what we can of this story by analyzing the nano-genes that sometimes resurface in his escapee's distant relatives. And . . . voilà!"

Montgomery gestures at Paulius like a magician producing a rabbit.

Kenna tries not to stare. "So you're a super-soldier."

Paulius whips the blanket off in response, displaying his body for Kenna's edification; he highlights his scrawny biceps, demonstrates the paunchy belly-bulge resting atop his storklike physique, runs his fingers through his unruly gray chest hair. All that, highlighted by the space-dark bruises and machine-tight stitches embroidering his re-created hip.

His eyes demand respect. "Do I look like a killing machine to you, O Prince?"

Kenna hands the blanket back by way of apology.

Paulius tucks himself back in as best he can, grunting as the pain drives him down. His pallid face flushes with the effort of covering his feet.

"No, Master Kenna. I'm no mono-browed thug with a penchant for pugilism. I'm the secret shame of a failed military program, a superpower watered down into disease. And I live with the consequences."

"So you . . . part the dimensions and step onto another biomass?"

"*I* don't do anything." He slumps back into the bed, speaking in a resigned monotone as he tries to regain strength. "From my perspective, it's more like a . . . a seizure. It happens every few seasons, whether I want it to or not. And—well, maybe it's more like a sneeze in that I have some control over it, if I sense it coming. And I have them in spasms, so I've usually gotten there and back. Though that's not guaranteed. Sometimes, I've wound up seven solar systems away and had to hitchhike back. Yet the charge builds slower if I work. Sleep just seems to empower the damned thing, so . . ."

His smile is a rueful twitch. "I did a lot of drugs. Then I discovered how easy it is to stay awake for sixty hours when you're creating something beautiful."

"Which makes it easier to stay put," Kenna finishes.

He taps Kenna on the nose fondly. "Precisely, my sweet prince.

I have experienced many foreign cuisines, most accidentally." Then he sighs. "One day, I'll disappear, and no one will know where I've gone. So I made myself big enough for someone to miss me."

Kenna looks around at the docbot's monitors, realizing they now have full records of Paulius's medical status. "But . . . why promote this clandestine nature of your . . . condition? Will that government track you down to dissect you, or . . ."

"Oh, probably." Paulius makes a disgusted snort. "The bigger deal is investment."

"Investment?"

Scrimshaw makes a distasteful little cough. "No serious investor would sink money into a celebrity chef who might disappear. They're already leery of his tendencies to go on daylong benders where he cannot be found."

"If I feel it coming on, I pick a fight," Paulius admits. "I fling plates. Then I retreat into my private lair before I vanish. Mostly, they think I'm temperamental."

"You *are* temperamental," Scrimshaw adds.

"That has nothing to do with my condition and you know it, you penitentiary proctologist! I am temperamental because when I ask for the finest vichyssoise and some oaf hands me a bowl of *paste*, she should—"

Scrimshaw lowers her horn-rimmed glasses, eyes woeful, stilling Paulius with a draconic glance. "Would it kill you," she whispers, "to thank me for funding your dreams? Just once?"

"Fine." Each word is strained, as though stepping through a minefield. "I . . . am . . . welcoming of . . . your . . . money."

Scrimshaw actually hisses, whirling around as though she intends to summon a storm of hypodermic needles from the docbot's walls and plunge them deep into Paulius's heart.

"*The point is,*" Montgomery says, her voice cleaving through the tension, "Ol' Walkabout here's getting worse. His spasms are speeding up. He travels farther with each warp. Putting his broken ass into the Escargone is asking for ruin."

"I can control it." Kenna has heard that unrepentant begging in Paulius's voice from rich children, wheedling their parents to buy them an exotic pet they can't possibly take care of in a transport ship's cramped confines.

Scrimshaw taps Kenna's shoulder, then grimaces with satisfaction as she sees Kenna understanding the infeasibility of Paulius's plan.

"Hel*lo*!" Montgomery rattles an IV hooked into Paulius's arm; Paulius cringes, grasping his needle tight to protect it.

A brief regret flashes over Montgomery's face before she bellies up to the bed.

"You couldn't control your space-hop when you were *well,* you glorious egomaniac! Shoving you into the Escargone when you're hopped up on pain pills? In full bed rest, *sleeping* all the time? That's asking for another discharge while you're in the time-fields, and look what happened then!"

Paulius's panic changes pitch. "Putting me into the Escargone is the only way to get this boy his meal! I can't work like this." He palpates his hip, hyperventilating as he traces the extent of his injuries, then lies back on the thin pillow, spent. "Please don't fight me, Montgomery. You need to shove me inside that capsule, turn it up so months pass over minutes, and let me heal this ruinous injury before tonight's service."

"You *will* teleport inside that time-capsule, Paulius. And we've already seen how the Escargone's time-enhancing effects don't play nicely with your dimensional splitting."

"I'll stay still this time! I panicked, and, I . . ." He huffs, furious, embarrassed. "Walked into things. At . . . great speed."

"And if you'd teleported *into* the oven instead of next to it?"

Paulius extends his arms to Kenna, imploring him, begging to come stand on the bed's other side to face off against Montgomery. Kenna feels the gravitic pull to comfort Paulius—

—but an almost subliminal squeeze from Scrimshaw's spidery fingers tells him: *Not yet*.

Paulius's mouth draws into a fearful frown when Kenna does

not come at his beckoning. He reaches back to draw his long white hair over his shoulder, braiding and unbraiding it like a man plucking at a violin. And like a violin, his edginess resonates through Kenna's body, making them both nervous at the same pitch.

"He needs the meal." Paulius's voice is a soft monotone, but his fingers yank his hair into agitated knots.

"You've made hundreds of meals," Montgomery says.

"Those merely make money. This meal makes kings. It—"

His voice quavers, and as it cracks he tugs his hair out into a messy gray feather-spread. He spreads the hair out with an irritated flick, looking down at it as though he hopes to find a speech written in it.

"The boy's been here for three days, yet already he's found his Philosophy. That's just from a bowl of broth. Yet what would we be if we stopped? He needs our nourishment to feed not just him, but his Philosophies. To make him not only wise, but *great*. I will *not* send him off to rule millions before I connect him with his ancestors' strength, because—because if we abandon his Wisdom Ceremony, we . . . abandon Kenna."

His voice cracks again as he speaks Kenna's name.

Kenna shivers: Paulius believes in him.

Paulius believes in him so thoroughly, he's willing to risk his life in the Escargone to deliver Kenna's meal. Paulius reassembles his silver strands back into a braid, hiding behind his hair, humiliated by his revelation: *Yes, I am a monster,* that shivering gesture says. *I break men to create great art.*

But I break myself to create great men.

Paulius scrubs away snuffled tears with his palm; Kenna recognizes the gesture as a reluctant confession. Yes, Kenna is but one of Paulius's pet projects. But those projects are how Paulius atones for the necessary cruelty of destroying men to create perfect meals. He needs projects overwhelming enough to incinerate his mortal fears, subsuming himself as he extracts flawness cuisine from a fallible world—

Yet he also spends precious hours sifting through pretentious speeches made in the confession booth, fast-forwarding past greedy thrill seekers in the hopes of finding someone worthy of love, of grace, of salvation.

In this way he does his best to bend his merciless culinary arts toward compassion.

Warm, surprising tears spill down Kenna's cheeks like a burst dam. Paulius plucked Kenna from an endless stream of pretentious confessional booth monologues because yes, he saw something worthy in Kenna.

Kenna thought he'd worn his heart on his sleeve, yet now he realizes how much adoration he's been holding back. Kenna *is* special, Kenna *is* beloved, all this affection given to Paulius has been returned to him . . . If only Paulius knew what a filthy liar Kenna is.

Then Kenna realizes Paulius wouldn't care about the lie.

Of this, Kenna has never been more certain of anything. Unlike Mother and Father, Paulius couldn't care less about the Inevitable Philosophies: he just wants Kenna to be happy. And brave. And wise. If Kenna managed that working at The Sol Majestic, or hitchhiking through space, Paulius would be equally thrilled.

If he admits his Inevitable Philosophy is a lie, he can stop Paulius from continuing with this damned-fool Escargone plan.

"Paulius." Kenna clutches Paulius's bed rails, feeling like a penitent shriving himself at an altar. "The comestibles you've prepared. It's—it's not—"

"How are those robe sales coming along, Scrimshaw?" Montgomery's voice is as cutting as a blowtorch.

Scrimshaw snaps her smartpaper open, scrutinizes it ostentatiously. "Hardly a single buyer."

"Oh, for pity's sake, you human abacus!" Paulius snaps. "The boy's trying to reveal something, and you're bothering us with a balance sheet?"

But the damage is done. The bed rail gripped in Kenna's palms

no longer feels like an altar; it has the cold feel of expensive technology, a reminder of the bills piling up at The Sol Majestic. He
could tell Paulius about the ceremony, but Paulius would refuse to
condemn Kenna to a lifetime of lies. Paulius wouldn't care about
the robes, or the money, or the damage to the Majestic's prestige;
he would shut it down in a fit of righteous anger, just the same as
he'd tossed that gravity-bowl aside in the orchard.

"I didn't taste the duck." He lies quickly, before he can regret it.

Paulius goes so pale, the docbot's monitors flare. Tranquilizing
needles curl outward from the wall.

". . . you didn't taste the duck?"

"I needed to be there." Kenna is surprised to find this true. "To
see it made. You can't just hand me the food, Paulius. I . . . I have
to watch it happen. The creation, it . . . it inspires me. Without
viewing the entirety of the process, anything you give me might
as well be—a nutricracker."

Paulius swallows, a choking gesture; Kenna's knees hit the floor
as he grasps Paulius's hand, begging forgiveness. Paulius squeezes
back, but turns away from Kenna to stare haggardly past the walls,
across the station, toward The Sol Majestic.

". . . Are you saying you need to see how it's done?" he asks.
"How it's *all* done? Concept to finish?"

He'd say anything to stop Paulius from throwing his life away
in the Escargone. "Yes."

"Then this is . . . unthinkable." Paulius does not fight as Scrimshaw waves a sedative-needle into his arm. "It'll take months of
Escargone-time to perfect the dishes. We can't cram a boy into the
time-ship to watch that. Not when he's growing. It'd be like . . . a
bonsai tree stuffed in a cube. That hellhole's suffocated my best
cooks—how can I rob Kenna of his best years? We can't . . ."

His chin thumps against his chest as the monitors turn a cool
blue. "I don't know how, Scrimshaw. I can't make him a meal—
the meal—in five uncompressed weeks . . ."

The beeps tracking Paulius's heart rate slow as Paulius nods into a troubled sleep, his face lined with despair.

Montgomery sets the cask on the floor; Kenna hadn't noticed how she'd hugged it to her chest like a frightened woman clutching her baby. She slumps to sit on the cask, digging elbows into lanky knees, massaging her pallid cheeks to bring blood back into them.

"Well, *that* was easier than I'd thought," she mutters.

Where Montgomery looks exhausted, Scrimshaw looks grim. "I'll start the paperwork."

"The paperwork?"

Scrimshaw sucks in air through her teeth, examining Paulius's prone body.

"To shut it down." She rolls her shoulders as if preparing to lift heavy weights—and charges out the door.

13

Halting State

To shut it down.

Kenna can't fit that sentence into his brain. What's she want to shut down? It sounds like she's discussing The Sol Majestic, but . . . Scrimshaw couldn't destroy all that beauty with no ceremony, could she? If you're going to condemn a space station to economic ruin, you should hold a moment of silence, prepare people for this collapse with speeches, give them the space they'd need to mourn . . .

But this is Scrimshaw.

"*Kid!*" Montgomery yells, grabbing at him as he bolts after Scrimshaw; this time Mother's training kicks in and he squirms out of her grasp. Scrimshaw barrels past, already out of the waiting room and striding past the police station's steel slats, her black robe fluttering in her wake. A few drunks lined up outside the police station report stolen smartphones, muttering into the flatscreen reporting stations as voice interpreters struggle to transcribe slurred complaints.

"*Hey!*" Kenna yells, all his studied politeness boiled away.

Without so much as glancing back, Scrimshaw flicks up a single index finger, an imperial command of *not now*, never slowing as she glides past the drunks.

Kenna tries to match her stride, but her legs are too long, and within seconds he breaks out in a run. "*Hey!*" When she doesn't stop he grabs a double-fistful of her woolen robe to haul her to an angry stop. "*Don't you dare—*"

Her head snaps around.

Kenna's heart turns to gelatin. He knows the fear a rabbit feels when the hawk's cool shadow crosses its back; there is no mercy in Scrimshaw's dinosaur gaze, just a cruelty accreted from firing a thousand men. Scrimshaw has killed hundreds, and never regretted it—not with a knife, no, but she's stared straight into the rheumy eyes of alcoholics who won't survive without her help, and kicked those sad bastards out the door.

Without Paulius, The Sol Majestic has ceased to function. She will sell its corpse for parts.

Rough fabric slides through his fingers.

Scrimshaw gives a satisfied little nod—then sweeps away, smooth as death.

Kenna trots along beside her, a humiliating compromise between a flat-out run and a stride, hearing the drunks snigger. "How can you shutter The Sol Majestic?"

She glares straight ahead, as if looking away from The Sol Majestic would cause her to weaken. "It was doomed the moment his hip shattered. At least I stopped the old fraud from throwing his life away in some vain attempt at recovery." She grinds her teeth. "Not that he'll thank me for it . . ."

"But . . . the Wisdom Ceremony . . ."

"Managing that kitchen is like herding cats. Without Paulius, the meal *will* fail. Given that more people would be watching *this* meal than ever before, even a mediocre review would destroy our reputation."

"We should at least *try*." Anger clenches his stomach.

"Between the robes' financial ruin and the impending Wisdom Ceremony disaster, The Sol Majestic is scrap metal. Yet we have a graceful excuse to close the kitchen: Paulius hovers between life and death. We can't keep up our level of service, not without our head chef. No one will blame us if we shut down before we tarnish our reputation—which means we can open further restaurants down the line. *Far* superior to serving deteriorating meals, watching the critics take our Firewar Stars back, following the sagging arc of our credit rating . . ."

"Fuck your reputation."

Scrimshaw flinches.

Kenna comes to a stop so abrupt that Scrimshaw is yanked to a halt by his denial. *This* anger is as cold as a comet's ice, encrusting him in armor so thick that Scrimshaw's expertise cannot touch him.

She stands stiffly, clenching and unclenching her bony fists. Her eyes dart from side to side, seeking escape.

"You asked me to risk it all." Kenna's hoarse whisper cuts through the air. "You asked me to live a lie so massive I'd carry its toxicity to my grave. You asked me to mislead the starving millions. You asked me to sell out the philosophy of *my ancestors* to keep your tattered corpse alive, and by all the Gods wheeling in the heavens, I agreed."

He takes a step forward; the dragon retreats.

"So when you tell me you've a reputation to protect? No. You don't get to keep a reputation. You manacled me to this sinking ship, Scrimshaw—and if I had to auction off my future to try to save this bedamned locale, then so do you."

Kenna walks up, aims one index finger at her as though it were a sword-tip digging into her wattled throat:

"You owe me a chance to keep it alive."

In the days to come, Kenna wonders what would have happened had Scrimshaw disagreed with him. After all, she had absolutely no obligation to risk her financial empire on Kenna's uncertain talents.

Yet as Kenna speaks, there is no uncertainty. The universe has lined up behind him, every planet at his back to amplify this inevitable morality that *I deserve a shot,* and Scrimshaw can no more escape that judgment than she could squirm out of a black hole's event horizon.

Scrimshaw crooks her own finger, as if preparing to riposte Kenna's audacity—but regret steals across her face. The stiff haughtiness melts away to reveal a sad old woman who's worn a dragon mask for so long, she's no longer certain how to abandon it.

She curls her hands around his index finger, formally requesting his absolution.

"I cry your pardon, Master Kenna." She bows. "If I asked you to risk your dream for mine, then yes. It is only fitting I bet my dream upon yours." She swallows convulsively. "If The Sol Majestic must die a slow death by incompetence, then so be it."

"It will not die by incompetence." Kenna's voice booms like an announcer, but the Inevitability he felt trickles away word by word; the decision's weight settles on his shoulders. "The Sol Majestic is more than Paulius. It is the people who make it."

Though as Kenna says this, he wonders who else he knows in the kitchen. Benzo? Montgomery? The . . . fromager? Someone gave him a joint, but he can't remember her name . . .

"Then go choose his successor," Scrimshaw tells him. "They're finishing up the night's service."

And Kenna realizes the trap of defying the dragon: he has informed her that he—a spacebound hobo who's yet to eat a salad—knows better than a woman who's devoted her life to funding restaurants. If Kenna will challenge her authority, then he must take up the mantle of proving her wrong.

He scours her face for any kind of malice, but there is only a grave sadness—that sense that The Sol Majestic is so utterly doomed that what harm can it do to take a risk like Kenna?

Kenna recognizes what he must do.

To save The Sol Majestic, he must learn its trade.

Scrimshaw releases her grip upon his finger, her hands floating away from his like two ships drifting away from a docking bay. Her grip settles into a position halfway between a welcoming embrace and a what-can-you-do shrug, as if asking: *Are you sure you want to do this?*

"No," Kenna says. "The kitchen's spent. We'll discuss the challenges with the staff come the morning."

"Very well, Master Kenna."

14

Five Weeks Until the Wisdom Ceremony

Kenna's spent most of his days curled up in rusted crevices, clutching his possessions against his chest, seeking out hiding spaces from bullies.

Yet now, as his fingers hover over the sapphire keypad to his parents' hotel room, Kenna realizes poverty lent him freedom. Nobody in charge cared where he was, and his parents couldn't afford implant-trackers, so Kenna could disappear so long as he found a space to squeeze into.

When he types in his hotel passcode, a signal will alert his parents to Kenna's return. There is no sneaking, not at this pay level.

Kenna tugs experimentally on the engraved titanium bars, seeing if he might somehow bypass them; a security camera stirs, its red eye flaring into a hooded wakefulness. It's security theater, of course—there are much better cameras inset where no one could disable them. This camera's the guard-AI's way of telling Kenna *Don't think I didn't see that.*

Kenna's hopes of escaping an argument die. Mother and Father will not be pleased to hear that instead of meditating in the room as they intended, Kenna will return tomorrow morning to lead The Sol Majestic's kitchen.

He maps out the arguments in his head. But this will come down to screaming.

He's not good at screaming.

Before he can ponder retreating, Kenna punches in his code. His best bet is to surprise Mother and Father, so he'll storm in to inform them that he will *not* stay here.

The corridor's just long enough to make him regret not fighting more with Scrimshaw. She'd insisted Kenna sleep with his parents tonight, saying his arrival would rouse the kitchen, cause them to pester him with questions about Paulius. If Kenna won't make his decision tonight, Scrimshaw told him, give them all the rest they can gather. They'll need it.

He pulls down on the doorlatch, and is tugged off balance as it pulls inward. He feels Father's Inevitable strength yanking Kenna into the room.

Father has stepped inward as he opened the hotel room's door, almost hiding behind it like a bellhop, giving Kenna space to enter. Father's stern face is wreathed in a secretive grin, beaming approval; his uncharacteristic jocularity makes Kenna want to run.

Mother sits cross-legged on her bed, frowning at the smartpaper—then looks up with such delight that Kenna glances over his shoulder to see who's standing behind him.

"Come in, O Prince." She places a kind emphasis on those last two words. "You'll need respite before your sojourn in the morning."

It's stupid, standing in the hallway, but Kenna feels stronger out here. Arguing from inside their territory would mean conceding some crucial ground before the argument starts. And they can't yell at him out here unless they want to wake the neighbors.

"There will be no sojourn. In the morning, I will return to The Sol Majestic." Kenna wonders if they hear the quaver in his voice. "I shall study there, not here."

"Of course."

"No matter what you believe, I shall—wait, pardon?"

Mother's forfeited the argument so thoroughly, she doesn't even look up from checking email. "We possess no debate, My Prince. That woman explained your position to us."

"How lucky we were," Father says, "to find a follower of the Inevitable Philosophies working at The Sol Majestic!"

Mother spreads the smartpaper primly across her lap. "We understand, O Prince. Seeing the slaving kitchen laborers fills your heart with sympathy for the starving millions."

"We shielded you too much from them," Father says. "It's true, the trades will taint a Philosophy, but we coddled you. Their suffering is the lens through which your Inevitable Philosophy focused itself."

Except Kenna's attention has been caught on one word: *slaving*. The Majestic's kitchen isn't *slavery*. *Benzo* is in slavery. The kitchen is the *escape*.

Kenna charges into the room like a cop making a bust. "That's not—"

Mother and Father look up, and their sharp gazes are like the security camera whirring: a warning, presaging dire consequences.

"—not kind of you, to think of those wretched souls so cruelly," Kenna concludes. "They are misguided, and we must have mercy in all things to lead them properly."

Father's face clenches in that old scowl Kenna's used to—then he shakes his head, beads rattling, a beatific surrender-grin hidden beneath his hair.

"Oh, Mother." He extends his hand to hers. "You see? Do you see?"

She stretches out across the bed toward Father, practically purring. Her body flows as she grips his fingers, as though they are magnets completing a circuit. "An Inevitable Philosophy. It bears no argument."

"You no longer fear us, Kenna." Father crooks his free hand toward Kenna's, inviting him; Mother sways toward him like a radio antenna swiveling to face a new signal. "*That* is what makes you a prince."

When he takes their hands, he can feel the strength in Father's arms, can feel the sinewy vigor in Mother's limbs, and wonders what they feel in him. They squeeze their eyes shut in bliss—but their chins lift up as if to better ignore the world beneath them, so confident in Kenna's shared bliss that they never note his disbelieving squint.

You would have taken no pride in my disagreement if I'd told you of manual labor's beauty, Kenna thinks. *Yet Rèpondelle can control you like a videogame character, simply by feeding you justifications that reinforce your beliefs.*

Is that Inevitability? Or blindness?

Though the comfort-crèches knead his shoulders with hypnotizing movements designed to induce rest, Kenna's sleep is splintered with nightmares. Whenever he drifts off, he imagines the Majestic's gleaming countertops—every knife in its storage block, every scrubbed pot put away, every stasis cube stacked into its recharge-slots.

But no one else stands with him.

They have left him to cook the meal alone.

The comfort-crèche plays comforting susurrations, floods his chamber with warmth. All the technological lullabyes cannot get him to sleep for more than half an hour before nightmares tug up out.

It's time to go to The Sol Majestic.

The bed's fuzzy surface has hardened to a pebbled vinyl as his appointment draws near, so it is no effort to leave it. Yet the only noises in here are the ones he makes—no Father's gentle snoring, no hushed carpet-rubs as Mother does her morning stretches.

He dreamed of being alone, and he woke alone.

But he expected that, at least; Mother and Father couldn't stop babbling about all their new appointments, the Majestic's clients asking them how the Inevitable Philosophies might help them appreciate their meal better.

Kenna realizes he stands alone because he is terrified he'll go to The Sol Majestic to find that Scrimshaw has abandoned him.

Then he thinks: *Benzo will help me.*

That gives him the strength to get dressed.

Yet as he pads through Savor Station's cold hallways, now brightened to their midmorning cycle, his stomach cramps from remembered hunger. He remembers willing himself to confront the bullies who stole his nutricrackers. Knowing he might get beaten. Knowing he *would* get beaten.

Scrimshaw put him in charge of the kitchen. But as he plods past the food market, he scrutinizes the black-hooded customers who hang their faces over bowls of edible smoke, tries to track the butcher's cleaver as she debones a once-extinct dinosaur resurrected through genetic reconstruction.

He despairs as he realizes half the stalls don't list prices.

If it's down to haggling, how could Kenna run The Sol Majestic on his own?

Mother and Father had never told him a trade could be as complex as a Philosophy. They made it sound like animals could do it, had *called* the common man animals, snidely shrugged aside mercantile skill.

If Scrimshaw is vindictive, then Kenna is doomed.

Why had he spoken so sternly to her? Why had he contradicted her? Why had he risked alienating her?

Are the Inevitable Philosophies flashes of madness?

And when he makes his way to The Sol Majestic's chipped obsidian entrance, Scrimshaw stands there, as immobile as a lamppost, drawn to her full height. All that moves are her watery gray eyes, tracking Kenna's approach like a spaceport's LADAR tracking incoming ships.

As Kenna stumbles toward her, knees weakening with relief, he realizes he should have known: Scrimshaw is like the metal beams that frame the station. She was the first thing placed here, and will crumble to wreckage before she allows it to collapse.

She may be shackled to Kenna's lunatic dream, but she'll enact it as best she can.

"They're waiting for you." She unfurls a new robe with a crisp *snap*. "I'll do the talking. You wear this."

Kenna scratches the broth-stain on his chest, scenting a puff of leftover sanitizing mist—but there's a hint of luscious chicken still clinging to his robe, Benzo's reassuring scent.

"We have enough issues with Mother and Father treating their robes as dispensable as napkins." Kenna speaks as low as a man at a funeral, contradicting her softly. "Until we have procured proper funding, I shall make do with this."

Her disappointment is so grave it registers only as a tremor-like shake. "Don't be ridiculous. One free robe to you won't break us; it's the other eleven hundred in unsold inventory that will snap our neck. If you're going to motivate the kitchen to work twenty-hour shifts, I need you looking prim as a soldier."

She drapes it across him. The new robe registers as a cool breeze tented across on Kenna's fingertips, it's so light. Whereas Kenna's robe not only has the wrinkled broth-stain across its chest, but the sanitizing mist has smeared the butterfly-bright patterns.

". . . I cannot." Kenna hands the new robe back.

She flips up her palm, refusing delivery. "We need them committed to making a meal for a prince. You need to look like a prince."

"And what, pray tell, does a prince look like? Just one of a thousand rich ogres they've already wrecked their lives to please."

Scrimshaw snorts in response, itching her upper lip as though she wants to rub off a stain.

"They've witnessed me already, Scrimshaw—stumbling into their kitchen in robes far more tattered than this. They've seen me so starved I nearly passed out from drinking soup. If they shall be inspired, they must needs take me as I am *now*."

"That's not why you're refusing the robe," she snaps. "You're refusing it because you want five final weeks where you don't have to pretend you're a prince."

Kenna holds the new robe between his fingertips like a used handkerchief, extending it toward Scrimshaw.

Scrimshaw crosses her arms, abdicating responsibility. Seeing her refusing him makes Kenna's skin clammy: how far can he push her before she abandons him?

Yet if Kenna does not resist her now, then he will never truly be in charge.

He opens his fingers; the feather-light robe expands like a rainbow jellyfish, billowing as it drifts downward, then slides like a multicolored ghost across the floor.

Scrimshaw gives the robe the feigned indifference of a cat watching a mouse scurry away. Her crossed arms tense inside her woolen robe, her neck twitching as she tries to suppress her distress.

Kenna takes a single, experimental step toward the back entrance.

And Scrimshaw breaks. She bends down to scoop it up in her arms like an abandoned child, shaking the dust off before refolding it into a resalable commodity. She's so humiliated she can't even look at Kenna, hunching over the robe to inspect it for nonexistent flaws.

"You and Paulius," she mutters darkly.

"I know what you do for this place."

Scrimshaw's whole body contorts, pulling inward, holding the robe before her like a shield. Her eyes dart back and forth, untrusting.

It would be unkind to speak. Scrimshaw is like a spaceship probe specialized to function in harsh vacuums, so adapted to punishment that a compliment might destroy her. But Kenna breathes in through his nostrils, Mother's meditative technique, and when he breathes out Scrimshaw breathes with him.

He holds her gaze, unflinching: *You care so much for this place that you act without ego. You have the courage to cut out whatever threatens The Sol Majestic, no matter what the cost to you or anything else. You let everyone else believe this restaurant is invulnerable, while you alone stack bills behind that lonely red door and stare at the slim margin of error that stands between next month's service and financial ruin.*

You alone looked at 100 percent truth, until you entrusted that to me.

She crooks her fingers into claws, ready to scratch his eyes out should he try to express this. To speak that aloud would make her seem like a wretched thing, whereas what makes Scrimshaw untouchable is that she has abandoned all pride.

But Kenna's silent acknowledgment is far more than Paulius could ever do.

Scrimshaw growls. "Is that all?"

Kenna reaches out to smooth the robe she clutches, erasing the rumpled furrows she left when she pressed it to her chest.

She rips it in half, a tattered remnant curling longingly around Kenna's wrist before sliding downward to fall in a heap upon the metal floor.

Kenna is too shocked to protect what's left of the robe. But as the fabric drifts away from between them, she pulls herself to her full height and gifts Kenna with one crooked, bitter smile.

"Let's do business." She heads for the kitchen.

Kenna lopes behind her, having to jog to keep up with her long-legged stride. She straight-arms her way through the door, revealing The Sol Majestic's employees standing at their stations—the front-of-house staff clustered at the entryway, boot heels touching, each chef waiting before their empty cutting counter. Some tremble with exhaustion.

Such a waste, Kenna thinks. They could have been creating things. Instead, they've killed time, literally killed it with boredom, waiting for Scrimshaw to arrive.

Kenna looks around, cataloguing familiar faces: only Montgomery is absent. But then again, as she's so fond of reminding everyone, she's not an employee. Benzo catches Kenna's eye, kips up cheerily. The chefs surrounding him press their palms against their serving stations, as if trying to smother Benzo's enthusiasm.

Scrimshaw clears her throat.

When Paulius addressed the kitchen, the staff turned to face him with a rock-concert excitement—slack-limbed but ready to explode into action. Even when Paulius said nothing, they bounced from toe to toe, chopping vegetables to drain off nervous energy, looking up recipes on the embedded monitors, dipping tasting spoons into sauces.

This? The kitchen now resonates to a more martial tune; the stations are polished to a gleaming readiness, empty of ingredients, not a chef in here willing to put anything out for consumption without Scrimshaw's say-so. They stand with their palms pressed flat against the counters, their knives lined up in perfect parallel, faces carefully neutral. Like dolls, waiting to be switched on.

Yet they give each other quick little elbow-jabs, jerking their chins toward Kenna as if to ask *Why is he here?* then glancing back toward Benzo with raised eyebrows. Benzo wipes down his station, studying his reflection.

He'd thought once he became a true Inevitable Philosopher, people would talk to him instead of about him. Now he finds there's no escaping that fate.

Kenna hates it.

Scrimshaw walks past them without acknowledgment, taking her position at the red door. They turn to face her as she passes, like solar mirrors tracking the sun, visibly relieved when she walks by without comment.

It takes a moment for Kenna to realize she expects him to follow her.

Of course Scrimshaw stops at the red door, snapping on one heel, whirling to face them. She taps her boot heel, indicating where Kenna should stand, but not how; he clasps his hands behind his back, decides that's too military, but his hands feel dangly when he lets them drop by his sides, and when he clasps his hands over his belly he's holding hands with himself. By the time he puts his hands on his hips he looks like some weird superhero cartoon, but the kitchen is already chuckling good-naturedly.

"*Really,*" Scrimshaw says, that word so cold it condenses into chill fog. The staff's nascent laughter, on the other hand, condenses into sweaty prickles, their smiles replaced with tight-lipped moues of regret.

Kenna preferred the laughter. It wasn't mean. He remembers the cleaning up after that first night's service, where the insults felt as warm as hugs, everyone fondly poking fun at each other's shitty alcohol tolerance or their huge nose or their regrettable tattoos, and when they mocked you that meant they knew who you were.

"Morning," she says.

"*Morning!*" They bellow it as one.

"About last night's service:"

It is remarkably difficult, Kenna thinks, to pause a real-life sentence with an audible colon, but somehow Scrimshaw bends grammar to her will.

"Paulius would have been proud."

Some break formation to stifle incredulous grins with cupped palms. Far in the back, Kenna can make out a series of low-fives.

"We didn't lose ground," Scrimshaw clarifies. "But we didn't gain any, either. In most cases, if we are not on an upward trajectory, we are descending into the low-class hell that is Belle du Balle. Still, given the . . . shock Paulius's injury inflicted upon you, I feel he would have broken out a round of champagne.

"Instead, I shall break out a round of promotions."

Two chefs, junior black-stripers, burst out into an embarrassingly isolated applause, which almost dies out until Scrimshaw inclines her head. Then everyone applauds, and does not stop until she flicks her fingers.

"Keffen did an excellent job last night, stepping into Paulius's shoes to run the kitchen." Scrimshaw adjusts her glasses, focusing the kitchen's attention onto a large-breasted woman with short-cropped hair and a chef's jacket bound so tightly that Kenna wonders how she can breathe. "He's done so before, but never under such trying circumstances. As such, he will serve as head chef until Paulius returns."

Kenna wonders why Keffen is a "he" until he realizes Keffen must be transitioning genders. The crowd applauds this time, a ragged joy that demonstrates how artificial the last applause was.

Scrimshaw announces a few more temporary promotions to handle Paulius's duties—someone must monitor the booth to determine which of tonight's supplicants is worthy of a free meal, another must talk with the orchard gardeners to reconstruct Paulius's plans for the next three weeks' plantings, still another must comb through old menus to select tried-and-true dishes to replace the on-the-fly amuse-bouches that Paulius created nightly to fill the gap between courses #8 and #9.

Scrimshaw's words carry the low hum of a damaged ship dropping into hibernation mode: life support and vital functions only. The chefs fidget, restacking their spice jars, an unconscious rebellion against Scrimshaw's order. They did not come to The Sol Majestic to re-create old recipes, like some bar band churning out the last decade's hits: they came to ride cuisine's cutting edge.

Kenna, too, simmers with fury until he realizes what Scrimshaw is doing:

"And now, let us discuss Prince Kenna's Wisdom Ceremony."

The chefs close their eyes as they scent a fresh challenge.

Montgomery saunters in through the side door, puffing a cigarillo, fingers curled around her cask. She prowls in catlike, stretching out her long legs on the black-velveted sink, spitting on one thumb before squeegeeing mold off her goggle-lenses. She crooks her neck, her thin lips curled up in a *this oughtta be good* expression.

"There has been scuttlebutt that I planned to cancel the Ceremony," Scrimshaw says. "Scurrilous lies. Yet without Paulius, the question remains: who of you can head up a meal worthy of The

Sol Majestic's name—a meal that does not compromise our vision, nor betray the Inevitable Philosophies' gloried history.

"Therefore, in three days, on The Sol Majestic's nominal rest day, each chef at yellow-stripe rank or above will present a sample Wisdom Ceremony meal to Prince Kenna. Prince Kenna will then judge which dishes are worthy enough to make their creator his Wisdom Ceremony's steward."

Kenna flinches: *I will?* He tugs Scrimshaw's fingers like a small child begging his parent for help.

Scrimshaw is impassive as a gargoyle. She takes his hand in hers, tightening her grip as if reluctant to leave him so alone. But she does not return his imploring gaze, staring at the kitchen staff as though the chefs are a lifeless desert they will die crossing.

Of course she believes this is a hopeless task, Kenna realizes: Scrimshaw was so convinced there was no one to lead the Wisdom Ceremony that she'd planned to euthanize the Majestic. She has set Kenna up for his best chances of success, but had she ideas herself she would have enacted them.

If someone *is* hidden in this kitchen who can make the Wisdom Ceremony happen, it's up to Kenna to find them.

The chefs look at Kenna with astonishment, as though Scrimshaw had informed them Kenna would be cooking the meal himself. Then they twist around to extract an answer from Benzo, the lone person in the kitchen who's actually fed Kenna, as if to confirm Kenna's palate was more than a desolate wasteland worn to pockmarked ruin by Frosted Chocobombs.

By way of answer, Benzo tugs his shaggy curls over his eyes.

Montgomery's barking laugh breaks the silence. "*Oh* yeah," she purrs, clutching the cask to her chest like a popcorn tub. "This is gonna be *such* a clusterfuck."

15

Four Weeks and Four Days Until the Wisdom Ceremony

In all the years Kenna had starved, he had never once dreamed he would come to dread a meal.

Yet over the last three days, a funereal tone has stolen over The Sol Majestic. The impending Wisdom Tasting—a name everyone has somehow settled upon—has riven the kitchen, separated it from one unified organism into competing factions. Not that there haven't always been jealousies simmering under The Sol Majestic, Kenna realizes, but those struggles had clear victors. Either you lived up to Paulius's exacting standards, or you were wrong.

Kenna's judgment carries no such confidence. He can tell by the way each chef tugs him aside for hushed conversations; they do not look panicked, as he'd expected, but instead have the look of learned professors about to help their student pass a test.

They all start the same way: "We cannot view this meal through the mere lens of food," they explain. They are kind enough to not say *they* could describe the Wisdom Ceremony in food, but Kenna wouldn't know a flank steak from a pork chop. "No, we must transcend the ingredients, make this dinner about re-creating your experience. *Something* in The Sol Majestic's cuisine lifted you up high enough to reach your Inevitable Philosophy."

Had Kenna thought he would spend these five weeks at The Sol Majestic being honest?

He swallows back laughs until they turn to molten steel bubbling in his stomach.

They always lean in close then: all the chefs, fat and lean, Gineer or Intraconnected, yellow-stripers or red-stripers. And if any had that merchant's odiferous air of advantage-seeking, then Kenna would have sent them packing.

But no; they treat Kenna like he holds The Sol Majestic's greatest treasure. Trembling smiles dance on their lips, shy in the presence of greatness. And then they ask the same question, every time, in the same damned way:

"What did you learn here?" They always lick their lips then, almost touching foreheads as they try to divine Kenna's secret. "What *is* your Inevitable Philosophy?"

They seek it as though it will save them: just like the bhelpuri merchant, just like the emails rolling into Father's account, just like the starving millions who looked to Mother and still went home with empty bellies.

These chefs have greater dreams than he ever had.

"It'll help them if you tell them, Kenna," Benzo had urged him, one late night when they slumped down against a dormitory wall, his left knee touching Kenna's right knee. "A good meal isn't just a bunch of dishes—it's a *story*. Anyone here can put together a plate that'd make Her mouth water. What they need to do is bring the diner through your journey: start with your humbled starvation, then culminate in a flurry of tastes that *confirms* your Philosophy, *celebrates* it."

Kenna doesn't know how a meal could accomplish that. But Benzo believes it can, and so do the other chefs: they cluster around Benzo, interrogating him as to every speck that Kenna's eaten since he arrived. Now no one criticizes Benzo's too-fatty chicken stock; instead, they dip spoons in, debate how this fattiness might have affected a starving young boy. They usher bowls of Benzo's broth out to the orchard like servants carrying a king on a palanquin, reenacting Kenna's enlightment.

(But they do not go into the Escargone, though its industrial transport-space remains empty. They shiver at the thought. That's where Paulius almost died, they say. Even though Scrimshaw displays diagnostics from local repairmen showing nothing is wrong with the Escargone, they treat it like it's the beast that cursed this kitchen.)

"You should tell them, Kenna." Benzo reaches over to slide his blistered fingers between Kenna's. A day ago, that tender touch would have shorted out Kenna's thoughts; now Benzo's touch makes his skin crawl, because Benzo's beautiful skin is pressed against Kenna's foul filthy liar fingers, and God, how could he kiss Benzo when his very soul is as fake as a VR game?

That vomitous revulsion saves him as each chef bends forward as if they can pluck the secret from Kenna's brow by mere proximity. Kenna turns from them, lest his stinking breath pollute these earnest men and women.

He'd understood he'd have to guide them one day.

He'd never realized they would impress him.

Yet it is he who must impress them. If they realize he has no Philosophy, they will realize he has no story, they will be unable to cook. He doesn't understand how they form a narrative from food, but he knows *they* need it. They need this *place*. They're so dedicated, so creative, and Kenna doesn't know what would happen to them without The Sol Majestic to shelter and encourage their instincts. When Scrimshaw spits the words of their competitor, "Belle du Balle," Kenna envisions a cringing restaurant that crawls on its knees to its customers.

Unless he can provide them with the proper inspiration, the Wisdom Ceremony is doomed, and The Sol Majestic is doomed, and Savor Station is doomed, and how does Scrimshaw ever live with this apocalypse held inches above her head?

Mother and Father made employment seem trivial, but no wonder you cannot hold both a Philosophy and a trade. A trade clutters the brain; solving the puzzle of creation occupies so many CPU cycles that there's no room left for lofty ambitions, only the hard-scrabble search for survival.

He looks to the red door for answers, but Scrimshaw has holed herself up, having placed The Sol Majestic's fate upon Kenna's impoverished tastebuds.

"I've *told* you I cannot discuss my Philosophy." Kenna always raises his voice now, so the others in the kitchen will hear, and maybe they will stop trying to pry this nonexistent secret from him. "It's customary to reveal the Philosophy only at the Ceremony."

This is not strictly true, and everyone knows it. Montgomery is right; the Inevitable Philosophies still have youth's pliable traditions, and some Philosophers have blabbed their ideas. Kenna wishes someone would slam him up against the wall to growl, "You could tell us!"

But no; they *respect* him. Like the Philosopher he is not.

And always Montgomery lurks nearby, thrusting her tasting spoon into dishes, shaking her head and chuckling. The chefs bristle, calling Scrimshaw over to ward her away, but Montgomery doesn't work here and without Paulius, no one can control her.

Yet Kenna stares at her, she licks her long-handled spoon and giggles, those insectile black goggles dark and mocking.

Kenna's surprised to find himself grateful at her amusement; one less person to lie to.

Though whenever he goes to talk to her, she's never around. Which isn't a surprise; she doesn't work here. But he could surely use somebody to brainstorm what his Inevitable Philosophy *might* be.

All the comfort-crèche's electronic balms cannot lull Kenna into sleep. He keeps juggling potential Inevitable Philosophies, grabbing them and then tossing them into the air: "to feed the starving"? No, that's Mother's philosophy. "Teach the lost to make art"? He'd die if he had to peddle that crassness when all he can make is shoddy lies. "To devote oneself to perfection"? That feels like a winner, but then he can't devise a good answer for when someone asks him to define perfection.

He wants to yell at Montgomery: Inevitable Philosophies aren't a catchphrase. They're *fractal*, a never-ending spiral of decisions unspooling off one simple thought so meaningful it guides all his future steps.

His proposed Inevitable Philosophies are vapid corporate slogans.

He longs to give the chefs an Inevitable Philosophy to guide them, but whatever he tells them is a lie he'll be lashed to all his life. Yet without it, the kitchen cannot judge. If they at least knew what his Philosophy was, then it would take the place of Paulius's stern judgment; they might disagree on a given dish's quality, but they would at least share the same goal. Now, Kenna hears the chefs bickering, arguing what they believe a boy like Kenna might like, how could they possibly think that gearlike display of fiddlehead ferns represents the Prince's Philosophy?

Kenna fears he will pick the worst dish. If he chooses something the kitchen deems unworthy, then the chefs will not respect him, and The Sol Majestic will tear itself apart in drama. Yet if he asks for assistance, then he will be seen to be choosing favorites, and The Sol Majestic will tear itself apart in drama.

Scrimshaw is right: without Paulius, The Sol Majestic cannot survive.

So the jealousies boil over when the Wisdom Tasting arrives. Kenna's whole body shrinks with embarrassment every time the chefs approach the long, linen-draped dining table.

Scrimshaw has arranged for the tasting to take place in The Sol Majestic's bar, which—Kenna is told—is not so much a bar as a staging area, an introductory space where new guests can acclimatize themselves to The Sol Majestic's ethos.

Had this been Kenna's introduction to The Sol Majestic, he would have fled screaming.

The dining room is an auditorium, a space so vast that each step into its emptiness lets you feel yourself shrinking into insignificance. Curtains sweep shut the moment you enter, engulfing you in a velvety black; AI lights set high up in the ceiling track your progress, casting a maddeningly dim ghost-light upon you that allows you to see a footfall ahead, fluttering murky shadows upon a black carpet—but the moment you look up to see where the light comes from, it disappears before you can get your eyes on it, leaving you stranded in darkness. Audio-suppressing walls sop up the echoes, let your voice call out once before being silenced forever.

You float through emptiness, a small asteroid, becoming smaller.

Then, as your eyes adjust, you take in the arc of the bar, a window as big as a movie screen, a prickling of starlight as you realize you are looking out into empty space. Fitted beneath is a slender strip of polished onyx countertop, dim as dawn, where a lone bartender services your needs.

Benzo has told him the isolation is the experience. The Sol Majestic is a state of mind based on the immensity of space, both in volume and time—the transience of all things heightens appreciation, and you are meant to feel small. The chairs you sit on are dismantled after you rise, the glasses you drink from smashed. Everything crumbles.

Destruction brings Kenna no pleasure. Instead, Kenna clings to the sight of that bar, the colored rows of bottles that speak of work and creation. He longs for the kitchen's crowded comfort, but Scrimshaw insisted a kitchen tasting was not fit for a prince.

So he sits at the table as the chefs approach with clasped hands— a trio of waiters carrying elaborate meals. The dishes are deposited upon his table with the curtness of bombs dropping, each course a pointed rebuttal of someone else's best efforts.

Whatever he chooses today will save or damn The Sol Majestic.

Kenna's inexperience betrays him the moment he picks up the fine-boned chopsticks.

The long sticks squirm between his fingers, duck breast chunks slithering out from between the rounded tips to spatter back on the plate. Why did they give him chopsticks? Everything he's eaten has been unpeeled from crinkling plastic wrappers, crammed into his mouth with bare hands. The chopsticks amplify Kenna's weakness, taking something he's done all his life and transforming it into an alien experience.

The courses come, clad in sauces dark as night, sprinkled with flecks of glimmering gold, served in woven fibrous vegetable bowls. The chefs announce the ingredients with the pride of a butler announcing debutantes to a ball, but the words are meaningless— citronic effusions, ambar-salted garum, turpenol, red-shifted iron flakes. Kenna strains to hear each syllable, as though they are magic incantations that will unlock the dishes' beauty, but they slur into a glossolalia.

"As you can see, this peacock-egg dish is rusted," a yellow-striper says, presenting a single blackened egg on a red porcelain plate.

"Rusted?" Kenna's curled up to sleep on many rusted floors, but had never thought to eat the flakes. "How do you rust an egg?"

"Rustic," the chef snaps, squeezing her hands as though she wishes she were strangling Kenna.

"Oh." Kenna looks down at the mottled egg. "I don't suppose there's a cooking technique where you rust something . . ."

"No."

This boiled egg tastes like a burnt match. Is that how it's supposed to taste? Kenna can't imagine the chefs presenting him with a dish that's anything other than they intended, but he heard someone cursing from the kitchen as the deadline approached; maybe the burnt match taste is a mistake, and choosing this dish will tell the other chefs their best efforts won't matter. Or maybe it's the height of cuisine, they've eaten so many peacock eggs that an egg that tastes like a burnt match is a glorious change of pace, and Kenna should choose this sooty egg to demonstrate his worldliness.

Kenna wishes for more burnt-match dishes. If all the dishes were awful, then he'd feel good about choosing at random. Yet the truth is, the instant he manages to negotiate each bite up to his tongue with these clumsy chopsticks, time freezes.

The dishes, they *are* stories.

He takes a bite of a duck stew, and at first it's a light cinnamon dusting, then the rich duck taste, then a light blossoming of flowers across his palate like an orchard blooming. Is this bowl too simple?

Some dishes are engineering feats that seem cold: glistening artificial grapes that dissolve into salt-sprays of foam when they warm on Kenna's tongue, crackling into a fizzy heat when he inhales. Others grow in complexity with each course, beginning with a bowl of clear broth as the chefs slide an ingredient into the tureen between Kenna's sips until the bowl brims over with a spicy meat stew.

Still others seem needlessly flashy; two waiters haul in a flower pot of periwinkle orchids, then pluck the blossoms from green stalks to assemble a salad, the "dirt" at the bottom of the pot a peppery seasoning. The petals evaporate on his tongue, empty perfume puffs.

Yet when the inevitable lacquered duck appears, it seems leaden in the wake of that salad's flower-play. It's just a *duck*, and yet that oily mouthful is so rich and crackling with fat that it's almost a gamey assault after the delicate blossoms . . .

Which dish is worthy of The Sol Majestic?

He cannot dare to *enjoy* them. He rolls the sauces over his tongue, *judging* them. Will this culinary story keep these ever-imaginative chefs employed? And all the while, he remembers:

He's the ignoramus who asked about a rusted egg.

The words bounce around in his skull, becoming louder and dumber with each iteration: *How do you rust an egg how do you rust an egg how do you rust an egg*

All those years starving, and he never imagined a time he'd want to *stop* eating. Yet each course is a mystery to Kenna; he has never eaten glass noodles, let alone decided whether these are the universe's *finest* glass noodles.

The chefs scrutinize his every bite, Kenna's every hesitation transformed into free-floating terror. *They* know when he should be closing his eyes in bliss: when Kenna does not match their scripted reactions, their hands tremble.

How do you rust an egg? They knew they were doomed then.

And just when Kenna is about to vomit on this fine white cloth, Scrimshaw grants mercy.

"That's the last dish," she tells him. "Have you made a decision?"

It is not so much a question as a command: *Guess quickly, and choose this killing meal.*

Kenna lifts his head to Scrimshaw, begging her for assistance— *tell me what to do*—but she steeples her long fingers before parting them apologetically: *I told you I could not help.*

Kenna is not a Philosopher. Nor is he a merchant.

He is nothing.

The chefs stand in the soft darkness, the tracking lights above reducing them to ghostly blurs. They pretend not to listen, but their faces are masks of suppressed horror. Scrimshaw snaps around, interposing her grand matron's body between them and Kenna.

"So the boy needs more time." She makes shooing motions. "Give him time."

They walk into the bar's darkness, fading away, swallowed up by the stygian gloom. Within moments, only Scrimshaw stands by this long table, which seems to float like the sole thing in the universe, the stars mockingly distant.

She turns to leave. Kenna realizes with horror that she expects him to make his decision *here*. In this silent void. And why not? The chefs are toking up in the kitchen already, commiserating . . .

"*Wait!*" he cries.

Scrimshaw is nothing more than a gray, distant smear—but she stops. Kenna tries to sound bold.

"May I kindly make my decision in the kitchen?"

The embarrassed rustle of feet on carpet. Kenna realizes the chefs have heard him; the bar's track lighting had hidden them from view, but not from earshot.

Scrimshaw lifts two fingers, an administrator's signal for the AI, and the overhead lights flare to a cold fluorescent. The darkness vanishes, revealing thirteen chefs facing Kenna, squinting in his direction, hungry for gossip—then, their machinations revealed, they straighten, rebuttoning their chef's jackets to regain their dignity.

"My apologies, Kenna," she says. "Perhaps more illumination will help ease this decision . . ."

"No, no." Giving enough light to see the scaffolding overhead, the empty black carpet below, is somehow worse. It's like being backstage during a play after a performance, a dead space Kenna does not know how to bring to life. "I can't. Not here. The kitchen is . . ."

Kenna wants to say *The kitchen is my home.* But a true Philosopher wouldn't destroy his home with guesswork. A man of real strength would shut down the Majestic at the peak of its power, like Scrimshaw would, but no—Kenna is a child too in love with his pet to accept euthanasia as the kindest choice.

"This must happen in the kitchen."

"Kenna." Scrimshaw pads her words in velvet. "We can't leave the chefs in the kitchen with you. Not now." *They might tear you to shreds.* "And it's heaped with dirty dishes . . ."

"I'll do the dishes."

He feels better, saying that. He is nothing. Manual labor is what a nothing should do.

"*Kenna.*" Her hands crook into claws. "You can't clear out the back room just to—"

"The kitchen is where I started." Kenna rises to his feet. His stomach has a sick water balloon weight, threatening to burst. "It's where I'll end this."

"You can't—"

He waddles past the thirteen chefs, who have frozen in place like bowling pins, so Kenna must walk through them. The heavy black curtains that separate kitchen from staging area lift as he approaches, sensors guiding him through the deep night to The Sol Majestic's kitchen.

Kenna's never seen the Majestic after a bad service, but the subtle changes are in place: there are no popped champagne bottles spattering fizzy toasts into crystal flutes, just shots of cheap arrack swallowed hastily as painkillers. Elbows are kept close to their sides as the chefs scrub down their stations like men strangling lovers. The laughs are sporadic as gunfire, bitter as black coffee.

Then they see Kenna, and even that loose camaraderie decays.

All sound stops, except for the soapy water pouring into the pot-filled sinks. Their hands each stroke their own personal injuries: massaging the aching biceps from stirring stew for an hour, injecting anti-radiation medications to prevent side effects from the stasis cubes, rubbing ice over the steamed fingers that boiled a hundred eggs to make the perfect one for Kenna.

They sacrificed their bodies to give him perfection.

They know he did not comprehend the gift.

They each take tentative steps toward Kenna then flinch back when no one steps with them, no one quite ready to rip the skin off this illusion. No one has yet dared to say Kenna is a fraud, not out loud.

No one can yet acknowledge this Wisdom Meal is a failure. Yet the illusion of success is so delicate a scornful cough might destroy it—

Before someone can be so foolish, Kenna taps a dishwasher's back. Her waist-deep sink is stacked high with filthy pots.

"May I . . . ?"

She makes confused scrubbing gestures in the air, unsure what he desires. Kenna removes the brass scouring pad from her fingers.

"I need to do something," he explains. "Something useful."

The dishwasher mutters protests, but falls silent when Scrimshaw's gaunt shadow falls over her.

Kenna turns his back on the kitchen to thrust himself shoulder-deep into the steaming water, welcoming the pain shooting up his forearms. It distracts from the half-digested food sloshing at the back of his throat; when he breathes in, he feels his stomach fighting his lungs for room. Who knew being full could be worse than starving?

He feels like vomiting, but—

How do you rust an egg?

The kitchen's attention is hot on his back. Throwing up their work in front of them would be worse than the sickness.

He grips the scouring pad tight enough to hurt, picks up a saucepan.

He will cleanse the kitchen and destroy himself.

How do you rust an egg?

The burnt-match egg or the clear broth that evolved into a stew? The evanescent grape-salt chemical cuisine, or the duck's simplicity? Does he choose the simple meal his ignorant palate liked, or does he choose the flashy meal that impressed his ignorant sensibilities?

How do you rust an egg?

He bears down, shaking caustic soda onto the pans' steel surface before scrubbing them clean, his fingers numb from the near-boiling sink. He smells reminders on every pan: the garden-fresh scent of the stew still clinging to the tureen, the thick dark lacquer glazing the saucepan . . .

How do you rust an egg?

His robe is a ruin—slopped with dishwater suds, smeared with grease. He does not look up as the chefs approach him, one by one, to deposit their pans apologetically into his sink.

He will never bring enlightenment to anyone. He will never

inspire anyone. He will scrub dishes until his fingers are raw, turning soiled dishes white again, and he is surprised to find there is a deep satisfaction in scourging both himself and these pans.

It's not his fault he can't judge. Who could do this but Paulius?

How do you—

A familiar hand rubs his back. Benzo. Kenna closes his eyes, lest seeing his friend rob his strength.

"Don't," Kenna whispers. "Please."

Benzo steps toward him, and for a moment Kenna feels Benzo's hands sliding around his belly, drawing him backwards against Benzo's lean body. But it's just a fantasy. He needs to scrub pans until his Princely veneer falls away, until he becomes another manual worker, becomes nothing . . .

Instead, Benzo squeezes his shoulder and pads off.

A layer of pans later, Kenna realizes: he hears no other noises. The clatter of women recalibrating the gravitizer has ceased. No shots are being poured. No cook is frying up a quick post-service meal.

Kenna's fingertips are sodden, wrinkled, shredded by the scourer. He is, for the first time, nothing more than a body; his thoughts have been scrubbed away like the grime on the pans.

No. No, that's not what's happened at all. That's what he wants to happen. The truth is, immersing his hands in caustic water has not transformed him; his thoughts still dance through his head, even as his body places the pans into the autoclave. Dishwashing does not transform him into the brute he longs to be, leaving him to find inspiration somewhere before morning, and—

The hollow *thump* of wood against steel. A cask, slammed onto the sink.

"You need to look after this for me."

Montgomery affects casualness, balling one fist into her bony hip, but she leans on the cask a little too heavily, masking her body's sway. Kenna can't make out her eyes through her goggles' smoked-glass lenses, but he'd bet dimes to dinari that her pupils are blown wide on some drug.

"Watching your possessions is not my task," Kenna snaps.

"It's not mine, either. *I* don't work here." She tosses the words around him like smoke rings, taunting him. She's no longer in her mold-stained chef's outfit—instead, she's dressed to party in a bright red, faux-leather skinsuit, with so many buckles across her ribs it hurts Kenna's fingers to think of her squeezing herself into that thing. "I need a guard for my party. My usual suspects are too traumatized—you're the only one left standing."

She shoves the cask against his chest and stumbles for the exit, leaving Kenna to grab for the Bitch before she hits the floor. He feels the loose slosh inside the cask, hears a soft *meep* of complaint.

"I have dishes to wash." *And a decision to make.*

She teeters back on too-high heels, her ankles flexing as she swaggers toward him. She snatches the cask away, almost toppling over backwards. "If my precious gets stolen while I am dancing among the stars, I'm blaming *you*." She emphasizes the "you" by thumping the cask against his breastbone. "Do your dishes. Do your duty."

She pivots away, but Kenna has known Montgomery long enough to sense the challenge buried in her words.

"What kind of party?" he asks.

She heads for the door. "A very illegal one. Packed chock-full of drugs your parents would disapprove of. Involving carefully applied vandalism in the service of art. Or kink. They're the same at heart, really."

"I can't look after the—" He doesn't want to say "the Bitch" out loud. "I cannot vouchsafe your cask during your escapades. I wouldn't know how to feed her . . ."

She turns to fire a laugh in his direction. "I wouldn't leave her with you all night. I need someone to come with me. I don't know when I'll get vacuum-sealed—they've spent *hours* setting it up— but when it happens, I need someone to hand her to right away."

"Why do you require a party? Tonight, of all nights?"

Her utter indifference stills Kenna's tongue. She does not, as she is so quick to remind people, work here. She scratches the tip of her nose.

"To answer your *question* . . ." She pulls herself up on the counter, crossing her legs underneath her. "People find out who they really are at parties. At least the parties I attend. Unfortunately, *some* people discover they're unscrupulous bastards who steal your shit. Hence my need for your pathetic ass."

He waves at the remaining pots. "I promised Scrimshaw . . ."

"You're a good boy, Kenna." Her words form a compliment, on the surface. But the way she grimaces reminds Kenna of the dismissive look Father once gave him . . .

I love you now as I would a pet, Father had said. *But I hope one day to love you as a man.*

When she says "good boy," it carries the fondness of a woman petting a faithful hound. He *feels* the cage of being a good boy, that itching sensation that he'll do what's expected of him.

And for what? All this punishment? These dishes aren't getting him any closer to making a decision, yet he's shackled himself to this sink as though The Sol Majestic will somehow be better if he destroys himself in some sad semblance of repentance.

What does he have to lose?

"All right." As he straightens, he does not feel Inevitable. But there is a new strength in his spine; his arms are wrinkled with foul physical exertion, yet he has remained Kenna. Since he cannot erase himself, maybe he should discover who he is at parties.

Montgomery hops off the table, landing nimbly on spiked heels. She does not waver. She is not on drugs. She never was.

She tosses him the keg. "Let's get starbound."

16

Half an Hour Until the Party

Trailing behind Montgomery as she leads the way to the Illegal Drug Party, all Kenna can notice is her skinsuit's shining red curves. He's clasping the Bitch to his chest, but it's hard because the wooden cask keeps slipping against his soapy robe, grinding sauce-stains deeper into the thin fabric.

A thin worry surfaces, swells, pushes his other thoughts away: is he stylish enough to attend this party?

Kenna has never been to an Illegal Drug Party. He's watched people piss away the hours on drugs, of course, but that's never been cause for a party on the transport ships; drugs were both tedious and omnipresent, all tin-foil packets and cracked glass pipes. After you took them you laid down in filth and let the light-years slide beneath you.

The hopheads kept telling Kenna drugs were phenomenal—and they *looked* phenomenal when you saw people doing them on the holovids, where rich children snorted smart-drugs engineered to make them witty before the world came alive for them in psychedelic bursts.

But on the transport ships, drugs just made people giggle at rust stains.

The idea that one could celebrate drugs is as exciting as celebrating food. Yet if the Illegal Drug Party is like dining at The Sol

Majestic, maybe Kenna is underdressed. He can't afford to rust another egg.

Maybe he should get a new robe from Scrimshaw. Montgomery's dressed to kill, even if she can barely amble about on those high heels. Will he look stupid?

She leads him into Savor Station's utility tunnels. She teeters down hallways crowded with snakelike bundles of power cables, the oil-slicked walls crammed full of access panels and emergency release valves and industrial plugs.

She taps her forearm three times. A map evanesces across her coppery skin, a green knot of hallways flaring with dangerous red cones sweeping back and forth. She brushes the map away before shoving him against a steam pipe, fingers clamping tight over his mouth.

A bright yellow maintenance bot cruises down another corridor, a massive engine suspended from a track on the ceiling, blocking the corridor. It sways pendulously, rattling as it drags a thousand thin antennae along the walls and floors, sensors analyzing for pipe breaks, open hatchways, severed cables.

Kenna tenses to run. If it turns left in their direction, it's big enough to smear their bodies along the walls.

"Don't," Montgomery whispers, flattening him against a pipe's scalding heat. "It's shit at hearing, but its eyes are real good at picking up motion. If it gets you on camera, you're getting thrown off this station."

"*Thrown off?*" Savor Station is a way station situated between empires, nested in a solar system with no habitable planets. Stations are governed by no laws but their captains' whims, though he's heard Captain Lizzie is a reasonable woman as captains go. Would she really eject them into the vacuum?

Kenna looks down the winding corridors, tries to remember which way they'd come from. Could he find his way back to safety without Montgomery's help? "Why would—"

"This isn't like you sneaking into the loading docks, kid. Worst you could do up there would be to steal some spices. Down here in the station's guts, you could blow the whole thing up. Captain Lizzie takes that real serious."

"Why did you—"

She presses him harder against the wall, not quite shaking him, but reminding him not to move while the maintenance bot is within reach. "I *told* you this party was illegal, kid. Did you think I meant we had a couple of smokes? There's a reason you find out who you are at my kinds of parties."

"Surely you wouldn't—"

She rolls her eyes so hard her head rocks back. "No, we will not blow up the ship." She speaks mechanically, as if reciting a denial to a cop. "Okay, we might cause a *little* explosive decompression. If we're stupid. But we're not stupid, we've read up on this."

This fails to reassure Kenna.

The maintenance bot whirs, jiggling on the thick bundle of cables that tethers it to the ceiling. It reaches down with an octopoid-like series of actuators, picking up the cables strewn on the floor beneath. Then it rolls away from Kenna and Montgomery, straightening the cables as it retreats into darkness.

"I cry pardon for the misunderstanding, Ms. Montgomery," Kenna says, and for the thousandth time he hates that stiff, prissy tone in his voice. "But I agreed to watch your fungal child, here. I did not agree to have the station chief view me as a saboteur. The restaurant you work for—"

"I keep telling you, *I don't work for them.*"

Kenna lets the matter drop. "Regardless. The Sol Majestic depends on me, and I cannot afford to take risks."

Montgomery sighs and flops back against the far wall. She holds her index finger and thumb together like she is aiming an imaginary dart between Kenna's eyes, viewing him through two pinched fingertips.

"See? *That's* why nobody trusts you."

When she speaks, it's like The Sol Majestic speaks through her.

She knows all the gossip. When she tells him that, her words thump against his heart.

Kenna's soap-damp robe feels clammy at the thought of the next morning's decision. He hugs the Bitch's splintered cask, retreating behind it.

She rips it from his arms, stealing his shelter. She looks for a safe place among the cables to rest the Bitch, then, finding no place she deems adequate, decides to berate Kenna some more.

"You can't make a decision because you don't have enough experience. And you don't have enough experience because between Mommy, Daddy, and this terror of somehow betraying your sad-ass heritage, you have been terrified to do anything that could get you in trouble."

I thought about kissing boys sometimes when Mother made me meditate, Kenna thinks sullenly. Then he realizes how pathetic a rebellion that is, and slumps back against the pipes.

She slaps him.

"*See?*" she hisses, not quite daring to yell with the maintenance bot rattling around the corner. "Anyone can shut you down by thumbing your 'guilt' button. Everybody loves having you around, because you're like an appreciative ghost, always smiling, never getting in their way—but your cheerful agreeableness will *destroy* The Sol Majestic when you become their manager.

"Those kids who starved you for three days," she continues. "They beat you up, stole your nutricrackers. Betcha dimes to dinari they fucked over other kids, too. Why didn't you form a rival gang and get your fellow losers to beat the crap out of them? You acted like some poor scared *asshole*!"

Hot, embarrassed blood pours into his cheeks. "Forming gangs was illegal. We could have gotten thrown off."

Montgomery's cynical smile could slice a heart in half. "And those other kids weren't a gang?"

"They were . . ." *They were friends,* Kenna starts to say, but his lungs deflate as the realization digs into him. They *were* a gang.

He'd been such an obedient son that he wouldn't have recognized them as such unless they'd walked up and introduced themselves to say, "Hi, we're a gang."

He looks up, expecting to find Montgomery sneering at him through those cold black lenses. Instead, her mouth is set firm, like she's biting back an anger she does not want to unleash on him. She stares down the access tunnels as if she wishes she could set them aflame.

"You don't even know there's two pathways here, let alone that you're on the wrong one." Her voice is a choked whisper. "It's stupid, the rules rich kids get to play by. If I do drugs, I'm experimenting—but if *you* do them, you're an addict. If I hack into an ATM, I'm young and foolish—but if *you* do it, you're a criminal."

She leans back against an access hatch, stroking her cask like a pet. "I thought everyone got away with shit. And I didn't even know what happened to those poor bastards until I saw what happened to some friends who didn't have an auntie to bail them out."

Kenna has the uncomfortable feeling of watching a holovid, seated as the lead character reels off a soliloquy. As long as he stays quiet, she'll reveal her darkest secrets, and never notice he's there.

That's not fair to her, though.

"It's not your fault," he offers. When did Kenna feel sympathy for the rich? But knowing she's wealthy snaps Montgomery into clearer focus. She has all the hallmarks of a trust-fund kid: a flagrant disdain for money, the boredom of someone who's seen too much, too easily—

"I didn't say it was my *fault*," she hisses.

—the angry independence of someone determined to prove she needs nobody's help—

"The point is, I'm *better* for breaking rules. I've refined my methods for getting away with shit. You, Kenna, gods *damn*—they have beaten *all* the risk out of you. Someone shakes a rule at you, you piss your damn pants. You think Scrimshaw got where she did by following orders? That *Paulius* did? No, the rich are entrepreneurs because they spent their childhood getting away with shit, and now they know how to get results.

"But goddammit, they've terrified you poor shits into following rules designed to fuck you over—which, sure, maybe works if you'll never amount to anything anyway, but you? You're trying to become a *prince*. And what kind of prince can you be if all you ever do is what people expect?"

Kenna thinks how he's killing himself to help Scrimshaw, to keep Paulius safe, to keep Mother and Father occupied, and realizes how right she is. The more axes of interference he adds, the more likely he'll snap.

"But I know not what this celebration is like," Kenna says. "Risking getting kicked off the station, losing The Sol Majestic and my religion and Mother and Father for—for something I don't even comprehend . . ."

He hugs his knees, braced for Montgomery's blows. Instead, she crawls over to sit next to him, her hip against his—and unlike sitting next to Benzo, which feels soaked in tension, when she taps her knee against his playfully, he understands what it's like to have a sister.

She sighs, stares at the far wall, shaking her head as though there's some joke neither of them quite get. "You never know what any party's like."

Kenna peers at her, expecting her to continue. But after a moment she hugs her long legs against her, mirroring his quiescence.

She won't move until he does, he realizes. And if he shuffles back toward the Majestic, she will go with him, and deposit him back in the kitchen to make his decision.

Or he can be her guard. She didn't choose that word lightly. She's going someplace dangerous, and needs someone to have her back.

She wants to make *him* dangerous.

He extends his cupped hands. She deposits the cask into his grip; the Bitch burbles happily at his touch. He can feel the Bitch's weight crawling up the wooden staves, responding to something new within him.

Montgomery doesn't look back. She's bringing up the luminescent map on her forearm again, a wrinkle appearing between her eyes as she figures out the quickest route to the party, this party that Kenna knows nothing about and is feeling better about knowing nothing about.

"I'm gonna get naked," Montgomery says.

He feels a little less better, but follows, hearing the distant clatter of other maintenance bots rattling toward them.

17

Twenty Minutes Until Explosive Decompression

WASTE REPROCESSING.

The sign is almost obliterated under a garbagey smear, the edges gnawed by rust. The processing plant is squat and heavy, a large bunker jammed between an emergency power generator and an oxygen scrub-station. This patchwork architecture is not unusual in space stations: even a large outpost like Savor Station is assembled one module at a time, prefab units flown in from distant factories orbiting resource-wealthy planets.

The corroded green BIOHAZARD WARNING sticker slapped across the door, however, makes Kenna pause.

"That doesn't mean poop," Montgomery tells him. "I wouldn't party in poop."

"Oh, excellent."

"It means dead bodies."

Kenna hears a dim rhythmic thumping that might be a bass beat, might be the oxygen reprocessor reclaiming the station's air. The Bitch lurches in the cask, her weight like a dance partner flopping into his arms, and Kenna realizes he has never danced. Is it like practicing judo katas?

Mother taught him katas. Does Mother know how to dance?

Would Mother dance among dead bodies?

"There's no stiffs in there now." Montgomery squats down so low her skinsuit squeaks like a young girl rubbing a balloon; she leans around a corner, directing Kenna's attention to a lone camera sweeping back and forth. "Savor Station's a way station, barely knows what to do when a tourist dies."

"So they don't warehouse bodies there?"

Montgomery's fingers close into a triumphant fist. "They have a body catapult that slings corpses into the goddamned *sun*."

Her forearm pulses green. She raps the cask once, twice, an executive calling the meeting to order. "Camera's jammed. Chop-chop."

Kenna tenses to run—but Montgomery sashays toward the door, stepping carefully so Kenna is forced to stay behind her, the debutante ready to make a grand entrance. Someone on the inside unlatches a door bolt with a hollow *clank,* which then creaks open like the entrance to a tomb.

Inside is a rusted tomb decorated with Christmas lights, the floor packed shoulder-to-shoulder with young dancers thrusting their hands into the air.

How do you rust an egg? His voice echoes in his skull, sounding louder and more backwater-hick with each repetition. His robe has always been sheer, but now it feels translucent as he walks into the party.

"Do you know how hard it's been holding this for you?" a skinny Gineer kid snaps. His cheeks are taut as plastic wrap, his straight black hair bound up into a pigtail corona. He wears a stained lab coat two sizes too small, designed to show off his artificially engineered muscles. "It took us two hours of this twelve-hour shift to install it . . ."

"I paid for the parts." Montgomery holds her chin high as she glides into the crowd, easing onto the dance floor with the stiff reticence of a woman lowering herself into chilly water. "I go first."

"Tell that to the other Sensates!" The Gineer kid shuts the door before the camera sweeps back across. "I've been offered the most *outrageous* bribes to try this out! Mutating AIs! Dance lessons! A flourishing dabhand! A *dabhand* for a pet, Montgomery!"

"You can hold the Bitch for a while, if you want," she says, flopping a hand back toward Kenna as she strides toward the far wall, then mouths: *Don't let him hold the Bitch.*

Kenna elbows his way past the squirming throng, feeling the wooden staves creak as he hugs the cask, excruciatingly aware how fragile the Bitch is; a dancer's bumping hip could jolt her out of his arms. The booming bass resonates through his rib cage like a second heartbeat.

The room is an effluvia of rot and sweat and rust and sex, this filthy organic churn—yet his body reacts to it, pores opening wide. This is the odor of life, a commodity so rare among the sterile microbiomes of transport ships, and having this chaos infiltrate his nostrils reminds him *life is short, let us dance while we may.*

And they are dancing. And making love. And licking eyedroppers filled with drugs, and squatting down to program on flickering green screens, and assembling robots. And their body language is always inviting, hips turned outward, heads craned upward, always looking for someone who might want to join in.

"Hey, cutie!" a squirming naked couple calls out to Montgomery. "Wanna join in?"

"I've tried sex already," Montgomery shoots back. "What else ya got?"

Kenna can't peel his eyes away from two muscled men pressed against a stack of plastic containers, kissing frantically, oil-stained bodies grinding against each other. He can smell their sweat as he squeezes past; he stiffens, thinking of Benzo.

And as he imagines Benzo, his fears of rusting eggs dissipate. All the drug parties he's seen on the holovids are vapid affairs, kids skating through malls. This is a working-class party, the folks here so bored after a ten-hour shift refitting pipes that they're desperate to create.

The waste reprocessing plant is crowded, but they have built tiny enclaves around the garbage compactors and plastic extractors and dump-chutes, constructing tiny tents and covering the controls with sheets of thick plastic so no one sits on the wrong button.

Everything is dirt-brown, lent color-blooms by the firefly glows of strung Christmas lights.

Yet as Montgomery makes her way toward a giant hatch at the back of the plant, the partiers watch her pass and lower their eye-droppers, close their laptops, dampen their armflail dancing to gentle hip thrusts. Kenna realizes all this furious activity has been killing time—whatever Montgomery will do with that hatch is the thing they all came to do.

I go first, Montgomery said. How long had she kept this party waiting? All so Kenna could clean enough pots to catch him alone? As the lovemakers sigh, uncoupling to prop themselves up on an elbow to watch Montgomery, Kenna's heart wells over with pride: *She's my friend, and she's going to do something awesome.*

Carefully applied vandalism in the service of art, Montgomery had said. *I paid for the parts,* she'd said.

The Bitch hisses through a hole in the cask, exhaling peppery blue fungus that knifes Kenna's lungs. The choking panic reminds him Montgomery is a Sensate, having consumed all lesser thrills, and nothing but inherent death may satisfy her tonight.

A few partygoers set down their drinks and scurry out, their attempts at a quiet exit foiled by the creak-and-boom of the door's bolts unlocking. Montgomery takes advantage of the noise to hold her hands up, an old-fashioned cop halting traffic. The thumping music cuts off. She leans backwards lackadaisically, leaning against the long horizontal handlebar jutting out from underneath a black cloth.

She whips off the cloth with a matador's flourish.

The hatch beneath is a dented, coffin-sized rectangle, inset into the solid metal wall. The black coffin is tilted out at an angle, providing an industrially chilled chest big enough for someone to dump a body into and shove it against the wall like a file cabinet, thus ejecting the corpse.

Except now the coffin's interior is heaped high with bungie cords, attached to the corners by freshly welded chains. And someone's mounted a seven-foot-wide monitor on the wall above it, showing a blazing sun hanging in black space . . .

Wait.

Now that the crowd is quiet, Kenna hears the white noise of oxygen jetting out through the sides of that "monitor," sees the flapping duct tape where they've taped over the tiny cracks in the porthole.

That's a window straight into space.

Kenna turns to bolt for the exit. He can tell which partygoers are lifelong spacers—they're the ones poised to run, scanning the walls for reflective yellow. Reflective yellow is the rarest color on any ship; even anarchist pirates follow the rule that *nothing* on board is reflective yellow except for patch-kits and alert-boxes.

Find the yellow, save a fellow. Kenna's first memories involve transport captains squirting compressed air in his face when he was barely old enough to walk, thundering if he ever heard that noise, *yell yellow.* At six years old he learned to read, write, and apply patch kits. The stereotype was that planetside folks were egomaniacs, spacers were humble, but you *had* to be humble: you were trapped in a reinforced box floating in hard vacuum, billions of miles from help, where any structural failure would kill everyone. Your home could crumple like a paper bag. Everyone had to pitch in to ensure the ship held tight against space's murderous emptiness, and if you died hitting that yellow alert switch, you died well.

Montgomery and her friends have cut a fucking hole in the ship and patched in a *window.*

"I believe in informed consent," Montgomery says, pressing her palm against a leak like she wasn't practically sticking her arm out into the void. The sun sweeps across the window, an accelerated dawn-to-dusk as the station rotates fast enough to provide the equivalent of gravity. "What we're gonna try here could lead to explosive decompression. Rakesh's crew does good work, but we didn't exactly have Captain Lizzie's blessing here, so yeah, this window could give, and though we have compressed oxygen to tide us over, once the revelries start, that vacuum-proofed door"—she gestures at the thick bulkhead they'd entered by—"stays shut. Worst case, this room's a write-off, but we won't take the station with us.

"So. If you want to leave, go. If you're staying because your friends are calling you chickenshit, come to me and I will handle your idiot friends. This is as safe as we can make it, but that doesn't make it safe."

She takes off her goggles and makes pointed eye contact with every partier as if to say, *I mean that.*

"Now." She peels off her skinsuit. "As to why we'd do this damn fool thing, easy answer is 'I'm a Sensate.' But I don't go for *any* new sensation: otherwise I could settle in a farm town and spend my life licking different barns.

"No, what I'm looking for is *enlightenment.* And that out there"— she thumps on the window hard enough that everyone flinches—"is *reality.* We cling to our little air-filled, heat-filled outposts, but the truth is the largest inhabited planet is a speck of sand floating in an ocean. What's out there is what the universe really *is*—a place indifferent to life, quintillions of parsecs of emptiness, and *you have never seen the universe until you have touched that.*"

She's topless now, kneeling down to unbuckle her boots. "Me, I refuse to cling close to the skin of this world. So Rakesh here is about to catapult me into the void on a carefully preplanned trajectory. I'll shoot out a couple hundred yards from the station, then bungee back into this ejector like a pool ball into a pocket, all in under a minute. Humans can survive in space for three minutes, so . . . plenty of room to maneuver, right?"

She stands naked before the crowd, one candy-red thigh-high boot dangling from her hand. Her eyebrows are raised high in anticipation of a laugh that never arrives. She stands proudly bare before them, which should be a majestic thing—but her scarred body is a scrap of flesh framed against endless space.

"Anyway." She chucks her boot into the corner. "Y'all are welcome to do this too, if I survive. It's an experience you'll get nowhere else."

She jumps into the coffin like a luge competitor hopping into the sled. Rakesh and the other techs bend over, strap nylon rope around her.

She calls Kenna over. Walking toward that hissing, broken window is like fighting gravity, his feet slipping backwards, away from this childhood danger. It's easier because the only exit is clogged with people, half the people at the party filing out; all this vacuum-jumping seemed like fun until all that stood between them and an icy, gasping death was a piece of plastic.

He justifies stepping near the emptiness by telling himself he is bringing the Bitch to her caretaker. They bind Montgomery's legs with straps, yanking on the welded eyebolts to verify they won't snap free to send her tumbling into the void, testing the air-jets that will shoot her out into space.

"Why are they—"

She has crossed her arms across her chest like a mummy; Rakesh is spooling cords to press her hands to her clavicles. "Told ya, kid, it's a *carefully* preplanned trajectory. They shoot me out, I bounce back; me flailing when I'm unconscious will ensure I never make it home."

"Unconscious?"

"Humans can survive for three minutes in space, but we only stay conscious for about twenty seconds." Kenna does not understand how she can speak so calmly. "That should get me far enough away for me to know what it's like."

"Out in space." The words feel like a curse when he speaks them, wishing ugly death upon a friend—but other revelers jostle close around him, their breath heavy and thick as porn, necks jerking around to take in every detail. They throw rock, paper, scissors, determining who gets to go after Montgomery. They discuss the work they've put in, comparing approaches, discussing how to improve the process for next time . . .

These people are insane, Kenna thinks. *I have to get out.*

"Bring me my girl?"

Kenna assumes Montgomery is asking a technician for something, but the happy burbling purring against his chest indicates the Bitch heard her. He nudges past the technicians to hold the cask near Montgomery, straight-armed—he can't bring himself to step one foot closer to the window's sucking noise.

Rakesh pushes her down into the coffin, but Montgomery shrugs—or tries to, but her shoulders are strapped into place. "She's *hungry,*" Montgomery laments, and Kenna realizes why Montgomery wears her goggles all the time. While she's trained her voice to be flat as cardboard, she has the delicate face of a Gineer debutante, cursed with eyes that reflect her every emotion: without the goggles, her desires are broadcast to the world.

"Can you get her some potassium?" She's trussed so tight, she can only flick her eyes in the proper direction. "A brown packet in my left-thigh pocket . . ."

"Sure." Kenna is glad of any excuse to back away. Her empty skinsuit is disturbingly flesh-warm; concealed within are bewildering assortments of unguents and nostrums and crushed-up pills. But he ferrets out a small banana-scented packet.

"Just a sprinkle," she instructs him.

"Montgomery," Rakesh warns her. "We need to adjust your thrusters."

"This may be our last moment together, your schedule can wait. That's right, Princey, dust a thin coat across her." The weight in his arms shifts as the Bitch deliquesces, spreading across the cask's bottom. "Good. She's preparing to bud. Could you . . . ?"

The words make no sense, but without the goggles, all her desires are made manifest. He inches closer to that vastness beyond, holds the cask next to her face. She rubs her cheek against the knotted wood.

Then she glares at him. Webbed and bound, eye contact is the best she can manage, but her gaze is hot as a ship's thrusters. "You need to go?"

It's not a kind choice to offer. He'd much rather she had bullied him into it; he could blame her, then. He can imagine that window shattering with the first thump as she's flung toward the stars, all of them sucked out of the room, their lungs bursting, his eyes crystallizing with frost . . .

But he feels the liquid weight of the Bitch relaxing into jelly, realizing she would not survive without Montgomery. He imagines ferrying her away, then Montgomery dying in this explosive decompression, then him seated in The Sol Majestic, offering bits of bread to a Bitch turning black with death.

It is a strange bond they share, but she has pledged never to abandon the Bitch—and if Montgomery dies then she and the Bitch should perish in the same violent vortex, and he realizes that yes, he's staying.

His head is a balloon when he nods, light and empty.

Her expression softens into happiness when she looks at him: all the others get hard *hurry up* glances, but she shares her enthusiasm with Kenna. Yes, it's a lunatic's dream she's enacting, one that sets Kenna's bladder shivering with the need to void, but he realizes she vibrates with excitement, she's eager to face the universe's cold hollowness and welcome it into the scrap of pulsating meat that is her body.

Though he does not understand, he accepts.

Doesn't he have to make a decision about The Sol Majestic?

If distracting him is her intent, she has surely succeeded.

They double-check the automated winches that will haul her back in, fuss over her positioning in the coffin. Kenna wonders how far the cords extend; if he cranes his neck, he can make out the edge of Savor Station's solar panels, glinting in the sun's light, the station endlessly pinwheeling. Watching the vast outline of Savor Station, he realizes what holds his feet to the floor is not gravity, but rather him being spun rapidly enough that he's being centriped-ally shoved against the station's walls, and if that wall gave way he'd drop into space, and the fine meals of this evening burble in his stomach at the thought of his body turning into a frozen pork chop orbiting the sun . . .

"Shit," Rakesh mutters. "Security's on their way."

"How the fuck?"

"Couple of idiots got caught by the maintenance bots. Captain Lizzie's coming down to investigate."

That was the problem with Savor Station; even though it was gigantic by station standards, it was only a mile across. Kenna could flee to its furthest reaches and security would still be a twelve-minute jog away.

Kenna remembered Lizzie's stern kindness when she'd overseen Paulius's surgery, and his guts squirm at the thought of her confronting him. This was her station, and Kenna knew from experience how hard it was eking out a living in the void: she'd made savvy deals, pinched and saved to purchase each of these waste processing plants and oxygen reprocessors and solar panels, worked to shield this outpost from politics and wars and economic fluctuations. She'd provided a home for Paulius and his madman's orchard and this restaurant.

Wasn't that why his belly was stuffed full of thirteen chefs' food, anyway? To save Savor Station?

No wonder Mother and Father would have berated Kenna for coming here. This party isn't saving the starving millions. He looks at the tents and the sprayed-over consoles and the twinkling lights. Now all he sees is selfish vandalism, and who'll clean this up when they're done?

"Goddammit. Abort." Montgomery's fists clench inside the web-bing, the only frustrated gesture she can make. "Scatter. By the time Captain Lizzie arrives, she'll find a gift of a new porthole and no people."

"No."

Rakesh's denial is a judge's gavel, hammering a close to arguments. His grave certainty thumbs the pause button on Kenna's concerns; there's another side to this story, and judging from the way the partygoers nod their heads solemnly in agreement, Kenna's misunderstood what's driving this party.

"We worked for *months* to pull this off, Montgomery. Scouting the territory between shifts. Scanning accurate plans. Planning how to mod the hatch safely. Christ, do you know how many people worked to inset this porthole in less than two hours?"

Montgomery squeezes her eyes shut; it looks like she's wincing, but she doesn't want Rakesh to see into her. "She's gonna catch you, suckbrain. She's gonna jail you, maybe even space you if you don't have the cash . . ."

Rakesh grabs the netting on her chest, not quite yanking her out of the coffin, but tugging the webbing upward as if he hopes to haul her around to his way of thinking. "*Let* her. Everyone's devoted their spare time to this, dropping by after work to tool up the proper parts, running kerbalsims to dial in your trajectories, researching ways to suborn the security cameras—a battalion's effort poured into this once-in-a-lifetime hack. We got the cannon in place, Montgomery. You're telling us we don't even get to fire it?"

Montgomery's upper lip curls upward, snagged halfway between a smile and a sneer, squinting up at the concerned people leaning in to beg her approval. Her golden eyes dart around in confusion.

"This is insane." She seals her eyes behind her eyelids, but a dab of moisture wells up in the corner. "I'm a Sensate. I'm crazy enough to risk my life on this shit, but—but I was gonna go alone. I can't let you get caught for this, I don't even know why you'd—you'd want to . . ."

Kenna understands.

He understands everything.

He leans over into the coffin, placing a gentle palm over Rakesh's angry fist; Rakesh's face flushes dark at the interruption, then melts into a quiet hope as he remembers this weird, cask-toting kid came here with Montgomery. He releases his grip, and Kenna instead leans down to slide Montgomery's fingers between his.

"You're not entrapping them in your own needs." He squeezes her hand, indicating this is kindness he is conveying. "They're satisfying their own. Witness them, Montgomery. They—they're sweating hours at menial jobs, too poor to afford a flight off-station, trapped in a tin can and wondering why their lives are spent on such small dreams. And you gave them such a ridiculous challenge—who in dark blazes would punch a hole in a working spaceship for *merriment*?"

Montgomery's muscles slacken in gratitude, her sinking back into the coffin. "All to shoot a bitch into space."

She shakes her head, or tries to; they've put her in a neck brace to minimize motion.

Kenna exhales a ragged laugh. "It's not wise. Yet nobody else has done it but them. That is, in fact, why they're doing it." He squeezes her hand again, then lets go. "You're not being selfish."

Her tears overflow, trickling in rivulets across Montgomery's sharp cheeks.

Kenna is certain that if he were to check the insides of her brass goggles, he would find a salt-crusted rim: the residue of too many hidden tears.

Then her hips heave upward, her laughter seizing her whole body, thrashing with amusement like a fish in a net. "All right. Let's do it. Let's shoot me into fucking space!"

The twenty or so remaining party members don't laugh—they choke out one disbelieving sigh, resigning themselves to failure one more time, sallowed eyes glistening with an uncertain hope. But Rakesh thumps them in the chest with a datapad, driving them back:

"Get the fuck out." He swats them toward the door; they cover their chests protectively before retreating with the frail disappointment of people used to being given orders. "Check those mounted cameras above: I've just shot you their addresses. I can do this solo, and the rest of you can watch from your bunks."

Kenna thinks of the sad rows of hot-beds that merchants and travelers rent to sleep in at Savor Station—he'd seen merchants crammed in narrow tubes with a ratty pillow and a marker-scribbled vidscreen mounted four inches above their noses.

Those hot-beds are smaller than the coffin Montgomery's stuffed into.

No wonder these people were so eager to do something amazing. *"Go."*

Kenna thinks Rakesh is exhorting them to leave—then realizes *he's* the one who's spoken. How in the stars has he become this cabal's co-leader? Yet Rakesh has batted the crowds toward the exit with limited success. When Kenna speaks, the room turns to look at him, giving him silence to hear what he might say next—

And he realizes that he is no longer Kenna. He is the Inevitable Prince. If he says they should go then he *must* know—he's wise, he swayed Paulius into a once-in-a-lifetime meal with the power of his Philosophy. They offer him tentative smiles before they exit, hoping to impress, then bolt out at full speed.

Rakesh slams the door shut. "Comfort her while I dial in the last-minute adjustments. If she pukes, the weight difference will throw off my calculations."

The duct-tape-covered porthole hisses as the air bleeds into the void, rattling in its frame. Kenna picks his way among the spare parts rolling across the floor. The room *feels* evacuated, and Kenna is robbed of protection; the crowds had made death seem less likely. A room full of people dying seemed like an impossible Grand Guignol tragedy.

Three people, however, could die easily.

That hatch will cause a pressure differential. If anything sucks that window out, Montgomery's launch will do it.

Montgomery's frazzled hair is damp with fear-sweat. Her body is stiff from her fingers to her toes, seized with the paralytic surrender of a woman freezing as wasps crawl across her skin. Even as Kenna leans in, she keeps a wide-eyed gaze fixed on the hatch—the hatch that, in under a minute, will tilt down to eject her into space.

"You look as terrified as I feel," Kenna says.

"Scared is good." She hyperventilates, staying as still as possible. "You have to be a little scared all the time."

It doesn't feel right, condemning a woman to death by decompression without understanding her. "Why do this?"

"Have you figured out what meal you'll choose?"

The question skids off him like fingernails off plastic sheeting. It doesn't even make *sense*. Then he recontextualizes her query, and somehow tomorrow's problems fail to evoke terror when his blood could boil away into vacuum.

She sees his perplexed recollection of stale fears, then grins. "Life-threatening risks pare your anxiety back to the essentials."

He tries to evoke his fears of faking his Philosophy, of rusting eggs, of condemning The Sol Majestic to a slow death; they shrink to a pinpoint when actual death rattles in a loose porthole inches from your face.

If he can get through this, The Sol Majestic will be *trivial*.

"You find out who you are at my kind of parties," she murmurs, a slow grin spreading across her face. Kenna feels her Philosophy mingling with his—she's shared something essential by bringing him here.

Rakesh adjusts a thruster strapped to her left shoulder. "Okay. You have to breathe out, and keep your mouth open. Any air in your lungs, you risk fatal aneurysms. You ready?"

Montgomery sucks in a wad of air to push back a bolus of vomit. "As I can be."

"It's easy for her," Rakesh mutters to Kenna. "She'll be unconscious in fifteen seconds."

"Goodbye, Bitch!" Montgomery howls, tensing her muscles. "Kenna, you take good care of her until—"

Someone bangs on the door, commanding them to *stop this now*.

Rakesh slams a big red button.

The hatch drops open.

18

There Is Only Now

For the rest of his life, whenever Kenna feels terror, he remembers the hollow *boom* as Montgomery was shot into space.

That boom was every noise Kenna feared: heavy metals slamming into each other at ship-crumpling speeds, the roar of wind pouring through the hatch, the thump of the porthole window flexing inward as the pressure differential hit.

Kenna screamed, his ears popping, the tornado sucking his fluttering robe downward into the breach . . .

Then he looked out the undulating porthole—which was, against all odds, holding—and saw Montgomery sailing toward the stars.

Her smooth arc outward was like watching mathematical formulae and aesthetic theory fuck. The long bungee cords unspooled behind her like ripples in a pond, the sun spinning into view just in time to illuminate her bronze skin, this dot of humanity rocketing through the cold void like a middle finger thrust against the universe's emptiness.

Her expression was rhapsodic, her fears melting away into the galactic wonder spinning around her.

Whenever Kenna fears the worst is going to come, he remembers Montgomery, how everything bad turned out okay, and holds fast to a faith that things will be all right.

19

Thirty Seconds Until Captain Lizzie

The soles of Kenna's feet vibrate from the automated winches on the other side of the hatch pulling Montgomery back in. He presses his hand against the porthole, his palm sending hoarfrost blossoms curling across its surface—but he feels a connection to Montgomery, now unconscious, as her body sails back under the shadow of the station's great solar panels, air-jets hissing crystallized plumes as they slow her return.

Then the meaty *thump* of Montgomery impacting the coffin as solidly as a baseball in a glove. Kenna rubs his ribs, imagining her bruises.

"One minute, sixteen seconds." Rakesh's voice taut as a mooring cable; he jams the handlebar down so hard his muscle-strained laboratory coat rips.

The trip took sixteen seconds longer than anticipated, and Montgomery could well have had an embolism in space—but Kenna's skin tingles with a post-orgasmic bliss. When that coffin flips back inside, she will be all right.

She flops back into oxygenated space, her cheeks bulging like swollen tires, her dark-peach skin now a mottled violet and puffing up through the space between the straps. Her bloated tongue is rimed with ice; it obstructs her airway, makes hideous sucking noises as Montgomery's lungs whoop in deep breaths.

He can *smell* space on her, a chill Freon odor, like old refrigerators.

Rakesh hip-checks Kenna aside, palpates her bruising body. Her skin makes squishing noises. His explorations come to a stop; he peels a hand away from her to clap it over his mouth, making high keening noises at the back of his throat.

Kenna grabs his arm. "Is she . . ."

Rakesh seizes him, pulls him into an encompassing hug, thumping Kenna's back in an exultant drum solo. "We did it! We *did* it!"

Yet Montgomery looks like she's gained twenty pounds in the void, her lumpy skin mottled, bruises veining open underneath the straps. "*Is* she . . . ?"

"Yes, yes." Rakesh fumbles at the latches, knuckling aside Montgomery's puffy flesh to set the cables free. "We anticipated this could happen. If there's rapid decompression, sometimes—"

"This isn't unusual."

Kenna barely has time to recognize the voice before Captain Lizzie leans between them, pops the remaining latches with nimble fingers.

His calm bliss-armor sublimates away, replaced with a numb floating dissociation.

Captain Lizzie examines Montgomery's naked body like a mechanic troubleshooting a blown engine. Though Captain Lizzie is practically naked herself. She's wearing a white camisole with thin straps and mismatched red jogging shorts, tugged-on sneakers with no socks, a holster strapped across her shoulder.

We must have roused her from bed, Kenna thinks. He imagines Captain Lizzie tumbling awake to a terrorist alert blaring across her datafeeds, sees the three officers standing with drawn Tasers pointed toward the floor, waiting for their captain's command.

Yet Captain Lizzie has no embarrassment about being half-naked in front of her crew. She stands before the hatch like she owns it. She *does* own it. If she wanted to walk naked through Savor

Station's food mall, then she would do it with the unashamed nature of someone walking into her shower.

She owns the air here. If she ejected Kenna into the sun, not Paulius could countermand her, not Mother, not Father, not anyone.

She finishes inspecting Montgomery, purses her lips in a frown. "Seen enough decompression injuries to know that some swell." Her flat tone suggests joining in on this conversation could be fatal. "Passes in thirty-six hours, usually. Most don't even get stretch marks." She clucks her tongue. "She's fine."

That curt *she's fine* gives Kenna the feeling of sliding out from underneath a warship's shadow.

She clasps her hands behind her back, standing at attention, directing their gaze out the duct-taped window. "You boys take my station's defense systems into your planning?"

Rakesh opens his mouth, as if to ask Captain Lizzie for clarification, then recognition blooms. He makes a strangled noise.

"I thought maybe that's why those six new broadcast nexi opened up as you started these shenanigans; I thought, *Well, these folks are surely asking me to turn off my automated meteoroid defenses.* Or maybe they're just *very trusting* that our systems are set to let fast-moving debris stay intact within station range."

She grants neither Kenna nor Rakesh the relief of eye contact. As she breathes through her nose, watching the porthole intently, Kenna looks out into the blackness, imagines an alternate history where Montgomery's body sailed out gracefully toward the sun and was obliterated.

"I . . ." Rakesh reaches out to embrace Montgomery in apology, then realizes she's not conscious yet. "That wasn't on the schematics . . ."

She turns her head to glare at him, her motion as precise as automated laser-banks. "I don't annotate my defenses for my enemies' convenience."

Rakesh shakes his head.

"I hired you to run my waste reprocessing plant, Rakesh, and you've repaid my kindness with injured women and wrecked equipment. This is at least ten thousand dinari of damage punched through my wall. I'm gonna tally this up and see if it's worth shipping you off-station, or whether I just stuff you in that damn coffin and show you what you woulda done to her."

She looks down.

"And as for Little Miss Sensate here, she'll wake up on a ship bound for home. Scrimshaw'll kick up a stink. Miss Montgomery's auntie will file formal protests. But hell." She scratches an itch under her left eye. "Figure if I don't kick someone with connections out once in a while, they won't take me serious."

Rakesh's index finger is crooked, almost registering an objection, but his opposition wilts under Captain Lizzie's cool gaze.

Lizzie turns to Kenna.

"Get back to the kitchen. You got decisions to make."

It hurts to breathe, looking her in the eye; it's like inhaling in a high-pressure atmosphere, everything wanting to collapse. Yet he struggles to get words out nonetheless.

"I . . . cry your pardon, Captain Denahue, but . . ."

But what? What she's doing isn't right, but he doesn't have an argument, just tattered ideas flying around. There's something in this chaos that'll convince her, he's sure, yet all he can do is grab at the nearest idea and hope it leads him to a useful conclusion . . .

"I'm afraid I must take full responsibility for this project," he concludes.

Captain Lizzie's measured blink is more surprise than he's ever seen from her.

She runs her fingers along the hatchway rail, eyes marking every patch, following every fresh welding groove. She taps the porthole thoughtfully, then rests her hand on her hip as though Kenna is more of a puzzlement than this portal.

"These refittings are at least six weeks' work. You've been here ten days."

But her gaze has turned expectant. The ache in his lungs eases as she authorizes him to speak.

"No. I've not been aware of this project for ten hours, truth be told. But . . ."

He swallows.

"I am the Inevitable Prince. When I discovered the nature of this gathering, I should have made to contact you. Had I done so, none of this would have happened. So as the sovereign representative of the Inevitable Philosophies, the full burden for this foolhardiness should fall upon me. If you eject anyone, I request it be me."

His conclusion stuns himself as much as it does Captain Lizzie. He hadn't *planned* on offering himself up as a sacrificial lamb, yet it was the inevitable conclusion of the argument he'd started.

But if he doesn't know where he's going with this, neither does Captain Lizzie. Her mouth twists up in wry amusement. She leans back on the hatch rail, as if taking a seat to watch a play put on for her benefit.

"And if I did allow that," Lizzie asks, "what would you say in your defense?"

Kenna takes in the spare robot parts heaped on the floor, the waste reprocessing controls sealed away behind thick Lucite layers, the lights twinkling above them. "I'd say . . . this party took place in the proper court for you to judge."

"How so?"

"We stand in Waste Reprocessing, Captain Denahue. You helm a station the size of a city, teeming with the garbage of thousands, and yet . . . what you actually throw away can fit in a small box. You repurpose, recycle, transform."

Her fingers drum upon the hatch rail, informing Kenna he's headed down the wrong track. "That's something your dirter parents mistaught you. Reuse isn't laudable when you're light-years from fresh supplies. It's survival."

Montgomery's breathing loses its hoarse, tongue-stuffed gasp and eases into a steadier rhythm, as if to confirm Kenna is on the right path. "And what happened here is an abundance of misplaced talent. They were bored, working jobs that didn't ask much of them. So when they were offered a challenge, even an insane one, they rose to the occasion."

She rips a strip of duct tape off the window, lets it flap in the air-sucking gap for a moment before letting it go. The silver strip sails into the void, catching a flash of sunlight before disappearing from view.

"Pretty shoddy work for the occasion," she concludes.

"Mayhap," Kenna allows. "But they accomplished that in under two hours."

She cranes her neck to look back to Rakesh, gives him another long, slow blink. "Your crew cut a porthole into my station in *two hours?*"

Rakesh crouches behind a control panel, head poking out as if he's not quite willing to engage with her without cover. "I had a twelve-hour shift," he snaps. "Two hours to install the hatch, eight hours for the party, two hours to remove the hatch and patch the hull."

Her face is blank with disbelief. "You were gonna patch this up."

"I had a *plan* to, yes."

Lizzie holds his gaze, but this time Rakesh does not back down: his exasperation at not getting to carry his grand schemes to fruition holds him fast. She steps away from the rail, then turns to examine the porthole with the knowledge this had been done in less time than it takes to watch a holovid.

"That's why this isn't sealed tight." She runs her hands around the porthole's perimeter. "You've got explosive bolts on the outside holding it in. When this is done, you send that tumbling toward the sun, and replace it with . . ." She scans the plant, finds a great metal sheet welded to a larger metal sheet. "You set that up against the porthole, blow the porthole, the air pressure sucks that patch into place, and you weld it in tight. You barely lose any air if you do it right."

Rakesh straightens from behind the console. "That wasn't my idea." He snorts, debating whether to say more. "We iterated through a lot of plans before settling on this one."

She steps back, taking the whole room into perspective, her frown no longer an angry captain's scowl, but an engineer working out a complex problem.

"Except this hole still weakens the plant's integrity, Rakesh. It'll hold for daily wear, but if something with any mass impacts the hull, it . . ."

"I admit it's not a perfect solution," Kenna interjects, before an argument breaks out on approach. "And it is, to be honest, a fairly insane problem they set out to solve. But I think Mr. Rakesh and all the people who helped him are stupefied by tedium. I think they burn to work upon something meaningful. And I think their lives will be enriched if you can guide them toward better projects."

Lizzie's sigh is all the concession she's willing to give. "The problem is, most of them work on the necessary projects. Waste processing isn't sexy, but someone's gotta helm it. What these people want is something crazy to work on, and I don't always have the cash to outlay for the exciting bits."

"It may have escaped your notice, Captain Denahue, but this hasn't cost you a dime."

Her flesh goose bumps beneath her camisole, muscles tensing for battle, and Kenna remembers she didn't want to run down to the waste reprocessing plant at two in the morning. "*This* has installed a person-ejector I don't need. That *nobody* needs. So why would I add another layer of administration, sorting through a thousand brain-fuzzed ideas to find one I'm okay with? If I'm going to let them cut up my ship and hold maker parties and authorize new construction, what's in it for me?"

Kenna now knows what his final argument is. He doesn't want

to give it. Captain Lizzie is rightfully angry at being yanked out of sleep to roust a bunch of malcontents who've weakened her infrastructure.

She has every reason not to be the person Kenna hopes she is.

"What's in it for you?" Kenna asks. "Well—you'll likely see less vandalism around the station. And you'll get friction from turning them down all the time. And I acknowledge the ones you *do* allow will have them working on a hundred projects you have no interest in, and once in a while they might even work on something you genuinely needed. Probably not that often, though."

Captain Lizzie punches her thigh. "That's not all, boy. Finish your thought."

Kenna sighs. "Mostly, you get to make people happier."

A rasping noise from the coffin panics Kenna, until he realizes Montgomery is laughing.

Lizzie leans back on the railing, massaging her neck. For the first time since she arrived, she looks tired—like a woman tasked with running a monstrously complex set of moving parts, both politically and physically, who wants to do the right thing by all of them.

"I'm not gonna talk about this now," she allows. "But I'm not gonna start spacing people, either. Rakesh, you and I are going to have a talk in a few days, and you'd better come up with some projects that intersect with both your people's fitful needs and my practical inclinations. If they're good, maybe you get to stay. Maybe."

Rakesh looks relieved as Captain Lizzie's men haul Montgomery and the Bitch off to the docbot. "Should I, uh . . . get people in to patch the hole here?"

She plops down onto a pile of plastic, staring at Kenna. "Not yet. First, the Prince is gonna return the Waste Reprocessing Plant to its former condition. All this mess cleaned up, all my control panels returned to working conditions."

"We had plans for that," Rakesh says. "I can get my—"

His voice drops like a cut speaker when Lizzie turns her still-sharp gaze in his direction.

"The Prince claims he's responsible," she says. "So the Prince can clean it up."

"But that'll take hours for one boy to do," Rakesh objects.

She gestures toward the plastic. "This is comfy. I got the rest of the night to watch. Ain't like I'm getting back to sleep, anyway."

And when she makes eye contact with Kenna, it is not a hard captain's gaze, but another, wearier question buried in her cool brown eyes: *Do we have a problem here?*

Kenna looks at the sprawling mess the party left—shattered eyedroppers, used condoms, piles of equipment that he has no idea whether they belong to the party or the waste reprocessing plant. He doesn't know how to peel the plastic covering off the controls, either. He's not tall enough to reach the twinkling lights overhead, and Lizzie said there were six camera feeds to be taken down but he can't see any of them.

Mother and Father would tell him manual labor is shameful.

That doesn't explain Kenna's smile as he gets to work.

20

Three Hours Before Kenna Is Released from Jail

Savor Station's jail cell holds everything Kenna finds comforting: it's tiny, maybe six feet by six feet. The walls smell of rusty piss, masked by bubbling gray paint. There's even a cot to curl up in—a luxury on a transport ship, seen as necessity here.

Yet above all, Kenna loves the Plexiglas wall that stops him from walking over to the Majestic and damning it with his foolish decisions.

He pushes his face into the cot's taut burlap, feeling the empty squirm in his stomach. As long as he pretends to be asleep, they cannot make him choose. Last night's party was a detour, but with morningcycle's cold light comes The Sol Majestic's execution.

He remembers each dish: the chemical grapes that dissolved into salty foam, the tureen full of broth that turned into a stew, the lacquered duck, the pot of delicate flowers, and

How do you rust an egg?

He shivers. As long as he does nothing, he cannot harm The Sol Majestic.

Except the bill for the robes is coming due, and the chefs must have time to prepare, and—

The monitor embedded in his cell wall flashes. It must be Captain Lizzie. She'd seemed dubious about his request that she lock him up, informing him that if she needed the space to hold the day's drunkards she would boot him out.

INCOMING CALL: The Sol Majestic (Montgomery)

Kenna's muscles lock. If he stays still, the monitor won't register his presence. Nobody at the Majestic will know he's ignoring them. Except he is locked in jail, and the operator wouldn't have routed the call to an empty cell.

He's stalled the decision until the afternoon, but now he will have to go to The Sol Majestic to guess their legacy into oblivion.

He groans and taps the "answer" button, hoping maybe it's Montgomery making a private call. But no, the camera angle is high in the kitchen, showing the chefs working on the evening's service, clad in their striped chef's outfits, chopping and comparing tastes and reducing sauces and debating.

Except when the jail cell's visuals flicker on, the flashing knives still, the staff's faces going dead with uncomfortable stiffness. They brush off their vest-fronts, jab the ones deep in concentration to look up. Burners are turned low as they stare up at Kenna's image.

He ducks his head. He wants the kitchen to proceed as though nothing's different—though the boy who'll pronounce judgment upon them has no hope of that. Only two people treat him normally: Benzo looks up from today's broth to jump up and wave at the camera, and Montgomery thumps the screen as if to ask *Is this thing on?*

Montgomery's goggles barely fit across the distorted landscape of her depressurization-swollen cheeks, her unwashed hair sticking out in all directions. She turns to three of the chefs—chefs who brought him audition dishes last night, why can't he remember their names?—with the preening confidence of a woman about to settle a bet.

"Greetings, O Prince!" Her greeting has a strained jocularity to it, an un-Montgomery-like friendliness that sets Kenna on edge. She jerks her thumb toward the chefs, who stand with their arms crossed as though barring Montgomery's entry to the kitchen. "These yokels refuse to believe we made a decision last night. If you can believe that bullshit."

". . . The decision," he echoes.

"Yeah." She pulls her goggles down, revealing her imploringly wide honey-drop eyes. "You know. The Wisdom Ceremony decision."

Kenna feels the numb weightlessness of placing his fate into someone else's hands.

"That—yes," he says. "A very difficult choice. Yet, I think, perhaps, it would be best if you explained our reasoning to the staff. You're more conversant in culinary languages . . ."

She sags for an instant, and Kenna wonders if he has said the wrong thing—but she nods once, then snaps her goggles on. They click their heels to attention as she chops her flat hand in their direction, calling them out like a sergeant ordering armies into position:

"Right. Weimer, that potted plant bullshit is fine for an amuse-bouche, but passing that perfume-puff off as a full dish is a travesty and you know it. You find some way to make that into an actual course, we'll slot that in. Gates, that lacquered duck is tasty, but one bite and we know every flavor in the duck. You don't sleep until you find a pairing that elevates the dish beyond expensive takeout. Fargo, the broth-that-becomes-a-stew is a nice idea, but that's not gonna carry the Prince through eighteen courses, so we'll set that into the table like a bouquet and simplify it into five tastings—reducing it to a flashy palate-cleanser that gets more complex as the meal does. And Bosworth, the Prince's fuckup is legend now, so you find some way to *rust* an egg."

The thirteen chefs are unified in their dropped jaws, their disbelieving silence. Bosworth, the most stunned at having her dish wiped from the tasting menu, waves both hands in a "Hold on" gesture.

"Scrimshaw told us the Prince would pick *a* chef to run this meal."

The cocky tilt of Montgomery's hips chews up Bosworth's nervous flailing. "He did. That chef is me."

"But you weren't even auditioning!"

"So?" Without looking back, she snaps her fingers in Kenna's direction. "You all saw the videos from last night. He crashed a maker party, shot me into space, then took responsibility for the whole damn thing. Now Captain Lizzie's taking suggestions for crowd-sourced station improvements. You think a prince like that cares for *rules*?"

The adulation they pour through Kenna's screen unnerves him, until he realizes why: that was the look they'd given Paulius, the first time he'd entered the kitchen.

Bosworth tears off her hairnet, slams it into a countertop full of diced onions. "You don't even *work* here!"

The kitchen falls quiet except for the sizzle of garlic.

Montgomery looks down at her chef's outfit, the front flap hanging open, covered in electric violet blue Bitch mold. Her thin eyebrows constrict in mild vexation—*how did that get there?*—and then she buttons her vest, taking her time, the snap of each button audible even through the tinny speaker Kenna listens through.

She fastens the top, conspicuously drawing attention to the black top-chef stripes decorating her breast. Then she strides over to Bosworth's station, taking rangy long steps like she owns every countertop, to snatch the hairnet off the table.

Bosworth stays still, bracing for impact. Kenna wonders if Montgomery will shove Bosworth against the stove the same way she slammed Kenna up against the wall.

Montgomery leans over, snaps the hairnet back across Bosworth's head, tugs it down into place. She leans in, daring Bosworth to peddle her brand of rebellion:

"Who," she says, "told you I didn't work in this fucking kitchen?"

There is a single clap. Benzo, at the back, bouncing up and down on his toes, applauding. The clap spreads like wildfire, and the chefs' backs stiffen in a standing ovation even though they were standing already, stepping away from their stations as if to welcome Montgomery in. Montgomery shakes her head, refusing the acclaim, but even though her head is bowed Kenna sees her suppressing a smile.

She snaps her fingers at another chef. "Yo. Bodard. That duck stew was amazing, but let's talk improvements."

The kitchen returns to work.

21

Three Weeks Until the Wisdom Ceremony

"This is mint." Benzo plucks a dark green leaf from the orchard's herb garden and swallows it as though he's disposing of evidence. "Yeah. Chocolate mint. It creeps all over the garden if we don't watch it. If Paulius is mad at you, he'll send you out to weed it out, you gotta dig up every last tendril . . ."

Benzo never stops moving as he works his way down the herbs' hydroponics trays—plucking at a stray vine, wiping moisture off on the towel at his waist, absent-mindedly checking the stasis cube filled with this morning's broth that hangs off his shoulder.

Benzo's never-ending commentary might seem friendly to an outsider, but to Kenna the words feel like a barrier—a steady monologuing flow like a river around a castle, never giving Kenna an opportunity to say anything meaningful.

They used to be so good with silence. But as The Sol Majestic has tensed itself to plan out the Wisdom Ceremony, Benzo's picked up on the kitchen's panicky energy, has begun filling every spare moment with words.

"Benzo," Kenna whispers; Benzo works in noisy pantries where raised voices don't even register as rebuke.

Yet Kenna's patient silence evokes guilty twitches; he notes Benzo's shoulders tensing, before pulling the stasis cube's strap over his shoulder.

". . . what'd I do now?" Benzo asks.

Benzo's shy grin is like a sun-rim peeking over an eclipse—a bright reminder of the friendship they'd once shared. Kenna could forgive anything as long as Benzo gave him that grin.

Kenna chuckles—not because he wants to laugh, but because he should set Benzo at ease. Yet the laugh is as fake as nutricrackers; Benzo's pale face squinches up.

He squeezes Benzo's shoulder. ". . . You—you forgot to give me a taste of the mint, is all."

Benzo's tremors calm at Kenna's touch. But not in a good way. Like an engine shutting down.

"I mean, you know," Kenna says, and he can *hear* himself babbling, *hear* himself throwing up walls of words against this weird disharmony that's seeped into their relationship, "You're supposed to be educating me in high cuisine, and I know you're quite eager to return to making a new batch of broth, which is why I said perhaps you shouldn't cook for me today, we'll consume raw ingredients in the orchard . . ."

. . . and maybe you'll be inspired by the warmth of the sun and the chlorophyll-scented breeze and you'll hold me and we'll kiss away this weird tension . . .

". . . but I hold a deep longing to, you know, actually taste the foods. If that's acceptable."

"Of course it's acceptable." Benzo lurches free, but unconsciously strokes the place on his shoulder where Kenna grabbed him. He hauls out a piece of mint, holds it out between thumb and forefinger toward Kenna.

Can he get away with cupping Benzo's hands in his, like he did with the spoonful of broth once? He doesn't dare. Instead, he pulls the mint leaf from between Benzo's fingers, closes his eyes, places it in his mouth. He chews slowly, tasting the wet leaf's peppery bite, thinking, *slow down, Benzo. Stop obsessing over the Wisdom Ceremony and the broth and stay with me . . .*

He doesn't open his eyes until he has licked the last shred of mint off his teeth.

Benzo has walked away, rooting up a bouquet of herbs, sampling several at once.

"Benzo."

To his horror, he speaks Benzo's name with Mother's stiff disappointment.

Benzo had been plucking plants with a frantic energy, but at Kenna's sharp tone he draws himself up straight, all gratuitous motion extinguished. He pulls the herb bouquet to his chest, elbows tucked in . . .

Benzo's blue eyes have grown hooded, his friend replaced by a servant.

He's a slave, leased to The Sol Majestic, Kenna realizes. *Snapping at him reminds him of Her orders—*

"I'm sorry," Kenna says. "I just—something's wrong, and I don't fathom its depths."

"Nothing's wrong." He rolls the herbs between his fingers until they turn to pulp. "We have the Wisdom Ceremony in three weeks, is all."

"I know. And how shall I appreciate it when I don't know what I'm eating?" He takes the herbs from Benzo, sets them aside. "I've—I've already rusted too many eggs. I need you to teach me, to be *here* for me . . ."

Because this is all the time we'll ever have together. But Kenna can't bring himself to admit that, because saying it would make it too real to bear.

Benzo knows what he means, though. He licks his lips, finally tasting the mint. Then he cups his fingers under the broth stasis cube, stroking it with the tenderness with which he used to touch Kenna, his gaze drifting over toward the entryway to the Majestic's kitchen.

"I gotta . . ." Benzo grips his forehead. "I gotta get the broth right."

"Except you don't." Kenna's watched Benzo snort drugs to stay up until five in the morning, making two broths after dinner service and one broth before. He wishes he could understand why Benzo has become so obsessed—more obsessed—with perfecting the broth all of a sudden. Then again, the entire kitchen's on edge as the Wisdom Ceremony draws closer, with Montgomery shouting orders and Scrimshaw stalking the halls berating people for wasting ingredients and chefs getting into screaming matches. Perhaps Benzo is hoping to contribute what little he can to Kenna's exultation . . .

"It'd be lovely to sup your broth as the climax to my ceremony," Kenna says carefully, "but . . . I'm not even certain they'll *utilize* broth in the final dishes. The courses seem absurdly complex, and I haven't witnessed the kitchen using much broth in the course of the normal service . . ."

"What in the void do *you* know?" Benzo's cheeks prickle in a flushed sweat. "You've been here three weeks and you think you know the kitchen!? Sweet void, that's why Paulius made me teach you! You, the lost Prince!"

Benzo is as taut as a mooring cable, his sneering mouth half-open and ready to unleash another round of insults . . .

Then he frowns as he finds nothing within Kenna but sympathy.

"I'm sorry," Kenna says. "You're correct; I don't have the measure of how this works. I'm not trying to insult or demean you. You're my friend, and I . . ."

I don't have many friends, Kenna wants to say.

Of course Benzo knows that anyway. The thought seems to still him, biting those luscious lips as he swallows back words. Then he shakes his head, a dazed alcoholic shaking off a regretted bender.

"I just saw Montgomery." He pushes past Kenna toward the kitchen door. "She hasn't tasted today's broth."

Which one? Kenna wonders, knowing Benzo's made at least two batches today.

He trails behind as Benzo stumbles toward the Majestic's

frosted glass door. His gut twists around a scant bellyful of herbs as he nears the kitchen's frantic labor.

I took you out to the sun-warmed loam because I wanted you to relax, he thinks. *Nobody is relaxing in there.*

The door swings open and The Sol Majestic exudes its sweet scent of broiled snakefruit and the oily heat of seared pterodactyl, but now there's a sour sweaty note laced through the air. Knives have always chopped, yet now the cutting holds a flat machine-gun anger; pots have always rattled, but now they're slammed into stoves like criminals flung into the backs of police cars.

Time is running out, and it's taken the kitchen's laughter with it.

Kenna threads his way through the kitchen's clockwork chaos; before, he'd had to dodge red-hot pans because the chefs were so busy they barely noticed his presence. Now they're on the defensive, treating any intrusion as an incursion, and they whip pots of boiling pho across Kenna's path as if daring him to reap the blistered rewards.

Their chefs' outfits are immaculate; that much Scrimshaw demands of them. But greasy tangles rest beneath their hairnets, and the chefs wobble on their thick-soled boots, blanching vegetables in a daze as they contemplate ways to perfect the Wisdom Ceremony.

Montgomery stomps back to her station at the kitchen's rear, back near the Escargone's bulky black hatch. Her arms are heaped high with squirming starfish and jars of grainy red paste. She slams them down into the station, blinking her eyes twice as she refocuses on a recipe flashing across her biometrics, then snatches a fresh pan and drizzles citrus oil across its face.

Benzo slows as Montgomery grabs a jar and twists it open as though she was wringing a bird's neck. He had held the stasis cube out before him like he'd brought a gift to royalty—but as he watches her flick the paste into the pan, he holds it protectively against his chest.

Montgomery's head tilts a fraction in his direction.

Benzo bobs his head in apology. "I'm sorry, Montgomery—I just wanted to know if you, you know, might—"

"Taste your fucking broth?"

Benzo looks so stricken, Kenna's arms itch to hug him. ". . . yeah. If it's not . . ."

"Sure, sure." She snatches the stasis cube. "Maybe something will surprise me in a *good* way."

Benzo cracks his knuckles as Montgomery withdraws a steaming cup of fresh broth. She swirls it, staring into its depths like a fortune teller reading tea leaves, her brass goggles whirring as they refocus. She holds the cup pinky-out, sips noisily.

She bends over convulsively and spits it into a nearby sink. The Bitch makes a keening noise as Montgomery wipes the broth off the cask in the sink as though Benzo's broth were a toxin.

"Sorry, baby," she whispers, before whirling on Benzo. "What the fuck was *that*?"

"My broth." Benzo breathes in carefully, trying to calm his hitching chest. "Paulius isn't here, so I thought maybe you'd judge it for me . . ."

"I'm not your fucking backstop, Benzo. *You* have to judge first." She shakes the cup at him, spattering golden broth across Benzo's black-striped vest. "Are you telling me *this* is Majestic-quality broth?"

He smears broth across his chest like he is trying to claw off his skin. "I . . . I wasn't sure . . ."

"Like fuck you weren't. You're hoping if you hand us enough cups of crappy dishwater, eventually someone will tell you you're a chef. You're not. You're moving *backwards,* you little twerp. This is worse broth than you were making a month ago, and you know it."

The chefs flinch at Montgomery's accusations, attesting to their accuracy; each raises a hand from their cutting boards in a half-hearted attempt to interrupt, but their hands lower as they realize no one can defend Benzo's cooking skills.

Worst of all, Benzo sees them coming to his defense and backing off. *They like having you around,* Kenna thinks, *but they can't justify you as a chef.* Which, to a boy who's here to win a bet with his master that he is a worthy cook, is a damning sin.

Benzo studies his shoes, gulping back sobs.

"Now, Montgomery," Kenna snaps. "There's no need to humiliate anyone in the course of duty—"

He barely dodges the broth she flings at him.

"I'm not *humiliating* him!" she screams, clamping her arms against her side lest she start flinging knives. "I'm pointing out the bleeding fucking obvious—he's not good enough! They're all staring because *they're* not good enough! The Wisdom Ceremony's in three goddamned weeks, and the dishes we have are not good enough, the concepts we have are not good enough, the chefs are *not good enough!*"

She swivels her head around, glaring at the chefs. Daring them to contradict her. The best they can muster is a muttered gripe: "What do you want of us, Montgomery?"

With a growl, she storms over to the Escargone's hatch, grabs it with both hands, slams that black maw open with a *bang.* She aims one hand at the cramped kitchen:

"I want you to get in this goddamned machine and buy us more time!"

As Kenna looks back over the kitchen, he realizes almost no one stands near him—everyone has switched stations so they're as far away from that ugly machine as possible. Only the lowliest prep cooks work beneath the Escargone's shadow.

That jagged hatchway is a mortal wound, Kenna realizes. He doubts the chefs even realize they've rejiggered their workflow to avoid going near it—yet that hulking pile of circuitry is a reminder of their lost invulnerability.

Locking themselves into this stoop-shouldered torture chamber for months on end had destroyed The Sol Majestic's best chefs.

But Paulius had entered this time-mangling device and come out smiling—proof they were blessed.

Now Paulius had gone back in for more corrective surgeries, and the Wisdom Ceremony was imploding, and the Escargone had come to symbolize all their failures.

Paulius could dispel this sour fog in minutes. He'd walk into the kitchen, smile, and tell them *every* service looks this bad three weeks before its debut. He'd sample their dishes, garnish the chefs with bright advice, challenge them in ways that kept their heads buzzing with new ideas.

Montgomery can't do that. She knows what's riding on this next Wisdom Ceremony—and though Benzo snuffles back tears, Kenna cannot blame her for hurting him. She's like a feral cat backed into a corner.

The longer Kenna stays, the more he realizes how carefully Paulius's delusions have been cultivated. Yet he also realizes how this kitchen runs on delusions. They've only achieved the impossible because Paulius, and therefore they, are shielded from knowing the consequences of failure.

Kenna misses Paulius so fiercely his chest hitches. Not the drugged patient in the docbot bed: the real Paulius, the Inevitable Paulius.

Montgomery slams the door again, a hollow boom; the chefs' knees flex as though they might dive for cover. "*Who?*" she bellows. "*Who'll get in this fucking thing?*"

One wrings her chef's cap in her hands. "It's not safe in there, Montgomery . . ."

"It's perfectly safe!"

"It mangled Paulius," another chef says with horror.

"You can't trust tech like that," a third chef interjects; her friends nod in agreement. "Paulius made some hefty bargains to get Captain Lizzie to allow that thing on her station, most sane empires have banned time-tech . . ."

Kenna almost corrects them—the machine didn't fail, Paulius teleported out—then remembers: Paulius doesn't want anyone to know about his Niffeneger syndrome.

So what if Paulius is embarrassed? he thinks, ready to spill the truth, then remembers: no one will invest in The Sol Majestic if they know Paulius could disappear forever. People have committed to years' worth of slow travel to taste his food—would they do so, knowing the head chef could evaporate overnight?

Telling the staff what really happened that night would condemn The Sol Majestic to a slow death.

How have lies held this shivering wreck together for this long?

Rage boils up inside. All his choices involve deciding when The Sol Majestic will die, and he needs to find a way to make his beloved home survive—not for a few weeks, not for a few years, but *forever.*

Montgomery slaps the hatch. "We can't do this in three weeks. You need to slip in there and squeeze out a few months to nail your courses down . . ."

"If it's so safe, why don't *you* do it?" Bosworth snaps.

"Because I'm a fucking *Sensate!*" Sensing distress, the Bitch squirts green puffs of air. "The same room every day? That gastronomic jail cell would fucking *kill* me, you assholes!"

"If you won't risk your life for the meal," Bosworth replies, "then why should we?"

"When moral courage runs thin," Scrimshaw says, "perhaps financial incentives can purchase backbone."

Kenna shouldn't be surprised to find that Scrimshaw, towering as she is, can move with such deathly silence that even Montgomery hasn't noticed her creeping into the kitchen.

She carries a robe—an Inevitable robe, butterfly-bright against her dull black coat—spread wide in her clawlike hands. The fabric hangs down like a burial shroud. When she sweeps that horn-rimmed, merciless gaze across the kitchen, it is though she is a detective, wondering who murdered this place's future.

She rubs the thin fabric between her gaunt fingers, affecting an air of calculation. Then she jerks her chin toward the Escargone's interior.

"Relative time," she says.

Kenna does not know what that means, yet judging from the way the staff exhales in a low whistle, everyone else does.

Scrimshaw paces slowly around the kitchen, slinging the Inevitable robe jauntily over her shoulder. "I do not misspeak. Traditionally, laboring in the Escargone paid you according to our time-flow's rates: if a month spent inside took four hours out here, then you got paid half a day. And when Paulius was well enough to teach you, that was sufficient: you were getting an extended master class, so why should we pay you for the privilege?"

She weaves her way around the aisles, encouraging someone to speak out as she passes. But as she glides by, each of the chefs holds their breath, examines their ingredients, terrified she might make a direct request.

"Yet with the . . . changes . . ." she continues, "mayhap we must offer fiduciary gain. So now. Spend a month in there, you'll be paid a month's wages, no matter how little time passes on the outside. I know many owe debts to your culinary arts schools, spent yourself to ruin to purchase a trip out to this distant outpost. With proper discipline, you could earn a year's salary in a week."

Mouths open as if to speak, then shut when people stare into the Escargone's shadowy maw. Bad enough when Paulius locked his employees in that cramped hole until the relentless cycle of *cook, sleep, cook, sleep, cook, sleep* drove them gibbering with claustrophobia—but to do that and think it might malfunction? To be sealed away in there like a pharaoh in his tomb, clawing at the walls, your bones drying to dust as aeons passed inside, yet mere minutes passed on the outside?

"A year's salary, I should add, that would be well-earned. Young Kenna here—the Prince"—and here, she kneels to spread out the robe before his chest, an oddly tailor-like gesture—"deserves a meal worthy of both his heritage . . . and ours. I dare say anyone who braves the Escargone's challenges would have a bright future at The Sol Majestic. A bright future indeed."

She sweeps the robe shut like a curtain, then turns to face the kitchen.

She sucks air through her teeth as her staff turns into fleshy mannequins.

She whips her glasses off, squeezing her eyes shut as she cleans them, as if hoping clearer lenses will reveal a more courageous staff. When she slides them back on and finds everyone still frozen in place, a guttural growl wells up from her wattled throat.

"Take a ten-minute break, everyone."

The head chef Keffen rests his hand on a mixer churning aerated batter. "Ma'am, some of the dishes are time-sens—"

"Take a ten-minute break."

The kitchen scatters—even Montgomery clasps her cask to her chest like a refugee grabbing possessions, hauling a stunned Benzo out with her before he can say something stupid.

Kenna makes for the exit, too, but Scrimshaw catches him by the scruff of the neck.

"You," she snarls. "Stand still. I need to copy your stains."

Kenna wishes that once, just once, he felt competent around Scrimshaw. He has to labor to force the question past his lips. ". . . what stains?"

Scrimshaw kneels, holding the robe up to Kenna's chest again. She licks a finger, runs it across Kenna's belly, pops it into her mouth.

"Lacquered duck sauce and soap," she mutters, then paces the stoves, searching for a panful of lacquered duck sauce.

"What stains?" Kenna repeats. But Scrimshaw is rattling pans in the sink. She scoops a thick dollop of glistening brown sauce, smears the sauce into the robe's front with the care of an artist putting a brushstroke on a portrait. Then, looking back at Kenna as a

reference, she grabs a palmful of dirty dishwater and wipes it across the robe.

"What are you doing?"

She snaps the robe in his direction, spattering soap in his eye. "Selling our first Inevitable robe."

Kenna's sudden grin makes his eye water even harder. "The word's getting out. They're starting to sell."

She digs through the garbage, hauls out a pallid chicken from Benzo's broth attempt this morning. She plops the boiled carcass onto the robe and rubs it around in circles, an insane dead-chicken dance.

"The family that purchased this robe," she says, grunting with the effort, "admires your efforts in bringing enlightenment to the working poor of Savor Station. They scrimped and saved for weeks until they were able to afford a single robe. They are, they tell us proudly, the first in their village to afford such an expenditure. But they desire the robe as you wear it now, marked with the sacrifices you have made for your people."

His robe crawls across his skin. He feels every clotted sauce-bump, every sodden water-stain.

Someone wants to be like him.

Him, a liar who only wants to sell robes to keep some snooty restaurant alive.

He's seen the starving millions—never met them directly, Mother would never dirty herself to walk among them, but she watches newscasts before bed. Many of them are mechanics and construction workers, housed in filthy company towns, paid in useless scrip, tasked to work on the assembly lines until they drown in oil and sweat. Others live in the deteriorated shadow of what had been thriving industry until the corporations extracted the last value from the land and then left, abandoning proud laborers to live in debris and famine.

Yet though her Philosophies technically embrace all the infinite flavors of downtrodden misery, Mother always meditates upon the plight of the farmers.

Kenna knows how little the farmers are allowed to retain of their own efforts—the emperors always take their food-share, and the armies take their share of food, and the landowners take their share, until the people who stand waist-deep in vegetable fields starve.

And for a starving soul—any of the starving millions who one day hope to become Inevitable—to deprive themselves of even more food, to wear a robe, to carry his symbol back to the fields as a symbol of, what—Hope? Joy? Respect?

Suddenly he is glad he ate almost nothing with Benzo out in the orchard. His growling stomach constricts, hollow as his philosophies. He has nothing to offer them—no political power, no connections, no diplomatic ties to stop a march to war—and yet they're so famished for dreams, they map their own need for greatness upon him.

I did this to sell robes, he thinks. But he thought he'd sell robes to the rich fashionistas who used to wear Inevitable robes, not to the starving millions. These poor souls must have eaten crickets to save up.

But they're selling, now. *The first in their village,* Scrimshaw had said. That meant more were saving up—and there were starving *millions,* he reminded himself, trillions of downtrodden subjects who'd watched his videos, there must be thousands hoarding their spare funds—farmers salting away their post-harvest dinari, mechanics requesting triple shifts, miners checking exhausted seams one more time in the hopes of extracting a last payout, all to wear the Inevitable Prince's robe . . .

"It's good." He lifts his own robe away from his chest; it feels foul, a charlatan's costume. "This is—it's a prerequisite. To market the robes. To save The Sol Majestic."

Scrimshaw makes a dreadful hacking noise, rolling into a fetal position.

It takes Kenna a moment to realize she is laughing.

"To save us?" She accents the word *save* with the guttural noise of a woman tearing a contract in half. She digs her fingers into Kenna's wrist, drags him stumbling into the locked storage room.

Scrimshaw has stacked the robes into one towering heap brushing the warehouse's ceiling. The pile of unsold merchandise leans forward, threatening to topple upon them, enough robes to bury them in a silken cloud.

A red placard is stuck into the pile, high enough it threatens to slit Kenna's throat.

"That." She flicks the placard. "*That* is how many robes we must sell to dodge bankruptcy."

"We've sold the first. In time, we'll—"

"*Time?*" She pulls out a roll of smartpaper from her pockets, unfurls it like a courier about to recite the news. "We have nine days to sell enough robes to pay the manufacturer. Given our sterling reputation, having never been so late as a single day with a payment, I can obfuscate that out to twelve days. But then people will know. At this rate of sales, we won't *make* it to the Wisdom Ceremony—we won't be able to afford the ingredients."

"But the villages," Kenna protests. "They're saving up for—"

"Yes." Her smile is as sharp as a slipped razor. "*Saving.* Fractions of their tiny, tiny paychecks." She holds up the robe daintily. "These purchasers were the lords of their village, the best off, buying to show off. The rest? It'll take them months before they can afford their very own Kenna-robe. And by then, it won't matter *who* they buy them from, because *we* won't be here."

She taps the smartpaper, brings up Kenna's Q-rating graph—years of dormancy, followed by a sharp spike after arriving at The Sol Majestic. The spike sharpens after the broadcast with Captain Lizzie, where Kenna's name recognition now approaches 96% in maker circles. Kenna has vaulted up to minor celebrity status, and yet he hasn't had an email address since his smartphone was stolen months ago.

Scrimshaw snaps the paper, revealing the financial demographics of Kenna's fans. That line barely rises above the ragged floor of abject poverty.

"Your videos went viral," Scrimshaw sneers. "You couldn't have appealed to the wealthy, somehow? Not millions of hitchhiking hackers and underpaid waiters, but folks who might actually *dine* here?"

Kenna slumps. Mother and Father would disapprove—they *had* disapproved, telling him more or less the same thing when they'd watched the videos of him facing down Captain Lizzie:

You were filmed consorting with criminals? Father had roared, Mother curled up weeping in the corner, Kenna's feet tangling as he tried to stand tall like a prince before Father's rage-darkened face.

They weren't criminals, Kenna had protested. *They were talented people who had no outlet for their—*

They broke into a plant, drilled holes in the wall like terrorists! Didn't we warn you the bloggers were thirsting to drink your fine reputation up before you even began?

Father had brandished the smartpaper at him; Kenna had watched the emails pouring into Father's inbox, all Father's old contacts who'd finally deigned to return his correspondence. Mother and Father had been negotiating their rise back to relevance, Mother gleefully discussing how once they caught the right ears they could save the starving millions . . .

. . . And the old viziers and vice-presidents and CFOs were sending concerned emails about Father's wayward Prince. They'd seen him clad in a filthy robe like some hick, assisting addicts, and was *this* the new face of the Inevitable Philosophies? The bloggers were dissecting Kenna's behavior, the webs ablaze with essays debating his bravery or recklessness or immaturity or just plain slovenliness.

Well? Father's voice had been colder than Montgomery's frost-rimmed flesh when he'd hauled her in from space. *Is this low behavior an expression of your Inevitable Philosophy, Kenna? Or one last burst of rebellion before you settle on the path to wisdom?*

Normally, when Father had chastised him, Kenna had felt like an empty bottle crumpling under a boot heel. Yet he had been surprised to find himself not sinking into apologies, but standing straighter. Every word Father had spoken demonstrated ignorance, showcased how he refused to hear Kenna's side of the story . . .

Captain Lizzie did not believe me foolish, he had said. *And she runs a far greater domain than you have ever ruled.*

And oh, how Father's mouth had snapped shut.

This had not been triumph. Father had never been a violent man, but he told anyone who would listen that it was correct to dispense pain medicinally. Though the truth was, Kenna realized, that Father resorted to might when logic failed. As Father's jaw clenched, Father's corded muscles gearing into violence, Kenna vowed that this time, he would block the blows until Father's height and experience overwhelmed him.

Oh, Kenna. Oh, my sweet boy.

Mother's voice had been sweet as sugar syrup, uncurling from mourning to embrace her son. There had been something in the way she held her arms out wide, as if offering him temporary harbor, that had made Kenna stop and walk, hypnotized, into her hug.

She'd clasped him to her breast, running her fingers through his hair, untangling his fretted knots.

I know Captain Lizzie must seem like true power to you, she told him. *And why not? She's the first official you swayed with your Philosophy. Don't you remember that first time, dear husband?*

Father had grunted a mild assent, then turned to answer emails. Mother had kissed Kenna on the forehead, her lips still damp with tears.

But you think small, my darling boy. Captain Lizzie owns a mile-wide hunk of metal, so distant from the populated systems that no one bothers to fight her for ownership. She commands no armies. The slightest rebellion would topple her.

Kenna had stopped breathing. *You're not suggesting we—*

No, no. Mother's serene smile had filled Kenna with uncertainty. *I'm saying a woman in such a weak position* must *compromise, my sweet boy, or she'll lose her position.*

That hadn't rung true, even then. Captain Lizzie struck Kenna as someone who would fight to the death for what she believed in, no matter the odds. Yet Mother had spoken so certainly, as if her Inevitable Philosophy was calming his jumbled thoughts . . .

But the people who hold true power? she'd continued. *They don't compromise. The folks you must sway rule nations, corporations, confederations. And if you side against them, well . . . as we've learned so painfully, they can shut us out.*

But we're Inevitable, Kenna had protested, even though he wasn't Inevitable. *They can't stop us if we are true.*

Yes! Mother had said, tapping him on the nose fondly. *But do you think you'll* remain *true, rubbing shoulders with these planless wastrels? Why irritate the powerful men capable of creating true change, all to associate yourself with people who can't muster enough of a Philosophy to escape a menial job?*

Yet even now, when Kenna thinks of Mother's argument, his brain feels clogged with so many competing thoughts that it's like a meteor shower inside his head. There's something wrong with her logic, yet she's so clever, so Inevitable, it's hard to muster the right arguments . . .

Go work, she had told him, pushing him off her lap. *Watch the laborers. See their shabby dreams made manifest.*

And Kenna had gone to Benzo, hoping to drink in his friend's kindness . . .

Yet as Scrimshaw shakes her smartpaper to reveal the Majestic's balance sheets, Kenna feels himself crumpling under pressure again. Except this time, he is crushed by robes; that teetering heap of clothing, that one bloodred card jutting out at throat height as if to rebuke him for his foolish decisions.

Scrimshaw is right: what does it get you, appealing to the poor and the powerless? If only Kenna knew how to appeal to the rich. But maybe that's Mother's secret: she has a Philosophy, he doesn't, and that's why he's buckling under these flimsy robes . . .

Benzo braces himself against the warehouse's doorframe as though expecting to be ejected. "Scrimshaw," he says insistently.

Scrimshaw whirls around like she intends to rip off his head—then lowers her hands when she sees it's Benzo.

"I'll talk to Montgomery after the break," she mutters to him, facepalming as though she's got too much to do already. "I agree, Benzo; she's growing abusive. Especially since she's not—"

"I'll do it."

"—technically, a member, of this, kitchen." Scrimshaw's sentence stumbles to a halt. She blinks, once, twice, a great blink magnified by her owlish glasses: "You'll do what?"

"The Escargone." He creeps out to stand before Scrimshaw, hands clasped behind his back, vest smeared with broth. "I'll go."

"Oh, Benzo." She covers her kind smile, fearful to show the depths of her gratitude. "You know I won't pay you for that." She shakes her head. "Not one dinari."

Kenna frowns. "If Benzo jails himself in the Escargone for a month to rescue the Wisdom Ceremony, he's earned the cash."

He looks over, expecting to see gratitude from his friend for standing up for him. Instead, Benzo bares his teeth at the ground, staring at a spot on the floor as if he hopes Kenna will evaporate.

"*He* won't earn a thing, Kenna," Scrimshaw explains in a funereal tone. "Part of our agreement is that every dinari he makes goes to that frigid bitch who owns him. And I will *not* give that glorified slaver a dime." She kneels to shake Benzo gently, like a woman hoping to wake a sleepwalker. "Benzo, I know you want to earn enough money to set your family free. But the Escargone isn't that path."

Benzo works his hands behind his back like he's trying to free himself from handcuffs. ". . . Didn't say it was."

"Then why?"

"I just . . . I want to perfect the broth. In there."

"We have no *need* for broth, Benzo. Not for the Wisdom Ceremony. And . . . sterner men have gone mad in that damned contraption. There's no sense risking you for something we don't even need."

Benzo gives Scrimshaw such a clear, fearless look that Kenna's heart dubsteps, Benzo's blue eyes bottomless as black holes. "You need people to get in there, don't you? You already asked the kitchen. See any volunteers?"

She sucks air through her teeth. Scrimshaw loves it when foolish people correct her, but loathes being contradicted by the competent.

"Thought so," Benzo finishes.

"Benzo." Kenna creeps behind Scrimshaw's black robe, giving Benzo the space to show the affection he's desperately concealing. "You don't have to go in there. We'll find some other way . . ."

"I'm not doing it for you!"

Benzo's face is red as boiled lobster. Benzo pounds the air, once, twice, redirecting his anger inward. When he speaks again, it's as if he's strangling on his own hatred:

"I'm the kitchen fuckup. My palate sucks. I have *no* skill. And if—if I can come out of that triumphant, then won't that get them in there like you need them to?"

Kenna creeps out from underneath Scrimshaw's coat, expecting to watch her contradict Benzo—but instead, her wrinkled features are placid, contemplative.

Kenna's arms ache to hug Benzo, to pull Benzo to his chest, to stroke that wild blond hair until Benzo's anger pours itself out.

Benzo brings up one fist across his chest.

"I don't give a crap about the Wisdom Ceremony." Benzo speaks the words with the slight amplification of a rehearsed speech.

"Kenna will—he'll be okay no matter how that goes down. He doesn't need me."

"I—"

"No, Kenna." Benzo sounds so bone-weary, so exhausted, that interrupting him would be like tripping Paulius.

He steps around Kenna, making his plea to Scrimshaw. "This is just for, you know, it's for me, nobody else. And I'm gonna—I'm gonna take it. Tomorrow morning, I'm going in. I'm *staying* in until I make the broth. And if you think it's a bad idea, Scrimshaw, then you'd better stop me now, because I'm going in before tomorrow's prep work starts and I'm coming out with the broth The Sol Majestic deserves."

He faces Scrimshaw down until she bobs her head in acquiescence.

When he turns to exit, he flinches at the sight of Kenna. Kenna can't help but think Benzo scripted this whole encounter, but Kenna's presence throws off his bold speeches.

"You'll be fine," Benzo mutters. "Fine."

He walks away.

22

Three Hours Until the Escargone

The white linen cots in The Sol Majestic's sleeping chambers are neither numbered nor marked. Anyone could sleep anywhere on any given evening, given that all gear must be stowed away in the staff lockers, and the cots' sheets are washed by the laundry service every morning.

Yet the staff has firm opinions on who "owns" which cot, constantly jockeying for position next to the room's heater or next to their lover or away from the shower-stalls—a consensus arrived at by political machinations Kenna does not understand.

And so Benzo, who used to sleep close enough to Kenna that they could brush their fingertips, has relocated to the room's far side.

Kenna lies on his belly, trying to glimpse Benzo in the dim nightlights. The gauzy not-quite-privacy curtains billow as the heater kicks on: drunken waiters stumbling into their beds, giddy new lovers creeping in with dirtied outfits from the orchard, the fingernail-tap of sleepy dishwashers composing smartphone emails home.

The lights above Benzo's cot have dimmed.

It would be rude to go over, Kenna tells himself. Benzo had refused to talk to him after he'd announced he was going in the Escargone tomorrow morning. Benzo had stomped off to bed, his stiff demeanor like yellow caution tape wrapped around a repair site.

Everyone had watched as Benzo had laid down in his cot to stare grimly up at the ceiling.

Despite the flimsy curtains, Kenna's sure they see him watching Benzo's darkened sleeping area. The kitchen runs on black coffee and gossip.

Can Benzo see him?

Does Benzo care?

He blinks into the stirs of shadows, hoping to pick out Benzo when he comes over to talk to him . . .

"Hey."

Benzo's whisper prods him out of a sleep he hadn't realized he'd slipped into. The low rumble of deep-REM snores tells Kenna it's about three hours before the service preparation starts, well before the station's dawn-lights glow on. Cards slap on the table in the kitchen outside, a gambling session turned into a drunken all-nighter, but everyone else is asleep.

Kenna almost leaps out of the cot, but Benzo's hoarse whisper pins him to the sheets. Benzo stands an arm's length away from Kenna, clutching a black cardboard box, straight and still as an emperor's guard. His face is a composed neutrality—an expression Benzo has practiced in the darkness as he's stood by Kenna's bed.

Kenna doesn't smile, instead reflecting the studied concern Mother and Father use when listening to important political advisors.

Kenna's silence seems to throw Benzo off-script. He turns the glossy cardboard box over in his hands, something flopping damply within it—it's a Majestic carryout box, stenciled in silver. Yet Benzo shows no inclination to give it to him.

"Can you, uh, come with me?" Benzo asks. "I have to make a . . . visit. Before."

Before the Escargone, Kenna thinks, but the thought is obliterated in a firework explosion of happiness; *Benzo needs me.*

He smashes his grin into a pillow before following Benzo out of

the sleeping chambers, out of The Sol Majestic, into the station's
neon-glowing hallways.

The station's filled with the usual late-night detritus of red-eye
flight arrivals eating sauerkraut at the all-night booth and drunks
sopping up the alcohol with bowls of noodles. Benzo carries the
box high like an offering.

Kenna doesn't need to ask to know where Benzo's headed: he
knew the moment they passed their first docbot sign.

His giddiness fades as they head for the hospital, a procession
of two, Benzo holding his black gift box. His hands tremble like a
man off to face his firing squad, and Kenna realizes that to Benzo,
he will be locking himself in the chamber that mangled Paulius,
and oh, he is so very scared.

Should he tell Benzo the truth?

He tries on explanations, but his conversational gambits wilt in
Benzo's solemn march. Quiet will harm no one. They still have
hours before Benzo steps into the chamber.

They pad through the waiting room, Kenna wrinkling his nose
at the disinfectant smell. Benzo allows the hospital's scanners to
trace identifying rays across his retina; the door to Paulius's room
slides open.

Paulius is, of course, asleep.

The old man's mouth hangs open while he sleeps, a silent cry
of anguish; he's doped to the gills on painkillers, the gyroscopic
needles in the wall darting out to numb him as the sensors pick
up pain-flares. His stout belly is deflating like a souffle, his ribs poking out from underneath the pale flesh, the scars peeking out from
underneath his hospital gown's recyclable white.

Paulius has only two states now: in physical therapy and passed
out. The docbot has just six bays, and the station can't afford to
have one slot filled up with a long-term recovery. So despite the
massive soft-tissue damage caused by the crushed hip, despite his
body doing its damndest to reject the artificial bone, Paulius must

get up every six hours to walk. It is, Paulius has told Kenna, like his bones have turned to knives.

Benzo bows to Paulius, then lays the box upon his chest. Paulius stirs, placing one hand on the takeout box before drifting off again.

"He hates stasis cubes." Benzo stares down at Paulius, his expression unreadable. "Says they make food taste like burnt hair. He's got no choice, because fridges won't keep ingredients fresh across long journeys, but . . ."

"What did you prepare for him?"

"Pierogies." A gentle smile floats across Benzo's face. "His favorite food. I probably did a crappy job, but . . . He'll taste the love."

"Benzo, you'll be back to watch him eat them. Months shall pass for you, but . . . you'll return before noon."

The smile flickers off. "Sure."

"The Escargone is *safe*."

"That's what they say."

"No, it's *verifiably* safe. Paulius is—" He looks down at Paulius, wondering how he'd react if he spilled his secret in front of him. "He's got a condition—"

"For fuck's sake, do you have to ruin *everything*?!"

Benzo shuts out the world, hyperventilating into his palms; the monitors in the room cycle from green to amber, needles creeping out of the wall as they debate whether Benzo requires sedation.

"I invited you because—I wanted you along on this last bit." Benzo's fingers muffle his voice. "And all you do is *talk*. I don't want you to tell me how safe the fucking thing is, I don't want you to reassure me, I just—I want you to be my friend. Can you just fucking do that? In these final hours?"

"But it's not your—"

Benzo claws at his face, turning his anguished howl into a gurgled choke lest he wake Paulius.

"Hey, hey." Kenna grabs Benzo's hands and scoops him into a tight hug. Benzo's back as taut as mooring lines.

"It's all right," Kenna whispers, waving the needle-bots away. "I won't—I'll say nothing. I'll stay with you until it's time to go. Not another word."

". . . promise?"

Benzo has been trying to be so strong for this, but Kenna realizes he has a choice:

He can understand why Benzo is so scared, or he can give Benzo the peace he needs.

He cannot have both.

"I promise," Kenna whispers. Benzo sags into him, pushing his face into Kenna's throat as if Kenna can hide him from the world. Kenna rubs Benzo's steely neck and tries his best to channel love through touch, compassion, silence.

After a while, Benzo sniffs back the last of his tears, squeezing Kenna's hand before turning away. They walk back to the kitchen in silence, but Kenna can sense how honored this silence is. Kenna's presence soothes him.

They file into the kitchen, where the Escargone's door yawns open.

Benzo opens up the Majestic's vast pantry, filled with mazelike rows of stasis cubes stacked high in charging crèches, the low thrum of stopped time prickling Kenna's hair.

At any other time, Kenna would have wandered lost through this labyrinth of ingredients, marveling at The Sol Majestic's immense stockpiles. This is a periodic table of cuisine, allowing the Majestic's cooks to fashion any meal a guest requires. There are boxes containing a single truffle—and though Kenna has never had a truffle, he knows for that truffle to earn a place in The Sol Majestic's pantry, it must be the finest truffle.

These cubbies of galangal and nightlace buds and mélange spices are each trophies, judged worthy by Paulius's fine palate, authorized through Scrimshaw's thrifty expenditures, endless corridors of mouthwatering foods that Kenna the transport ship prince never could have imagined.

Yet Benzo slumps through the corridors as though inured to joy, glancing at the glowing LED readouts on each cube until he finds the label he is looking for: CHICKEN (WHOLE).

The LED readouts are identical as far as the eye can see. He and Benzo stand before an imposing wall of time-frozen chickens.

Benzo extends his palm. The biometric scanners identify him, check his permissions, log the access for Scrimshaw's perusal.

The cubes unlatch.

He detaches the first stasis container, hands it to Kenna.

They haul the first batch of chickens back to the Escargone.

There are hundreds of whole chickens to be hauled and dumped into the Escargone's old-style bucket freezers—and the chickens must be dried off to avoid freezer burn, stacked carefully so as to avoid bruising the tender flesh. The flesh is sun-warm underneath his hands, blood pooled in the stasis cubes; sometimes the chickens twitch as he picks them up, their final death-throes having been trapped in stasis.

It's not so bad, lugging the stasis cubes, though Kenna's arms ache from the effort.

Yet with each trip, he dreads entering the Escargone more and more.

This shouldn't be a problem, he tells himself. *I grew up on transport ships. This is just another cramped place.* But the light here is strangled, the mounted spotlights on the walls obstructed by the supplies necessary to survive here, chopping the cigar-shaped room into blinding light and pooled shadows.

Seventy-two chickens decanted and defrosted. Seventy-four.

So many freezers are strapped into the ceiling that Kenna must bend, stoop-shouldered, to make his way to the back. They work back to front, loading the supplies in the rear, and soon Kenna's knuckles are battered bloody from hauling the stasis cubes through the narrow twin-corridors of the ship. Either he bangs his hands on the dented copper prep-table running down the Escargone's center, or mashes his fingers against the push-up stove on the other side.

One hundred and sixty-four chickens decanted and defrosted. One hundred and sixty-six.

The *air* is different in there: a subtle reek of burnt grease and body odor masked by aggressively lemon-scented cleansers. Kenna's robe sticks to his skin like plastic wrap as the freezers' exhaust fans blow stale hot air across him. How bad would it be once the stoves were fired up? How did Paulius handle it?

How would Benzo?

Two hundred and fourteen chickens. Two hundred and sixteen.

The repetition gets to him—he bolts to the hatch when Benzo nods to tell him these chickens are stowed properly, gulping in whoops of clean air. He wants to suggest to Benzo maybe they should pack onions, or celery, but Benzo is an automaton. Kenna notes the clockwork pause he allows himself after each delivery, the way he rests his weight on the hatchway's frame for precisely three seconds, emitting one exhausted sigh before plodding out again.

He's steeling himself for repetition, Kenna realizes. *He's prepping himself for the insane orderliness he'll need to survive within.*

Kenna does the math: 214 chickens is seven months' worth of effort, assuming Benzo makes a single broth a day. But Benzo will do nothing but make broth. By now, Kenna knows every inch of the Escargone, and has seen no other entertainments aside from the single smartpad affixed to the wall. Paulius let men bring in their own smartphones, yet Kenna realizes Benzo does not dare allow himself distractions. There will be a smartpad for notes, two confessional camera-stations at either end of the ship where Paulius endlessly stockpiles footage for his blog, and cooking.

Endless, endless cooking.

Two hundred and eighty-six chickens. Two hundred and eighty-eight.

Kenna's hands are slimy with chicken feathers, his robe making sickly squishing noises as it detaches and affixes to his thighs with each step.

He plays games to keep himself sane: He inventories the supplies, one per trip. The hammocks are stowed against the wall. The showerhead and toilet are almost hidden behind the great stack of cleaning supplies; they'll be working overtime to keep this place sanitary.

"Wait," Kenna says, his bubbling thought breaking the silence. "What will you consume while you're in here? You can't live on broth."

Yet Benzo's not mad. His grim smile is knowing. He leans down to pull the tarp off a case stowed underneath the copper prep table . . .

"Nutricrackers," Kenna says.

"Another thing to remind me of you."

The air shimmers with the potential of a tender moment—but Benzo sighs and gets more chickens.

Kenna's not even taking a trip inside the Escargone, and the preparations are driving him mad.

Three hundred and sixteen. Three hundred and eighteen.

And with each trip, the chefs line up outside the Escargone. They arrive one at a time, scratching their armpits as they yawn to take in the kitchen—yet when they show up, the others elbow them into silence. They take up position like soldiers, standing shoulder-to-shoulder.

At first, Kenna feels a dull anger—*why don't they help?*—but with successive trips the skin on his back prickles into hives at the thought of entering that beast, a whole-body allergy to the ship. The chefs are equally fearful.

They cannot go in, but they can acknowledge the men who can.

Kenna wishes someone would smile. Yet even Montgomery has taken off her goggles, nodding to Kenna with each trip.

Three hundred and forty-two chickens. Almost a year's worth of supplies.

Could Benzo withstand this isolation?

As they hoist the last packed freezer to the ceiling mount, Kenna allows himself one question:

"*Do* the stasis cubes impart the taste of burnt hair?"

Benzo's chuckle is like hearing a champagne cork pop. He shakes his head in disbelief. "I dunno if you've noticed, but Paulius isn't always in touch with reality."

Kenna wants to laugh. But Paulius's fact-defying certainty has hauled The Sol Majestic through soul-destroying times.

Benzo cannot survive for a year in the Escargone. Paulius went into the Escargone with dreams to buoy him. Benzo's trying to carve weakness out of himself. Inside that dark ship, Benzo's self-hatred will feed on every failure, grow to suffocate him . . .

I believe in Benzo, Kenna thinks. *I could keep him going.*

"Come on," Benzo says, slouching out the front door. "We need to get the root vegetables."

Soon, Kenna will haul the last onion into the Escargone, and then he'll leave Benzo to spiritual starvation. The Escargone will devour his confidence and spit him out broken, so broken his Mistress would drive him to suicide with the lightest of touches . . .

Does he love Benzo enough to lock himself inside a room as tight as a straitjacket? To be so close to Benzo that there would be literally nowhere to get away from him for months on end?

To abandon his Philosophic dreams to boil away his thoughts in the monotony of manual labor?

That's ridiculous, he tells himself. *This isn't a commitment. If it gets to be too much, stop the ship and get off.* Yet Benzo, he is certain, will stay until every last chicken is cooked or he achieves perfection.

Would it be worse to abandon Benzo in midjourney?

It would.

If he does this, he has to commit as much as Benzo.

And as he hauls the crates of onions in, he ponders time's immensity—months drained away inside a six-meter-by-five room.

That hellhole's almost suffocated my best cooks, Paulius had moaned.
How can I rob Kenna of his best years?

By the time they take in the three sample containers of broth—
made by Keffen to give Kenna something to compare to—it is midmorning. Even Scrimshaw does not complain that the day's
preparations have not started yet. She kneels before Benzo, a queen
kneeling before the brave squire who might save her kingdom—
an image strengthened by the rows of The Sol Majestic's staff lined
up before them, fretting.

"Is there anything you need from us?" she asks. "Name it. We'll
make it happen."

Benzo's movements are slow, waterlogged, like a boy drowning.
"I need Kenna to . . . to sit there." He walks over, drags a stool
in front of the porthole. "I need him where . . . where I can see his
face. So when I look out, I can watch him watching me."

Yet he never looks at Kenna. His gaze falls into the Escargone's
abyss. And Kenna imagines Benzo stealing up next to the porthole
once a day to steal a glimpse of his friend's time-slowed face, only
to return to the dread routine of chopping and boiling and searing and dying . . .

"I'm coming with you."

The kitchen murmurs its approval. That, he realizes, is what
they were waiting for: for someone to accompany Benzo.

Benzo's sleep-darkened eyes go wide with horror. "What? No."

"I'll become your soup chef."

"That's *sous* chef!" Benzo paces in tiny little circles, tearing at
his hair. "And I—I don't need any preparations! You can't cut! Your
dishwashing, it's—it's terrible! And your—"

"That's not what you need," Scrimshaw says. Benzo's fingers
slump defeated at his waist, claw at the air, scrabbling for a counter-
argument he can't find the strength to muster. "You need friendship in there. And Kenna's your best friend."

Benzo shakes his head so violently that sweat-drops spatter
against the hatchway.

"*No.* No, no, *no.* I'm going in alone. I don't need—I don't—I don't need—"

"He's the Prince," Keffen, the lead chef says, with the gentleness of honey poured into tea. "He helps people. When he's scared, he does dishes. When he sees beauty, he takes control of a party and talks Captain Lizzie into changing the rules. Benzo, I know you're scared to let him help you cook, but . . ."

"Helping people's what he does," one person murmurs—no, two people, three people, half the kitchen speaks as one, then each looks surprised at each other to find they all quietly shared this faith.

Montgomery lets loose a low whistle.

Their confidence knocks Kenna out of his body. He feels as light as a hologram, an illusion they're projecting onto him. *I don't have a Philosophy,* he thinks.

He burrows away from their plaintive gazes, retreating into the Escargone, which seems a blessed sanctuary now—he'll have months before they unveil him as the swindler he is . . .

"Well, he's in there, Benzo." Scrimshaw's voice is rimed with an icy amusement. "Will you haul him out?"

"He shouldn't *be* there!"

Scrimshaw lowers her voice to an angry whisper, but Kenna hears her voice echo within the Escargone: "He's making a sacrifice out of love, Benzo. Will you throw that in his face?"

"But I . . . I . . ."

"Then go."

Benzo's stammering subsides to wordless negations, and soon even those objections wither before the crowd's confidence. And though he knows this will be for the best, Kenna feels sorry for Benzo: his single triumph in saving the kitchen has been turned into a referendum on whether he is a good enough friend.

It's all right. They will make the perfect broth. With three hundred and twenty attempts stockpiled away, surely one batch will be good enough.

The kid was just short of six years before Paulius took him aside, Benzo had said. *Said his palate wasn't good enough . . .*

Benzo storms into the Escargone as Scrimshaw slams the hatch shut behind him. Kenna offers a gentle smile as the great engines warm up.

A deep thrumming rattles the chickens in the freezers as Benzo sprints down a corridor, hands crooked into claws.

The metallic rattling drops an octave, the lights blue-shifting to a sickening violet as time outside slows and Benzo slams Kenna up against the cleaning supplies, bars of soap tumbling to the ground:

"*What did you do?*" Benzo's voice is choked with despair—no, not despair. He mutters through stiff lips, hiding his mouth from the cameras, almost subvocalizing so the embedded microphones won't pick his voice up. "*What did you* do?"

Kenna coughs as Benzo's forearm squashes his Adam's apple. Benzo slams him up against the boxes again before collapsing back down to the rubber mats on the floor, curling up into a fetal position.

Kenna falls on top of him, hugging him. Benzo stares at nothing, his skin a cardboard gray. The tension he's held all these weeks has ebbed into a limp surrender; Kenna rubs his shoulders, but his touch inspires Benzo's tears.

"What *did* I do?" Kenna asks.

"The outside door's broken." His voice is soft as a death rattle. "They can't get in, or shut it down."

"How do you know—"

"Because I sabotaged the door." He pauses long enough to register the shock on Kenna's face, then glances over Kenna's shoulder at the camera twisting to focus in on them. Paulius's automated blogpost-scanners, hunting for juicy footage. He speaks lower, encouraging Kenna to keep their secret between them. "By the time they realize things have gone wrong and shut the Escargone down, we'll have spent centuries in here."

"Can we—" Kenna feels the ship's weight closing in on them, looks at the thick glass porthole, imagines trying to smash his way out. He looks at the frozen chickens they've packed into the walls, realizing just how tiny their food supply is when compared against eternity. "Can we get out?"

"We weren't *supposed* to! I was supposed to be trapped and *die!*" He scrubs tears off his cheeks—but when he looks at Kenna again, his face is a portrait of regret.

He's concealed his impending suicide for a week. The brusqueness, the anger—Benzo was pushing him away, distancing himself from Kenna so he wouldn't be as sad when Benzo died . . .

"But *why?*"

"She's called me back."

"Who called—"

"*She.*"

He pronounces the word as if there is only one "she" in all the stars. Kenna realizes that to Benzo, there *is* only one: his master. The woman who owns Benzo, Benzo's family, Benzo's future children.

"She sent you here to become a chef," Kenna says. "She—"

"She knows we're going under."

A hard terror punches the air from Kenna's lungs. If Benzo's master knows of the Majestic's financial struggles, then who else knows? The merchants must be circling The Sol Majestic, watching for signs of weakness—Kenna pities Scrimshaw, who's been waging a secret battle to camouflage their fiduciary weaknesses . . .

"Between Paulius going down, and, and rumors she heard, She thinks we're going to tank hard. So She called in her marker last week. Scrimshaw talked Her into letting me stay through the Wisdom Ceremony, but . . . after that, She's bringing me back home. And I . . ."

Benzo throws his head back to inhale, a ragged half-cry like something horrible has been unstoppered.

"I lost the bet."

"The broth." Kenna curls around Benzo, so close the soft stubble of Benzo's cheek rubs against his. "That's why you were devoted to preparing so many broths these past few days. Because . . ."

"I thought I could win." Ironically, Benzo regains strength as he talks; he's been holding the anguish in for so long, sharing his impending horror has become a confession. "But now I've indentured my family, for generations. She'll pile on the interest for sending me here, bury them in debt. And every time I serve Her, I'll see Her smirking, me unable to say a damned thing lest She penalize me for insubordination, watching Her lap up my suffering . . ."

"You could make the broth," Kenna says. "We have a year."

Benzo compacts a planet's weight of self-hatred into one bitter laugh.

"There's no way in hell I can make that . . . broth, Kenna. I've known that for months. Everyone's nice to me because they know I'll lose. I've been struggling to make the simplest dish for three years, and *I can't do it.*"

"You could—"

"But I could wall myself away in here!" He mashes his face into the rubber mat to keep his words from the probing cameras above. "I secretly damaged the inside latch so everyone would think that poor, clumsy Benzo got accidentally trapped inside and was too stupid to fix the door. And I'd waste away, and everyone would have blamed it on a malfunction. Nobody could blame me. Even *She* couldn't make that bet hold up in court once I'd died in the course of duty. And my mother would be free of this debt I'd incurred, and my brothers would be free, and . . ."

". . . And then *you* showed up!"

In those words, spiteful though they are, Kenna hears the warmth of grilled cheese.

Benzo interlaces his scarred fingers through Kenna's, sinking down onto the mat.

"I was supposed to lock myself in and never come out," he

whispers. "I was supposed to die in an accident, so She couldn't say I lost. And then you had to come here and *ruin* it."

He shrugs Kenna off, heaving himself onto his knees, headed to shut down the Escargone and open the door.

"We could make broth," Kenna offers.

Benzo's smile is both genuine and exhausted. Kenna feels humored, as though Kenna had offered to fly to the sun to scoop gold from its surface.

"Not in a year, not in a decade, not in a century. I lack *talent*. I cannot—" Benzo swallows. "I *cannot* open that door and have them look hopefully toward my empty hands. I *cannot* walk out into a life where my failure dooms my family forever. I can't—"

That goofy grin peeks out from behind Benzo's anguished façade. Kenna realizes that even though Benzo is committing suicide, he's still happy because he doesn't have to pretend anymore.

"I'd rather die, Kenna," he whispers.

Neither can stand fully upright without banging their heads on the overhead lights. The ship's tinged with a penumbral violet, the claustrophobic blackness of space, closing in around them. The cameras whir like clockwork snakes, triangulating their position, recording their data for future entertainment.

Kenna imagines staying here forever.

All they have is nutricrackers, and chickens, then slow starvation. He imagines their bodies deliquescing on the floor, fruiting molds, whole new ecosystems blossoming in the Escargone's closed environment as decades pass, centuries, the recycling fans breaking down, bacteria mutating, new lifeforms forming a ghastly terrarium . . .

He imagines Benzo, stumbling out of the Escargone with a ragged beard and empty hands. He imagines the intake of breath as the kitchen prepares to cheer, the way their enthusiasm softens as they mark the gaunt failure etched into Benzo's face. The reluctance with which they approach Benzo, biting their lips as they try to think of something kind to say, settling on a mild congratulations as they mark that Benzo has, at least, proven the Escargone is safe.

Safer for better chefs to cook in.

And all the while, numbers pile up in a bank account in a rich woman's servers, Benzo's debt accruing, his Mistress selling his family members . . .

Why shouldn't Kenna stay in here? The restaurant is doomed. He has no Philosophy.

What better way to spend his life than helping his friend?

"I'll stay," Kenna says.

Benzo is afraid to acknowledge what he's heard.

"I'll stay." Kenna squeezes Benzo's hand. "That door will never open until you repair the lock yourself."

Benzo grabs Kenna's robe, as if to protest—then squeezes his eyes shut, scowling in self-hatred, knowing his friend has offered to give his life for people he's never met, knowing he cannot turn him down.

Kenna cups his palm across Benzo's cheeks, feeling the clammy wetness of too many tears.

"It's okay," he reassures him. "It's okay."

Benzo sobs now, his body rising and falling like the tides, and Kenna's back aches because he cannot stand straight to hold his friend like he needs to and oh God how long will it be before they finally die.

23

A Long, Slow Infinity to Die In

Benzo lies facedown on the thick rubber mat, propped up on his knees so his body weight mashes his cheek into the sticky floor-pad. He looks like a beached whale, having collapsed where he fell last night.

Kenna cannot tell if Benzo is breathing.

The Escargone is filled with noises—the freezer-banks' hiss, the generators' clunk-and-ratchet, the life support's whirring ventilation. And above all, the slow-motion sway of the Escargone, causing the wall-strapped cargo to creak like an old ship at sea.

Kenna had tried to escort Benzo into the pull-out hammocks—but Benzo had wept until his water was gone. He'd sagged limp in Kenna's arms. It had been all Kenna could do to draw a cupful of warm water from the reclamation tanks and force Benzo to drink it.

As Kenna creeps down the sliver of space between copper countertop and the enameled freezer-banks, making his way toward Benzo's body, his lungs cut out like a bad circuit. If Benzo is not breathing, then neither can he.

He pads up to Benzo, feeling himself splitting into two futures; one where Benzo snorts and wakens at his touch, and another where Benzo has died of heartache, and . . .

Kenna pushes a crate aside to look at his friend's face.

Benzo stares blearily back at him.

Benzo blinks reluctantly, resentful of his body's blank insistence upon living when he spent the night corpse-quiet.

Kenna's exhale feels like a ball dropping into the winning slot on a roulette wheel. He's seen that stillness on transport ships before; a few days after the ship left port, you'd find those men curled up in the corners like cockroaches, having distilled disinterest into death.

Kenna stands up, hoping the quick motion will inspire Benzo to mirror him.

"Leave me alone," Benzo mutters.

Kenna had seen addict-brothers pacing the transport ship hallways, pushing their necks underneath their friends' armpits, sweating as they hauled their friends around. "Stop moving and you're dead," they'd mutter, even though their overdosed brethren were usually too far gone to hear.

Benzo has overdosed on despair.

Should he march Benzo around the tiny track circling this copper table? Would Benzo fight him? Kenna tries to map out how to drag Benzo to his feet without smashing Benzo's cheek on a storage case.

Kenna inventories the ship's supplies to see what might be of assistance. He unsnaps a stewpot from the wire rack, running his fingers around the cold ceramic rim; maybe he could cook a chicken to inspire Benzo?

But that would destroy one chicken. They have three hundred and forty-two on-board—except when the last bird is gone, then so are Kenna's hopes of escape. He would die to protect Benzo's family—but lying down before the last broth has been wrung from their bodies is too much to ask.

"Benzo." Kenna taps the bottom of the empty stewpot like a drum. "Benzo, come on, just one broth."

Benzo's body caterpillars into a shrug.

"Teach me." Kenna drops the stewpot to hold out his wrists, offering himself to Benzo. "Teach me to make the broth."

He needs Benzo's strong fingers guiding his hands—his strength would flow out through his skin and into Benzo's heart . . .

Only Benzo's mouth moves, compressing into the ghost of a smile. Benzo has woken up every morning for three *years* now, trying not to remember his family in hock, trying not to remember his insufficient taste buds, pushing aside the weight of a thousand failures to convince himself that today would be different.

Kenna's asking Benzo to lift a weight that's already crushed him. Asking for more is the cruelest of kindnesses.

Kenna inventories his options, searching for something to spur Benzo into action. The serpentine camera at the Escargone's entryway cranes around with a tiny whirr of gears, the AI's insectile lens focusing in on the movement.

That's it.

Kenna falls to all fours, pressing his cheek against the copper table so the cameras cannot read his lips.

"She's watching, Benzo."

Benzo twitches like a man awaking from a nightmare.

"Or She will be." Kenna's body spasms as he digs his voice into Benzo's ear like a knife sliding under an oyster's shell. "Do you imagine She won't at least review the tapes when you pass on? What will her impression be if She sees you dying before the first attempt is made? No, no, Benzo—you've committed to three hundred and forty-two illusions . . ."

Kenna hears the harshness in his voice and realizes: he is channeling Scrimshaw.

"*All right!*" Benzo lurches to his feet like a punch-drunk fighter, snatching the stewpot off the floor so violently that Kenna dances backwards to avoid getting clobbered. "*Fucking!—get a chicken!*"

Benzo slams the stewpot down on the countertop. He roots his feet onto the mat: *I'll make the damned broth, but you will fetch me every ingredient, every knife, every pot.*

Kenna senses much dishwashing in his future.

Yet opening up the refrigerator feels like opening a tiny hatchway back to Savor Station.

Benzo hauls the chicken carcass across the countertop, leaving a smear of lumpy blood and befouled feathers. He shoves the stewpot toward Kenna: "Fill it."

Kenna dribbles it full from the reclamation tanks. The entire time, Benzo remains immobile, glaring down at the chicken like an oracle reading his future from its gizzards. The stewpot sloshes with water, enough to drown a bird; Kenna strains to bring it over without spilling any, but the pot is so large it seems to have its own tides. When he sets it down before Benzo, a tiny geyser splashes up Kenna's nostrils.

"Not there. There." He jerks his chin toward the pull-down stove. Kenna lowers it into position—the stove feels so low-tech after The Sol Majestic's smooth wonder.

Benzo closes his eyes to shut out Kenna's embarrassing idiocy. "Turn it on."

Kenna sees the wavering hiss before the flame lights up in a blue ring beneath the stewpot. Shadowy numbers coalesce along the pot's enamel sides: the rising temperature, the oxygen saturation, the water's impurities.

"Stabilize it at one fifty," Benzo says, gripping the chicken in his hands.

Kenna assumes Benzo means *degrees,* but the stewpot's choked with readouts. "How?"

Benzo shoves past Kenna to glide his fingers near the stewpot's surface. He doesn't need to touch it—the motion yanks a temperature gauge into position like gravity tugging a moon. "The stove is synchronized with the pans."

He snaps his fingers, and the temperature gauge locks into place.

The pot's user interface is some arcane gesture-language Kenna has never learned. He speaks basic UI languages, but every manufacturer has their own dialects.

Curls of steam plume off the water. When it reaches 150, Benzo snaps again to gain Kenna's attention, plunges the bird into the water, jiggles it with a curt jerking motion. He yanks it out again, dunks it back in, jiggles harder as if to say *Like that*.

He tugs a feather out; there is no resistance. He tosses the limp corpse to Kenna to pluck; Kenna never realized how many slimy crevices feathers can hide in. Benzo keeps pushing the bird back at him, jabbing at the unplucked areas until Kenna has rendered the bird uniformly, translucently pink.

He's never watched Benzo make a broth from start to finish. He wishes this could be something they shared, as opposed to something Benzo inflicts upon him.

Benzo splays the bird open, dissects it with a cold anger.

"Stop calling it broth," Benzo hisses, even though Kenna hadn't said a word. "We call it broth around you because you don't know any better. It's consommé."

"What's the difference?"

Benzo plucks out the organs like fruit, lays the chilled heart in a wide roasting pan. "Consommé is distilled from broth. It is clear as whiskey. It has no fat clogging the surface. It has no filmy residue swirling in dirty tornadoes."

And just as Kenna channeled Scrimshaw a few moments ago, Benzo adopts Paulius's theatrical tones. It is heartening to hear enthusiasm from Benzo, even artificial enthusiasm, as Benzo arranges the wingtips, the legs, the neck in a ghastly mosaic around the chicken heart.

He grabs the cleaver from his waist, chops off the chicken's legs. Then he flips over the cleaver, uses the blunt side to smash its webbed feet.

"Collagen," he says, taunting to demonstrate how little Kenna knows. "For the soup."

Even though the olive oil and salt are in tiny alcoves a mere step away, Benzo demands that Kenna hand them over. He drizzles the meat in olive oil, sprinkles it with salt, instructs Kenna to shove the pan into another oven he's set to 400 degrees.

Runnels of sweat gather in Kenna's cornrowed hair. He can feel the heat, the air in the Escargone heating up from the flame—and they have not yet begun to cook. He knows from the kitchen gossip that the Escargone's ventilators are inadequate, the temperature will rise dish by dish until the room swelters like a sauna . . .

Benzo snaps his fingers, leaning back against the stove like a sultan. "We clean as we go."

Kenna scrubs the boiled feathers out of the stewpot, hearing the hollow gurgling as the cramped sink's drain empties back into the nanofiltered reclamation tanks. He digs out the cleaning flakes and disinfects the copper table.

When Kenna is done, it's time to haul out the browned chicken bits. Benzo hunches over the pan, not flinching as popping chicken fat sizzles onto his cheeks. He moves his head in tiny circles, swooping over it like a military satellite analyzing enemy territory.

He glares at Kenna, furious this is something he cannot order Kenna to do, and then tilts the pan over the sink so a hair-thin trickle of fat seeps out. Benzo is as tense as a man defusing a bomb; it is as if the slightest wobble will cause all the flavor to spill out.

That fatty chicken taste infiltrates the Escargone's every crevice. Against that simple backdrop, the other buried scents come alive like a spotlight has been shone upon them; the stale odors of mummified dishes, dead herbs rising from the grave one last time to breathe their memories into Kenna's nostrils. Kenna feels surrounded by wrecked meals, feels the decades that have passed within this confinement, wonders whether their broth will leave its mark in the complex weave of Escargone-scents . . .

Your biggest contribution will be your rotting bodies, Kenna thinks.

Satisfied, Benzo scoops the roasted chicken bits into the stewpot, not trusting it to Kenna. He fills the stockpot with fresh water, holding up three fingers to demonstrate what depth to cover the bird in. Glittering jewels of fat swirl around the inside; Benzo scowls them down.

He instructs Kenna to bring the pot to a boil—and the moment bubbles break the surface, he gargles terror and swipes the stewpot down to "steam." He rests a pot lid askew on top of it, like a rakish hat.

Benzo fences off an area around the stove with his hands. "Do not," he says, "come near. Do not stir the broth. Do not jostle it with your footsteps. Do not *look* at it."

Kenna isn't clear why Benzo feels better imitating Paulius, but whatever gets his friend functioning. "What now?"

Benzo pulls his chef's cap out of his pocket, then puts it over his face, leaning back as if to doze. "We wait."

"For how long?"

"Overnight."

Kenna opens his mouth, preparing to ask, *So what do we do to kill time?* But Benzo's reproachful silence cuts his words: *You made me do this. I won't do more.*

And Kenna realizes: by using Her as a scourge, he had inadvertently become Her enforcer. Now Benzo treats Kenna with the sluggish responsivity any slave owes his master—he'll do the job, might even pass the time with Kenna if ordered, but no amount of goading could compel Benzo to enjoy enforced labor.

Kenna had threatened Benzo's family.

He hadn't. Not really. He was trying to get Benzo moving, to save himself, and that was . . . well, maybe it *was* selfish, as Kenna was saving Kenna, though there's a bolus of fury lodged in Kenna's throat he cannot swallow.

So Kenna watches the steam waft off the broth, watches the rise and fall of Benzo's chest, watches the cameras twitching.

When the time is up, Benzo dips a spoon into the amber broth. Kenna has been with Benzo long enough to read the stages of tasting on his friend's face: first he dribbles it to the back of his throat to check for silky mouthfeel, then to the sides to check for salinity, then rubs his tongue along the roof of his mouth to ensure the proper density.

All the while, his lips are pursed tight, as though he holds the broth prisoner.

When Benzo has sprinkled salt and tasted and simmered it down, Kenna stifles a groan as Benzo demonstrates how to chop the onions, curling his fingers back over the onion slices protectively—his blade moving in an assembly-line blur that Kenna is certain will draw blood.

Somehow, this isn't done yet.

Benzo crushes juniper berries with the side of the knife, scoops the remains into the pot. He takes out leaves with an herbalist's reverence, lays them in the soup like he was tucking in a lover. He swirls in the mashed chicken feet.

More time passes. Still Benzo says nothing.

At some point, Kenna feels he must be forgiven, but no remorse crosses Benzo's beautiful face.

He instructs Kenna to haul out a plastic tub, which they line with a strainer and a linen. Kenna ladles the chicken mixture through the filter one precious bowlful at a time, moving at snaillike speeds lest he stir up the sedimentary layers at the bottom of the pot.

"That's broth," Benzo says. But he rests his fists on his hips; despite himself, he is pleased.

They chill the broth in mason jars.

They separate out egg whites, the yolk's brilliant yellow nearly blinding Kenna. They fetch a leftover chicken breast from the fridge, cut it into finger-sized strips. They chop tomatoes, more herbs. Benzo obsessively tastes, trying to get the balance right.

They pour the broth into another, colder, stewpot. They blend the egg whites and the tomatoes and the herbs and the meat into what Benzo calls a *raft,* and then they pour that mixture into the broth and Kenna has learned how to set the stockpot on medium, and Benzo yells at him to stir, stir, stir, these graceful sweeping motions around the broth as it heats up with the egg whites, the egg whites trailing through the broth and catching the suspended solids like a great trawling net, stirring and stirring and stirring until the raft is a layer of detritus hovering over the perfection of the clear consommé like a garbage storm cloud.

He sags, flicking his fingers toward the strainer. Except now, he's not ordering Kenna around; he is paralyzed by fear.

"We strain it through another linen." He enunciates each word, as if they might stampede, panicked, out of his mouth. "Then we'll know."

Kenna stares down into the broth—no, into the consommé. He's devoted their last eighteen hours to assembling this monstrosity, which left him no time to contemplate whether it was any good. It's like running a marathon, yet being judged as a ballet dancer; simply finishing this should be enough, and yet subtle errors they made half a day ago could have destroyed this consommé's chances to set them free.

Kenna realizes: The consommé's clearness is designed to leave them no place to hide. The consommé is a single note struck with no chords to camouflage it.

It's like shooting a bullet at a star light-years away. You can't get lucky; your only hope is precision.

At last, he understands why Benzo despairs.

"That's a middenheap of work." Kenna's words his attempt to let Benzo know he comprehends the pressure Benzo is under . . .

The bleary gaze that Benzo shoots back speaks of years dissolved in drowned chickens, his family dying broth by broth.

He shakes his head: *No. You don't understand.* Then his chin dips, his floppy curls dropping down to hide his wide eyes: *I never wanted you to understand.*

He grips the handles, peering down into the pot like a fortune teller auguring madness.

"You don't know how much work." His voice is tender—but as Kenna reaches out for him, he deposits a ladle into Kenna's hand. "But you will."

24

Zero Seconds to Disappointment

Of course the consommé is cloudy.

25

Six Weeks in the Escargone

Six weeks in, and everything is boiling over.

Benzo starts a new consommé every eight hours—so three of the four cooktops are simmering broth, turning the Escargone into a chicken soup sauna. The ventilators fight mighty battles, but thyme-scented droplets collect on the roof, wet their necks with weak broth.

They breathe in clouds of rosemary, their movements stir wispy billows of stale chicken. Sweat prickles Kenna's skin, the temperature inside the Escargone always rising thanks to the banked stove-fire rings—and when he wipes the perspiration away, his wrinkled fingertips come away flecked with browned chicken particles. It is as though he is sweating soup . . .

Yet his mind remains his own. He *is* learning a trade, and yet while Mother and Father would have him believe the work demeans him, the truth is, the work barely touches him. If anything, he has *more* time to ponder Philosophies, his contemplation twisting into spirals—

If only he could think about anything but Benzo.

They scrub the surfaces with disinfectant, wiping away mold. They clean towels in the tiny washer, yanking them out as soon as they're done, pressing the dryer-warm terry cloth against their cheeks to remember what dry feels like. They check off the datapad's daily maintenance tasks, ensuring the antiquated machinery that *can* function inside a time-sped field *keeps* functioning.

The work is hard, made harder by Benzo's fumblings. There is but one pathway in the Escargone, a cramped loop around the copper preparatory table. Simple courtesy would dictate Benzo keep his elbows close to his sides, keep his workspace tight, flatten himself against the freezer doors whenever Kenna moves near so he might slide by.

Yet Benzo ambles about the ship slack-limbed, backing up in a panicked scurry whenever Kenna moves in his direction. He is forever misplacing his tools, forcing them to hunt behind every freezer for wherever Benzo left the spare hexagonal bolts.

The last time Kenna misplaced something, he starved for three days.

He could forgive Benzo's carelessness if Benzo would stop treating this operation like it was a military procedure. The cooking itself is like war: violent bursts of activity followed by soul-sucking dullness. There are things they could do, while the stocks simmer; the smartpads have a slim selection of old-style flatfilms. Kenna has found a deck of cards scrawled with GOOD LUCK, KID stashed behind the detergent.

Yet Benzo spends his spare time cross-legged on the countertops, scrutinizing the steaming pots with a faint frown—as though he could somehow expunge impurities through willpower alone.

Kenna too sits cross-legged on the floor at the Escargone's far end, linked to Benzo's motions; he cannot get up unless Benzo does. He wills Benzo to embrace him, to tell him a joke, to do anything that's not cooking-related.

He grasps Benzo by the shoulder after another failed consommé. He feels Benzo's momentum carrying him away before he jerks to a stop.

Benzo reaches back, patting Kenna's fingers uncertainly. More moisture prickles on Kenna's cheeks; it takes him a moment to realize these are tears, not lukewarm soup.

This touch is a lost man trying to find his way home.

Benzo turns, blinking too rapidly—then his eyes slide off Kenna to stare at the floor, as though he doesn't know how to talk to Kenna when not barking orders. "Yeah," he says, a hushed whisper vaguely inflected as a question.

This sudden softness startles Kenna. "I . . . perhaps we could . . ."

"No."

Benzo nearly swallows that single syllable of denial, but it's unassailable.

". . . I just want to *do* something, Benzo . . . A game . . . we have cards . . ."

Benzo's lush lips twitch into an unhappy frown before solidifying into a sour denial. "I can't."

"But *why?*"

A spatter of brown condensation dampens Benzo's blond curls. "If I look at the consommé, I think about consommé. If I play cards with you, the world opens back up again, and I think about my mother, and my brothers, and my family, and Her . . ."

He reaches up to squeeze the soup from his hair, then wraps his fingers around the roots and pulls until Kenna hears a thick tearing noise like carpet being pulled up. Blood dribbles down Benzo's forehead; Kenna grabs his friend's wrist before he can do more damage.

"I've got one shot to save everyone," Benzo whispers. "That's why I didn't *want* you here. Distractions unman me. I don't need a friend now; I need a kitchen to save my family."

I need a kitchen to save my family tells Kenna where Benzo's priorities lie.

Those priorities do not include Kenna.

Stunned, Kenna sits back down. He tries to meditate, but all his thoughts involve Benzo's body; the feel of Benzo's muscular midriff, the scars on Benzo's fingertips, the taste of Benzo's drenched hair.

He meditates for hours, trying to clear away these carnal thoughts—yet when he opens his eyes, minutes have passed.

How can he feel so achingly lonely? Didn't he spend his life trapped alone in small places?

But he never had anyone he wanted to *be* with before.

And Benzo only wants to be with the soup.

The silent minutes pass like sandpaper, rubbing at Kenna. Eroding his love for Benzo.

A few weeks later, Kenna sits down, feeling the cardboard box of cards pressing into his hip. He gets the box out and turns it over and over in his hands, wiping moisture across the cellophane covering.

He could play cards.

He's been imagining playing cards for days. He'd crack the seal on this thumb-worn box, then lay out the cards on towels—the waxed cards would stick to the soup-dampened countertops. He'd sweep Benzo's stray knives off the table, clearing a space in Benzo's gods-damned clutter.

Playing cards would be so much better than this bubbling silence.

And every time his thumbnail slips underneath the little red wire stub that would open the cards, he freezes—hoping Benzo will see how lonely he is, grab the cards from his hands to pull him tight against his chest—

Yet Benzo is lost in souply meditations. Cross-legged, as always. Peering into steam, as always.

Insensate to Kenna, as always.

Kenna puts the cards away, again, for the hundredth time. Benzo's misery has tainted Kenna's mood; Benzo's silence has stilled Kenna's voice. The Escargone's slow grind has compressed their feelings into the same diamond-hot anguish—but at least that's something they have shared.

Playing cards would decouple his mood from Benzo's.

Kenna clambers up, the black mat oozing wetness beneath him, and walks back to the scratched glass circle looking out into The Sol Majestic's kitchen.

Even though Kenna knows the kitchen is well-lit, viewed through the hatchway it is penumbral, shadowy, a maze of statues. The light from outside moves slower, robbing the kitchen of luminescence, color, motion—but if he looks out in the gloom until his eyes ache, he can make out Scrimshaw and Montgomery's gaunt silhouettes, hands flung high in the air, frozen in midair as they leap toward the kitchen entrance.

Away from the Escargone.

"Everything is so still out there," Kenna had once marveled to Benzo.

"Well, yeah." Benzo had focused on the chicken, bracing for another argument. "We need to be dead within an hour. Or they'll have time to fix it."

And as Kenna brushes his fingertips across the ice-glazed window, he wonders if Montgomery and Scrimshaw are running because they have discovered Kenna's sabotage—but that can't be. It's been weeks for Kenna, maybe months, yet minutes have passed in that free-roaming kitchen.

You made a vow, Kenna thinks. *You vowed to die in here to protect Benzo's family.*

Another thought fights that one: *You could walk out.*

He's watched Benzo maintain the freezers, swapping out motors; Benzo is no mechanical genius. Kenna's certain he could undo Benzo's sabotage, shut down the time-field, run out into the kitchen's cool air, his legs pumping as he runs through Savor Station's beautifully wide corridors . . .

The cards are in his hand again. He doesn't remember taking them out.

But if he plays cards without Benzo, then he might as well watch flatfilms without Benzo. And if he watches flatfilms without Benzo, he might as well form a life in here that's independent of Benzo—

—and Kenna knows *that* path leads to not giving a fuck about Benzo and walking out of the ship.

Already, he grows to loathe Benzo. Benzo and the way he leaves his tools everywhere and Benzo who leaves nutricracker leftovers on the table until they go fuzzy with mold and Benzo who, when Kenna damn near chopped his thumb off dicing the stupid carrots, tossed him a blue bandage and said, "Congrats. You're a real chef."

He didn't even look at Kenna's wound. He went back to mashing berries with his knife.

Paulius, he was sure, would have been more thoughtful.

He misses Paulius. Paulius explained himself as though he were narrating his own movie. When Paulius broke down, he exploded outward; Benzo's implosion feels like punishment.

Yet the worst thing—the thing that drives Kenna to this cool window to contemplate escape—is Benzo's incessant, prissy slurping.

Every eight hours, they try another consommé, each flawed: tiny shot glasses glimmering with fat, dark as maple syrup, light as machine oil. Benzo runs each through the machinery of his tasting factory, tossing the consommé into his mouth for a steady gurgle.

Kenna clasps his wrists so he won't hit anyone, counting down Benzo's gurgling inanity. And it lasts thirteen seconds, always lasts thirteen seconds, and Kenna guesses someone told Benzo how to do this once and this is how Benzo does it, how Benzo will always do it.

How could he have loved someone so stupidly plodding?

"It's too salty," he says. Or too light on chicken flavor. Or too saturated with juniper. He defrosts a thimbleful of Keffen's perfect consommé, holds it up to compare his wretched effort to this perfect centiliter.

And *every time* he stomps away, Benzo realizes he can stomp four paces away before he's standing in the shower, then covers his face and crouches below the copper workspace like a child playing hide-and-seek.

Kenna always sneaks up on the consommé, as though it were a grenade that might cover him in Benzo's madness. His fingers curl around the sweaty shot glass. He sips.

No matter how far away you are, your mouth will bring memories flooding back, Paulius had said. *Food is how we find our way home.*

Benzo's broth had once been his home. The garden's radiant sunlight had been suspended in that amber liquid, warming his belly, embracing him in love . . .

Now the soup lies cold in his gut, and his cheek is cold against the hatch.

The ice is bumpy; he pushes his fingertips into the coolness until they go numb, feels them sink deep as his body heat melts indents into the chilly scrim. He keeps coming back here for the cold, or so he tells himself.

The Sol Majestic is so close.

And—

"—the fuck?"

Kenna yanks his fingers away at the sound of Benzo's voice, his mouth already forming the words *I wasn't doing anything.*

Except Benzo crawls down the narrow pathway, like a grimy werewolf shambling on palms and knees. He growls, yanking out the largest boxes in the supply racks, sending smaller supplies rolling beneath the countertop.

The cameras snake back and forth, cataloguing this abundance of movement.

Benzo pounces atop the larger box, pinning it beneath him, reading the container. Then he rejects the box, shoves it back behind him toward the shower and sleeping quarters, not caring what breaks, and proceeds forward.

It'll take us hours to repack that, Kenna thinks, then feels shamed *that* is his first thought instead of *Benzo has gone mad.*

Kenna slams his palms down on a box of air-scrubbers just in time to prevent Benzo from heaving it over his shoulders. "Benzo, *stop!*"

"*Where is it?*"

Benzo's scowl slackens into a helpless confusion; his gaze bounces from Kenna's nose to his lips to his knees, as if Kenna's presence is some puzzle he cannot quite solve—

—*the soup,* Kenna thinks. *He's gotten so lost in his broth, he's forgotten someone else was here—*

—and Kenna's belly prickles as he realize how soulless and cruel he's been, Benzo's never grown up on transport ships, he's never been trapped for weeks at a time, and if Kenna is going mad then the relentless pressure must have cracked Benzo wide open.

His palm slides up Benzo's shaggy neck to press his friend's cheek to his shoulder, their bodies fitting together like puzzle pieces—

Benzo shoves him away. "*Where's the toilet paper?*"

Laughter sprays from between Kenna's lips like pressurized air— he didn't even know they *had* toilet paper on board—before a lightning-jolt of adrenaline courses through him.

Laughing at the space-crazy is a good way to get stabbed.

He's seen people 'roid out on the transport ships about the silliest things—a joint that won't stay lit, a neighbor's sniffles, a vending machine's rattle. Yet it's not the soggy joint that sets them off: boredom and cramped quarters turn trivial annoyances into excuses for murder. And it's not funny when you have to sleep in yesterday's crime scene and you're picking blood-flecks out of your hair.

There are knives scattered on the counters.

Benzo is crouched on his palms, ready to spring at Kenna—but he sucks steam between his teeth, his chest spasming like he's about to retch.

"It's not *funny!*" Benzo shrieks; Kenna suffocates his laughter. "I have to—I have to crap, okay? And I used up the last of the rolls! So where *is* it, Kenna? Where's the extras?"

Kenna swallows an urge to chide Benzo—doing weekly inventory is part of the maintenance. They've scanned every cupboard, and Benzo should know there's not enough room for Kenna to hide a box of toilet paper as a surprise present.

"I wasn't aware we had any," Kenna says.

Benzo's accusatory finger trembles before Kenna's eyeball. "Yes you did. There were six rolls. Behind the toilet."

Benzo draws back his finger as though he plans to jab it through Kenna's eye. Yet Kenna's body refuses to believe it's been threatened—Kenna is slack-limbed, unable to comprehend how Benzo is that mad about something this inconsequential. He wonders whether the murdered men died with this stony disbelief.

Kenna raises his hands in surrender—and then, moving in slow motion, he sweeps his palm across his face to nudge Benzo's fingertip aside.

"Perhaps there were rolls," Kenna says, dimly recalling his surprise someone had stashed luxuries on a stripped-down mission. "I wouldn't know. I don't use them."

"Then what do you use?"

Kenna holds up his left hand.

Benzo leans in to see what Kenna is holding—and then, when Benzo realizes Kenna's hand is empty, his lips pull back in disgust. Kenna watches as Benzo scrutinizes Kenna's short-cut fingernails, as though Kenna could be so filthy as to not wash his waste off properly.

"That's disgusting."

Kenna rotates his palm, looking at it with airy disinterest. "It's what is done upon a transport ship. We can't afford to haul tons of wood pulp when a hand and a chemical sink will do the job with equal efficiency. I thought you were a slave, Benzo."

Benzo straightens, trying to seize the high ground by accentuating his height. "I am."

"A slave with *toilet paper*?"

He rubs his forearm across his head, squeegeeing off droplets of sweat. "All the slaves have toilet paper, Kenna, it's not a big thing—"

"My mother toils to save the starving millions." Kenna slices through Benzo's feeble justification like a blade through fresh celery. "And I can tell you—they squat in fields. No one brings them cottony sheets to wipe themselves. You arrived in a ship stocked with *toilet paper*?"

Benzo wipes off his forearm, which looks ominously like a man dusting off his sleeves, readying for a fight. "I was *brought* here in a ship that—"

"Did you get *fed* on this onerous journey?"

"We ate cold offal." Benzo throws down a gauntlet with each syllable. "Mashed up with stale bread—"

The thought of a bowlful of meat swamps Kenna's tongue in drool. "I starved for three *days* before I got here, Benzo! You know what a luxury meat would have been to me? To *anyone* in the passenger hold?"

"Well, you got to go where you *wanted*! *You* could fly anywhere in the stars! Me? I—"

Benzo splutters as the words abandon him, then yanks up the blue Kevlar scrubs he's wearing.

In all their time together, Kenna has never seen Benzo shirtless. He's always drawn the curtains on the sani-shower, always gone to bed in a thick nightrobe. Looking at Benzo's bare chest, Kenna realizes why:

Benzo's ribs are etched with black-and-silver nanofilaments, stark against his milk-pale skin.

He twists, and Kenna tries to follow the movements as the nanofilaments flex along with his body. The glimmering black ink loops in and under his muscles, the technology sunk deep into his body, then emerge elsewhere as though someone had strung his rib cage like a violin. Kenna envisions Benzo's beating heart struggling tight in those nanofilaments, a fly in a spider's web.

"She can shut my organs down at will!" He digs his nails into the black fibers, raking through them until his skin tears, then holds up his hands as the fibers knit themselves shut. Blood oozes down over his stomach. "No ship would take me! She's *marked* me! Every RFID scanner marks me as *cargo*!"

All Kenna can see is the soft bulge of Benzo's belly—that doughy layer of fat Benzo takes for granted.

"*That's* slavery?" Kenna scoffs. "Not choosing where you *journey*? Mother and Father never asked me where I wanted to go— and there were days I would have sold myself for guaranteed meals!" Kenna lifts up his blue scrubs; even after weeks of eating, he can still almost fit his fist beneath his rib cage. "I locked myself in here because I thought your family was suffering in *servitude,* Benzo! I didn't jail myself to save some gaggle of pampered house-slaves!"

Benzo slaps his chest, the nanofilaments seething protectively in writhing tendrils. "She breeds us like animals!" He grabs his crotch. "She neuters us like animals!" He pounds his heart. "And when our ratings fall beneath Her thresholds, She *slaughters* us like animals!"

"Then perhaps you'd better treat me better."

The words spill out of his mouth like a fuel leak, hot and hateful, each word igniting the next.

"I've watched men flood their veins with drugs until they turned purple and rotted. I've watched babies get smothered because there wasn't enough food to last the trip. And I am *done* feeling sorry for you and your family. All you've done since I've imprisoned myself with you is ignore me—"

He leans in close, his breath on Benzo's ear, tilting his head so the cameras can't read his lips:

"And you want to think *very carefully* about ignoring a man who holds the fate of your family in his hands. I could repair your feeble sabotage while you sleep. I could tell Scrimshaw of your plan. You'd never touch a stewpot again."

Benzo's fingers clutch at his breast, struck so dumb by Kenna's threat that he needs to brace his heart. The nanotendrils corkscrew underneath his fingernails, drawing out thin threads of blood as they deter Benzo from touching the bonds She has placed upon him.

His gaze ping-pongs around the Escargone's rat-trap mechanics, looking for an escape. His eyes come to rest on a space behind Kenna—and then look elsewhere.

Kenna's caught him staring at the knives.

Kenna grabs Benzo's shoulders, feeling Benzo's dim panic resonating up his palms. He tugs Benzo against him, rejoicing in Benzo's newfound pliability, he's been watching that stiff spine for weeks, maybe months, begging Benzo to pay attention—

Now Benzo has to.

"You could try," Kenna whispers, suffocating Benzo's embryonic plan. "But you'd better come at me fast, Benzo. Because if I see you coming, I'll yell what you're trying to do. The cameras will record my murder, and the reason for it. And *then* what will you do?"

Benzo goes limp. Kenna shoves Benzo backwards, steps over his friend's sobbing body to snap down a hammock. He rolls into the warm fabric, rigid as a stone, crossing his arms over his belly, the fabric taut against his ears to shut out Benzo's cries.

Kenna's been suffering mutely for weeks, maybe months, to ensure Benzo can rescue his family—and Benzo's family had full bellies, had beds, had *toilet paper.*

Once Benzo dries those gummy tears off his cheeks, he will ask what Kenna wants. He will crawl here to ask Kenna what must be done to satisfy him.

Kenna stares at the ceiling, not blinking as condensed droplets plop into his eyes, contemplating all the things he will make Benzo do when the new Benzo rises.

26

Unknowable Months in the Escargone

It's hard to tell how much time passes in the hammock; all Kenna can see above him is the shower head, bolted into the wall, and the access panels of the Escargone above. He's read their torn labels a thousand times since he crawled in here—a blue sticker reading PLUMBING ACCESS, a scratched red bar code reading H026P3, a tiny label reading WARNING: THESE SECONDARY SYSTEM(S) MUST BE CONNECTED TO A GROUND ELECTRODE.

On the far side of the ship, he hears Benzo sobbing into a towel, muffling his anguish. Occasionally there are metallic clanks.

It's been so long since Kenna's moved that the rigidity has permeated his limbs. There's a grim satisfaction in staying motionless even as the steam condenses upon the panels above him, breaks free to plop on the water-resistant hammock, slides down to soak his underwear. He can feel his ass turning pruny, but refuses to give in to the urge to get out and towel this dampness off.

It's starting to feel foolish.

Initially, Kenna stayed put because he'd been waiting for Benzo to come to him. He'd spent so many hours watching Benzo stare into steam that he figured he owed Benzo a few minutes of stony silence. Benzo would crawl beneath the hammock—he'd never dare look down into Kenna's space, not when Kenna had the upper hand—and he'd beg in a broken whisper, "What do you want me to do?"

The inflexibility had felt correct, then: he was an idol, waiting to be worshipped. Motion would have signaled compromise; it was time for Benzo to serve him.

Then Kenna realized he'd have to answer Benzo's question: What did he want?

He wants Benzo to fry him up a gooey grilled cheese sandwich, like he'd done before all this foolish consommé concern. But there was no bread in the ship, no cheese.

He wants Benzo to beam that crooked, lush-lipped smile down on him, but Benzo's face is a gauge that reports his emotions. Benzo could be compliant but never convincing—his lack of artifice why Kenna holds Benzo's friendship so dear.

Kenna comes to realize that what he craves is Benzo's company, yet what he has created is a hostage situation.

His body weight settles deeper into the hammock, the taut fabric squeezing his arms so the muscles strung beneath his shoulder blades twitch in rebellion.

Yet if he moves, isn't he stepping away from Inevitability?

He envies Mother and Father; for them, Inevitability is a quality they possess, not some thought that slithers away when they're distracted. Kenna remembers feeling the stars align behind him as he commanded Scrimshaw—Scrimshaw!—that *The Sol Majestic must stay open*, and even as he probes his feelings he feels not a speck of doubt that The Sol Majestic must grind itself to bits or reignite its glory.

Whatever Mother does, she *commits*. And she too has worked miracles, standing outside great politicians' offices, telling them she will not be moved until the vice chancellor sees her or jails her.

No argument has ever swayed her.

Yet an hour listening to Benzo's muffled tears has boiled away Kenna's conviction. He makes excuses for Benzo: yes, his family's bellies were full, but what other depravities did She inflict upon them? He remembers Benzo licking his lips as he struggled to find the right words, then Benzo all but howling as his anguish had overridden his thoughts. Kenna hadn't asked how She had neutered them, what other horrors those nanofilaments inflicted, had handwaved the thresholds and the tests She inflicted—no, he'd simply spoken more incisively about *his* pain.

Kenna had won the argument by dint of being *clever.*

A droplet plunges into Kenna's eye, salty and stinging.

Even if Benzo's family *had* been as spoiled as Kenna had believed in that moment, would that have made it okay for Kenna to demand Benzo choose allegiances? Benzo loves his mother and brothers deeply enough that he'd starve to death to rescue them.

When had Kenna begun to grade levels of suffering? If Benzo was truly his friend, wouldn't Kenna cease to care about how much Benzo should *be* hurt, and worry about how much Benzo *was hurting*?

His fingers spasm; Kenna locks them tight. Moving now would acknowledge his mistake, and Kenna is not quite ready to relinquish victimhood's pleasant illusion.

He sags in the hammock, coming to realize the indignity: he's spent years batted about by Mother and Father, by transport ship staff, by diffident politicians. That submissiveness became incorporated into his very DNA, blinding him to the possibility that some day he might gain potency. He had sat waiting for Benzo to acknowledge him because he could not comprehend there was anything to do *but* sit and hope his friend would grant him an audience.

Yet when he achieved unquestionable power over another human being, he became a monster.

This, Kenna realizes, is not Inevitability—or if it is, then he wants no part of it. Setting aside his justifications is like plucking burning coals from a furnace with his hands—there's anger, so much anger, over what Benzo has done to him, and he is right to *be* angry. But nothing can justify threatening Benzo's family.

He fights his way to the unsatisfying truth that everyone is to blame, but the only thing he can change is his faults.

And so Kenna wills his cramped legs to swing out of the hammock, getting up to beg forgiveness of a man who has hurt him.

As the hammock tilts, a skin-warm flow of sweat and condensed steam streams over him, spattering onto the drains beneath like a blister bursting.

He rises, sweeping his gaze across the quarters to find Benzo—

And Benzo is naked, slumped shoulder-first against the hatchway, staring down at his bloodied wrist. He's gripping his maimed wrist with his good hand, staring befuddled down at his wound, so wracked with grief that his body has seized up like an engine without oil.

His chef's knife lies on the ground before him, its sharp edge rimmed red. Sluggish drops of blood hang off of Benzo's elbow, his albumen-pale forearm limned with dark red streaks.

"*Benzo!*"

Kenna dashes toward Benzo, but his legs have gone numb; he tumbles face-first into a crumpled detergent crate. He shakes the soap granules off his eyelashes, feeling his guts congeal with the realization he waited too long to apologize . . .

"*Benzo!*"

Benzo jerks back in an apology so apocalyptic that he bangs his scalp against the bulkhead.

"Sarri." Benzo's tears dissolve his once-strong voice—or is that the slur of blood loss? "Sarri. I trieda fixit, but I din wanna disturb you . . ."

"Fix *what*?" But Benzo's so ashamed he clutches his injured hand to his chest to hide it from Kenna. Kenna grabs for it, hoping to see how deep the wound is—Benzo flails at him, making whimpering animal noises. "Benzo, fix *what*?"

". . . the dammij . . ."

Benzo slides down the wall, his head thumping against the sabotaged access panel. There are gleaming slivers of freshly exposed metal knifed across the panel's dull sheen; one of the nuts fastening the panel to the hatch has been screwed off, the second is smeared with blood.

Has Benzo been trying to cut the panel open?

"Benzo, if you wanted to repair the lock, the . . . the screwdrivers are right over there." As he points toward the tool case, Kenna sees the red steel bolted next to the shower, not six inches away from the hammock, and realizes Benzo was too terrified to get the tools and rouse Kenna.

That's foolish, Kenna thinks, then realizes he's not spent his life under a slavemaster's whims.

A full belly didn't mean Benzo didn't have his own torments.

"Benzo, I'm not . . . I'm not Her." Benzo wails and pulls in tighter, sobbing, and Kenna realizes channeling Her power had flooded Benzo with traumatic memories. He imagines Benzo, trembling as he summons the willpower to disturb the man who controlled his family's fate, trying to convince himself that Kenna didn't mean it, breaking down from the strain of rebellion.

"Gods, Benzo, I'm so *sorry*." Kenna is filth, he is waste, he has harmed his friend who has accidentally cut himself open trying to fix the Escargone with a knife . . .

The knife.

Benzo had slashed himself trying to pry open the hatch.

Which meant Benzo had given up hope of the perfect broth. And rather than dying in the Escargone, he'd injured himself in a frantic attempt to set Kenna free.

Except he's not injured, Kenna realizes, the bile boiling in his throat. The nanofilaments are writhing across the cut like worms, repairing the damage—of course She wouldn't allow Her slaves to destroy themselves . . .

"I couldn't . . ." Benzo wheezes like a broken accordion. "I *tried*, Kenna . . . Either you died or they stayed in Her hanz . . . I hadda *choose* . . ."

He wails the words, tilting his head back so his throat will open wide enough to let loose his sorrow, and only now does Kenna realize the pressure Benzo's been under. He'd thought Benzo was only concerned for his family, but Benzo had been terrified about killing his friend—and why not? Benzo would get to watch Kenna starve to death, or watch Kenna slit his wrists, or see Kenna swallowing back tears as he plunged the knife into Benzo's throat to end it.

"Only way I could save both aya wasda cook a perfect broth," Benzo mumbles. "I hadda winna bet to keep everyone alive, and I . . . I . . ."

Benzo chews his mushy words into a defeated silence.

Despite the moist heat, Kenna's breath flash-freezes into liquid nitrogen. Benzo's devotion to the task was his way of *protecting* Kenna, how could Kenna not have understood, Benzo was drowning his affection for Kenna in consommé because cooking was his best chance to get Kenna out alive, and . . .

God, Kenna has been such a child.

Benzo gulps in hitching breaths, his lungs too shriveled to hold his sorrow. He grasps Kenna's blue Kevlar gown, pulling his way up Kenna's body, and with relief Kenna sees the gash on Benzo's wrist is shallow.

Benzo's tension slackens as he sags into Kenna's arms.

"I can't do it." Benzo's voice sounds like a broadcast from a distant star. "Open the door. Send me back to Her. I'll be a talentless fool, but I won't have murdered you . . ."

"Benzo . . . your family . . . is it . . . ?"

Benzo nods, shivering, cutting off Kenna's query: *It's that bad there.*

Kenna looks over Benzo's shoulder, through the dimmed hatchway window, imagining unlatching the Escargone's door to walk into freedom. He envisions taking that first breath of dry air, not filling his lungs with this moldy chicken-steam, feeling sweat prickle off his arms instead of dribbling back into his robe. He imagines stretching his arms out without banging them into the freezer, running down the hallways . . .

He tries to imagine Benzo's family. He can't; Benzo has never spoken a full sentence describing his mother before his throat swelled shut with remorse.

Yet he can imagine the merry light in Benzo's eyes forever extinguished by lifelong failure.

"Then you must do this." Kenna tugs Benzo, jerking his whole body toward the remaining chickens. "You must at least try."

"Then you need to give it to me."

He speaks as though it's obvious what Kenna should give. "I'm uncertain what you . . ."

His laugh is bitter as a bullet. "It's why I envy you, Kenna. We struggle to serve Her, working eighteen-hour days, jolted awake by electrical shocks—"

Benzo traces his fingers over his squirming nanofilament bands; they lap up the blood, fed by his body to dominate his body.

"She tracks our hormone levels, our blood pressure, our EKGs— punishing us for *feeling* resentful. She won't tolerate anything but pure adoration. It took me years to trust that Scrimshaw had disabled Her trackers so She couldn't steal the kitchen's secrets. I had nightmares that I went back, and She'd recorded everything, and She would shut down my eyesight, deactivate my mother's pancreas, destabilize my brothers' immune systems . . ."

Whenever Kenna had imagined Benzo defying his Mistress, he had envisioned that bet as a huge showdown—Benzo flinging trays to the ground, shouting defiance. Now, he realizes Benzo's rebellion had been a subvocalization—a stray thought he had refused to take back, a pebble in his Mistress's shoe that She had reacted to by forcing him into monstrous bets.

Kenna envisions himself as Benzo, trying to crawl across the Escargone to get to the man who'd threatened his family. His chest itches with flashbacks to biological punishments a creative sadist could hand out, knowing that even reaching for the knife without Kenna's say-so must have been overwhelming . . .

"But I saw what they did when they united behind me, Kenna. When I made a—a *bet*." His lips purse into a silent whistle, still amazed after all these years. "I know they still think of me back in Her corridors. They toil under Her quarterly deadlines in the hopes that I might prove Her wrong. I'm the steel beams in their structure, Kenna, I'm why they don't collapse inside.

"And I . . . I don't *have* that strength.

"I've been trying for three years to make one perfect dish, and everything has boiled away in that pot—my arrogance, my confidence, my *hopes*. I've got nothing. But . . ." He smacks his lips. "You, Kenna. You stood up to Captain Lizzie. You stared down Scrimshaw. Nothing can stop you . . .

"I can't do this without a Philosophy. Give me yours."

Time slows. He knew he'd have to lie to millions to become the Fraudulent Prince, yet he'd never imagined the first person he'd lie to would be his best friend.

Why did you ask for the one thing I cannot give?

". . . I can't."

Benzo's beautiful body falls into Kenna like an asteroid tumbling into a sun's gravity well—and he *croons* in a cracking addict's voice. "Kenna, please, I *need* to know what you know . . . What makes you Inevitable . . ."

Kenna shoves Benzo away, repulsed—not by Benzo, but nauseated by how worthless he is, how all his lies have been exposed. But Benzo keeps crooning, begging, until Kenna shouts:

"If I had any Inevitability about me, would I have lost my temper at you?"

Kenna fears he'll have to explain further. But it's a small mercy that Benzo knows him well enough to understand what he's admitted.

And it is heartbreaking, seeing Benzo abandon his own pain when he recognizes Kenna's anguish.

". . . but how?" he asks. His blue eyes are so earnest, he's like a boy asking to be told how the magician's trick was pulled off . . .

Kenna can't stare into that beautiful trust. He looks away into the shadowy murk of The Sol Majestic's time-slowed kitchen, feels the sharp electric shame as he thinks of the chefs out there who believe in him . . .

He drops his chin, studying the wriggling black filaments embedded in Benzo's brawny chest.

"Paulius bought so many of these bedamned robes, he put the Majestic into hock," Kenna says. "And the only way to sell enough robes—to save the Majestic—was to fake a Wisdom Ceremony. So I did."

It's a much shorter speech than he'd thought it would be.

Lifting up to look at Benzo takes more effort than anything he has done in his life. He doesn't want to stare into Benzo's bleak despair as his friend realizes nothing can save them . . .

Instead, Benzo's face blossoms into a grin. "You've got nothing."

Benzo speaks as though he has just been told the funniest joke in the world. Kenna should be shamed by this accusation, but . . .

Instead, he thumps Benzo's bioengineered chest. "Well, *you* have no talent."

And Benzo burbles with laughter, a high and joyous titter flowing out of him, spilling into Kenna and Kenna is laughing and it feels like an old clogged engine spitting out dust. "We've got no hope!" he cries.

Benzo nods happily—he's staring the worst-case scenarios in the face, but it's okay because he has Kenna. "We're going to die."

"We are going to die so horribly," and when Benzo says it this absurdity is a thing of beauty, and then he mutters, "Come here, you," to pull Kenna in for a kiss.

And Benzo kisses him, and Kenna worries that his mouth tastes foul, his robe is sticky with chicken-sweat, Benzo's wound pulses blood down the side of his neck—

But when he feels the soft tip of Benzo's tongue slide into his mouth, all that is swept aside. It's like being struck by lightning, *love* lightning, that Inevitable certainty that once they've stripped away all hope they *still* have this love, so why not fuck madly and wildly when there's nothing left to lose?

Benzo strips Kenna naked, and everything is beautiful.

27

The Morning After

Kenna has discovered how paralytic orgasms can be, and he never wants to move again.

He lies with his cheek pressed against the black rubber floor mat, every muscle so slack he's certain his bones must have dissolved into semen. The warm steam traps the feel of Benzo's strong hands on him, his limp cock sticky and rubbed blissfully raw. He and Benzo had drawn pleasure from each other's bodies, stretching their desire out like spun cotton candy until they'd been reduced to twitching nerve bundles . . .

Benzo had come first. Kenna's mouth crooks up in satisfaction at that memory. But Kenna had come instantly after, the pleasure boiling up and out of them. Everything had erupted out of him, all their stress, all their concern, and he'd flopped to the floor.

He's drooling. Like a baby.

Yet eventually, the rattle of pans and the hiss of boiling water rouses him from the dream. He could sleep, but his love—yes, *his* love—has stirred, and he needs to see what Benzo is doing.

He pushes himself up, the soft suck of the rubber informing him that he's been happily comatose for hours.

Benzo is stark naked, knife in hand, whistling as he spreads another chicken across the table.

He moves, loose-hipped, among the stations, cutting the chicken open and then swaying over to chop the celery. Benzo had always had a grim assembly-line rhythm. Now, he bobs up and down, his blade seesawing through the onion to a secret music.

He sees Kenna stirring, winks, shoots him finger-guns. He does a little salsa backstep, shoulders dipping, encouraging Kenna to join in. Kenna staggers over, his legs weakened when he imagines his palms on Benzo's bony hips again—and Benzo spins the knife down the table before sweeping Kenna up in a drop-kneed tango.

They dance, pressing their thighs together, Kenna's hands moving across the nanofilaments on Benzo's back, shifting between the cold feel of his lover's embedded technology and the kiss-hot patches of skin. Benzo massages Kenna's neck, his touch melting his muscles—

The pot boils over.

Benzo breaks away to wave frantically at the pot, instructing the UI to lower the heat—then shrugs a goofy smile in Kenna's direction.

"The chicken's gonna go bad if we fuck again," Benzo says.

Kenna shivers at the word; *fuck* feels so deliciously naughty, and yet so workaday. He'd heard Mother and Father making love sometimes—you couldn't help overhearing things in transport ships—but they'd never spoken of it. Any desire that distracted from their Inevitability was—well, not quite shameful, but certainly impolite.

Benzo's word unseals a whole new world for Kenna. It speaks of a servant's crudeness, a plain talk that trades elegance for practicality.

Kenna loves to fuck. He tries on the words.

They suit him.

Kenna fetches Benzo's chef's coat off the floor, wraps Benzo lovingly in it. Benzo leans against him, purring. "Covering me up so you're not tempted?" he asks.

"Making sure you don't cut that beautiful cock off," Kenna ripostes.

Benzo's laugh is a shy snort, his thighs pressing together at the thought that anything he has is beautiful. Kenna intends to lavish praise on him every day; now they're in love, he will adore every square inch of that wondrous body.

Benzo has yet to move, dazed by the compliment. Kenna smacks him on the ass: "Cook."

Kenna leans back, the metal chill against his bare ass, thrusting his hips forward; his nakedness feels like a glorious advertisement. Perhaps he's enticing Benzo with a reward for an exceptional job done?

Benzo works efficiently, hoping to finish the broth to get to Kenna. He cooks the chicken, dices the carrots, bopping along to that jaunty tempo. He retrieves a palmful of juniper berries from the fridge, their deep-space purple laced with frosty nebulas.

He winces. "Ugh. I can't stand the way these things smell."

Kenna pulls himself up onto the counter, then regrets it as his ass squeaks across the metal; he'll have to sanitize the hell out of this spot. "So don't."

Benzo's eyebrows knot in confusion. "Don't what?"

"Don't use them."

He holds the berries out toward Kenna as though the fruit alone should make the argument for him. "They're in the recipe, Kenna. One tablespoon juniper berries, crushed." He speaks with the low reverence Father drops into whenever he quotes Grandfather's scripture.

"Who cares about the recipe? Perhaps you'll discover your *own* perfect broth—I mean consommé."

Benzo shakes his head—and they're out of synchronization again. "That's not how this works, Kenna. This broth is flavor-neutral. It's designed to slip into hundreds of The Sol Majestic's recipes—if I change it, I change the delicate balance of flavors. This isn't some hidden creativity test—it's about technical accomplishment."

Kenna realized he had been holding on to some vague fantasy of Benzo forging his own glorious path—but Benzo's right. That clear, amber fluid is a test designed to magnify the slightest flaw.

Still, the first task Benzo had handed off to Kenna was the juniper—he hated the sticky pine-juice on his fingers.

"So don't do it today," Kenna offers. "You want to touch me, don't you?"

Benzo's smile is as delicate as a consommé.

"Fine," Benzo says. He chucks the berries extravagantly into the disposal. "One consommé, no juniper. A distinctly imperfect broth."

"You don't have to call it broth."

"What do *you* call it?"

Kenna's eyebrow twitches with embarrassment. "Broth."

"Then it's broth."

Kenna remembers Benzo snapping at him—*Stop calling it broth. We call it broth around you because you don't know any better*—and realizes that Benzo remembers too, that Benzo has been shamed since they crept into the Escargone. That shift in vocabulary is a request that all sins be forgiven.

"I can live with broth," Kenna says. Benzo dips his head in acknowledgment: *Yes. Yes, we can.* "I love you, you know."

"Show me how after I finish this pot?" And Benzo's eyes linger on Kenna's mouth, and Kenna remembers that Brillo-like friction of Benzo's not-quite-a-mustache rubbing against his lips, the softness of his tongue, and he aches hard for his lover.

"Promise."

Now the waiting is delicious.

They fuck. They cuddle. They exchange boyhood stories; Benzo finally finishes a sentence describing his mother. They clean each other. They sanitize the kitchen. They pick up the mess Benzo made, Kenna reinventorying to account for damaged goods.

Except now the chores feel cozy. They're building something together—and that something may be a bower for their corpses, but they're okay with that.

When the timer goes off, they taste the juniper-free consommé out of habit.

Benzo doesn't even put the consommé through his usual thirteen-second slurping factory. He tilts the shot glass into his mouth, moving toward the plastic tub to empty the botched batch into the sink . . .

And cruises to a stop like a robot with a dead battery.

"Are you all right?" Kenna asks. But Benzo's pink tongue laps up the consommé residue on his lips. He plants his hands on the countertop, shutting down his body's balancing mechanisms so he can better process this odd taste.

"Try this." He hands a fresh sample to Kenna with a purposely diffident air, reluctant to taint Kenna's reaction with his own.

Kenna slurps a swig. He's imbibed enough consommé to sense a clean flavor unsullied by fat globules, to press his tongue against the roof of his mouth to check for the silty particles, then to roll it to the back of his tongue to hunt for the telltale tastes of burnt chicken.

This consommé is . . . acceptable. There's nothing he can point to that Benzo did wrong.

Yet it's . . .

Shallow.

There is a solid chicken flavor—but it slides off the palate, as ephemeral as a swallow of saliva. The onion and celery flavors weave their way underneath the chicken, trying to knot it into place—but the chicken taste disappears like water down a drain.

"That's weird," Benzo mutters. He gives the consommé the full thirteen-second assembly-line tasting, sucking and glugging and swishing . . .

"Did you ever make it without the juniper before?"

Benzo sucks the broth back in, coughs in surprise. "Who'd do *that*?"

"People experiment."

"It's the *recipe*, Kenna." Benzo looks around as though there might be a smartpaper the recipe is written on, then sighs in aggravation and settles for quoting it to Kenna. "One tablespoon juniper berries, crushed."

"For what reason?"

"Because it *says* to."

"I am aware, Benzo. Why *does* it say to?"

Benzo lets loose an aggravated huff. He glances back toward the inventory system, as if wondering whether the recipe might be in the ship's databank.

And Kenna realizes: Benzo doesn't know how to question.

Benzo's spent a lifetime being cattle-prodded by his Mistress for the slightest clarification. She'd fashioned a world where requesting explanations is rebellion.

So Benzo follows orders—has followed orders since he's walked into The Sol Majestic. He's made consommé after consommé, but he has no idea what the ingredients do—he just puts exactly this many in.

—goddammit, they've terrified you poor shits into following rules, Montgomery had said.

Hot on the heels of that realization comes another one: that's why She was so confident in sending Benzo to The Sol Majestic. She knew She'd burned the playfulness out of Her servants, leaving Benzo a lackluster boy who could follow instructions. Experimenting was a privilege reserved for masters.

Kenna inhales, anger stoking his belly. She'd crippled his lover and sent him off to fail.

"The juniper." Kenna catches Benzo before he fetches a tablet to verify its existence. "Have you ascertained what it did here?"

Benzo drums his fingers on the consommé shot glass, squinting like a man investigating a crime scene. ". . . It's different."

Kenna wonders how Benzo has survived in The Sol Majestic without developing a vocabulary to express the flavors he must sense—and then realizes Benzo's been faking it all these years. Formulating tastes would involve creativity.

How has no one recognized Benzo's lack of talent? he thinks—and then remembers The Sol Majestic's fierce competition. The chefs worked to best each other. A compliant boy like Benzo, who never questioned orders, was like a miniature vacation—when the other chefs suggested spices and sniffed haughtily as if they could do better, Benzo would never contradict them. His placid agreement was a certain yes in a chaos of *no*s and *maybe*s, and he'd been so affable nobody had noticed he was too timid to *change* anything.

Kenna presses the shot glass into his lover's palms. "The lack of juniper makes it less complex," he explains. "Something in the resinous taste deepens the chicken flavor—some melding that makes them resonate. Try it."

When did Kenna learn to speak this language? He must have picked it up around the kitchen. He angles a glass to fill Benzo's mouth with more consommé, and when Benzo tastes this time it's not the mechanical slurping of a man going through the motions, but the fluid sips of someone *experiencing* the soup.

"It's different," he repeats. His brow furrows. "It . . . washes?"

Kenna would clap happily at any word Benzo used as description, because that silly word presages a new thought process blooming in Benzo's brain.

"Huh." Benzo's tongue mops the inside of his mouth. "Juniper . . . does things."

"Yes."

"So . . . onion. Must. Do things."

"Yes." Kenna suppresses his instinct to connect the dots for Benzo—Benzo must make this leap for himself. He is crucified upon The Recipe's rigid cross, and must free himself to discover the principles that make recipes worthwhile . . .

Benzo peers into the soup for minutes. Kenna silently chants *come on come on come on* as Benzo wanders away from the soup, lost in thought, trailing his fingers along the pantry doors.

"Maybe . . ." Benzo raps his knuckles on the door. "Maybe we should make a batch without onions."

"A bold venture." Kenna grabs Benzo's hand and leads him toward a fresh chicken. "Let's cook."

Now introduced to experimentation, Benzo takes to it rapidly. He pan-sears the chicken, looking down into the pan as if he can't quite believe he's doing this. He rolls his palms over the garlic cloves, crushing them instead of chopping them. He shoots Kenna a mischievous wink before waving at the stockpot, sending the tender broth into a rolling boil.

The consommés are terrible. But the sex is great.

Their cramped day is held together by the same routine— endlessly cooking, endlessly sterilizing, endlessly maintaining—but graced by the joy Benzo experiences pulling apart this recipe, it feels like they're building a home. Obligations bloom into rituals— Kenna cheering after Benzo announces what new way he's going to fuck up *this* broth, the gentle kiss Benzo plants on Kenna's forehead after they make love, the way they each cup the shot glasses in their hands and pray loudly to the Soup Gods before trying Benzo's wretched failure.

Following The Recipe led to stagnant death. Tearing it apart creates a vibrant shared culture.

But straying from The Recipe's golden path proves Paulius's wisdom. Pan-searing the chicken creates a dishwater-thin broth. Smashing the garlic leaves an acrid taste. Boiling it both leaches flavor and turns the broth milky—which surprises Benzo, who'd never been careless enough to let his temperatures get out of hand.

Each time they break a rule, they discover why Paulius made it. Who knew lawbreaking was such an education?

Weeks pass, soup melding into lovemaking melding into cleaning, and one day they sip a consommé to realize there is no flaw.

They cup the glass in numb palms, feeling the stillness in their throats. Saying anything would mar this moment.

This should feel extraordinary, Kenna thinks. *We've been waiting for it for months.* Somehow, once they've stopped expecting perfection to arrive, it has dropped into their hands. And the consommé vibrates across his tongue, a rich dark meat reduced to a supple liquid, but . . . the consommés have hovered so close to perfection that criticism had taken on the sourness of nitpicking. This is perfection, yes, but they'd been camped on perfection's doorstep for weeks.

Benzo inhales, closing his eyes, and when he exhales it is the soft breath of a man dying. And Benzo is dying, Kenna realizes—a good death that buries an insecurity.

Benzo tilts the cup in Kenna's direction. Then he swigs the rest down like a shot of whiskey, slamming the cup on the countertop like a judge slamming a gavel.

"Again?" he asks.

"Again," Kenna agrees.

It takes them three days to make another perfect batch.

They don't stop until Benzo can make it every time.

Kenna shivers as they step out of the Escargone, the air so dry it sucks the moisture from his skin. The tile floor flexes beneath his feet—not the unyielding metal floor he's trod on for months.

It's distracting.

The kitchen is a field of waving flags—reds and golds so bright, his eyes water. It takes Kenna a moment to resolve these colors into chefs' outfits, The Sol Majestic's staff shuffling uneasily from foot to foot, the bobbing motion dazzling after the Escargone's endless stillness.

What are they doing here? The ovens are cold. The kitchen staff stands in clumped groups outside the Escargone door, facing him, their elbows clamped tight to their bodies as if they're prepared to flee at any moment.

Kenna wonders if he's somehow crashing a party.

Then he realizes perhaps an hour has passed for them since Benzo and he entered the Escargone. They'd spent that hour waiting fretfully, tensed for the explosions from the Escargone's unstable technology, for Benzo to tumble out white-haired and mad from years of isolation.

Yet if they are waiting for his appearance, shouldn't they cheer, or clap, or do something? Only a handful have noticed him. They're tapping their neighbors' shoulders with the air of a person hoping to get someone else to solve this problem. The rest study their fingernails, straighten the spice racks, doing anything but look in his direction.

Then Kenna hears the yelling.

The noise seems dim, but Kenna realizes he's so overwhelmed by sensory input that his eyes have sucked up his hearing's processing cycles. He tunes into the argument like a satellite station, dialing in focus—

"—you unrepentant penitentiary! You open that door!"

"No."

Even after all these months, it's a familiar show.

Scrimshaw stands with crossed arms, a gaunt sentinel barring the way. Paulius is cradled in an elaborate motorized wheelchair, his sticklike body clad in a plain white hospital gown—yet he grips the armrests like he might spring out of the chair to throttle her.

The kitchen staff surrounds them, but they back away, signaling that Paulius has wheeled himself all the way here from the docbot.

"Why in the fuck-befouled stars would you ever, *ever*, let them go in alone?" Flecks of spit fly off his lips, land on Scrimshaw's robe like embers from a flaring bonfire. "They're *young*! They're not fully *formed* yet! You can't lock two young boys into a supply closet and ask them to *grow up* in there!"

Scrimshaw is still as a statue. "Benzo volunteered. To save the kitchen. To save the meal."

Paulius flings his hands into the air. "What good is it saving the meal if you destroy the Inevitable Prince in the process, you horripilating hound?"

Their gazes are locked like swords. Which is why Scrimshaw doesn't notice the employees waving feebly to redirect their attention toward Kenna and Benzo.

Paulius senses the twitching movements behind him, narrows his eyes. "No, of course the Escargone won't destroy *you*," he mutters to his chefs, making calm-the-waters motions. "You're dedicated. Grown men. But throwing someone like Benzo, who's wavered with uncertainty all his life, in to face his demons . . ."

Benzo coughs.

Paulius twists in his wheelchair, then lets loose an anguished hiccup. *His hip was smashed,* Kenna reminds himself—but he's been working with Paulius's recipe for months inside the Escargone, deconstructing that wise overlord who dictated The Recipe, and in his mind the jovial emperor of The Sol Majestic had healed.

But of course it's only been an hour.

Yet when Paulius sees Benzo, the pain leaves his face. He cranes toward them, his head moving back and forth like the Escargone's security cameras.

Paulius reaches back with trembling arms, heaves himself onto rubber-slippered feet. His center of gravity dips, legs bowing, before he jabs his cane into the ground and pushes fiercely upon it—his arms bearing the weight his legs will not.

Yet if Paulius is in pain—and judging from the angry red incisions sliced across his hips, he must be—he shrugs that aside to hobble toward them. His world has narrowed to contain only Benzo and Kenna, his breath shallow with apprehension.

Kenna steps forward to offer his shoulder—

But Benzo is dumbstruck by Paulius's concern. He clasps the consommé against his belly, as if worried Paulius might take his newfound triumph away.

"Thank you," Paulius says, gently waving away Kenna's assistance. He makes his way toward Benzo one hard-earned step at a time, half-bent, a supplicant approaching a king.

When he is close enough, Paulius reaches out abruptly to cup Benzo's cheek in one palm.

Then he looks down at Benzo, and Kenna realizes:

Benzo is naked to the waist.

His slave-tattooed nanofilaments ripple across his body—but Benzo stands straight, revealing his plight to the kitchen. The kitchen staff whispers to each other, shocked, having traded rumors of Benzo's slave status yet never having dreamed his body had been wired for Her convenience.

Benzo brings up the broth, offering it to Paulius. Paulius places his hand over the cup, refusing to look.

"You did it, didn't you?" he asks.

Benzo nods.

Paulius's smile is radiant as a supernova. He clasps Benzo's face in both hands, kissing his cheeks, cane clattering to the floor.

"She'll burn with anger," he sighs with deep satisfaction, taking the consommé from Benzo's fingers, twirling the shot glass as though he held up the Holy Grail itself. "I'll save that conference call and play it on cold mornings! 'Benzo won your bet,' I'll tell Her. I'll drink this broth, and savor it, and I'll offer to send this consommé to Her express mail. Do you want to be there for that call?"

Benzo swallows. "I do, sir."

"Let's fuck that cold cunt right in Her ear. I'll set up the call right now." And then he whirls to Scrimshaw, moving with a nimbleness belying his recovery, and snaps his fingers. "Scrimshaw! *Fetch me the uniform!*"

Scrimshaw is so overjoyed she doesn't quibble. She glides into the back, emerges from the red door of her office holding a clothes hanger with one neatly laundered uniform. Gold stripes race boldly across the vest and sleeves—the next kitchen rank, elevated from the lowly black-stripers who dice onions.

She holds it out for Benzo to step into. He does so, dazed. Paulius turns to present the upgraded Benzo.

"The first person has been reborn in the Escargone!" Paulius says. "Safe as houses! Now, I ask you—*who wants to unlock their true potential?*"

The clamor is deafening. Kenna cannot help but admire how quickly Paulius has transformed a soup into a celebration.

And Scrimshaw hands Paulius his cane, noticing he's leaning a little too hard on Benzo's shoulder, and Paulius escorts Benzo off to his private office where the leased ansible will provide an instant connection to Benzo's Mistress. The kitchen pops open champagne, the fumellier unlocking boxes of pungent bud, and they charge into the Escargone to clean up the mess and retransfer the remaining ingredients and argue over who deserves the next run, they can do this at least twice more today, who gets to perfect their dish for the Prince's Inevitable Meal.

Kenna, meanwhile, stands in the kitchen like a ghost. Someone presses a wineglass into his hand, someone else claps him on the shoulder—but the celebration rages around him, not with him.

Benzo is gone.

This is not an unhappy thought. Benzo is suffused with his wildest dreams, and Kenna does not need to be there to know how joyous Benzo must be in this moment. After weeks of cradling up in Benzo's arms, he does not need to hold Benzo's hand to feel him; if he closes his eyes, he can summon Benzo's touch. He could be ninety, arthritic and blind, and would still feel the firm curve of Benzo's biceps pulling them together.

But there is that gentle ache of parting.

A few cheering people follow Benzo into Paulius's office,

whooping as the connection protocols fill Paulius's screens—and Kenna is baffled to find himself inching toward the door, drawn to Benzo like a metal filing to a magnet.

He grips a counter, rooting himself.

Benzo is leaving, he thinks. *He'll be gone after the Wisdom Ceremony. And so will I.*

They won the bet, but the bet was never about freeing Benzo from bondage; this bet was to free Benzo's future generations, ensuring the interest on his debt would not accrue to his nieces and nephews. Benzo's descendants will have a pristine credit rating.

But Benzo?

His Mistress now has a personal chef trained at The Sol Majestic.

He and Benzo will make love again, of course. But Kenna can feel the sharp keen of that impending final separation. He will become the Inevitable Prince, and Benzo will return to being Her slave, and if he does not cut slivers of isolation into their bond now, while he still can, he will wreck himself when they part.

He watches the screens as the protocols resolve into a video feed—then notices the looming figure standing next to him, every bit as still and sorrowful as he is:

Scrimshaw.

"You're doing the right thing," she says.

Her arms are pulled tight over her belly, braced for isolation. Her bespectacled eyes gaze off into the distance, refusing to focus on him, her lips set bitterly as if she regrets speaking.

Yet Kenna finds that comforting: *I survive alone. So can you.*

He pulls his arms tight around his belly, like Scrimshaw. He blurs his vision, like Scrimshaw.

He hugs himself, like Scrimshaw. And hopes he can be as strong.

28

Kenna knows how bad this lecture will be by the way his parents have positioned themselves in the hotel room, waiting for his arrival: Father stands before the sleep capsules wide-stanced, arms crossed, braced to slap down Kenna's rebellion. Whereas Mother sits serenely cross-legged, breathing through her nose, readied to endure any foolishness Kenna might throw up in his defense.

His parents script out their worst reprimands in advance, like plays.

Father makes a curt, bladelike gesture, indicating where Kenna shall sit for his part in this performance. The security guard closes the gilded hotel room door, which clicks shut with a jail cell's finality.

"How long," Father asks, "did you poison your Philosophy, in that chamber, with that servant?"

He speaks so each clause rises in volume, the crime worsening with every phrase. Kenna contemplates an airy response, asking whether they want the answer in relative or local time—but Father's cheeks are flushed blood-red.

"Fourteen weeks," he says, cowed.

"Fourteen weeks," Father whispers, staring dramatically out into space. Mother nods. Kenna knows they knew this answer already. "With a *servant*."

Kenna's lips are still rubbed raw by Benzo's stubble. "What's wrong with a servant?"

Mother and Father exchange a startled look. Kenna feels pleased to have knocked them so far off-script in the first exchange. She unfolds her legs from beneath her knees, descends from the table—but their anger has evaporated, replaced with the concern of a doctor determining whether this growth is a mole or a metastasized cancer.

"They lack vision, Kenna."

He expects her to say more, but that is her full argument.

Kenna wipes the sweat off his upper lip, which still smells of bay leaves and chicken. He remembers Benzo, designing a gastronomic philosophy from the atomic components of dark meat, water, salt. He remembers Rakesh working to transform the waste unit into a technological party.

"They have more vision than you accredit them."

His head snaps to one side. He flops across the armrest, cheek stinging, Father's blow so strong it sent him flying.

Kenna's breath is jangled, his legs wanting to flee, his brain still spinning. Yet what turns his bowels to water is realizing Father is not angry. Father has tugged up one sleeve like a line cook preparing to clean a dish.

He would beat me to death and walk away from my corpse, Kenna realizes, cowed before Father's Inevitable strength.

Mother leans in close. "There is no wisdom in suffering, Kenna. Surviving a war does not qualify you to be a general. An empty belly does not teach you how to feed the starving millions. A servant's thoughts teach you how to serve, Kenna."

"I wonder." Father cranes his neck down. "Do we have an Inevitable Philosophy here . . . or a simple teenaged rebellion?"

Kenna hangs his head; his face feels like a curtain, easily parted to show deception. And once Father knows . . .

Father clasps his hands behind his back, content to have made Kenna squirm. "We have three weeks before your Wisdom Ceremony, Kenna. Three weeks. And while nothing would please me more than to have Mother and I guide you back to your Philosophy ourselves, the Wisdom Ceremony already attracts the bright flames of politicians. They arrive by the day, begging audiences."

"They wish to talk to *you,* of course," Mother says, "but we have told them it is tradition you be sequestered until you have voiced your Philosophy to the world."

They're alternating lines, back on script. Kenna opens his mouth, intending to knock them off course again, but his aching jaw silences him.

"So we spend our days in conference rooms, answering questions, preparing great men to hear your word," Father says. "And that word will arrive, Kenna. Our Philosophies are strong. Even as we speak to ambassadors and viziers, the universe has sent us the perfect instrument to repair your tattered ideology."

"Witness!"

Mother flings open the door.

A bright comet of fabric streams into the room—a woman, her hands held high in triumph as if she holds the sun between her palms. The woman whirls on one heel, transforming the Inevitable robe she wears into a Technicolor tornado, then stamps her foot into the floor as if the station itself would stop its motion for her.

"Your Philosophy calls, and the universe answers!" the woman cries. "For what are the odds a disciple of the Inevitable Philosophies would be waiting for you in your hour of need, Master Kenna?"

Mother and Father grasp the woman's shoulders as though she were a life raft. They seem to eclipse her and yet orbit her at the same time.

"You will remain here, and be taught," Father says. "The Wisdom Ceremony is a meal designed to demonstrate your mastery, yet you hold your chopsticks like a farmer. And all the while, um . . ."

They pause enough for Kenna to realize: *They don't know her name.* Kenna himself struggles to remember it; he's sure Scrimshaw's mentioned her. But the woman steps in with the grace of a dancer cutting into a waltz:

"All the while, I shall guide you down the paths you've strayed from. Your parents know the fine details of dining to impress; I shall impart that knowledge to you. When you eat like a prince, you think like a prince."

"Remember, Kenna," Mother says. "The reporters will circle you like warships, seeking weakness. They need you to be the country bumpkin—and you will be seated next to men who have been raised to the crown. Drink from the wrong glass and you will pay for that ignorance."

"But impress the right people, and they will be your levers to lift the Inevitable Philosophies back to ever-greater heights. Anyone can seduce a scullery boy. But can you speak to kings and never stammer?"

Kenna wants to say *Yes, yes he can,* but the back of Father's hand is aimed at his mouth.

"I'll sharpen the boy's good instincts." The woman places her hand atop Father's, gentle as a butterfly landing on a blossom. He relents. "Training, sixteen hours a day. No breaks. No . . . visitations."

Kenna hears a door slamming. *No more Benzo.*

He presses his fingertips to his collarbone, feels pain blooming from where Benzo sucked hickeys into his skin. *You can't give me anything to remember you by,* Benzo had told him. *She'll take it. And you can't mark me.* He'd looked down at the black nanofibers knotted through his chest. *But I can mark you for as long as we're together.*

Benzo had marked him whenever they'd made love. He knew their time had been short. But to have his marks fade while Benzo was a ten-minute walk away . . .

"We must start the mending immediately," the woman says— the lack of her name is an itch Kenna cannot scratch. She kneels down, revealing a sleek leather valise concealed in her robe, cracking it open to reveal fluted plates and gold forks. "The next six hours will be devoted to proper cutlery placement. You will not sleep tonight until you can locate the seven types of cold-service knives blindfolded."

She swivels to face Mother and Father. "Would you like to refresh your cutlery knowledge? Kenna would benefit from your heritage as we lay out the seafood spoons."

Mother and Father offer an embarrassed smile. "I'm afraid we have dinner with a suzerain."

"Perhaps you can tell us of the dishes when you return, then." She clasps her hands, steps in too close, driving Mother and Father back toward the door. "Bequeath to us your experiences of dining with power . . ."

"We shall see." Mother speaks in that strained tone that means "no." The woman grasps their fingers, kisses the tips, escorts them to the door as if she wishes they'd never leave . . .

The door closes.

The woman shrinks inside the fabric, her grand gestures folding shut like a mechanical canopy. To Kenna, her bright robe fluttering down feels like a curtain descending at a play's end, her body becoming an empty stage.

She steps with a curious grace over to the seat across from Kenna, birdlike, as if uncertain how to sit once Mother and Father have left. She stares down at her legs as if debating how to position them, her face expressionless as a mannequin. Her eyes flick up to Kenna like cold cameras—a blank attention that catalogues everything about him.

"You . . ." The only reason he knows her is that he's seen her wear this robe before. "You . . . danced in the procession when Paulius ushered the food in to the loading dock. You're the response team Scrimshaw assigned to placate my parents. You . . . *are* the person who talked them into letting me stay at The Sol Majestic, correct?"

"as a matter of efficiency, i do not believe in gods." Her voice is a monotone. "but at times i indulge in the concept of providence. i promise you, Master Kenna, you'll find no teacher greater suited to this moment."

"I . . ." Kenna wipes his palms on his robe, noticing how she notices it, his skin prickling with the sense she's taking in far more about him than he understands. "I hold no interest in forks."

"yet you are interested in faking a religion."

Kenna's lungs freeze. Who else in the kitchen knows? Has Montgomery told everyone? How much—

"no one in the kitchen told me. i know because of my upbringing."

Kenna grips the couch, his every motion betraying him. Her eyes flicker across his stiffened muscles, reading his mind through his body language. He speaks reluctantly into her stillness, lest she extract his fears from the motion of his lips.

"And . . . who . . . upbrought you?"

"the Allface."

"You're an *Allface*?"

Kenna's not sure what to say to an Allface. He can't be sure if he's ever met one.

The Allface specialize in trades among reclusive religious sects—the remote cults who have convinced themselves the unfaithful have been wiped out in a blaze of novafire, or who believe outsiders brought in a sin deadlier than plague. These settlements survive only because they cling to planets no one else wanted; scornful of technology, farming black ash, most die horrible wasting deaths.

The Allface take pity on them. But the only way to bring charity was to pretend to be one of a hundred different cults so flawlessly no local would suspect them for a heretic. The Allface studied scripture until they brainwashed themselves into temporary belief, exulting the Goddess on one world and cutting off their breasts on the next, tattooing and excoriating and reweaving body and brain alike to trade these stunted settlements the medicines that would let them survive another season, and let the Allface continue to operate their fleet of trading vessels.

The strain of constantly switching religions, it was said, drove the Allface mad.

"i was," the woman says. "i was an Allface, once. here, i will tell you my name. it is—"

She holds her breath.

"my name is Rèpondelle." She places her fingertips over her mouth as if she has breathed foul air. "there. i have said it. let it not be said again. names lure you into obstruction."

"Obstructions of what?"

"from now on neither of us will use names. we will be mirrors."

Kenna's not sure whether she's too mad for him to follow, or too quick. "Why would we want to be mirrors?"

"because your Philosophy is false."

She does not speak as though it were an accusation, yet Kenna feels framed in a spotlight. His lack of a Philosophy is a sickness; mentioning it holds the sick distaste of popping blisters.

"I can fashion a Philosophy," he protests. "We have three weeks. Surely, I can—"

"you would fashion a Philosophy to please others. that is not a Philosophy. you wish to leave the people who seek your empty guidance feeling beloved and fulfilled. this is what i did in my time in the Allface. this i can teach you."

"But how—"

"you must reflect what people want to see."

Kenna thinks of the bhelpuri merchant, needing to hear a Philosophy so potent it erases all regret. That man loved cooking so much, he'd abandoned whatever home he'd had for a coffin-sized sleep-cubicle and a food cart on a distant station, so desperate to seek culinary perfection he would warm his hands by The Sol Majestic. He could have thrived on some planetbound street, selling waxed cups of vinegar-soaked rice to workers who would have gobbled anything filling. But no—each serving he sells is an offering, given in the hopes of finding some appreciative patron.

The bhelpuri merchant already has a philosophy far more Inevitable than Kenna's—a mad devotion to a single dish.

What that merchant wants to hear is that if he just believes harder, he'll never regret sleeping in a cold torpedo tube, will never lament that lover he'd left behind, never fret over the stained clothes he cannot afford to replace.

The only way he'll believe that is if Kenna tells him he doesn't believe hard enough. That this regret is his weakness.

Except—

"it is not his weakness," Rèpondelle says, "it is yours. if you had something to offer, you could salve his pain. as things are, you must convince him the fault lies with him."

She's read his mind, raced ahead, devised counterarguments. This is, he realizes, what the Allface engineered her to do.

He goes still as a rat in a corner; his every twitch broadcasts his beliefs to her. She matches his stillness, though hers feels like a quiet computer bank devoted to analyzing his movements.

"extracting secrets from the physique is mere technique." Once again, she's extrapolated what he's thinking. "i will teach you how to pluck someone's fears from the muscles bunching in their forehead. i will teach you to ask a single question and let someone's eyes lead you to what they value most. but in your case—"

She lowers her head. Is she bowing to him, or expressing regret?

"i know your heart because what you express is the Allface's struggle. giving people what they want is still a gift. this is what you must tell yourself. without a burning faith, people wander alone through the universe, doubt corroding them. unpacking the secrets in their hearts and whispering them back into their ears makes them feel they are not a single string vibrating, but a chord in a song. they will forgive you any sin then. they will love you because they will mistake understanding for agreement."

She's expressing regret. He's sure of it. "Yet you left."

Her eyes close. "i did."

"You escaped to a restaurant because soothing an upset customer was better than convincing someone to believe in false Gods."

Her nostrils flare, her breathing turning ragged. "i took a name so they could never take me back."

"Then why are you eager to convince me to follow a path that destroyed you?"

She blinks twice. She kneels down, joints oiled, to place her cool fingertips upon him.

"do you not understand what you have promised?"

"No."

She angles her face back and forth to view him, clinically merciless as the Escargone's cameras.

Kenna realizes: *she can't believe how naïve I am.*

She pulls up his Q-rating: it's jumped to the thirty-fifth rank. Not quite global headlines, but enough he can be safely referenced in jokes. She lets the glimmering surface dangle between two fingers.

"you have told the wealthy there is a thought so potent they have traveled light-years to come see its birth. disappoint them and you pull back the curtain. once one prince's Philosophy is a fraud, all Philosophies could be frauds. your religion will be wrecked."

A relieved laugh sputters out. "I know *that*. I'm not afraid of some rich man's anger—"

"the wealthy are merely antennae. they will broadcast your failure to the galaxy's edges."

Kenna wants to draw away, but her fingertips have the weight of manacles.

"emaciated children go to bed hungrier because their community saves for a robe. your robe. their parents are despairing slaves serving callous powers—but because their great-grandparents were once nourished by the Inevitable Philosophies, they have chosen once again to believe. they believe your revelations will ease their pain. they believe your wisdom will guide their leaders."

Kenna thinks of the bhelpuri merchants, the creditor-slaves, the station's laborers—he's done practically nothing, tried his best to shrug off the dreams they've loaded onto his shoulders, yet they still believe in him. And yes, he'd known about the farmers and factory workers, but to hear of sacrifices made for a belief he'd done so little to cultivate . . .

"and when they discover that what you told them was a fraud to save a rich man's restaurant, they will kill you."

Kenna's stomach cramps at the realization.

Rèpondelle places her hand on his belly as if to urge him: *Yes, protect yourself.*

"your only hope is to become a mirror, Kenna. show them nothing until they look into you. feed them enough aphorisms and they might let you live."

It's true. There's nowhere he can run, not now. If he had fled when Montgomery had told him to, he might have escaped his fate—but his Q-rating has risen as the newsvlogs have tuned in, as Savor Station's residents have blogged about his adventures.

Before, boys had kicked his ribs and stolen his nutricrackers for the audacity of claiming to be a prince. Trapped on transport ships without the patronage of the wealthy, they'd tear him apart.

This is what Mother and Father fear, he realizes. All the while he'd seen their newsvlog terror as some prim vanity, but now? If his legend curdles into foolishness—or worse, into greasy swindling—the protection the wealthy have provided will evaporate.

"your lie has swelled to take on its own life. this is what lies do. now you feed it, or it devours you."

She's correct. If Kenna is seen through, there will be no more Inevitable Philosophies—there will be an angry ex-acolyte waiting in an access corridor with a knife.

"now." She retreats to her chair. "shall we begin?"

29

Two Weeks and One Day to the Wisdom Ceremony

Rèpondelle is a hundred different people. Her fingers stiffen into a cynical dock repairwoman's arthritic clutch, then extend into the delicate *please-slow-down-a-bit* gestures of a befuddled debutante. She paces across the beige carpet toward Kenna with the aggressive stride of a banker about to grasp Kenna's hand in a bone-grinding grip, then sidles up next to him with the smoky sensuality of a female vlogger hoping to dismantle Kenna's guard with some mild flirtation.

Yet for all the people she pretends to be, Rèpondelle cannot make this vast hotel room into anything other than a series of psychiatric duels.

Only the wealthy get to be alone, Kenna thinks. There is no motion here, aside from Rèpondelle's body language lessons and the microbots creeping out to scrub the carpet. Nothing is created here except what they make together—Rèpondelle's input, Kenna's output, no arguing couples passing by to break up the monotony, no maintenance men laser-scanning the walls for imperfections that threaten the integrity of Savor Station's hull, no burping men pissing in corners.

Mother and Father would tell him isolation is where great men develop great thoughts. Yet Kenna starves, living off his own echoes. He needs to defend his flighty thoughts against Montgomery's bitter cynicism, he needs Paulius's boundless confidence to shove him past his fears, he needs to simplify his theories into words plain enough for Benzo to understand them.

No wonder he has no Inevitable Philosophy.

She leaves every evening to preside over The Sol Majestic's daily service. He slams his palm against the door, but it is no longer keyed to his biosignature. Resigned, he carries out tedious exercises, synchronizing his expressions with computer-generated faces as booming voices tell him how he appears to outside viewers: COMPASSIONATE. SYMPATHETIC. WISE.

But no human speaks to him.

The only communication comes from the three daily meals, wheeled in by bodyguards on trays straight from The Sol Majestic's kitchen—a hidden language wrought in food.

Lunch is a grilled tomato-cheese sandwich and a cup of consommé, a signal Benzo is still thinking of him. Dinner is a more elaborate routine, the dishes swinging from forested salad ferns to bone marrow swirls corkscrewing through a bowl of gazpacho— Benzo's way of informing him what courses he's been allowed to assist on.

After four days, the consommés stop arriving.

Kenna is not sure what that means.

On the second day of no consommé, he frowns as he nibbles at the sandwich's gooey edges. Why would Benzo withhold the consommé? Is it a sign he no longer needs to make it? Ah, but Kenna's certain that even if the kitchen doesn't need the consommé, Montgomery would let him make it as a secret sign to him.

He's eaten the sandwich to the crust before he realizes:

This sandwich had no tomato slice.

Benzo knows the food is a message. This missing tomato is a new syntax, one Kenna is not sure how to interpret.

Is Benzo breaking up with him?

Why shouldn't he? They'll never see each other again. Benzo will return to his life as a slave. Perhaps Benzo is saying *Let's ease out of this.*

Or perhaps this consommé absence is a cryptic apology: *I'm working sixteen-hour days, Kenna, I have no time for romantic gestures.*

Rèpondelle trains him relentlessly in the cold read: she makes him repeat back her statements as if Kenna had known what she'd told him all along ("Yes, that's right, you've been troubled for a while now"), she trains him to speak in ephemeralities people will fill in with their own details ("You're on the cusp of a big decision"), she forces him to insert uncomfortably long pauses between his responses to pressure his subjects into offering more information.

"you must remove yourself to become them," she says.

Kenna tries to pay attention, but his mind keeps snapping back to the missing consommé, thinking of changes in Benzo's affection that might make him withhold their soup, and in the middle of a reflective questioning exercise he blurts out:

"Why did Benzo cease sending me consommé?"

Rèpondelle's posture had been that of a a glad-handing functionary, but she tilts back to put a cool distance between them, shrinking back to her baseline teacher's bearing.

"this is well done." She arches one eyebrow; on that tranquil frame, it feels like wild applause. "already you learn to conceal your emotions; i had no idea of your distress until you spoke."

I learned that on the transport ships, Kenna thinks. "And yet I repeat: Why isn't Benzo gifting me with our signature soup?"

Her shoulders roll forward, her mouth dropping open in a way to mirror his distress. Kenna realizes that instead of being comforted by her adopting compassion's trappings, he is cataloguing her technique.

"oh, Kenna." Emphasizing his name reinforces his importance. "this has nothing to do with Benzo. we are out of chicken."

"Out of chicken? The most common meat?"

She turns her face to one side, a dismissive gesture meant to establish authority. "supplies are always a problem for The Sol Majestic. we are light-years from fresh markets, and our clientele demand the finest ingredients—our vendors frequently fall short. with the impending Wisdom Ceremony, Scrimshaw frets about the quality more than ever . . ."

"*Scrimshaw.*"

Kenna can hear the way he grinds the syllables out between his teeth. Rèpondelle drops back into teacher's posture, scrutinizing him.

Her pause is an attempt to get him to volunteer the reasons behind his anger.

Yet Kenna is too busy translating the culinary message Benzo has, in fact, sent to him: *Scrimshaw's stopped buying chicken.* The lack of a tomato slice is a clear suffix: *she's taking other things away, too.*

There's no shortage of quality chicken, of course—not at Savor Station, not such a common ingredient. Scrimshaw is no pickier than her budget would allow.

She is quietly shuttering The Sol Majestic. Why replenish poultry when there will never be patrons she intends to serve chicken to again? Kenna suspects she's sandbagged enough chickens to keep the Majestic's famed spherified chicken alginate coming, but . . .

Benzo is informing him there are gaps in The Sol Majestic's inventory—gaps innocuous to anyone who doesn't know how precarious the restaurant's finances are, but are impending doom to those with the eyes to see.

Rèpondelle doesn't have those eyes. She sees Scrimshaw's tension, but doesn't know about the robes, the impending debts . . .

"I need a break."

"we only have so much time before—"

"I SAID I NEED A BREAK!"

Rèpondelle folds into herself, lowering her head into a bow as she glides backwards into the bathroom, her robe fluttering behind like a jellyfish squeezing into a hiding-hole. Kenna wants to feel guilty, but anger washes off Rèpondelle. There's not enough of her left inside for her to take anything personally.

Everything in this hotel room seems sturdy. But all this could be disassembled easily; space stations are too expensive to justify square footage that isn't bringing in profit. It costs money to pressurize empty spaces, maintenance to ensure they're not rusting. Having been shuttled through the cheapest routes, Kenna has watched dreams die before: once-bright shops dismantled by creditors' agents, men in hard hats carrying away anything salable.

He imagines the Escargone hauled away by bulk freighters to another client—someone who'll never know how he and Benzo had made love on that floor. He imagines the orchards Paulius had strolled through repurposed into mass agriculture, the herb gardens taken over by high-yield soybean crops. He imagines that kitchen stripped to bare metal and jutting wires.

He'd never had a home, before The Sol Majestic. But The Sol Majestic had birthed him. It would die as he became the Inevitable Prince, a mother bleeding out in childbirth, and a few weeks after that Wisdom Ceremony the creditors would come to strip it to the bones.

Unless he sold the robes.

He remembers standing in the shadow of that stack of fabric, the card that marked "profitability" sticking out at throat-level like a hatchet. That was hundreds of robes, each so expensive poor families had to save for months to afford them, and how could he justify selling hardscrabble workers a robe to save his home? He had no selling expertise, he had no—

He remembers the hollow *boom* as Montgomery was shot into space.

That boom had been the Waste Reprocessing Station imploding, Plexiglas rattling in the hole cut into space, Kenna's stomach clenching as his heart braced itself for death . . .

And then Montgomery's serene grace, a speck of living flesh engulfed by a great void yet refusing to bow to the emptiness.

Kenna grips the bathroom door frame. Rèpondelle sits cross-legged on the toilet seat; banishing her has left her unfazed, nor does her face register concern as he pulls her out.

"shall we continue?"

Kenna cannot save himself—but he must become a hollow salesman to save The Sol Majestic.

"What," he asks, "do rich people want?"

She smiles.

30

Two Weeks to the Wisdom Ceremony

Mother and Father would never allow Kenna to visit The Sol Majestic—with the Escargone, Kenna might disappear with Benzo for a few minutes and have it stretch out into Philosophy-corrupting months.

But not even they can refuse Kenna's request to discuss the Wisdom Ceremony with Paulius.

Paulius swats the bodyguards' ankles with his silver-tipped cane as he enters, head thrown back imperiously as he pushes between them. "What, you think someone would masquerade as a crippled old man? I'm *Paulius*, for Christ's sake—if you're stupid enough to request credentials, then you don't deserve to see them. Shut the door and leave me with my friend."

His final two words wrap around Kenna, warm as a hug: *my friend.*

Paulius thumps his cane upon the carpet; they leave. When they do he exhales, chin drooping to his chest centimeter by centimeter, nodding in fits and jerks as if reluctant to let his boisterous host persona lapse.

His head still bowed, he gives Kenna a shy wink: *I let you see this, you know.* Kenna finds his tension ebbing away; to gaze upon this weakened Paulius is to enter a secret club few are escorted into.

He takes Paulius's arm, guides him toward a comfortable chair.

Paulius pats his hand: "Good lad, good lad. With the Wisdom Ceremony coming up, I don't see why they keep you pent up in here, but . . . well, normally, I'd have Rèpondelle talk your parents into letting you wander free. But she's refused. She's usually malleable as a marshmallow, but every so often you bite into pure titanium."

His bushy brows lower in consternation. Kenna's mouth opens, halfway to telling Paulius that Rèpondelle is refusing because Kenna needs to learn how to become a charlatan—

But if he does that, then everything else he's been hiding will come spilling out and Paulius will shut the Wisdom Ceremony down.

Kenna can feel Paulius's fatherly arms wrapping around him— *Good Lord, Kenna, I won't condemn you to a life of lies! No restaurant is worth compromising your life. I'll start over somewhere else—*

His cheeks heat up like an oven. *Paulius* is Inevitable. He'd walk away and never look back.

(*That's easy for him,* a small nasty part of Kenna thinks. *He expects to teleport into a star any day now. He doesn't understand consequences.*)

Still. If Paulius believed for a split second that The Sol Majestic was complicit in fraud, he would fling it aside. Which sounds noble, but Savor Station has become a culinary trading hub based solely on Paulius's mad gastronomy—economies rest on this old man's whims. Without The Sol Majestic, Savor Station's bhelpuri merchants and traders and dock workers would starve . . .

As would Kenna's heart.

"*Anyway.*" Paulius waves his hand in the air, as if conducting some distant orchestra. "If you're looking to discuss the Wisdom Ceremony, you should talk to Montgomery. She's consulting me— but if you have a request, you need to go to her—"

"I fear I can't discuss this with Montgomery."

"You can. She's surprised me in how well she's taken to governing, once you coaxed her into ownership. I assure you, Master

Kenna—she'll make your Wisdom Ceremony as impressive as your Philosophy."

Kenna's lungs crumple, so shamed his body refuses to let him draw breath. Paulius takes his long white braid in his hands, twisting it like a schoolgirl hoping to draw favor.

"Though I will confess, I—" Paulius lets his braid slide from his fingers. "Well, I *do* crave a preview of your Inevitability. I've seen flashes—we all have—but no one's certain the meal fits the man. Is that—perhaps—why you wanted *me* here? To tell me . . ."

He digs his knuckles into his still-bruised hip, reproaching himself for pressing to know Kenna's secrets.

Kenna wishes he could tell Paulius. Rèpondelle had helped him debate which Inevitable Philosophy would befit his marketing plan, rhapsodizing over Mother and Father's Philosophies—"*i will save the starving millions*" and "*i will lead my people out of darkness,*" she'd gushed. *do you realize how perfect those are? they're meaningless. you can do anything and justify those philosophies.*

She'd flooded him with suggestions, like *I will lead the lost back to fruitful pathways* and *I will burn to fight the darkness,* but Kenna had felt too sick to continue.

He shoves that thought aside. He doesn't want to have to lie to Paulius yet. Not if he can avoid it. "Can I mandate what will be worn at my ceremony?"

"I assumed you'd wear your robe."

"No, I mean—can I compel *other* people to wear the robes?"

Paulius sucks air between his teeth. "Well, it's your ceremony, Kenna," he allows. "But . . . you do realize that of the two hundred invited guests, almost none are Inevitable Philosophers?"

Two hundred robes. Less than he'd hoped for.

"They shall be converted by the time I complete my speech," he lies. "Because these are not mundane robes I'm asking them to clad themselves in, Paulius. They're limited-edition robes. Three times as expensive as ordinary robes, hand-numbered—commemorating the birth of a movement!"

Paulius wraps his long braid around his knuckles. "Huh."

"And ten percent of the profits will go to fund my mother's charity. Feed the starving millions. Every robe sold will save a life . . ."

He squeezes the hair in his fist, as though massaging out some old ache. "I see."

"And I—I require you to fashion a blog entry to sell these robes to people who aren't in attendance. People—people everywhere shall need to be a part of this, and . . ."

Paulius cups a hand around his ear. "Scrimshaw? Is that you?"

Kenna should have known Paulius would see through him. But he hadn't wanted to lie. "This aspect is critical, Paulius. We must vend these robes."

Paulius sighs.

He reaches into his pocket, takes out a brown plastic prescription bottle, dumps out a palmful of pale blue capsules. Antianxiety medications. He dry-swallows them.

"Kenna, I . . ."

He tucks the pills back with the regret of a man who wishes he'd taken them sooner.

"I'm no fashion maven. I dress well enough, but . . . I purchased Inevitable robes to lend authenticity to a great meal, not because I had any sense for stitches. I can put you in touch with people who rejoice in the way silk hangs off someone's shoulder. Let them"— he shudders as though he'd swallowed a cockroach—"*promote* this beneficial robe. But that's not me."

"You don't have to love it, Paulius, you just have to—"

Paulius's merciless blue eyes shove Kenna's words back down his throat.

"Only suckers and the desperate sell things they don't love," Paulius says. "Instead, ignite your passion. Next, find a way to market the things you love. Make the money nourish you. Anything else auctions off pieces of your soul."

Paulius leans in, pushing Kenna's chin up with his cane-tip.

Kenna hadn't realized he had slumped in despair; he can hear Rèpondelle chastising him for not controlling his body language.

Yet as Paulius tilts his head from side to side, his eyes narrowed as he tries to extract the reason for Kenna's altered behavior, Kenna can read Paulius's emotions:

He's concerned.

Kenna can use that.

Kenna slides his palms up over his cheeks to hide himself from Paulius's vision, unknotting the tension in his shoulders as though Paulius has knocked through some final shameful barrier—

yes, he hears: Rèpondelle's voice. *lean forward until your forehead almost touches his, mirror his movements, offer your wrists to him—*

Yet as he shapes his movements to maximize empathy, a coldness settles over him. He is not betraying a friend: he is beginning a performance.

"That's not why I'm selling the robes," he lies.

Kenna twists his wrist, catching Paulius's attention. Paulius takes the bait, pulling Kenna's hands aside to get at what he thinks is the true emotion.

Revealed, Kenna draws in a ragged breath like Rèpondelle taught him.

"The truth is . . . ." Here is where a sad man would swallow back tears, so he does. "The truths I must speak are so—*different*—from anything I've voiced before, I'm worried people will reject them."

Paulius grips his shoulders. "Of course they'll believe you. You're Inevitable."

"How can they believe in me when I don't? I—my Philosophy's wavering, Paulius. And Mother, Father, Rèpondelle, they assure me I should rely on myself, but . . . I need to see how *someone else* sees me . . ."

Paulius smiles. Kenna lets that kind smile slide off. That smile won't save The Sol Majestic. "I can tell you that now."

"No. I hold fast to how you believe in me, Paulius." That, at least, is true. "Yet I must needs see how you sell me to—to other people. Because—because I'm going to make such a big statement, Paulius. I can't test-market this Philosophy—it's Inevitable. I'm terrified I'll speak and everyone will think me a fool. Perhaps I am."

Paulius speaks softly, as if trying to wake Kenna from a dream. "I believe in you, Kenna."

"That's the crux of this matter, Paulius. You know me . . . or at least the parts I wish most deeply to become. You fathom what made me special—you've always known, even when I can't see it—"

That part is also true, Kenna thinks, stuffing his self-loathing down deep.

"When—if—you were to produce a video that peddled these robes, I'd see you explaining what *I* meant to you—and I'd see in advance whether all these strangers would respond to the best parts of me. They won't even know what they're buying is not the robes, but my Philosophy, smuggled in gaudy cloth. And I—I—"

He pauses.

"You'd help convince me my Philosophy was something people needed to hear."

Appeals to ego, appeals to friendship, appeals to immortality in art, wrapped up in secret pleas that would make anyone feel flattered. A perfect weapon to mold Paulius to his will. Rèpondelle had helped him form this argument, and Kenna swallows back bile—in an ideal world, Paulius *would* be a part of his Philosophy.

Instead, Paulius is enlisted into his marketing scheme.

Paulius goes still, seeing if Kenna has more to say. Secretly, Kenna hopes Paulius smashes his skull open with his silver cane.

But instead, Paulius leans forward to embrace him, his hips popping in excruciating ways, pulling Kenna against him until he can feel his fragile warmth doing its best to melt Kenna's chilly performance.

"Of course."

As Paulius holds him, Kenna realizes how correct his parents were:

To be a salesman instead of a Philosopher is to be truly damned.

He'd thought Paulius would retreat to his quarters to record the blog—but Paulius had started production right in the hotel room.

Kenna hides in the bathroom, clammy with cowardice-sweat, turning on the shower to drown Paulius's stentorian attempts at narration. It's not long before Paulius cracks the door open; Kenna is hunched on the toilet like a boy with a bowel dysfunction.

"Don't you . . . want to watch me make it for you?" Paulius's hurt voice floats across the bathroom with a feather's gentleness.

Kenna remembers a lie he'd told, a long time ago: *You can't just hand me the food, Paulius. I . . . I have to watch it happen. The creation, it . . . it inspires me.*

"Not this time."

Paulius nods and retreats.

Kenna shivers, needing the touch of someone who cares. But Paulius's touch would unlock awful truths.

He keeps the door shut—but the frosted glass barrier doesn't block Paulius's shouts as he erupts in symphonies of curses, breaks out in mad-scientist laughs, flings his cane across the room, purrs in satisfaction. The glass lights up with a kaleidoscope of colors as Paulius fast-forwards through The Sol Majestic's archived videos.

Kenna presses his cheek against the glass, mad to know what Paulius assembles, feeling incomplete without seeing what clips he has selected, how he's rearranging them, what words he's choosing . . .

When did a lie become a truth?

He *does* need to see the beauty being made. The Sol Majestic has addicted him to the act of creation. All that keeps him pent in

this porcelain jail is the knowledge that what's being created is hol-
lowly rotted—Paulius struggles to create beauty, but the best he'll
manage is a tawdry huckster's pitch.

Kenna rubs the shower-steam into his skin, pretending it smells
like chicken soup.

Hours later, Paulius raps his cane on the glass door, so enthusiastic he threatens to shatter the glass. "Come, Kenna! Let me show
you who you are! Or at least as I see you!"

Kenna's hair drips with moisture, his skin beaded with cold
water, as though his whole body was weeping. But Paulius rushes
in, grabs him by the hand, leads Kenna out like a man starting a
parade.

"I did it, Kenna," he whispers, placing Kenna down in a chair,
getting him a towel to dry himself with. "I have distilled what you
do."

Kenna has seen this manic exhilaration before: when Paulius
brought him the lacquered duck. Paulius has once again assembled
scattered ingredients into beauty, and his eyes gleam as he queues
up the video.

"the highest art is to get someone to give you something that
grants them joy," Rèpondelle said, and he knows this is how she
justifies her manipulations: yes, she alters their mindsets through
flattery and lies, but it's all to make them blissful.

Though as Paulius dims the lights, to Kenna he has the drugged
look of a cow led off to be butchered.

The screen blurs into motion, and:

A camera poised high in the trees shows Paulius standing in a
tangled green garden, lit by golden sunshine, as though the heavens have chosen to illuminate him alone. He reaches back, clasping an emaciated boy in a wretched robe as though some great
electricity were being carried between them—and as he sweeps the
tip of his cane up, it's as though he's demarcating the heavens, his
face suffused with joy.

Kenna is shocked to see himself as he was when he first stum-

bled into The Sol Majestic—but of course Paulius records everything. If a lucky accident happens in the kitchen, Paulius wants to
re-create it, celebrate it, market it. But there is no noise except for
a howling wind that exists nowhere in the gardens.

"I was inspired the moment I saw Kenna," the speakers in-
tone.

Cut to a high shot of a cramped waste reprocessing unit, strung
with Christmas lights and half-empty beer bottles: Kenna stands
tall beneath Captain Lizzie, his robe fluttering dramatically.

He stands so straight. All he remembers from that day is terror,
confusion, desperation. Yet there he is, one finger raised politely
to contradict her, her anger dissolving into understanding.

"He's been here for only weeks, and he's changed the Station.
There's new policies been enacted, things that encourage the flourishing of . . ."

Montgomery, catapulted into space, a high angle from a low security camera.

"The strangest beauty."

Benzo is collapsed by the porthole, naked and weeping and
bleeding, clutching Kenna like a drowning man clinging to a rock.
Kenna, whispering something unknowable in his ear, his back
arched as if he intends to lift Benzo up.

"He unlocks potentials in people," Paulius whispers. "He takes
who they are, and magnifies the best parts of them. I don't think
he understands how powerful he's going to be. But . . ."

Chefs standing around a lacquered duck, engaging in inspired
debates over meals, an entire restaurant dedicated to turning Kenna's vague philosophies into food.

"We have wrapped ourselves deep in the Inevitable Philosophy
the Prince will manifest in two weeks. And he's asked us to make
available the opportunity for you to be a part of it in advance—a
special Inevitable Robe, made to mark the Prince's ascendence. If
you cannot attend, let this limited-edition robe guide you to the
destiny you deserve . . ."

Kenna squirms in the seat as the sales pitch heats up. Paulius chuckles. "You see it now, don't you, Kenna?"

He wants to be in the kitchen. He wants to be in places where people speak in practical languages, of temperatures and tastes instead of gossamer philosophies. He'd rather cut root vegetables than cut commercials.

But what he will get will be more cavernous hotel rooms. Meals he's never seen prepared. More time alone in rooms with people who, under different circumstances, he might be friends with, tricking strangers into doing him favors.

Yet The Sol Majestic will exist, he tells himself. *There will still be a kitchen, there will still be meals made, there will still be Paulius's mad vision.*

He will never be a part of them again. But they'll exist.

That will have to be enough.

31

Two Hours Until the Wisdom Ceremony

It is the night of the Wisdom Ceremony—and though a sumptuous feast awaits him, Kenna feels as though he has been prepared for the meal. His brain has become a thrashing database, so stuffed full of Rèpondelle's lessons that whenever he gets nervous, preloaded conversations of *engrams* and *narrative transportation* and *subliminal stimuli* shuffle to the fore.

After eighteen-hour days in Rèpondelle's simulations, he won't actually talk to people at the Wisdom Ceremony: he will regurgitate snippets of dialogue that Rèpondelle has poured into him, and they will repeat their lines back to him.

Rèpondelle fusses with the straps underneath his clothing, pulls tight until the thumbtacks she has wedged against his skin threaten to bleed. His body language has been a challenge—standing proud inside the cramped transport ships led to banged foreheads and bullies—so she's resorted to an old Allface trick of torturing him into a confident posture.

She circles him three times, hands clasped behind her back. "perfect," she sighs.

Kenna is unsure if the pleasure she radiates is accidental, or a tactic to boost his confidence.

"ready?" she asks.

He isn't. Yet he knows no amount of training could prepare him.

He remembers Rakesh leaning over Montgomery as she'd hugged herself, one lever-pull away from being dropped into icy vacuum. She'd worked for months to arrange this lunatic's dream, and yet come the day even iron-willed Montgomery had hoped someone would haul her out and tell her she didn't have to do this.

But Rakesh hadn't.

"Nobody cares about your needs," he'd told her. "They're satisfying their own."

She hadn't been ready.

She'd done it anyway.

"Yes," Kenna says, and when the words come out a whisper Rèpondelle pokes his thumbtacks to remind him an Inevitable Prince should speak clearly.

"then proceed, o Prince!" She sucks air into her lungs until the nondescript Rèpondelle becomes the acolyte Mother and Father entrusted their son to.

She thumbs open the door. Mother and Father loom like statues.

Father nods, once. "It's good to see you, Kenna."

Kenna can tell that Father has rehearsed those words.

Yet as Mother hugs him, Kenna reads a stiff reluctance on their bodies: not quite the open fondness they had for the brief period he was in their favor, but they do not clasp their bellies as if looking for excuses not to touch him. He will be neither favored nor shunned until he reveals his Inevitable Philosophy.

His Philosophy is, of course, stinking bullshit.

Rèpondelle and he have chosen "I will be a light to disperse the darkness"—a Philosophy so vague it can be applied profitably to any situation. He has memorized a platitude-filled speech designed to give people nebulous placeholder hope until he can talk to them in person and cold-read their fears.

Yet his distaste is only because he knows the tricks behind the speech. Rèpondelle has recorded his rehearsals for analysis, coaching him which words to emphasize, when to slow down—and the playback of his final reading brought him to tears, even though he'd been the one who gave it.

For the first time, Mother and Father's presence reassures him. He needs to look like the Inevitable Prince, and Mother and Father have spent their entire lives expecting to be treated as royalty. They fall into place behind him as he walks down the hotel's hallway, their presence a beacon that he is Inevitable, he is this religion's righteous owner, and even if it's hokum they're telling him it's right to be hokum.

Rèpondelle bolts down the hall, hands raised high like a sprinter crossing the finish line, her robe streaming behind her, and she slams open the exit doors.

The roar thumps him in the chest, a cheer so loud it ripples his robe, and the crowd is packed so tight the onlookers clamber over each other to get a glimpse of him, pushing their heads beneath other people's armpits, wriggling forward with the clumsiness of newborn kittens . . .

Yet though they're stuffed tight enough to cause transport ship riots, they're all grinning, eyes wide with hope. Kenna's too used to sedentary people waiting in line for paperwork, women smoking joints to pass the crushed hours packed inside the public spaces—this animated rush is a spark. He breathes in their excitement and when he breathes out he shouts greetings at them—

"*Salutations!*" he cries; they rush forward in praise. Rèpondelle produces a baton to push the crowds back, shouting "*make way for the Prince!*" and they clear a bubble for him to step through . . .

This can't be real, he thinks. *Scrimshaw must have purchased these crowds for me.* But Kenna recognizes some of the faces, janitors and merchants and mechanics, and realizes somehow his triumph has become their triumph, that when he becomes the Inevitable Prince they will have become enmeshed in his greater story. This is why they grab his shoulders, ask Kenna if he remembers them, their faces taut with the hope they were essential to this new and glorious movement he will unleash.

"Of course I know you!" he tells them, Rèpondelle's reflexes coming to the fore—*never dampen someone's enthusiasm when you can reflect it back at them*—and he watches them relax as he lies to them, each worried they had offended him by overlooking him when he was nobody, but he sweeps them up in happy Rèpondelle-shaped embraces designed to fill them with forgiveness, and his generosity confirms his reputation that the Prince loves everyone.

They walk away stronger for his lie.

And Kenna sees a Colpuran man with brightly braided hair skulking at the back of the crowd—

"I know you most of all, sir!" Kenna cries, carried along by some great wave of kindness, as if everything he sees today will help him heal someone, for of course it's the bhelpuri merchant he left behind.

He's been so selfish. Of course the bhelpuri merchant doesn't know Kenna's pondered his plight ever since. All he knows is that he offered a free sample to the Inevitable Prince, who ran away.

Kenna commands the crowd to bring the bhelpuri merchant here, whose eyes iris wide in wonder, and Kenna falls to his knees.

"You fashioned me a gift, once," Kenna says. "I was unworthy."

That is truth.

Yet there's no harm in using Rèpondelle's techniques to magnify the truth.

The bhelpuri merchant stammers apologies, and Kenna cries that this brave man followed his dreams to Savor Station to make the best bhelpuri in the galaxy, and the merchant demurs that Kenna never tried his bhelpuri and Kenna says, "Then we'll have to try it, shall we?" and promises to sit down with the merchant before he leaves and by the time Rèpondelle escorts Kenna away the merchant is overwhelmed with people demanding he get back to his cart and sell them his wares, the *Prince's* wares, and Rèpondelle winks in approval.

They make their way to the Majestic's obsidian cave entryway, which has been cleared by Savor Station's security personnel. The space has been lit bright for vloggers to record.

Scrimshaw, pulled tight in her vulturish black cloak, stands alone to greet him.

She steps forward, wreathed in hisses of random noise to confound the vloggers' recording devices, and produces a single blood-red index card, which she holds between two fingers. Scrimshaw bows, offering the card to him.

He takes it, turns it over: it's blank on both sides. Rèpondelle's spine stiffens, which he knows is her default behavior whenever something unexpected happens: clearly, this isn't part of the ceremony.

Scrimshaw's thin lips curl up into a cryptic grin.

He stares down at it, hunting for hidden technology. But it's an ordinary piece of paper.

Then he remembers where he last saw it.

He flicks the card against his chin, remembering how high this card had seemed when it was tucked into a stack of robes. This is her hidden signal: those robes had been sold, pouring enough money into The Sol Majestic's coffers to pay the robe-maker.

He tucks the card into his robe, glad of the keepsake—and realizes that as the Inevitable Prince he will no longer have to worry about bullies stealing his memorabilia.

"Did we turn a profit?" he asks. "They were triple-price. I hope that seals the breach in our financial interests . . ."

Her eyes flutter shut as she shakes her head in a tiny dream; Kenna can almost watch her savor a world where she'd be allowed to keep money. "There *were* profits. But then Montgomery and Paulius decided at the last minute the Ceremony they had wouldn't be right for you, and nearly bankrupted me with the architectural changes . . ."

Kenna frowns. "What did they do?"

She clucks her tongue. "They'd kill me if I spoiled the surprise. But they're awaiting you, O Prince. Everyone has arrived but you."

She bends down, her dry lips brushing his ear.

"Everyone but Benzo," she says. "Your parents refused to allow his presence."

Kenna slumps, the thumbtacks pushing deep into his skin. But Scrimshaw does something she has never done before:

She takes his hands in hers.

Her fingers are bony, her skin worn thin by age, but her grip is prepared to haul him away if Kenna whispers a single protest.

"Are you ready to claim your . . . Inevitable Philosophy?"

What a wonderful world, Kenna thinks, *where even Scrimshaw has a conscience.*

Of course he's not ready.

But Rèpondelle has taught him to lie well. He ponders the empty words he must speak until his dying days: *I will be a light to disperse the darkness.*

Such bullshit.

Such beautifully crafted bullshit.

He nods. Scrimshaw opens the doors.

32

Ninety Minutes Until the Wisdom Ceremony

Kenna has never entered The Sol Majestic through its front doors before.

For a moment, he thinks he has died.

Then he realizes: sophisticated audio countermodulators have dampened the noise around him, leaving him in such perfect silence he can hear his pulse quicken. Slow-light fields have absorbed every photon, plunging him into a velvety darkness so cool it wicks the sweat from his skin. The carpet is soft and springy, so each step loosens the bonds of gravity, propels him forward through the void. Mother and Father are behind him, but they could be a galaxy away.

Kenna treads forward; the sudden quiet has robbed him of the crowd's boisterous energy. He is, once again, reduced to a boy pretending to be a Philosopher.

There are supposed to be drinks before the meal. Kenna tries not to hold out his hands and stumble forward as though this were some haunted house; he clasps his arms by his side, retaining a prince's dignity. *Rèpondelle prepared me for the salad course, the snail course, the rusted egg course . . .*

Normally, he'd freeze before he crashed blindly into a waiter. But he trusts Paulius. He trusts Montgomery. If they ask him to walk through darkness, he will follow . . .

A laser inscribes a smoking inscription on the floor before him.

Welcome to the Inevitable Prince's Wisdo

Kenna stumbles to a halt. The laser stops writing. He chuckles, feeling silencing countervibrations penning his laughter in his chest, then clasps his hands to hug himself as he realizes: *this is the first of the wonders they have planned for me.*

He steps forward, following the laser's trail, and it continues writing for him in robe-vibrant letters, moving like a ballerina gliding ahead, an elaborate curlicue he recognizes as Paulius's handwriting:

> *m Ceremony! A glorious dinner awaits—but before you eat, you will travel the path the Inevitable Prince took to get here, reliving life as He knew it. But I warn you! Where He has journeyed, there is very little food . . .*

The words squiggle up from the floor, jumping as they trace their way across an airlock—

The bulkhead airlock to a transport ship.

The words pulsate, pointing to the entryway keypad with a puppydog enthusiasm that suggests tonight's guests wouldn't know enough to press their palms against a standard bulk-transport biometric access pad. Mother and Father stagger up behind him, faces contorted as though looking for the joke.

It's as though the airlock has dressed up for an evening out. A few snarls of graffiti lend it artificial danger, but not the graphic patina that builds up after months of boredom. There's no scent of rust and urine and dope. The biometric access pad gleams, not fogged with layers of skin oils.

Did Paulius understand who Kenna was?

This airlock's mockery has united them. Kenna looks to Father for guidance; Father shrugs, gestures for Kenna to access the lock.

They scoot backwards as it hisses open. Kenna knows what he will see inside; the cavernous assembly area, where ship security can round up the passengers in case of riot.

They await his ersatz wisdom.

I will be a light to disperse the darkness. He subvocalizes the words, remembering the rolling tones Rèpondelle has taught him to make this sham of a Philosophy sound as deep as oceans. He softens his gaze to make meaningful eye contact, prepares a cryptic smile to imply he understands his guests' troubles . . .

But no. Beyond the door is a washroom, complete with sordid squat-toilets and dry-wipe stations and graffiti-smeared bathroom mirrors. Which is ludicrous; no transport ship would funnel its passengers into alcoves that encourage them to freshen up. They're usually jabbing your back with plastic poles to push you in.

Who *designed* this stupid ship?

"The graffiti!" Mother stifles an un-Mother-like chuckle. Sure enough, the pastel knots of gang signs on the mirror wriggle like worms, forming new words:

As the Prince was anonymous when he arrived, so shall you be. Please. Wash your hands.

Father sticks his hands beneath a faucet. Mother and Kenna gather round him, curious to see how deep this charade goes—and sure enough, after ten seconds the water clicks off with a red buzz. Father flicks his fingers, pleased at least they have gotten this detail correct.

Except instead of a red laser light blinking YOU HAVE USED UP ONE UNIT OF YOUR DAILY WATER SUPPLY, the warning reads, *Please. Dry your hands.*

Father and Mother exchange a look, then Father crouches down beneath the bulky blast-dryers affixed to the walls.

Except the blast-dryers hiss like spray paint, a grid of lasers painting Father's face as the smell of burning plastic jets out from the driers.

A smooth white mask drops into Father's hands.

Father cradles it, the etch of a grin cracking his stern face. He traces the mask's fluted edge with his fingertips, marveling at the quality of the fabbed creation: one side is made of a flexible nylon, fitted to his face's contour like a sleeping mask, while the outside could have been a beautiful bust from ancient times.

"Go on," Mother says. "Try it on."

Father presses it to his face; it sticks. The mask obscures Father's concerned expression with a sculpted look that is penitent, gaunt, hopeful. "It's comfortable enough," he says; filtered through the mask, his voice has been modulated to sound like Kenna's.

Mother claps. "Oh, this will be so much fun!" She gets her own mask; curious, Kenna tugs at the bathroom door to confirm that no, they would not be allowed into the party until they have each donned their disguise.

Aside from being shaped to fit Mother's features, her mask is identical to Father's. In their robes, they look like assembly-line dolls.

As Kenna affixes his mask, the door to the bathroom clicks open. Mother and Father extend their arms, touching each other at the fingertips like swans in flight. They unfurl their free hand toward Kenna, who grasps them to welcome himself into the fold—

The thumbtacks jab his shoulder blades, reminding him of a true Prince's posture, reminding him he is here to lie.

"Let us go," Mother says, holding the door open for Father, the two sweeping through first, a silent rebuke for Kenna's impertinent lone entry into The Sol Majestic. Kenna holds his breath, preparing to enter into the great assembly area . . .

But no. Correctly, they exit into a crowded side corridor, swaying hammocks filled with gray-robed passengers exhaling plumes of marijuana, thick shielded cables for power and gas, floors with rubber mats so the pooled body fluids won't cause anyone to slip.

Not that there are any body fluids; transport ships are sometimes this clean, but only before a government sanitary inspection.

Yet aside from the fact that everyone is dressed in starvation masks and flowing Inevitable Robes, wandering through the corridor like excited children playing Blind Man's Bluff, this *could* have been his childhood.

A knot of tension in his chest relaxes: he'd been worried Paulius and Montgomery had turned his childhood into a grotesque stage play to entertain rich fools. But this area's accuracy is a secret signal to him that they can get the details right when they want to.

That thought lasts until a passenger leans down, his face made up in exaggerated addict's pockmarks, to croak, "A joint to put your mind at ease, guv'nor?"

It is the fumellier, spreading open a selection of weed in her fingers. They are rolled into stunningly perfect joints—which is almost enough to stop Kenna from protesting, "Who says guv'nor on a ship?"

Yet the fumellier waggles her eyebrows, directing Kenna's attention to Mother and Father behind him. Eager masked men in robes have caught them by the shoulder, asking, "So are *you* the Inevitable Prince?"

Mother and Father preen like tomcats, turning ever-so-slowly to acknowledge the question, tilting their chins as if long accustomed to possessing information others desperately seek. They lick up the way this crowd hunches in anticipation—

Kenna is gone by the time they turn to acknowledge him. He does not want to be the Prince yet, wants to luxuriate in the last moments in which he will not have to tell a lie.

He tiptoes through the corridors, feeling childish among these giants of industry. No one here is scrawny; the closest anyone resembles his shape are the clothes hanger bodies of models, who have sashed up the robes around their waists to highlight their figures. Actors and actresses have followed suit, rolling up their rainbow sleeves to reveal toned biceps, whereas the epicureans who've poured culinary fortunes into creating great jiggling bellies are content to wear the robes as is.

Kenna feels like he's moving in slow motion—everyone else darts past like amphetamine-crazed ferrets, opening every supply door and looking under every hammock. "It's a Majestic production," they mutter, moving through the marijuana smoke's blue haze. "There's got to be food *somewhere*."

Their speed turns this replica set into a musical. They feel the walls, looking for hidden doors with the wealthy confidence that something exciting lies around each corner, stifling giggles as they ask their fellow travelers if they are the Inevitable Prince. Whereas the transport ships Kenna traveled on were steeped in dullness, your options these gray walls and maybe a joint if you were lucky, the long hours wearing you away . . .

The cool nylon pressed to his cheeks feels like a barrier Montgomery has interposed between him and tonight's guests—Paulius and Montgomery's secret message that everyone wants to be him, yet will never see the truth of him.

Which is foolish arrogance. They built this replica to delight the guests. This is where Kenna's own needs will be sublimated away, Kenna vanishing into the Inevitable Prince.

His belly cramps. The air smells wrong. You don't live on transport ships without picking up a working knowledge of marijuana, and long-timers choose resins to deaden the stomach. The fumellier has chosen smokes that stoke hunger, so even the exhalations of other guests circulate and generate craving. Their merry games are deteriorating into a hunt for confections.

A flock of barefaced guests wave at Kenna, shooting him exaggerated *Isn't-this-fun?* smiles as they toke up in a repair alcove. Kenna pauses—why are they so eager to have him?—until a man huffs past Kenna, tearing off his mask.

The guests applaud, calling out his name—Kenna has seen this politician's face on the holovids, though he can't remember where.

The politician slicks back his hair, grabs a joint with irritation, and snarls, "I didn't come all this way to *not* be seen," before he joins the celebrities trying to sway people to their half-hearted rebellion.

A mask-wearing woman with flowing black hair runs into the room so fast she has to hold a bulkhead to catch her breath.

"Attention, starving Princes!" A person in his robes is calling for Kenna's attention with Kenna's own voice, and an irrational fear floods him that he is not himself. But the black-haired woman shakes her fists in the air with a quite-un-Kennaish restraint, vibrating as though she cannot contain herself. *"Someone's paying the vending machine!"*

The demasked protesters attempt to hide their excitement—but everyone else chases after the black-haired woman, looking like a river of flapping flags as their robes snap and unfurl behind them, leaving disconsolate celebrities looking bewildered no one wants to pay attention to them.

Kenna follows the stampede of trillionaires, buoyed by their excitement, needing to see what vending machines could inspire such passion.

Yet unlike the strips of Bark-Chew and SugarBomb vending machines that lined the transport ships' walls, this replica holds a single vending machine—and holds it in an amphitheater.

This towering vending monolith sits beneath a violet spotlight. It dwarfs the one woman standing at its base, who peers up at its rows of mouthwatering baked goods.

The confections are held in gleaming chrome crèches—fat pink cupcakes with striped buttercream curlicues, bowls of purple rice topped with mango, dense black aniseed drops that ripple with blue flame, a delicate cobweb of spun sugar.

Each dessert more unusual than the last. A crowd has gathered in a ring around it, swaying from smoke-hunger, pressing close like zombies about to break through the glass.

Except the woman paces up and down the rows with the irritated curtness of a lion stalking prey, clearing space for herself. She approaches a bowl of green foam fizzing over with sugar, glances up, winces, withdraws.

The crowd gathered in the amphitheater leans forward when she does, sighs in dismay when she backs off. One calls out, their voice turned into Kenna's by the mask, "*You said you'd made up your mind!*"

She shakes them off like a baseball pitcher waving away a bad call. "I said I'd made up my mind to *do* it," she corrects them, Kenna's voice chopped up erratically by a foreign diction. "Any of you lot feel like footing this bill, I'll choose right now."

Chastened, the crowd falls quiet.

The black-haired woman stands next to him. Kenna whispers: "Why does she hesitate so?"

The woman directs Kenna's attention to the vast screen hovering high above the vending machine: a trillion-dinari figure scrolls past as the woman's attention hovers upon a coffee crunch cake.

"Would *you* pay a trillion for a piece of cake?" she asks.

"A *trillion*?" Kenna splutters, expecting the rich men to whirl around, realize how shabby his robes are, notice his howling poverty—but they bob their heads as if to acknowledge how insane this is.

"For some people it's only a few billion," the black-haired woman whispers. "It's scanning our net worth. Making sure that whatever we pay for it *costs* us. That woman has to be unfathomably rich even by our standards, and she's determined to have the best dessert."

Kenna hunts for a pathway through the dense crowd, trying to make his way down to the auditorium. "She won't get the best. That's not what this is about . . ."

The black-haired woman tents her fingers on his shoulder. "*Sssh.* Let her learn."

Kenna should help this woman before she bankrupts herself. Yet he wonders how many in this crowd expect these jailed sweets to be as good as the cost . . .

"How many of them understand?" he asks, pained.

She pats his shoulder; that militarily-crisp touch has the sensation of having passed an audition. "We who grew up in poverty fathomed this trap." She crosses her arms, radiating grim satisfaction. "We've been waiting to see which one makes the Prince's choice."

Still. Even though Kenna understands the trap, he can't let anyone make the mistakes he would have made. "Wait—!"

But the woman has made her selection. The green figures turn gold, melting into red, dripping away into nothingness as the amount is subtracted from her accounts; her mask flakes away into gold filaments, dissolving to reveal an elderly Gineer woman with genetically taut youth.

She twirls, her robe opening like a blossom, drinking in the crowd's applause.

The vending machine makes a harsh clattering noise, gears ratcheting into place. The violet light snaps off, the glass goes dark.

The coffee crumb cake is plopped onto a paper plate, shoved toward her, its sharp triangle shape squashed into a heap.

She takes a plastic fork and prods it, as if perhaps there is some new trick hidden inside. But without the clever spotlights, it is merely a mass-produced, oversugared cake.

She takes a new bite in disbelief. "I paid a fifth of my family's inheritance to sample the best dessert in the galaxy . . ."

"No," the black-haired woman snaps. "You paid a fifth of everything you owned to fill your belly. Just like the starving Prince."

An argument ripples across the crowd: some grumbling *How dare Paulius do this to us,* others braying bitter laughter, folks rushing forward to try this sodden cake, the woman batting them away to savor every last gram of this trillion-dinari investment, licking the plate like a starving child as her peers try to snatch it away.

Kenna knows the scent of nascent riots. He balls himself against the wall, bracing for the first person to throw a punch . . .

The floor shakes: the booming shudder of transport ship docking maneuvers.

The cold violet light phase-shifts into a warm, golden radiance.

The crowd halts as a crackling noise booms down from the overhead speakers—an old-fashioned recording spinning to life:

I've had canned meat, dried noodles, pickled eggs. If I . . . if we . . . ever came back into favor, would I . . . appreciate anything else? I can't tell. All this surviving is killing me.

With a great *clack,* the vending machine sinks into the floor, and more of that golden light spills through into the cramped darkness. It illuminates the crowds' faces, their hateful sneers relaxing into drop-jawed wonder as they realize Paulius has played them like instruments, and their orchestrated anger was a part of the performance.

(Though Scrimshaw rushes in to grab the Gineer woman, whispering reassurances that of *course* they'll refund the money, actually charging her accounts for the full trillion was a clerical error, she'd talk with Montgomery about giving the impression they'd—ha ha—intended to *keep* the dinari . . .)

Then the rich chicken scent hits their nostrils and the crowd shivers in pleasure. Their bellies have been primed by the fumellier to short-circuit conscious thought when the hunger hits; their noses lift to follow this aroma, leaning forward to walk toward the luminous space opened up by the descending vending machine.

The sun-warmed scent of chlorophyll filters through; Kenna's eyes adjust to the patches of blue overhead, the green thatches, looking as beautiful as the first time he laid eyes upon The Sol Majestic's orchard. Although it's overgrown, with waist-high brush thickets turning the once-neat fields of olive trees wild and dangerous.

Paulius and Montgomery stand on a hill next to a gigantic bubbling stewpot, waving its scent down onto the crowd with great green fronds.

"Shall we gather by the river?" Paulius asks, waving his hand to encompass the heavens. Paulius's white suit is as clean as starlight, his long braid wrapped in gleaming silver, looking so hale

Kenna can hardly believe he had his pelvis sawed open a month ago. *"You have survived the Prince's travails!"*

"Now taste the broth that birthed the Inevitable Prince's Philosophy, and be reborn!" Montgomery's wearing an Inevitable robe—an act that makes her unsettlingly feminine after all her red-leather violence. The Bitch rests at her hip in a newly refurbished oak cask, her goggles clear of mold specks.

The crowd erupts from the transport ship's cramped confines, hands extended like zombies . . .

"Don't you dare bum-rush *this* show, my friends." Paulius's voice drops to a stage whisper. "This is a sacred experience. Come with cramped bellies, one by one, and let the Prince's Inevitable wisdom fill you." He points his cane at Kenna. "You, sir! Why don't you sup first?"

Kenna's skin prickles into chill goose bumps, cold as a corpse. His knees lock; thumbtacks jab into his spine, prodding him into the regal stance Rèpondelle taught him, but his body refuses to respond to Paulius's call—

And why not? When he drinks from that stewpot, Kenna will evaporate away like steam, leaving behind the Inevitable Prince's mirrorlike reflection. He will not officially become the Prince, not until he gives his *I am the light to disperse the darkness* speech after the meal, but . . .

Kenna's body refuses to attend his own funeral.

Montgomery slaps a silver ladle into his palm and steps away, abdicating responsibility for Kenna's choices. She knows his Philosophy is false, she has told him to run—and now she refuses to look at him, directing her gaze out over the crowd, her face contorted into a cultist's stiff grin.

She has orchestrated this for his benefit—but having catapulted Kenna into the adoration of the powerful, she has withdrawn her approval.

She's left before he can, which makes this easier.

Paulius, however, catches Kenna by the shoulder as Kenna leans down to scoop up the broth. He detaches the mask's mouth, freeing Kenna to drink—but Paulius cranes his neck to peer up at Kenna with a fierce pride, as if he wants one last moment to savor this dish before sending it out to the dining room.

Kenna stares into the soup, wishing Benzo was here to hold his hand.

The broth's surface wobbles with fat globules, swirling with nebulae of darkened chicken particles—imperfections Kenna never had noticed when Paulius first brought him the bowl.

Except they are not imperfections. They are Benzo's last lovenote: *I will be with you in your final moments.*

This is the last moment he will be Kenna.

He sips the broth, letting his lover fill him.

The mask dissolves into golden tatters, streaming away to reveal his face, the crowd gasping, Paulius waving his cane and shouting, *"Ladies and gentlemen, the Inevitable Prince!"*

Kenna closes his eyes as the mask floats away on the wind, saying goodbye to Benzo, to The Sol Majestic, to Paulius.

When he opens them, the wealthy line up to drink his broth.

He begins to become a salesman.

33

One Hour Until the Wisdom Ceremony

As Kenna spoons broth out to the Ceremony's guests, he appreciates Paulius's genius. *Do someone a small favor, and they become more willing to do you large favors,* Rèpondelle had said.

By allowing Kenna to serve the broth, he allows Kenna to dispense favors to the powerful. They line up before his stewpot, grouping into loose conversational circles as they assure each other that of *course* they wouldn't have paid a billion dinari for dessert, they were on to Paulius's foolhardy game from the beginning, detailing how they'd outfoxed the old man by making love in a hidden alcove . . .

But their feet move in lockstep. Whenever someone bows before Kenna to receive their broth, the others maneuver so no one nudges them from their place in line. They saunter away with brimming bowls as if this is trivial, but when they believe no one is looking they take belly-filling slurps.

They scrutinize him as Kenna fills their bowls with a silver ladle, and Kenna senses the flashpoint: if they feel judged in any way for their fears in the transport ship, their hatred will crystallize around him.

Instead, Kenna thanks them as they approach, as if they have done him a great service by attending his Ceremony. Their eyebrows knot as they examine him for sarcasm—but Kenna knows he is dressed in ragged robes, his scrawny body the picture of asceticsm, and he bends his knees to look as though he offers to boost them up.

"You're welcome," they say, and he can see them retranslating their discomfort into a nice thing they did for a wise man's pleasure, associating Kenna with regained dignity and power.

there are two kinds of rich people, Rèpondelle had told him: *those who earned their money, and those who inherited it. the ones who earned wealth are forever terrified someone will take it away from them, while the ones who inherited wealth are forever terrified someone will expose them.*

Kenna has returned power to the once-poor ones, and has ensured the always-rich ones feel like their discomfort was a performance.

By the time he steps away from the stewpot, ladle still in hand, he is surrounded by admirers. Presidents ask him, *Was it as bad as that on the transport ships?* And Kenna knows enough to demur: *I'm sure it was nothing you couldn't have handled.* Bankers ask, *Where will you go after the Ceremony?* And Kenna says, *Wherever I am needed most* and floats his gaze around the room to mark which ones stare longingly at him so he can corner them later. Nuvawood starlets sidle close to ask, *What will your Philosophy be?* And Kenna waves his hands in a circle as though opening a gateway and says, *You shall step through with me in a few hours.*

Except he doesn't know long it will be. Mother and Father keep hauling people over to him—the guests pause, chests puffed out as they offer themselves up for a scan, before Kenna tells them he has no bioimplants, please, he would far prefer to hear their name from their own lips. And when he does not recognize them—which is not often, as everyone here has made galactic headlines—he prostrates himself to play the "I am a humble traveler" card Rèpondelle taught him to use to deflect a potential embarrassment into an opportunity for them to train him.

For the opportunities also go in reverse: *Let them do you small favors, and they will be more disposed to do you greater ones.* It's all about playing on people's magnanimity, and Kenna discovers he is more adept at this than he would have dreamed—men and women hold his hand for a scandalous moment too long, he can hear them murmuring in approval as he steps away, and Mother's prissy over-politeness turns out to be suited to these environments.

And the people, well, they guard their decorum, but Rèpondelle's training allows him to see through them. He'd always thought wealth and power would be an armor to shield people from fear.

Yet most are like the people on the transport ships: worried about status, hoping they don't make fools of themselves, jockeying for position.

After a while, Kenna realizes the thumbtacks have stopped pricking him; being the Inevitable Prince isn't difficult.

It's actually an interesting challenge. He seeks out the cantankerous investor who'd shrugged off Kenna's charms and tries conversational approaches until he opens up the man's love of gambling. Kenna knows nothing but professes curiosity, and when he ambles away the investor has promised to take Kenna to an outlaw casino where you can wager your memories to win secrets.

Then the black-haired woman breaks through the crowd to bow to him. She does not bow deeply—but then again, nobody here does except for the actors.

"Finally," she huffs, flipping her long hair back over her shoulders; her face is beautiful in a cut-diamond sense, sharp and precise, genetically engineered in the Gineer fashion to have model-quality traits that blend together into a mélange that defies ancestry. Yet despite the fact that she's fit her features together like a puzzle, she's chosen a dazzlingly friendly smile. "I thought Paulius would never leave me alone. My name is Madison, and I wanted to thank you for helping me with my—is that a *frying pan* growing by your elbow?"

Kenna turns—and indeed, a bulbous copper frond on a thick green stalk appears to be blossoming into a frying pan.

This derails the conversation. Kenna gets on his knees in the soft loam, bumping shoulders with the cooing guests peering close to examine it. It's a budding pan; only the handle is fully formed, jutting out like a metal stalk. The copper cooking surface is curled, its tall sides unfolding as it pulses open.

"You can't . . . grow . . . cookware, can you?" an energy investor asks.

Kenna grabs the stem—and unlike the living fronds in The Sol Majestic's orchard, this is a hollow nanite tube dyed green. If he looks close, he can see the slender filament of gray nanotech goo pulsing up into the pan-blossom, pumped up from below.

Madison brushes her fingertips against the pan's dull burnish before drawing her hand back. "It's warm," she giggles. "Of *course* it's warm, it's moving like a living being, it has to radiate energy . . ."

Kenna feels the guests looking to him for explanations: *They think I'm in on this.* Which, now that he thinks of it, would be a sane assumption: Rèpondelle had trained him to master the seventeen-course dinner they'd prepared, but Paulius and Montgomery had assumed Kenna could wing this.

Not that he can find them. Kenna has trained three weeks for this party, but Paulius has devoted his life to dancing through cocktail hours—he is a soiree ninja, and when he moves to bow out no one can follow him.

Paulius has left Kenna to lead the festivities.

The pan has unfurled, facing him like a sunflower, its steep sides revealing it is not a frying pan, but a sauté pan. He grasps the pan's handle, smooth and Benzo-warm, tugs—

It's wired into the ground, tight as a merchant's electronic wares tethered to the shelves.

"Huh." Madison scratches beneath her ear, circling the pan as though it is a puzzle to be solved. "Do you mind if I try?"

Kenna realizes Madison has courteously outmaneuvered the other guests, who halt their forward lurches—they had each intended to haul the pan from the soil. By deferring to Kenna's judgment, she has installed a hierarchy and placed herself second in line.

Mother and Father cross their arms, hating Madison for wresting their scant influence away, unable to speak lest they deny their son's specialness.

"Of course," Kenna demurs, feeling the giddy delight of cutting his parents off.

She grips the pan as though she were an ancient warrior wresting a sword from a stone—but instead of hauling, jerks the pan upward in a brisk motion with no more force needed than to pop the cap off a bottle.

The sauté pan comes free.

She rotates it in one wrist, reflecting sunlight across the crowd, then reaches out to Kenna with it in a gesture mirroring a queen knighting someone with her scepter. She nods toward the ladle Kenna still holds in his left hand.

"You had a cooking implement already." She holds the pan, flat and at arm's length, sweeping it out toward the field—a green swath of high grass in which blossoming eggbeaters and measuring cups and immersion blenders bob on stalks. "I suspect we are intended to become your staff."

The guests charge out into the utensil field, racing to pluck the most interesting tools from the stalks, a few unlucky ones harvesting too soon to discover their nascent mandoline crumbling apart into black dust. Sure enough, once a guest has reaped a strainer, the other stalks become immutable as iron to them, waiting for some other guest to stake their claim.

The first harvests come easily, but the crops soon vanish, leaving guests sadly empty-handed; they laugh, but Kenna reads the embarrassment in their tight shoulders. They're all compensating, in their own ways: telling the empty-handed ones where to look, feigning boredom, unleashing snide putdowns of people who settled for a simple spoon, all as Mother and Father flatter them.

Even to the powerful, being excluded from a group stings.

"Come on." Once again, Paulius and Montgomery have maneuvered the guests into allowing the Inevitable Prince to lead them to their destiny. Kenna modulates his voice to be a dauntless young child who is certain new adventures lie over the next hill. "It's like gathering herbs. You have to hunt for them!"

Yet sure enough, the scarcity binds him and these guests together, Kenna feeling oddly protective—they can be guided so easily. Instill them with uncertainty and they'll follow anyone who presents them with a promising pathway . . .

He likes being their pathway. It nourishes his soul to have people looking to him for assistance, to watch them *acknowledging* him.

There are larger pieces, growing like mushrooms deep in the shadowed woods: ovens, roasting pans, a turnspit. Some require multiple people to heft them before they'll break free. Blossom by blossom, sloping down, the organic kitchen leads Kenna down an erratic pathway—everyone peering into the dwindling sunlight, making a competitive game of "Who can find the next one first," bellowing triumph as they find a curved countertop.

Kenna stumbles onto a cave flanked by a massive chef's knife sprouting from a reed.

Paulius reappears, his suit a blinding white in the penumbral cave, to snatch the knife free. "It wouldn't do to give such a competitive bunch a knife," he jokes, but holds a sober gaze upon Kenna before stepping into the cavern.

Oil-smeared maintenance workers toss off camouflaged ghillie suits, take the implements from the guests' hands with a polite bow, file into the cave. Kenna follows, palms feeling water-wet stone as the blackness deepens, bringing him in through a maze . . .

He stands upon stars.

Kenna's knees wobble as he sets weight on the polished clear platform, looking out into the violet-tinged emptiness. Back when

Rakesh's engineering was a poorly sealed window knocking against the vacuum, Kenna had felt terrified—

Yet the stars wheel beneath his feet, and now he feels propelled through space, whipped around like a yo-yo as the station whirls. He falls to his knees, presses his palms against the icy surface to see the frost radiate out from his fingers.

This is a beautiful high-wire act the station's artists have blessed him with.

He whirls around to hunt for Rakesh, to compliment him on this vast improvement he's made, to ask him how he and Montgomery leveraged Paulius's influence to convince Captain Lizzie this transparent floor was a good idea—

But Rakesh is flattened against the wall's knurled pipes, only visible because his chilled breath jets out into the cool room. Several servants bring in coats for the shivering guests, but Rakesh's sharp features are steely; he slumps back from a great control panel curved before him, offering weak high-fives to his fellow programmers as the three-dimensional images of copper sauté pans and stovetops twirl above them . . .

Then, with a great relieved sigh, they shut down the gray goo control routines and order the smart molecules to collapse into inert carbon.

He realizes with a shock that Paulius had asked Rakesh to work with *unprogrammed* gray goo. That stuff was tightly regulated; a subtle bug in its instructions could cause the goo to absorb and consume every piece of matter it touched until the station was a malignant tumor encapsulated by vacuum. Yet somehow he'd talked Captain Lizzie into this, and what had just happened was like surfing a supernova.

The guests hadn't understood what happened.

They hadn't seen the creation blossoming beneath their noses; just spectacle.

The maintenance workers assemble a small kitchen before them,

Madison and the others taking charge even though the workers
know how to do this, managing the stove's assembly, and as the
chefs bring out the duck, words float over empty stars as though
Kenna speaks to the galaxy:

".. . *you didn't taste the duck?*" Paulius's recorded voice asks.

"*I needed to be there,*" Kenna replies. "*To see it made. You can't
just hand me the food, Paulius. I . . . I have to watch it happen. The
creation, it . . . it inspires me. Without viewing the entirety of the
process, anything you give me might as well be—a nutricracker.*"

He'd lied once to Paulius about that, but his lie had become truth.

The chefs dunk the duck into boiling water to defeather it—but
when it becomes apparent this will produce no immediate dish for
them to sup, the guests converge upon Paulius and Montgomery
to congratulate them for this, as though the kitchen staff were some
extension of Paulius's will, as though the transparent floor beneath
their feet hadn't been installed by Montgomery and Rakesh and
the workers who'd understood this . . .

They didn't see the beauty.

(*Neither did you,* some small part of Kenna objects, noticing he's
not paying attention to the duck, he missed the nanotechnology
art, but by then he's scanning the crowd to find someone to use . . .)

The rich can't see beauty the way I can, he thinks, sweeping past
Madison as she attempts to start another conversation, *but that's
all right. I can aim them like weapons.* He remembers who he'd
discussed art with, plucking out the energy investor who enjoyed
funding unique approaches, and he pretends not to hear Madison
as he takes them by the elbow to say, "Excuse me, have you met
my friend Rakesh?"

Rakesh is starstruck; he daubs oil-streaked sweat off his cheeks
with a rag so filthy it moves the blotches around, but that's okay,
to this crowd a bit of dirt is *credentials,* and by the time he is done
Rakesh is not a worker with artistic expressions, he is an *artist.*

I am a light to disperse the darkness, Kenna thinks, realizing these
words are true in a way he'd never intended. The wealthy will al-

ways have money, of course—that's the darkness—but he can disperse that wealth to better hands, granting Rakesh and the bhelpuri merchant celebrityhood, shining lucre wherever he faces, and Kenna realizes the Inevitable Prince will be a force for good.

"Now that you have stood in the Prince's kitchen," Montgomery says dramatically, "we take the final step in the Prince's journey."

Kenna glances over at the sous station, confused; the lacquered duck isn't prepared yet—

Montgomery taps a button on her smoked lenses and darkness falls away, revealing a battered steel hatchway dripping with chicken-scented condensation, yawning open to reveal a cramped tube of refrigerators looming over a dented copper table:

The Escargone.

Kenna remembers kissing the scarred knife-ridges on Benzo's knuckles, and for a moment he wishes they'd never returned to The Sol Majestic.

"A properly lacquered duck will take hours to prepare!" Montgomery gestures into the Escargone's cramped interior, as if demonstrating she has nothing up her sleeve. The three chefs scoop up their ingredients and march into the Escargone; she slams the door shut, it hums with bright light, and the chefs walk out twenty seconds later with a hot duck sliced onto appetizer trays.

The guests descend on it, the broth not enough to stave off their hunger. Yet Kenna shrugs off Madison's third attempt at conversation to peer into the depths:

They've removed the shower at the Escargone's far end, refitted it with an exit hatch.

"The Prince spent months in here one day, giving of himself to help a humble kitchen staffer." Her dark goggles give away nothing. "And so you shall be given fifteen minutes alone in the Escargone with the friends you have made here tonight—fifteen minutes that shall pass in seconds."

Paulius chuckles as a hologram of Kenna, kneeling before a

slippery naked Benzo, flashes overhead. "And remember—whatever happens in the Escargone, stays in the Escargone."

A ripple of amusement flashes across the room, people stifling knowing smiles with their fingertips. Except it *wasn't* that way; that image was from when Benzo had slashed at the lock with the knife, bloodying himself in an attempt to free Kenna, and they were naked because they were desperate and dying . . .

Mother and Father move to flank him, ensuring he'll never have such adventures again.

"Line up," Montgomery says. Madison laughs uncomfortably as Paulius distracts her with a too-polite-to-refuse offer of lacquered duck.

The wealthy demurely feel each other out to see who might be amenable to amory.

The queue is brisk. Even clad in her Inevitable robe, Montgomery is a no-nonsense guardian, ushering folks in through the doors with a bodyguard's impassivity, slamming the doors shut, reminding them to exit on the other end. The line dwindles as Kenna seethes—

Yet isn't this the way it will always be? He and Benzo, they had once created something of immense beauty, burning away their imperfections until together they conceived the consommé that gave Benzo his victory against his Mistress. Perhaps this was Paulius's hidden message—yes, the plenipotentiaries you influence will never see things as you do, you will never be alone with anyone you love again.

Yet it is a sour mood, and by the time Kenna bumps up against Montgomery, he realizes he is last in line. Of course the Prince goes last. When he steps out, he will eat his meal, and become the light to disperse the darkness.

He moves to step across the entryway, Mother by his left elbow, Father by his right—but Montgomery stops them.

"Sorry." She sounds as apologetic as a jail door. "Only two in at a time: No more, no less. As the Prince once did."

"But we're his parents—" Father splutters.

"Which is why you will go before him. Use your time well."

Kenna laps up their discomfort. They are not Inevitable now, they are loose ends, and everyone knows it—their toadying has been ineffective all these years; it's Kenna's strategies that reignited the Philosophies.

Usurping them will be as simple as a speech.

They vanish with an Escargone flash. Yet he is certain that they'll spend the time mapping out a strategy to insinuate themselves within his Ceremony, so he braces himself for the pleasure of refusing them before an audience—

It is not until Montgomery slams the door behind him that he realizes he is not alone.

Madison stands behind him, backing up against the hatchway as she senses she is intruding. Kenna doesn't want to think of her as an intruder, but the Escargone is filled with familiar scents of sex and soup. This should be a temple to Benzo, not a meeting hall to gladhand people.

Yet gladhanding people is what he does now. He allows his features to relax for one pained stare at the far exit, one last honest expression to remember his lover, before engineering his body language to reflect cheery welcome.

She stiffens, glancing toward the Escargone's window before realizing there is no way to take her embarrassment out upon Montgomery. "My apologies."

"None needed." He glides forward to take her hands, the thumbtacks poking him back into a hospitable stance. "It's good to have company."

"I'm glad you feel that way." She snaps into the brisk stance of a stockholder making a proposition. "I didn't want to intrude. You've done me great favors already."

Kenna cocks his head. "Have I?"

"Oh yes." She shakes her head, a strangely girlish gesture for such a competent woman, as if to acknowledge this wasn't going well. "I just . . . I wanted to thank you for improving morale among my staff. My debtors are not gifted, yet you've managed to turn a D-grade employee into a chef worthy of my service."

Madison continues to talk: "So I was hoping to hear your suggestions toward improving my household staff's performance ratings . . ."

But her words gray out—her *tone* is what matters. Madison is being polite to him, even cheerful, and a woman like this *can't* be cheerful. Kenna knows who She is, he understands why She's been so eager to speak to him tonight . . .

"Her," he whispers. "You're Her. You're Benzo's Mistress."

34

Fifteen Seconds and/or Eight Minutes Before the Wisdom Ceremony

She flicks the name away with Her fingertips, attempting to scoot it out the doorway. "Oh, please don't call me that," She demurs. "That's what my debtors call me."

"Is that a nickname, then? *Her?*"

"Oh, God no. Not a nickname. 'Her' is the official name they're contractually obliged to call me." She offers up a peal of merry laughter, which dwindles into a quick silence when Kenna doesn't join her. "They can't afford to call me by name."

"You make them pay for the privilege of using your *name?*"

"It *is* copyrighted. Look, I'm sorry, O Prince—you took a debtor on the verge of being liquidated, and turned him into a vital asset. That teaching should become a seminar—"

"A seminar."

"Yes. I—" She smooths Her robe, hoping to brush away the awkwardness. "I'm sorry, O Prince, I suppose I should have anticipated this. You don't deal with debtors the way I do. My asset must have told you such sweet stories when you were with him, I—I should have foreseen you would harbor sympathies toward him . . ."

"Benzo." Each word is a bullet fired across a ship's bow. "His name is Benzo."

She purses Her lips, as if Benzo's name was a test She should have studied for. "If you say."

Kenna is about to shriek *How can you not know his name?* when he realizes:

Her slightest whims threaten to snuff out Benzo's life. Her tantrums might sell Benzo's brothers into new slaveries. Her snits condemned his mother to torture. She is the storm that can break Benzo, and so Benzo *has* to catalogue Her moods—to remember that half-hearted smile She gave him one sleepy Sunday so he can reconstruct what he did to cause it . . .

Whereas Kenna realizes She has destroyed families in a fit of pique and forgotten their destruction before noon.

He can see it in Her eyes: She doesn't even *remember* the bet. For Benzo, making consommé was a rebellion that took him a lifetime's courage to engineer; for Her, She gets a quality cup of broth or a few more generations of slaves, and She'll remember neither when Benzo's brothers tuck Her in at night.

She holds up Her hands in surrender; he realizes he has backed Her against the wall. "Now, I know you believe *Benzo* is special." She stresses his name, emphasizing She is taking Kenna seriously—yet She still pronounces "Benzo" like a commodity. "But his family took on *massive* debts. They borrowed cash from lending libraries at interest rates that you or I would never have risked—"

"For what purpose?"

Her studied diplomacy evaporates in a nova-hot flash. "Oh, *I* don't know. I could look it up, but—" Bright green bioware spirals loop around Her pupils, then contract into a flashing red "NO" sign. "There's no signal in here. But folks borrow for all sorts of unwise reasons. People get sick, and can't cut losses. They don't do the due diligence on some investment. They get sentimental about keeping homes they'd do better to move out of. In any case, O Prince, I've seen thousands of these cases and they are *never* prudent decisions—"

"So what you're saying," Kenna says, measuring each word, "is your slaves are people who cared for sick relatives in ancestral homes."

"If they were smarter, they'd have found better options," She snaps. "And they're not slaves."

"Not legally, no. Morally?"

"I don't buy them. They sell themselves *to* me. That's the difference. Benzo will tell you sad stories, O Prince, but somewhere his mother or his grandmother or his great-grandmother decided, *Well, I'll risk selling my childrens' children into debt.* And you blame *me*?"

So many objections crowd into Kenna's brain that he cannot fit them into his mouth. He blames Her for winding nanofilaments through Her debtors' bodies to control them. He blames Her for taking these children's children and using them as breeding experiments. He blames Her for letting their children's children *have* children, allowing Her slaves to fall in love because that gives Her greater levers to control them—

But he knows what She would say. *She has to make sure Her property doesn't escape, doesn't She? She paid for the right to future generations, didn't She? She didn't make Her debtors break company policy to fall in love, they could have spent joyless lives focused on paying back a meaningless debt passed on to them . . .*

He could tear Her arguments apart: She *does* buy slaves. Benzo told him how She finds pools of cheap debtors from bankrupt companies and snaps them up.

But Her real rationale boils down to one hideous truth:

She's better than they are.

She wouldn't have made these dumb decisions.

Therefore, Her debtors deserve what's coming to them.

And the reason She needs a *seminar* is because it's never occurred to Her that Her slaves might have inner lives worth cultivating; the people who work for Her aren't like the Inevitable Prince and Paulius and people of *import*.

The politicians and the bankers and the investors waiting for
his speech feel the same way. They might want to help the laborers,
they might want to exploit them, but they can come together to sup
drinks because in the end, they all believe their success *elevates*
them.

They don't see beauty because they don't see people.

And as She taps her foot, actually waiting for an *apology*, Kenna
realizes if he stays pent up in here with Her, he will strangle Her.
He imagines the crowds applauding as he leaves Her dead body
inside the capsule. Yet other creditors wait to pick up Her debts;
killing Her would just condemn Benzo's family to be split apart
like parts of a sold corporation, Her debtor-slaves re-homed somewhere worse.

Everyone here knew who She was. *Everyone.* Other people had
asked how Her businesses were going, and they'd not only toler-
ated Her, they'd accepted Her as a *colleague* . . .

"O Prince, you should know—you traveled on transport ships,
saw the bums—you can't just make *anyone* worthwhile!"

"You can," he says. "You just don't bother."

He slams the Escargone's stop button.

His back bleeds, the thumbtacks driven deep into his flesh.

And when he wrenches open the door, tumultuous applause
washes over him. Spotlights play across his robe, fill his eyes with
white heat—but he can hear chairs shoved aside as the Wisdom Ceremony witnesses get to their feet.

The applause rises to a thunder as he realizes the wealthy chosen ones he led through Paulius's adventures lead a much larger
crowd, standing proud—two hundred people have gathered in The
Sol Majestic's dining room, some vloggers with live ansible-feeds
broadcasting to all humanity, sending his words to people huddled
in tents tuning in to see the Inevitable Prince.

I will be a light to disperse the darkness. But those poor bastards in the tents will never see that light. Kenna will redirect
dribbles if he's lucky, teaching the rich they deserve to be rich,

teaching the powerful their half-hearted efforts are compassion, and by the time he speaks his belly will be full with the salmon course, the rusted egg, the layered broth . . .

Except Kenna is charging to the stage, the crowd's applause turning into a startled whoop as he knocks a chafing dish aside to bring this whole Ceremony down.

35

Wisdom

"I was going to tell you falsehoods," Kenna says.

He stands atop a mountain of polished wood. He grips the podium with both hands as though he wants to rip up the smooth mahogany and fling it down at the people below; from this high up, he can see white tablecloths like islands, floating in the darkness.

"Instead, let me tell you something true: there is dignity in work."

He closes his eyes, dizzied by thoughts of the bhelpuri merchant sleeping in his tube, the maintenance workers smuggling mad projects through Savor Station's hidden tunnels, of Benzo steamed lobster-red from broth . . .

"Every one of you fat bastards is here only because hundreds labored to make this world for you. They tilled the land to grow your food, they maintained the ships that delivered it to this door, they chopped the food to make it elegant, they built the station beneath your feet and GET AWAY FROM ME!"

Rèpondelle tumbles backwards, eyes wide, shocked into stillness by Kenna's rejection.

"All those people did the work," Kenna whispers, as though he'd never been interrupted. "Yet strangely, not a one of those laborers is in attendance. I wonder why?"

You could drop a knife into that silence and never hear it hit bottom. His audience's mute fear enrages Kenna; he pounds on the podium, furious they're so uninterested they can't debate . . .

"It's because you ignore them! You write off the men and women who didn't *want* to abandon family and friends and love in some mad dash for power! Or you sneer at them because they weren't lucky enough to start with the connections and education and money that you did! You don't want them here because you think you're *better* than they are!"

He whirls to point at Mother. "You know why you can't save the starving millions? It's because people like this won't pay them enough to *eat*! They've got enough wealth to make miracles like Savor Station happen, and yet they can't get a fucking kid some food?

"It's bullshit. It's all bullshit."

Something wet spatters on the podium's fine-grained surface. Is it tears? Holy Gods, Kenna is crying. But fuck it, let them see him cry . . .

"And I! I was going to stand up here and tell you people how beautiful you were. That I was going to be the light to disperse your darkness. Fuck that. You need *more* darkness. I'll become the darkness to smother your light.

"I'm going to tell everyone there is *no shame* in being a servant. That there is *grace* in being a worker. And that there is no dignity in greed. And I'm going to tell all those people—"

He points at the vloggers, who hold their cameras rock-steady because this is the sort of footage that gets billions of hits. A prince melting down before a live audience? This is what Mother and Father warned him about. What will he tell the starving millions now?

He has one shot to talk before he's never heard from again.

Fine.

Make it a good one.

"I'm going to tell them that if you don't give them dignity, they should rise up and take it. You don't have enough money to stop all of them. And they should tear you motherfuckers to shreds, because if you get in the way of billions of people's dreams of having enough food to feed their family and maybe a drink afterwards, then *you deserve to be cut down.*

"And—"

But his fury has choked him, turning invective into hitching nothingness, and he has no idea what's going on anyway because his tears turn bright spotlights into dazzling rainbows, maybe the audience is getting ready to throw plates at him, and Lord he'd had *such* a good message and he'd blown it on a tantrum . . .

Kenna flees the stage.

36

The Wisdom Ceremony

"*Keep everyone else out of here!*" Paulius roars. Kenna had never known The Sol Majestic *had* security guards, but of course several unobtrusive women block the entrance to the kitchen. Kenna sees vloggers rushing forward, Mother and Father pushing their way to the front.

A blacklight curtain walls them off.

"*You!*" Paulius bellows. "*What did you do?!?*"

Paulius grabs at his tie like it's strangling him, rips it off, flings it to the ground—and then takes an unsteady step backwards with the frail exhaustion that reminds Kenna that Paulius is still recovering.

The kitchen staff abandon their posts, dropping dishes to rush to Paulius's rescue. He waves them off, his cane clattering to the floor.

Paulius buries his face in his hands.

"Do you realize what you've *done,* Kenna?"

Montgomery creeps out from the garden entrance, clutching the Bitch's cask; Kenna cannot tell whether she holds it like a shield, or holds it out to Paulius as a peace offering. Yet she walks like a woman hoping to wake from a nightmare.

"It's my fault, Paulius—I shouldn't have put him in the Escargone with that bitch, I was so angry She showed up . . ."

He picks up his cane, flings it at her badly; it bounces off a spice pantry, scattering cinnamon. "Why do you think I kept Her away from him, you narcissistic fool? Kenna! Do you realize what you've *done*?"

A man who can lift you up can also cast you down. He'd seen Paulius's anger before, but Paulius's disappointment feels like gravity has doubled, Kenna shrinking beneath the terrible understanding of how much he has let Paulius down.

Still, he can't just take this. "They—they're wrong, Paulius . . ."

"You just destroyed The Sol Majestic!"

The words ring out like gunshots. The kitchen staff, who had been making half-hearted attempts to keep the meal preparation going during this ruckus, come to a stunned halt.

"Paulius, no—I—I got you the money to—"

"You just told the workers on Savor Station to tear Captain Lizzie to shreds!" Paulius thunders. "How long do you think she'll let me operate here when I've unleashed a rebellion? Her family's tended this place for *generations*! I'm surprised she's not evicting me *now*!"

The worst part is watching the workers back away as they realize their job has evaporated. A moment ago they'd been united to make a meal fit for kings—now Kenna sees them tabulating résumés, tallying finances, wondering if they can book a flight out before the rush causes prices to rise.

"No," Kenna protests. "I lied. I lied to save the kitchen . . ."

"Then lie again." Paulius sweeps the cinnamon into a pile—and that hurts most of all, feeling that he is less important than a random mess. "No station owner will let you board. And you just told every Inevitable follower your religion was a sham. You need to get out there and do damage control."

". . . damage control?"

Paulius rolls his eyes. *"Apologize,* boy."

"No."

He won't apologize. Not for the truth.

Paulius wipes cinnamon dust on his shirt, leaving brown smears. "Kenna. I'll accept the loss of my business. But not you. You're too young to understand what a short, brutish life you'll experience if you don't recant. You need to walk that back."

"I will not."

"Think of Benzo," Montgomery says, her voice wavering. "She knows it was your attachment to Benzo that triggered this. She'll torture him, Kenna, him and his whole family, until you write those words off as teenaged foolishness. You need to get ahead of this, before She tears him apart to change your mind—"

"She's torturing him *anyway*! She's torturing his family, and if I concede She'll *keep* torturing his family, and all the families She holds in Her thrall! All I'll do by 'walking this back' is make it easier for people like Her to keep Her staff in line!"

Montgomery snaps off her goggles. "I thought you loved Benzo."

"I do. I love him enough to know I'll crush the hopes of thousands of other Benzos if I yield."

Paulius sits down, collar askew, white suit streaked. "They're going to kill you, Kenna. They're going to kill us. They're going to find everything you love, and they'll twist it as hard as they can until you laugh that speech off. The Sol Majestic won't exist, your religion won't exist, your lover won't exist, and your corpse will be chucked out an airlock. Is that worth it for a speech?"

This decision would be so easy if he were not sitting in The Sol Majestic's kitchen. He can see the station where Benzo's stockpot stood, which floods him with memories of how good it felt to spoon up against Benzo's naked body. He can see the fumellier and the sommelier and the sous chefs and the dishwashers waiting for his answer; his refusal will scatter his newfound family to the winds.

Yet there are other places where the work does not unite you into a family, but makes men into monsters.

And when he speaks, he feels nothing left but this foolish resistance, so much a part of him they'd have to kill him to stop him:

". . . yes," he whispers. "It's worth it."

Paulius's head droops to his chest. He takes Kenna by the shoulders, tears trickling down his wrinkled cheeks:

"Then you're Inevitable," he says.

Kenna flinches at the word. Only Mother and Father can judge his Inevitability.

Then Kenna thinks: *If Mother and Father can refuse my Inevitability, am I truly Inevitable?*

Montgomery taps her bare temple knowingly, approvingly, as if she'd read his mind. He remembers what she'd told him long ago: *Back in the glory days, all a Philosopher needed was an incandescent willpower.* Even if Mother and Father mustered all their wealthy allies to stop him, Kenna would create a civil war to stop slavers like Madison.

He has reclaimed the Philosophies, and no one can make him give them back.

Paulius's laughter mixes with tears. He lifts Kenna to his feet, twirling Kenna to face the crowd as he thrusts his hand high into the air and shouts: *"He is Inevitable! He is the Inevitable Prince!"*

As the staff cheers, flinging their hats into the air, Paulius sags into Kenna, releasing the tension he'd felt over wondering whether Kenna meant that speech or had blurted out thoughtless anger, and Kenna remembers how many times Paulius had thrown that lacquered duck tantrum for the cameras . . .

"When did you know?" Kenna asks.

Paulius is almost too overcome to respond, refusing to relinquish his grip on the boy he loves. "Montgomery told me. After I wondered about selling the robes."

Montgomery is quelling the celebration, smacking people to rescue what dishes they can, yes the Prince is Inevitable but so is The Sol Majestic and they'll use the Escargone to save tonight's dinner.

"I thought . . ." Kenna swallows. "I believed Captain Lizzie would shut you down."

"Oh, *she* won't," Paulius scoffs. "I looked at a lot of stations before I decided where to settle. Most captains would have evicted me for this—and yes, you'll have to be picky about where you travel—but Lizzie's far too practical to let a little freedom afear her."

"What would you have done if I'd chosen differently?" Kenna asks. "If I'd given in?"

Paulius shakes his head, refuting the awful future that could have come to pass.

"I would have let you."

Montgomery gets the security guards to clear a path back to the stage, hauling Kenna in her wake, refusing to release Kenna's hand. She hoists his fist high in the air, brandishing her trophy.

As they clamber up the huge dais, she snaps her fingers: a hologram plays of Paulius, hunched over Kenna in the kitchen:

"They're going to kill you, Kenna. They're going to kill us. They're going to find everything you love, and they're going to twist it as hard as they can until you laugh that speech off. The Sol Majestic won't exist, your religion won't exist, your lover won't exist, and your corpse will be chucked out an airlock. Is that worth it for a speech?"

". . . yes."

Montgomery's grin is as bright as a supernova as she gives Kenna a high-five. She yanks her Inevitable Robe off, hurls it into the audience, lets it flutter down like a great butterfly set free.

"Ladies and Gentlemen!" she shouts, exultant. "I am privileged to inform you that despite your best efforts, there remain *some* people you filthy frog-fuckers can't buy, beguile, or browbeat! Kenna has asked me to announce his new Philosophy to you all: 'There is dignity in labor!' So allow me to present to you—*your Inevitable Prince!*"

Dinner is a mostly silent affair.

37

Five Minutes to Freedom

Kenna waits in one of Savor Station's docking ports, letting the luggage carts jostle him, ignoring the vloggers staring in his direction. He's come to understand this is the cost of blowing up his Wisdom Ceremony so dramatically; millions now follow him on 24/7 livestreams, certain he might do something unexpected at any moment.

Today, at least, they will not be wrong.

He takes the last bite of bhelpuri from the waxed container. He made certain the bhelpuri merchant—his name was Viaan—was his last stop before arriving here. Viaan had even allowed the Prince to fry up some crispy noodles as an experiment, much to Kenna's delight: one final morsel of enjoyment before a long cold condemnation.

Not the last joy, thankfully. Not yet. It feels good to be back among the passengers, lined up to get an outbound ship. There had been so many important guests arriving on-board for the Ceremony that Savor Station's private ports couldn't dock them all at once, so the traffic control stations play a complex and diplomatic game of chess as they balance everyday transport shipping with independent cruisers.

Yet Kenna finds being in the winding lines comforting. Weary passengers will spy him, his stained robe a beacon even among the chaotic docking procedures, and they'll frown as if to say, *That can't be him.*

Then they realize the Inevitable Prince is among them, and he shoots them a merry wink to confirm that yes, his place is in steerage travel, and they come over and shake his hand and tell him how they loved his speech. They assure him that if they're ever on a ship with him, they will fight the captains to prevent them from airlocking him. And he thanks them, telling them he is grateful for their support.

Then he asks them what they do.

They're always surprised by that. He wishes they wouldn't be.

And Kenna—not the Inevitable Prince, he assures them, just Kenna—is licking the last of Viaan's delicious bhelpuri off his fingertips when he sees Her shouldering Her way through the crowd. Her debtors charge ahead like a sports team to make room for Her, Her shoulders drawn in tight as though She's loath to touch the passengers.

Benzo trails behind Her, heaving the portable kitchen he uses to cook Her meals. He smiles, a fast-food-worker's gunpoint grin, dressed in an immaculate orange uniform; beneath the thick cloth, his chest glows, Her reactivated nanofilaments monitoring his moods.

Then She sees Kenna, and waves Her people to a stop. They pull up clumsily, a panicked team of horses.

The vloggers surround them, sensing confrontation.

"O Prince!" She gives a shining grin for the cameras: not quite as smoothly as someone trained by Rèpondelle would have done, but She's been schooled in PR. "Congratulations on your coronation."

"Thank you." He offers a genuine pleasure that leaves Her nowhere to take offense.

"So." She turns around to take in the vloggers, rising to the challenge of dueling with sheathed daggers. "I hear riots have broken out because of your—unusual—speech. You must be quite proud."

"Every benefit we take for granted was once spurred by riots. Employers prefer to spill buckets of blood rather than give up one drop of profit. I'm hoping, of course, the masters will see the benefits of giving in before heads roll—but that depends on them, not us."

"Or the quality of their masters. Some are beloved for different reasons."

Benzo's teeth clamp together as he staggers forward. Kenna wonders if later video analysis will pick up the faint green traceries beneath Benzo's jacket as She maneuvers him into place—but to the crowd, it looks like Benzo has obeyed his Mistress's orders.

She curls her fingers underneath Benzo's chin, an intimacy to remind Kenna he will never touch Benzo again. "Isn't that true, my sweet? Don't you love me too much to love some silly Prince?"

Benzo says nothing. Kenna loves him all the more for it—he knows Benzo is tormented by a thousand invisible anguishes, yet he refuses to speak the words his Mistress would have him say.

A few of Her slaves mutter "We love you, Mistress" in ragged syncopation. She frowns, cataloguing silences for future punishment.

"*Any*way," She sing-songs, "it's been delightful catching up, O Prince, but it *is* time for me to go . . ."

"I am aware. I wanted to ensure you left with the entirety of your property."

He whips his robe off.

Beneath, he wears Her orange debtor's uniform.

"That's . . ." Her confusion is delicious. "I'm afraid you're confused, O Inevitable Prince, you are not indebted to me . . ."

"I must debate that dubious assertion. I spent several months in the Escargone, trained in consommé by your servant. His mentorship came at Majestic rates. As a result, I am several hundred thousand dinari in his debt, which transfers to you."

He kneels at Her feet.

"You own me, ma'am."

The vloggers flick on their live feeds, subvocalizing commentaries; the passengers abandon their places in line to see whether the Prince needs rescuing. She hesitates, Her hands held up as if She wishes to slow this down . . .

"That's . . . absurd, O Prince. You have thousands of donations rushing into your account, the starving millions tithing their tiny paychecks to you . . . You're wealthy beyond redemption . . ."

"No, no, those weren't to me," Kenna corrects Her. "That was to the charity the ten percent cut from the Inevitable Robes went to. I left that in Scrimshaw's hands; she's investing it to create interesting market pressures. But I, personally, don't own a dinari. Which makes me yours."

He bows. She pales. "Then I free you. As a gift."

"That is merciful, but alas, I cannot accept. The others in your debt have no ability to pay their way free—so how could I accept freedom when others languish? Alas, I shall become a slave like the others in your care."

She bares Her teeth, Her PR façade slipping. "They're *debtors,* not slaves."

"Well. I suppose we'll have a spirited debate about whether there's an effective difference, won't we?" Kenna beams a gentle smile at the vloggers to encompass them in his "we," watches Her horror as She realizes She's only gotten away with Her abuses because nobody's cared.

But now the Inevitable Prince has an audience, and he will bring them into Her slave chambers. Though She'll try to lock the journalists out, they'll never stop hunting for exposés on the Inevitable Prince. They'll investigate the working conditions the Prince and all Her other slaves suffer under. They'll write op-eds on whether people should be sold with their debts. They'll call for legislation to break Her stranglehold . . .

"This is nonsense! I'm *freeing* you, Kenna!" She taps Her arm, spreadsheets blossoming across Her bioimplants, swiping green refunds across Kenna's name. "Your debts are erased!"

"Generous indeed," he says. "Yet you buy bad debt in bulk.

Scrimshaw's told me she's willing to sell me to you hidden among others, again, and again, and again. Why, you might spend your whole life purchasing me and releasing me . . ."

She leans in close, whispering so the cameras can't hear. "Walk away, you emaciated cretin. I'll lace you with tormenting nanofilaments until you *beg* to tell everyone that life with me is a paradise . . ."

Kenna knows what smile Rèpondelle would have him give to instill fear. Yet the unbreakable smile that rises naturally to his face forces Her to take a step back in terror.

"I'm Inevitable," he tells Her, and steps into Her circle to become a slave.

The cameras never stop rolling.

Epilogue

Eleven Years Later

They had traveled for three months to get to the funeral.

Kenna and Benzo had waited in the transport ship to let everyone else get off first, thanking those who came to pay their respects. And when the time came, Benzo had helped Kenna to his feet, put his cane in his hands, pointed him to the door.

Kenna had kissed Benzo when he got up, of course. They always did that, now that they could.

And waiting at the exit is Paulius—a little plumper around the middle, a little more wrinkled, a little slower to greet them. But it is still Paulius, in his gleaming white suit, still Paulius with that splendid grin, and Kenna realizes he hasn't seen his home since he sold himself into slavery all those years ago.

Paulius kisses them both on the cheek. "So proud," he whispers. "So proud."

Then he glances down at Kenna's infamously twisted knee: "Will you be all right? Can you make your way to the restaurant?"

"I can forge a path anywhere, if the need drives," Kenna says. Yet the effort costs him. Both his legs are in constant pain, the aftermath of Her—Madison—having all but destroyed his nerves to get him to recant. She'd turned to outright physical torture at the end, breaking out the hammers, but after eight long years Kenna's testimonies had led to new laws that had forced Her out of business.

He liked to joke that no man should be a cripple at twenty-seven—but if someone should be, that man should at least be In-evitable.

Paulius leads them through the station's corridors to The Sol Majestic—or what had once been The Sol Majestic. The obsidian rock in front is streaked with dust, the plants in the thin soil dying. The doors are padlocked—not because the biolocks can't keep people out, but because a thick iron lock is a sign prior reservations have been canceled.

"It's not entirely closed," Paulius says, fishing a key out from his vest pocket. "It's been like a going-away party, really. All those people I helped back in the day want to see me one more time before . . . well, before." The key sags in his hands, and for a moment Kenna worries he might drop it. "So . . . I've been cooking a few meals, sometimes. For the ones who could make it here in time. We talk about the old days, catch up on what they've been doing. Captain Lizzie has been quite generous letting me stay here."

"So they've left?" Benzo asks, crestfallen. Kenna knew how much Benzo had missed working in that kitchen. "All the staff?"

"I spent what I had on good severances. I gave them fine rec-ommendations. I repaid their dedication as best I could."

He pushes open the doors to reveal The Sol Majestic's degra-dation—a vast carpet that needs vacuuming, overhead lights that need changing, a wide bar with missing bottles. A lone table sits near the kitchen entrance, where this private service will be held for Kenna, Benzo, and Paulius.

It's not hard for Kenna to fill in the Majestic's gaps to remem-ber what it once was, but . . .

Benzo squeezes his shoulder. "You don't want to try."

Of course Benzo is right. Reconstructing The Sol Majestic would be its own bereavement, and they are here to mourn Scrim-shaw's passing.

"You mentioned a meal," Benzo says. "Would you mind if I cooked it?"

Paulius clasps his hands in silent prayer. "I was hoping you would lay the Majestic's kitchen to rest."

The table is laid out for nine courses—even in reduced circumstances, Paulius cannot bear to cut corners. He hears the *chok-chok-chok* of Benzo chopping vegetables in the kitchen—they'd become vegans after She had treated them as cruelly as livestock—and feels guilty for leaving Benzo alone with his memories.

Then he remembers Benzo is never happier than when he is creating. Tonight will be a simple soup, but Benzo will make it perfect.

Simpleness has become his husband's strength.

Paulius is halfway through uncorking the bottle before he hesitates. "Do you drink wine?"

"Upon special occasions."

Paulius tilts the label toward Kenna for his approval; Kenna nods, even though he knows nothing about wine. But he's certain this is the most precious bottle in Paulius's storage.

Predictably, it is delicious.

"Have you heard from Montgomery?" Kenna asks.

Paulius slumps back against his chair, grinning, the question flooding him with so many fond memories that he can no longer function. "Once she found herself, I couldn't keep her on staff. She does pop-up supper clubs now—one-time events held in secret places. She held a tasting menu in the heart of a comet once. She's done water tastings at the bottom of oceans. She sends me invitations. Sometimes I even show up."

Kenna spreads his hands apart, mimicking an explosion. "Do you show up via . . . ?"

Paulius sets the glass down. "The Niffeneger syndrome? You're asking if I pop onto a comet, and then pop back here?"

Kenna's legs ache; he imagines them throbbing in time with Paulius's reconstructed hip. "My apologies. I didn't mean to imply . . ."

"No, it's fine, it's fine." Paulius guzzles his wine, refills the glass. "That's . . . I almost forgot you knew about it. I'm on better medications for it, ones that don't quite destroy my palate. But the older I get, well . . . the worse my aim gets. I'm still able to hit planets if I concentrate, but one day . . ."

His gaze drifts out toward the deep space window. Then he shakes his head, smacking his lips in distaste.

"Doesn't matter. Without Scrimshaw, I'm all but forgotten anyway." Kenna is halfway out of his chair to comfort his old friend, but Paulius clamps him to the table with a warm touch. "It's all right, Kenna—I had a good run."

"How did . . ." He hasn't wanted to say it out loud; vocalizing it would make it too real. "How did Scrimshaw pass on?"

"She went doing what she loved," Paulius sighs. "Died at her desk. Officially, it was a heart attack, but realistically? Well, she was pushing a hundred and fifty. We'd gotten her the best gene rejuvenations, but something was bound to fail. Poor bird."

"And you . . . shuttered the doors?"

"I didn't *want* to." Paulius's voice rises peevishly, a little too exhausted for irritation. "But that first wave of bills came in, and I realized there was too much for a man like me to follow. She was a good investor—a *fine* investor—and, uh, a . . ."

His beetled brows knot inward, ticking his manicured fingernails against his glass.

"A fine friend," he finally acknowledges, tripping quickly through the words before draining the glass and refilling it. "But no. The Sol Majestic was a—it was a family business, Kenna. I could bring someone else in to run the finances, I suppose, but she's dead and I'll be dead soon, so . . . let it go out on a high note."

Kenna lifts his gaze to the tattered curtains overhead. "This is a high note?"

"This," Paulius says solemnly, "is the *echo* of a high note. But no matter. You know how distasteful I find money, and—well, I'd like to finish up the evening without fussing about cash. So since

Benzo will be a while making the peanut stew, would you mind going to Scrimshaw's office to transfer whatever data you need?"

Kenna was hoping to forestall that, but Paulius is right—Scrimshaw had managed Kenna's charitable funds, doing a herculean job for free, and even if Paulius would let his affairs collapse, Kenna should find someone else to manage his funds.

His parents still burned to take over. They'd been traveling the galaxy ever since Kenna disowned them, bringing shabby cases to insignificant courts, claiming they had rights to Kenna's charity.

Scrimshaw used to cut them checks, secretly gifting them enough dinari to book futile flights to toothless courts. Mother and Father thanked their anonymous benefactor in the few news interviews they could scrape up, never knowing how Scrimshaw delighted in watching them waste their remaining years away on slow-cargo ships.

"I'll be a few moments," Kenna says, heading for Scrimshaw's office.

"I'll be in my cups," Paulius says, lifting a glass.

Kenna kisses Benzo on the neck as he pads through the kitchen, wondering when the prep space had shrunk so small. Yet Scrimshaw's red door looms as large as ever.

Nobody ever went in there unless they were going out permanently, Kenna remembers.

As Kenna opens the creaking door, he half expects to hear the old dragon admonishing him that this is *her* space. Yet for all her secrecy, Scrimshaw's office is an ordinary office cubicle: a single monitor, a stack of smartpaper, no wall decorations. He was told death took her by surprise—but the office is perfectly filed, and Kenna suspects it had *been* perfectly filed for the last twenty years.

There is one envelope taped to the wall: "For Kenna."

Confused, he examines the envelope: the tape is yellowed, as if this envelope had been stuck up long time ago.

He looks around, expecting to see other envelopes—one for Paulius, perhaps—but this is all there is.

He blows into the envelope and takes out a note, written in spidery handwriting:

> *Kenna.*
>   *If you are reading this, I am dead.*
>   *If I have—*

He tears up, because until now he'd pretended she might shuffle through the door to greet him—but of course cold-eyed Scrimshaw would push him past pointless reverie.

> *If I have done my job correctly, everything is in order, and control of the Inevitable Philanthropy Association has passed to you. I have made copious notes about what political movements I have chosen to fund and why, about which people are not to be trusted, and about the best tax shelters to protect the funding we have gathered. I have also maintained a file of potential successors who could take over for me, updated every six months.*
>   *You ignore me at your own risk, of course.*

He can almost see her draconian lips curling into a smile.

> *But I have also willed my personal fortune to you.*

The paper trembles in his hands. He didn't want money. She knows he doesn't care about money. Of all the people in the universe, Kenna would rather have Scrimshaw alive than have her money. Perhaps that is why she gave it to him.

> *You're wondering why I gave it to you.*

He laughs. "Gods damn you, Scrimshaw."

It's because only you can keep The Sol Majestic alive.

Kenna reads the words again. Has she gone mad? He's the Inevitable Prince, not some financier—

You will object that you are ignorant. You will object that you are devoted to tending to the poor. I also know you are a quick study, and I know the Inevitable Philosophy is so entrenched in most congresses and courts that your presence is barely necessary.

And if you wish to sell the idea to your movement, you have always told them there is dignity in service. Serving great artists is still a service. Yes, you will tend to the rich and powerful, but I suspect your presence here will be a powerful reminder to them not to get too comfortable.

Also, remember that The Sol Majestic left one table reserved each night, free of charge, for those with the love to see it. You were only the most notable of hundreds of lives we improved in the course of our service. I only wish it had been my idea.

Were I there, you would tell me that this is mad, that money has never been your skill—but you were the one who marketed the robes. You were the one who got Montgomery to lead the kitchen. You're cleverer than you know, Kenna. You and only you could lead Paulius back to greatness, and become greater yourself.

I know you dreamed of being Paulius.

I'd like to ask you to become me.

Sincerely,
B. Scrimshaw

*   *   *

Kenna clutches the letter to his chest as he emerges. Paulius stands hip-to-hip with Benzo, a dollop of peanut butter on his index finger. He makes approving noises as he tastes Benzo's first pass at the peanut stew and suggests a hint of *chiles de arbol.*

Benzo carries the same serenity he did in the Escargone—that certainty that he would, one day, outcook Paulius, but relishing the pleasure once it has arrived.

Then they see Kenna's pallid face and rush to grab him.

"Are you okay?" Benzo asks. "Is it your knees again? Should I fetch your pain suppressants?"

"No." He doesn't have to tell them; he could stay quiet, and none would be the wiser.

But he'd never been content committing his life to steady courses.

"She left me her money," he tells them. "I've sorted through her funds. It's . . . a quite considerable amount."

Paulius claps him on the back. "That's wonderful, Kenna! After all you'd endured from that slave-addled maniac, how delightful must it be to have a rich bastard *give* you something for once?"

"She's . . . suggested I should take over as the Majestic's business manager."

Benzo drops his spoon, splattering peanut sauce across the tile floor. He holds his breath; Kenna knows how many times Benzo had longed to come work for The Sol Majestic, yet had never asked Kenna because he knew the Inevitable Prince's duties.

Paulius's mood, however, goes dark. "You don't have to, Kenna. I'll be all right."

You won't, Kenna thinks, noticing how the old man's shirt is already a little too rumpled, his belly a little too full. Paulius cooks small meals because he needs to make the world amazing for someone, even in the ass-end of a rusted station—

But Paulius would give that up if it made Kenna happy.

Just as he'd always done.

"You need someone to manage the bills," Kenna says. "And we need a home. Even three months is too long for a place this blazing to fall dark. I'll look into how to—how to manage the credit lines we'll need to reopen the doors. I presume there must be regulations, so I'll have to ascertain which merchants are worth dealing with—"

And because Paulius had been so somber a moment ago, Kenna is unprepared when the old man whirls him into a gleeful dance, high-stepping up and down the kitchen aisles, looking years younger than when he met them at the docks.

"You and me, Kenna! And Benzo! We three will fashion new dreams! We can't call it The Sol Majestic, of course—it won't be that, not without Scrimshaw. But we'll refit it. We can call it—" He sweeps his hand across the air, outlining an imaginary sign: "*Inevitable*."

"It kind of is," Benzo chuckles.

"Certainly." Kenna bobs his head, wrapping his head around creating a new restaurant. "That . . . actually sounds wonderful."

"We'll take the opportunity to refit the old girl!" Paulius says. "We've got windows into space—but everybody's got those now. We need to go next level. We'll get Rakesh to put twenty hatches into those walls, we'll catapult our guests out into the void so they come face-to-face with their own mortality, and then when they return even the simplest soups will seem so sweet—"

"What about the expense?"

Paulius blinks.

"Seriously," Kenna says, pressing forward. "Our funds aren't limitless. The construction costs alone risk bankrupting us. And the safety concerns of such an endeavor, I can't imagine what insurance contracts I'd need to procure . . . I'll have to look into it."

Paulius tosses his cane aside. "What is there to look into?"

Kenna watches the anger blossom on Paulius's cheeks as he bumps chests with Kenna, peacocking in absurd rage . . .

You and only you *could lead Paulius back to greatness.*

As Paulius's furor rises, happiness floods through Kenna: he understands why Scrimshaw left this to him.

"The budget," Kenna says loftily. "I'll have to investigate the budget."

"What? *An Idea* waits to be born, glorious and formless and infinite, and you'd weigh down art with tawdry remuneration?!" Paulius splutters.

"I wouldn't argue with him." Benzo stifles a chuckle behind a spatula. "After all, he *is* Inevitable."

"You . . . malicious manacle!" Paulius fumes. "You genitortuous jailer! You'd strangle art in the *womb*?"

Kenna smiles.

ACKNOWLEDGMENTS

I wrote the first page of this novel on the day I decided to give up writing.

Let's set the stage for you: it was 2014, I'd written seven novels, and not a one of them had sold.

If you're a writer, you know what it's like to inch along that painfully slow process toward "getting published"—and after many years, I'd gotten to the stage where agents now gave me personalized feedback before rejecting me. Getting gentle punches on the shoulder that said "Try again, kiddo" was admittedly better than the cold anonymous rejections—but seriously.

Seven books.

Twenty years of my life as a writer, and not a damn thing to show for it.

But I had great hope for that seventh book. Because as I was writing it, an agent was asking me, "So how's that book coming?" He liked the pitch I'd given him, and liked the novels I'd submitted before (though not enough to take me on as a client).

So when I finished that novel, a story about magical drug dealers, I sent it off to him in the grand hopes that I'd finally at least get an agent.

I sent it to him exclusively, but four months passed and he still hadn't read it yet. Which was fine; he was busy with his stable of

New York Times bestselling authors, I knew I was on the back burner.

But after five months, I said, "Maybe I should send this novel out to other agents." So I sent Novel #7 out, widely.

At seven months, and a plateful of agent rejections, I was realizing that Novel #7 was not, shall we say, an easy sell.

At nine months, *all* the other agents I'd sent it out to had rejected me. Every single one. I was down to just the original agent, the one who'd liked my elevator pitch, the one who'd loved my short fiction, so I waited by my inbox hoping, and . . .

At ten months, my agent got back to me. And he said, "I'm sorry, I've spent the last few months pondering how to revise your book #7 so as to make it something I'd feel comfortable pitching, and I can't think of a way to do that without destroying your whole plot. So . . ."

Reader, I felt my entire writing career implode in that moment.

I'd worked hard to be an author. So hard. And this Novel #7, my best novel, the novel I was so proud of, wasn't good enough.

I had to quit.

And I'm gonna tell you: I crept down into the basement so my wife wouldn't hear me, and I wept.

Because if I ever wanted to be a writer, I'd have to spend another year finishing a new novel, then another few months revising it, and then another year shopping it around to agents, and then—*if* one accepted me—they'd spend a year shopping it to publishers and I would not have a novel published for four years minimum if I was good enough.

Or I could quit.

And in that basement, I wanted to quit. I was so fucking tired of writing. I was so tired of pretending I had talent. I should just abandon it and find something else to do with my life.

I knew: If I did not start a new novel that night, I would never write again.

So I sat down. I had no plans for a novel, so I set it in the setting of *Sauerkraut Station*—my novella that had been nominated for a Nebula, which is an alliterative appeal to be sure. I didn't know what I wanted to write about, so I took my favorite restaurant and set it in space, and I.

Just.

Wrote.

If you feel Kenna's desperation in the opening chapters, my friends, that desperation is *very* real.

And to quote Lin-Manuel Miranda, "I wrote my way out." I needed a tale of hope, so I wrote a boy who found a place that was home to him. And that resonated with me, so I wrote more and more about food and love until it became my refuge . . .

And literally *two weeks* after I started writing *that* novel, I sold Novel #7 to Angry Robot, which became my debut novel *Flex,* which was successful enough to turn into a three-book series. (Go check it out, if you liked this; if this book is about soup, that series is about donuts. No, seriously.)

So I'm gonna acknowledge people in a bit, but first lemme just tell you what this novel taught me:

Don't quit.

You have something to say.

Write until you unlock that potential.

Anyway, let's talk about restaurants that inspired this book:

The Velvet Tango Room in Cleveland is routinely ranked one of the best bars in the world, and its owner is Paulius Nasvytis— yes, that *is* an homage. They make the best drinks I've tasted there, including a bourbon daisy with a twenty-second aftertaste that mutates on the tongue, and much of the philosophy of The Sol Majestic is taken straight from the VTR's devotion to the craft. It will be worth your while to make a pilgrimage to the VTR, but be on your best behavior—they expect you to respect the drinks, and so do I.

Joe Bastianich's Babbo, in New York City, was the first Michelin-starred restaurant I ever ate at, and it was a revelation in terms of service and attention to detail. I cribbed a lot of the atmosphere for The Sol Majestic from Babbo, which makes some damn fine gnocchi.

Eleven Madison Park is routinely ranked among the top five restaurants in the world, and they showcased that glory when they asked me, "Are you celebrating anything special at this dinner?" and I said, "I'm writing a science-fiction book on fine dining." And during my meal, they took me in back, made me and my wife frozen maple treats, and took us on a tour and answered all my questions. A lot of The Sol Majestic's kitchen look is taken from Eleven Madison Park, and man are they good.

Also critical to the world view of The Sol Majestic was the Cleveland Museum of Contemporary Art's showcase on Ferran Adrià's seminal restaurant El Bulli, which provided a lot of fodder for how Paulius thought.

And, of course, thanks to my mother and my sainted Uncle Tommy, who took a sullen kid out to restaurants when he was twelve because they liked fine food, and so gifted me with a great love that ignited this whole damn book.

(Note: all the restaurants listed here are expensive because The Sol Majestic is expensive. But you're not really a foodie unless you can appreciate the value of a well-made two-dollar hot dog. In fact, if you go to the VTR, one suggests stopping by Cleveland's stalwart Old-Fashion Hot Dog afterwards to get you some chili cheese dogs and a glass of cold milk.)

Thanks to Billy Martin, who, back when I was just a nobody blogging away on LiveJournal, told me I had a gift for writing about food. Considering Billy was a Published Author back then, that meant the world to me. If you liked this book and haven't read Billy Martin's Liquor series (written under his old name Poppy Z. Brite), then do so posthaste: your world will be expanded.

Thanks to all the people who helped me revise this book:

Matthew Duhan and his amazing introduction to sous vide cooking, Amy Aldrich, Geri Bressler, Darren Lester, Daniel Starr (who is *still* responsible for destroying Boston), Ingvild Husvik, Ian Griffith (whose Mage campaign is still responsible for kickstarting my book *Flex*), Raven Black, John Perich, Barbara Webb, Christina Russell, my old Clarion classmate Sarah Miller, and Ashley Thompson.

Thanks to the usual cast of suspects who held me when I was, predictably, freaking out over the book—Fox, Laura, Aileen, and Kalita. You helped soothe the worried weasel, and your unique flavors permeate the book in their own way. And thanks to Renee, who I was staying with when my agent's notes came in for this book, and who was tolerant enough to let me read the revamped first three chapters of the book to her so I could see whether it made sense.

As always, thanks to my, uh, best friend, Angie.

Thanks to my father, who has been relentlessly supportive of my career. Thanks to Evan Gregory, my beleaguered agent, who told me, "You *do* realize that most space operas are about starship battles, not soup, right?" and yet boldly got out there to sell this unwieldy sucker. And thanks to my editor, Diana Pho, who clasped this odd little soup-book to her heart and brought it into the Tor fold. (And thanks to everyone else at Tor who helped push this book out the door.)

And hey! Thanks to *you*. You read this! In an age where there's a new Marvel or Star Wars movie out every three minutes, that's a very kind usage of your time.

But last, there's thanks to the woman who I literally could not have done this without. The woman who, when I slouched upstairs to push the first 500 words of yet another novel into her hands, dropped everything to read it *right then* because she knew I'd stop writing if anyone else rejected me in any way. The woman who, when I said, "You know, we should spend lots of money to try eating at snooty Michelin-starred restaurants," became more enthusiastic than I did because *damn* that woman loves fine cuisine. The woman who yelled at me when this novel started to drift off-track and wrenched The Sol Majestic back into shape.

I love you, Gini.

Arf.

Ferrett Steinmetz
@ferretthimself on Twitter
www.theferret.com